The Missing Child

THE MISSING CHILD

A NOVEL

SANDRA BIRDSELL

LESTER
&ORPEN
DENNYS
PUBLISHERS

The Publisher wishes to thank the Ontario Arts Council
for its support.

FIRST EDITION

Canadian Cataloguing in Publication Data

Birdsell, Sandra, 1942–
     The missing child

ISBN 0-88619-242-0 (bound). – ISBN 0-88619-270-6 (pbk.)

I. Title.

PS8553.I76M58 1989   C813'.54   C89-094162-9
PR9199.3.B573M58   1989

Cover design by Gordon Robertson

Printed and bound in Canada

Lester & Orpen Dennys Limited
78 Sullivan Street
Toronto, Canada
M5T 1C1

This book is for Jan Zarzycki, who gave me another point of view.

The Author wishes to acknowledge the support of the Manitoba Arts Council, the Canada Council, the University of Waterloo, and the Ontario Arts Council; and to thank the people of St. Jerome's College for their encouragement and hospitality during her stay as Writer-in-Residence.

IN THE BEGINNING

On the final day of the valley, Minnie Pullman stands among the tangled growth beside the river, singing. She's an ordinary woman, not ugly or beautiful—indeed, except for the ribbon of silver in her dark hair, there isn't a single thing about her that makes her appear remarkable or chosen. Her voice is high and thin, ridiculous in its wavering falsetto. She kicks off a pair of heavy black galoshes, unties her apron, slips white buttons the size of silver dollars through buttonholes, and allows her flower-spattered dress to fall in a heap on yellow clay. Rayon panties slither down around her ankles. She fumbles with the clasp of her brassiere and it too flutters to the ground. Middle-aged Minnie Pullman stands naked. Mud sucks greedily at her feet, ankles, knees, as she wades down into the river. The rush of cold brown water swirls up around her hips as she pushes off. Then she glides out to midstream with a strange crawling stroke and rolls over onto her back.

Minnie squints up at the slate grey sky, at the solid crown of trees, where beyond squats the town of Agassiz, a pot whose surface churns with conflicting, diverse undercurrents. Where the Justice of the Peace, Mr. Campbell, sits behind his claw-footed desk and sucks on an unlit pipe. He cannot go backward and he cannot go forward. He is caught for ever in time because today the valley has been closed. He's a scrub oak tree, Mr. Campbell, like the stunted trees that lean towards the river, as he bends over his desk shuffling through mounds of paper, thinking: a water diversion project, a giant ditch is the answer to the water lapping up the sides of his house. He hears the scuffle of Etta's rubber boots against the floor as she passes through the cluttered, damp kitchen. She enters the room and plunks the pail she's been using to bail water from the basement onto the centre of the desk. "J.P.," she says, "I give up. It's coming in faster than I can get it out."

Minnie's soft white mound of belly and full breasts bob as she gulps her lungs full of air and floats. She twirls her hands at her sides, making lazy eddies in the water as she rocks gently. A pouty-mouthed catfish glides to the surface and drifts across her buttocks. Minnie, a glimmering sphere who has dropped down from a tongue-shaped leaf, is cupped now in the palm of the valley and surrounded on three sides by distant, smoke-filled hills. The hills grow beards of green forests and churning boulders of red and grey rocks—rocks seamed with sediment of an earlier lake and fossils and the scratchings of people who long ago scrambled across the face of them, climbed down into the valley, and will never be heard from again. In the far distant northland of the valley, a blue sea reflects the flight of pelicans, their broad wings moving in unison as they sweep silently across the face of an ancient cracked glacier. Beneath the icy waters a pod of beluga whales glides upwards towards the surface.

The earth of the valley is as heavy and thick as chocolate pudding. It spreads out beneath squares of yellow and green fields and above it, tonight, the concave sky will slide down into place for the last time and will reflect back the lights flickering across the valley from the blisters of towns, that rash of chicken pox creeping across and up the sides of the valley. Near its centre, a shapeless puddle shimmers like a blue topaz on a woman's finger and the river flows from it, turning brown with irritation as it nears the town of Agassiz. The river is dissatisfied with its status; it was at one time so much more than a river which the people spit into, curse, and refuse to drink, a breeding place for mosquitoes.

Like most of the towns near the centre of the valley, Agassiz stands apart from the river, allowing the banks of it to snake alongside the town's edges but never through its heart. A single street in the town, Ottawa Street, leads to the river, and at the other end of Ottawa where it joins Main, the J.P. Campbell house towers, weathered, but still imperious. Campbell's curled, arthritic fingers sift through a mound of papers on his desk. Two Mounties sit on straight-backed chairs, trying to ignore the sharp odour of urine rising from a ceramic pot beneath J.P.'s bed and stale whiskey that clings to the creases of his moulding and twisted body. Etta can no longer carry him up the stairs and so his life has been pared down to this one room at the front of the house. Through the vine-covered window across from his desk J.P. can see patches of Main Street, a broad strip of pavement which cuts through the town and stretches on beyond its limits becoming a highway, and beside the highway is a graveyard and across from it a sign which reads, "Welcome to Agassiz, Pop. 1,500". Beneath that the letters are scoured and defaced; some say it was Sandra Adam who did it, that Sandra the Singer had taken a rock on the day she was forced to leave the town and scraped off the bottom part of the message, "Drive Carefully, We Love Our Children".

The connections in the valley are clear in the grid of roads that divide it into neat squares of ownership. Up near the hills in the west, the squares of land sustain whole communities of Ukrainians; closer to the lake, Icelanders; to the south, French-speaking communities rub noses with colonies of black-clothed Hutterites and towns of German-speaking Mennonites. In the east, where the broad back of the stony shield is worn smooth by the wind and sand, there was once a designated square for the remaining bands of Indians. The Métis, first cousins to every race in the valley, live everywhere. Those who have become French or English or Indian are invisible. The others wander through bushland, along the edges of the hills, or near the shore of the north waters like a child's aimless song. Closer to the fertile soil of the valley's centre are the Scottish and British settlers and in the centre of the basin is the town of Agassiz—its only distinction being that it's a town which has caught the overflow of all these different communities and is a mixture of almost the entire valley.

As Minnie Pullman floats on the river and sings, it's clear to her that the neat lines of the valley, the charted ancestries of families, ethnic backgrounds, languages, quaint customs are going to be wiped out. The glacier is melting and the river is rising. It comes to Minnie then that she could try and warn them. She could ride a horse through the streets, down the wide centre of Main, past the Red and White store where in the window, blind, sun-faded mannequins shamelessly model Gothic cotton brassieres and where upstairs in a large unpainted room lined with caskets, Mr. Harrigan, the store proprietor, stands behind a purple curtain. He leans over a coffin and places sprigs of lily-of-the-valley between Sandra Adam's young fingers. Minnie might clutch a horse between her thighs and cry out as she rides, "Gather up your photo albums, your diaries, your histories of the valley and run for the hills." But they wouldn't listen. Her desire is lulled to death by the rocking motion of the river, by the inevitability of the rising water. She frog-kicks and glides forward swiftly and smoothly. She passes through the shadow of the steel bridge and feels the chill of its spanners cross her glistening belly. As she drifts through its shadow and out the other side, she sees the soles of Hendrick Schultz's boots as he sits on the top span swinging his legs back and forth. It's a lazy, hypnotic motion and if he should lean too far forward he would be carried away.

"Zechariah, chapter 2." Minnie's voice echoes in the steel girders of the bridge, accompanied suddenly by the dry fluttering sound of wings as swallows dart from their grey mud adobe nests beneath the bridge and fly off in a tight swarm down the breadth of the river.

The boots stop swinging. "No," Hendrick calls down.

"Daniel, chapter 9."

"No," Hendrick says.

"What then?" Minnie calls up.

"*And this is the song of songs, which is Solomon's,*" Hendrick says and begins to recite for the last time.

Minnie cups her palms, reaches up through amber chips of algae suspended in the water, and pulls hard. She shoots forward, gliding swiftly towards a curve in the river that leads away from town. She feels the tug of the current against her spine. The boy's monotone recitation fades as the bridge passes from view. "Oh, I'll swim in your swimming pool," Minnie sings, "I'll dance in your garden. All the pears in the window will be mine. And I will never, never again, choose to be born."

THURSDAY

1

On Thursday morning Minnie Pullman had been hanging the
laundry out on the line and when a pair of hummingbirds
appeared among Albert's star-throated petunias at the side
of the house, she wasn't surprised. She'd already seen their
gold-plated breasts flashing in the sun when she'd lain in
bed beside Albert earlier that morning, eyes closed, hands
reposed against her breastbone, barely feeling the bump
of her heart in its ribcage while she lay suspended inches
above the day waiting until she imagined Jeremy saying, it's
all right now, open your eyes. And when she did, she felt
herself sink and merge. Daylight filtered through the narrow
bedroom window that faced Ottawa Street. Beside the dust-
coated window hung the current month's chart and the pencil
dangling from a frayed string. Thursday. Rosella's bold letters
said so. THURSDAY. The day for the laundry and for cooking
pizza for their evening meal. But look, she imagined Jeremy
saying as she merged with Thursday, and when she closed
her eyes to look she saw the hummingbirds.

  She shook loose a pair of Albert's wide-striped boxer
shorts and held them up to the sun before pinning them on
the line. The look of them was so harmless, innocent—boyish,

in fact—that the sight of her husband's undershorts ballooning in the breeze was like Johann Kirnberger's "Lullaby" that Minnie's girls were learning to play on the piano. The way the youngest, Ginny, played it, a gentle, smooth touch fingering up the notes, a soft touch. Like that. And if Albert were here now, inside his shorts, knock-kneed, hair slicked into a salt-and-peppery wave, his face shining with expectancy, she'd pull the elastic from his waist, bend and stick her face inside his tent-like shorts, and smooch those fly-speck moles on his bare behind. The whole wide white expanse of undershorts, the yellowish stain in front, made her think of it: Albert's pink penis, its head tucked shyly in among the thick hairs of his leg, stirring up and out of that forest inside his shorts to the rising tune of Kirnberger's "Lullaby", a twig, pencil thin and stiff, nodding at her when she crawled into bed beside him. As it had done every night for fifteen years. At one time, she'd tried doing those exercises Albert had read about in the *Women's Monthly*. The pinching and releasing of muscles down there, holding them tight for as long as she could, willing herself to become smaller for the sake of Albert. But there was just so much of Albert which amounted to so little in the end.

A petunia blossom bent sharply and then sprang back into place, its petals shivering. The tiny birds had left the flowerbed, Minnie realized. She saw the quick, spoon-shaped flash of their tarnished breasts in the centre of the yard and then they were gone. She became aware of her tongue stinging with the roughness of the wooden clothes peg. She pulled it free and clipped Albert to the line. Thursday. The day for laundry and pizza. As predictable as the Thursday before it.

What was next? The girl's ruffled dresses, dish towels, or the bed sheets, blue-white and smelling of chlorine bleach, stainless, no tell-tale pecker-tracked sheets on her line. The order of the laundry on the line revealed much about a person. The look of it—long items strung together first then graduating down to the shorter items, the underwear and socks—spoke of an ordered life. Or should she, like June Marchand, do a collage of colours? No symmetry, but the whole look of the line—of the plaid shirts, yellow towels, red, blue, and white clothing—being perfect for the day, the sun-dappled foliage in the garden, and the spatter of dandelions in the lawn. Or would she today forgo the aesthetics of the clothesline and do a Mrs. Dorfman across the street: be more utilitarian? Kitchen with kitchen and bedroom with bedroom, for instance. The consequence being an orderly and more efficient manner of putting the house back into place. She decided. Random selection. It gave her more time to think. Albert's undershorts fluttered in a sudden breeze. With it rose the heavy sweet scent of his petunias. The people on Ottawa Street looked to Albert's pink and white star-throated petunias for reassurance. It was the only thing around the Pullman place they could count on. But they were wrong, of course. Every day was predictable. Today was Thursday; Rosella's chart said so. Wash day and—she glanced down at the palm of her hand—and pizza day. She closed her eyes to see what item she should pull next from the basket. Oh. Today she would hang one of Albert's aprons next to his undershorts. Perhaps that meant that later, after work, he was going to surprise her with a batch of carrot muffins. She untangled its strings and was about to pin the apron onto the line when she heard a strange gasping noise. The noise sounded as though someone had swallowed something too large and was in danger of choking. She looked up across the swaying shell of Albert's behind and saw the boy, Hendrick Schultz, walking along the road.

"Hoo, hoo. Is something the matter?"

Hendrick stopped short and reared his head, startled. He hadn't realized she was there. His face was red and swollen. He clenched his hands into fists and plunged them deep into his trouser pockets and veered away from the road, down into one of the gullies that lined all the dirt roads in the town of Agassiz, into the fox tails and purple thistles which bent and stuck to his legs.

"Has someone been after you again?" she asked. "Just say so, and I'll have Mr. Pullman look into it."

"I'm not talking." The boy's voice was sharp, the control forced. He climbed up the other side of the gully and stepped into June Marchand's yard that edged the east side of Minnie Pullman's. As he cut through June's garden, Minnie heard the choking sound again and although, as usual, the boy kept his head down, she knew by the jerking motions of his shoulders that he was crying.

"Jeremiah 50," she called because she knew that it helped. Ginny and Rosella had brought home tales from school of how the boy, who had been born, it seemed, with the entire words of the Bible miraculously committed to memory, would stick his fingers into his ears and chant Scripture when bullied or excluded from a game. "Why don't the other children like Hendrick?" Minnie had asked. "Because he dresses funny," Rosella had snapped. "Because they're jealous that he can do that," Ginny had said.

Hendrick swung about and faced her, planting his feet firmly among June's sprawling and unruly tomato plants. He pulled his hands from his pockets, clasped them against his abdomen, and squared his shoulders. But then his chest heaved and his shoulders collapsed and dropped forward into their usual slope.

"No," Hendrick said. "You can't make me. I'm not talking."

Across town, a dog crooned for a mate. Minnie heard Katie whine and claw at the door of the shed. She was glad then that she'd remembered to lock the animal up last night. Not so much for the sake of Albert, she realized, that he wouldn't have to carry a bulging sack down to the river, crying his eyes red, blaming Minnie for his bad dreams when really he should pin the blame on itchy Katie. Pudgy, doughy Albert with his translucent, freckled skin, sitting on the bridge over the river and nudging the warm, squirming bodies inside the sack nearer and nearer the edge and closing his eyes as it rolled off the bridge and, ten seconds later, hit the water. She was glad that she'd remembered to lock Katie up because the dog was just no good with a full swaying belly. Into herself and unsociably nippy. Katie whined. Hendrick stared at the shed in the back corner of Minnie's yard. He frowned and flicked a heavy blond curl from his forehead. "She wants to run," he said.

Minnie watched as the boy turned then and strode through June's yard. He crossed an empty field behind their street. Heading off towards the fairgrounds, Minnie realized, and wondered what was the attraction of that broken and abandoned place. A mosquito hummed about her face as she shook Albert's apron loose and pinned it on the line. She closed her eyes and reached for another item in the laundry basket.

"It appears that you're not as invisible as you think." Annie's raw-sounding voice startled Minnie. Her eyes flew open to the sight of Rosella's Sunday dress dropping down onto the grass. As she bent to retrieve it, she looked up at her friend Annie at the same time. The old woman's hair had escaped the navy woollen toque she wore day and night, both summer and winter, and the tangled mass of grey, steel wool hair crackled with static electricity. Annie squinted down at Minnie and her hazel eyes glittered in their mucus-rimmed slits, the look of pain in that glitter too strong. It became stronger every passing week.

"I was lining my windows with newspapers so's I could sleep," Annie said. "Take a look at what I came acrost. I thought of you, right off." Between blunt fingers, knuckles rough and seamed with pond silt, she held a newspaper clipping.

"I never once said I was invisible," Minnie said. She reached for the clipping and then thought better of it. Only bad news happened in newspapers. She never read them.

"I never said you said you were invisible. It's just that the way you walk around half the time up there inside your head—well, sometimes I think you think you're invisible."

Minnie shook the creases from Rosella's Sunday dress and hung it on the line. Rosella's dress alongside Albert's apron. What could that possibly mean? "I'm doing random selection today," she said through a clothes peg clenched between her teeth. "I haven't done that for ages."

"That oughta keep them guessing."

"Who?"

"Maybe they'll let you off the hook with this one and put it down to being premenstrual," Annie said.

"Go away," Minnie said and laughed. "People have better things to do than keep tabs on my clothesline."

"Minnie Pullman," Annie said, "you just won't smell the coffee, will you? They say every town's got one and as far as this town's concerned, you're it." Her voice cracked and she turned, hawked, and spat. Minnie saw the string of blood in the mucus as it dropped to the grass. Annie wiped her mouth on the sleeve of her jacket. "Here," she said and stepped towards Minnie waving the clipping. A musty odour emanated from her clothing. Apples, Minnie thought. That Annie was an apple going soft inside.

"This could have waited until I went for my walk tonight," Minnie said.

"It's the type of thing you gotta read during the day." When Minnie didn't take the clipping Annie began to fold it down into a square. "If it's enough to get me out of the house in the morning, you can at least read the damned thing." She jammed the clipping into the breast pocket of Minnie's dress. She turned and walked back across the yard, rubber boots thumping with a hollow sound against the hard, packed clay of the driveway. "I see Albert's 'tunias are their usual blooming fools," she said.

"You up for a visit tonight?" Minnie called.

"I'm onto something," Annie said. "A new cure. Come over and see."

Minnie waited until the pea green plaid of Annie's jacket was hidden by a clump of caragana bush which separated June Marchand's yard from the Standings'. Annie's boots slapped against the sidewalk and then she was screened from view. Minnie took the pen from her pocket. The nib tickled the palm of her hand as she wrote the letter "A" beside the letter "P". The reminder wasn't really necessary as several times a week, automatically, her feet took her down past Annie's shanty. And she could always just go back into the bedroom and look at the chart on the wall to see what she was supposed to cook for supper. But carrying around clues on the palms of her hands helped her to relax and write the test of the day, the answers often coming without the prompting of codes scrawled across a lifeline. And it gave her more time to think and talk to Jeremy. She pushed the pen back down into her breast pocket and became aware of that square of paper pressing against her bosom. The heat from Annie's fingers still clung to the paper as she unfolded it. The words darted across the sun-bleached newsprint.

MINNIE, IF YOU'RE READING THIS, IT'S TIME TO COME HOME.
Very Sincerely, J.

Well. She hadn't realized that she'd been sitting in the basket of wet laundry until the dampness began to seep through to her skin. Well. She should really rush inside the house and chop peppers and shave cheese for the pizza. Ta da da da da tum, ta da da da tum tum ta tum. The song circled up from the top floor of the house, up there in the part that Albert had never gotten around to finishing. The song had been in her mind because Ginny played it on the piano. The girls had claimed the room, hung blankets over raw studding, arranged books about the edge of the floor, pushed doll carriages into corners, set the little porcelain tea service Albert's Aunt Violet had mailed from England out on a table. Putting the piano up there had been Albert's idea. Ta da da da tum tum, tum tum ta tum tum. Ginny, the skinny little darling, had the song down pat. The melody repeated itself in the bass and then the treble changed and off it went, swinging and cute.

MINNIE, IF YOU'RE READING THIS, IT'S TIME TO COME HOME.
Very Sincerely, J.

A mosquito hovered about Minnie's ear, its hum becoming the whine of a chain saw. J. "Jay," she said, the name popping forward out of nowhere. Tears pushed behind her eyes. Stop it, stop it, she told herself. She must never, never cry. There was simply no need for it. "J.", she read. Which J? Jeremy or Jay? It had to be Jeremy. Ginny's music circled the air above her head. Johann Kirnberger. She remembered Jeremy saying the composer's name with scorn. "Listen while Johann tosses off another weary sonata," she said aloud and Katie, hearing Minnie's voice, begged to be released.

The clasp on the shed's door clattered and then the hinges squealed as Katie bounded through Minnie's legs. "Ta da da da da tum tum," she hummed. The tears broke loose and ran down her face. The window in the playroom reflected the sun and she could not see through its solid glare into the face of her oldest daughter, Rosella, who had heard Minnie speak and had come to the window and looked down now at her mother, who was knee deep in the flood of memory.

The memories, like children cartwheeling across the roof of a house, could not be ignored. They tumbled across Minnie's roof, its cedar shingles only a spotty and fragile covering against the thump of them. A house with missing shingles. A chicken wire fence. A sand box. A white dress with strawberries along the yoke and hem. Minnie pressed her hands against her eyes. Pasquia Hills, she told herself. Pembina Mountains, Porcupine Hills. She recited aloud the names of the ridges on three sides of the valley. Mountains riding, Duck mountains flying with heights and depths of mystery and discovery, and beyond them, Jeremy. But an image of a red truck leapt forward behind her hands and a man stepped down from it. He walked towards her through a billow of steam, the grimace of pain twisting in his bloodied clown's mouth. Jay. The hair on Minnie's arms prickled. "Go away," she said. Her hands dropped to her sides. The sun pushed through her eyelids and the world inside turned soft and pink. She saw the wind sweep down across an opaque cliff of glacial ice. She sighed with relief and opened her eyes. Well, of course. It *was* Jeremy. Jeremy had used the newspaper to contact her. He couldn't speak to her directly. Not yet. Albert's white boxer shorts snapped in the wind. Well. It was clear now. She couldn't have sex with Albert any longer. The contract with him had ended. In her mind. More or less. If only she didn't have the girls.

Across the yard at the Marchands' off-kilter cottage the day gave the impression of being the same as the one before in June's voice rising up the scale inside the house. "I told you and told you," June cried, and sure enough, both the front and back doors were flung open at the same time and June's four offspring fled in every direction. Their brown knees pumped as they vaulted hedges and tomato plants, half-eaten sandwiches grabbed in haste from the table clutched now in their grubby fists as they ate on the run and vanished for the day to the far corners of the town. June's voice followed, a rooster priming up to let fly with an early morning cry of: "Oh, I can't, I can't, I can't dooo it!"

Minnie held her breath and waited for the sound of glass shattering. But there was a sharp thud instead and then a light clatter as a dish bounced off a wall and shimmied to a stop against the floor. Plastic. It was the work of that snotty little Sandra Adam, June had complained to Minnie. It was Sandra's idea. She tells August to come down to MacLeod's store and check out the new everlasting, non-breakable kitchenware and save a few bucks on polyfiller.

"Rosella?" Minnie called for her eldest. Wouldn't hurt none for Rosella to get a little morning sun. Likely had her nose stuck in a book anyway, Minnie thought, thinking then with a smile how like Annie she sounded in her head. How it happened that she seemed to take on anyone who came within a three-foot range. She wiped her eyes on the hem of her dress.

The music stopped.

"Ma?" Rosella called down from the top floor.

"Why don't you go and get a drinking glass from the cupboard and take it on over to the Marchands'?"

"No way," Rosella said.

"The kids are gone," Minnie said, "so there's nothing to be afraid of."

The music carried on from where it had stopped. Kirnberger had made Jeremy frown and pinch his nose in irritation. The composer was so full of himself, Jeremy had said. "Into himself," Minnie said. "Right? Inspired by himself and being correct," she said.

The window upstairs slammed shut. Those two girls of hers were all common secrets and silent rebellions behind their over-starched dresses. Rosella saw to the starch and sprinkled water on the dresses Aunt Violet mailed out yearly from England, wound them up into damp bundles to be uncreased while Minnie pulled on her galoshes and went out for her nightly constitutional. Down to the river with her little bar of soap to wash the ink from the palms of her hands. When it grew too cold, the firehall, kept open all night, had a sink and warm water. Rosella hung the dresses from the kitchen cupboards on hangers. When Minnie returned, the smooth, crisp look of them was supposed to shame her into good behaviour. But these things escaped Minnie's attention. She never noticed that the girls dressed differently than the other children in town. That they seldom went anywhere. At school, during recess, they huddled against the fence at the far end of the yard holding hands, waiting for the bell so that they could once more escape into the pages of their lessons. Minnie just thought how responsible Rosella was and what an exemplary job Albert had done to equip the girls to live out their lives in the valley. She pulled one of their dresses from the laundry basket. Her hands shook as she pinned it to the line. She saw suddenly a mousy blonde pigtail shifting between angular shoulder blades. Freckles on a nose. Her throat closed. She couldn't leave the girls. Ta da da da da tum tum. She closed her eyes to the music and saw once again the wall of ice, a blue waterfall roaring down the face of it. She looked down and saw a puddle spread out at her feet and then a fish, its gills pink and raw looking, flopped down into the grass. She watched as it found a current and swished away into the garden.

"Oh, I can't, I can't, I can't dooo it!" Minnie heard herself cry. Even if there was a way to get back to Jeremy, she had the girls.

Rosella turned from the window at the sight of her mother at the clothesline, the hem of her flower-spattered dress pulled loose on one side and riding the top of her ridiculous, ugly galoshes. "Go get a drinking glass from the cupboard and take it on over to the Marchands'," Rosella mimicked her mother's voice. "Why should I?"

Ginny missed a note, went back, and corrected it. She couldn't stand it when Rosella got like that. Huffy, pacing, knocking things over. "Because she said to," Ginny said and straightened her back once more into the music and curved her bony wrists over the keyboard.

"She's talking to herself again," Rosella said.

"She's our mother," Ginny said. "It doesn't matter."

Rosella's footsteps echoed in the hallway. She paused at the top of the stairs. She slid her fingernail beneath a piece of wallpaper hanging loose at the seam and yanked. "Are you sure about that?" she said. "She says she's our mother, but how can we really know?"

"I'm telling Albert," Ginny said.

The strip of wallpaper reached the ceiling and fell free to the floor. "And he'll write a letter to Aunt Violet. Period." Rosella stirred the strip of paper with her toe. "Ginny," she said, "haven't you ever wondered about us?"

"No," Ginny said, knowing what was coming next.

"It's not normal," Rosella said. "We don't have anyone. No grandparents or aunts or uncles or cousins. No one but Minnie and Albert."

"We have Aunt Violet," Ginny said.

"I'm not so sure about her either," Rosella said as she went down the stairs. She paused at the bottom, in the hallway, and then stepped into her parents' bedroom. Aha, she thought as she looked at the chart. Minnie had forgotten to mark off the day.

A cloud of mosquitoes had risen from the damp grass and billowed up around Minnie's face as she bent over the clothes basket. Their wings fluttered against her nose, ears, bounced off her eyelids. It had been years and years, but suddenly she wanted to sing. God only knew what. Some nursery rhyme Albert had taught the girls. Or perhaps a hymn she'd learned when she used to go to the United with Albert. Before the Sunday school had begun to influence the girls against Jeremy. Jesus Saviour, the pilot, guiding. She couldn't remember. She tried, but she couldn't recall any song she'd learned when she'd lived with the Mennonite couple in Yarrow. Or even the gospel song John the Baptist had taught her. The one that had been playing on the radio when she'd walked in off the highway that night in the heat of summer. The night she'd left behind.... Gene. Gene Lacroix. Of course. Gene had taught her something in French. She opened her mouth, but nothing came out. She couldn't remember it either. She swallowed. Hum, hum, she sang in her head. The melody would come eventually. And when it did, it would not be something she had learned in the valley. It would speak of chimes and varnish and wavering images dancing through sepia ink and a cuttlefish scurrying through sand in a glass tank. Something from her time in the hills with Jeremy.

"Virginia?"

The music stopped.

"Please don't play that man's music. He was so full of himself."

"I thought you said you liked it."

"Play something by Mozart instead. Jeremy seemed to think he had great potential."

"Oh no," Rosella's voice rang out from the screen door. "Not Jeremy again."

Across the sagging wire fence on the west side of Minnie's yard—the fence held upright by a profusion of phlox which had seeded themselves over the years, concealing beneath their purple and pink flowers a mound of ancient garbage, broken bits of pottery, roasting stones, leftovers from another world—was Delta William's yard. The woman herself came out onto the back step and stood for a moment, hiked her stretch pants up over her pot belly, placed her hands on her hips, and looked over at Minnie's clothesline. She shook her head and went back inside the house. Minnie hadn't seen the woman. She stared at the row of maple trees growing their hearts out in a straight line across the back of the yard. She'd seen the flare of a white skirt with a swirl of red strawberries bordering its hem. She turned away and then back again, quickly, and from the corner of her eye she saw the flash of a silver button on a black patent shoe.

"Ma?" Ginny's voice. "Ma? You okay?"

A bug in her eye. That's what it was. Minnie rubbed and felt it swim across her eyeball. She opened her hand. P. "Ginny, honey, would you be a good girl and go down and start peeling the potatoes for our supper? Put them in a pot and cover them with water so they won't turn brown."

"It's Thursday." Rosella's strident voice snapped at the summer air.

"Yes, well, what I meant was, would you be a good girl and chop the peppers for the pizza? I want to go for a little walk."

"Now?"

"Yes, why not?"

"Well," Ginny said, "it...it...it...it isn't night."

"I know that, dear."

Ginny's voice dropped to a whisper. "But Ma, someone might see you."

"I want to have a little talk with Jeremy," Minnie said, returning the whisper.

Rosella's voice rose in an exclamation at this and then she muttered a string of sentences amid the clanking of water glasses knocking against one another in the cupboard.

"I'll tell you a story later on for being such a good girl," Minnie called up to Ginny.

"It's okay."

Minnie sighed. They used to pester her for stories. Now they didn't want them any more. But once it had got so bad that she was glad in the end for the play closet. Because they'd wanted stories of happenings before they were born. I found your mother in a potato patch, Albert had told them. Barefoot. With no shoes on. She couldn't remember summer from winter, and so I bought her the galoshes, he'd said, because she can wear them year round. That must have been—she searched her memory—at the Churchill farm. And before that the MacKenzie place and before that, Yarrow and the Penner family. John the Baptist. Gene Lacroix. And then, of course, Jeremy and his mother, in heaven.

The girls had wanted stories about after they were born, not trusting their own good memories, and so Minnie told them, "Oh, I pushed and pushed and out you squirted. Still covered in blood-tinged mucus, you swam across the sheets towards my feet and said, 'So long, it's been good to know you.' Good thing your father was there. Both times. He caught you just before you went out the door, wrapped you in warm flannel, and made you stay put for a time." Once Minnie's girls laughed at what they thought was the absurdity of it. Now they were resentful, feeling that their arrival was of such little consequence that she could scarcely recall it. And that was the truth. She couldn't recall much. Except that Ginny, the skinny little darling, had the colic and cried for three months straight and Albert had taken leave from the lumber yard to swaddle the child and jostle her in his arms while Minnie tramped the woods beside the river waiting for the child's cries to subside before she could go back home. But it was all part of the contract. Albert, she'd said, all right. I'll have babies. But I can't stand crying. All in all though, big or little consequence, both vanished from her memory as quickly as the next consequence arrived.

She used to tell the girls, "I was once in the circus. I rode an elephant and stood on my head on its back. I swung upside down from a trapeze thirty feet above the ground while the crowd ate popcorn and held their breaths, thinking I was going to fall." And she couldn't be certain if this was true or not. Every story she told them seemed to scratch at some memory lost in the back of her head. "I used to tie my legs in knots and put them behind my neck. I was made of rubber, you see. Once I lived in a man's car in his driveway for a month and he never knew it. I lived off his garden. One time I was caught in a rain storm and I began to melt. Another time I hid a stack of quarters in an oven and said, 'Abracadabra!' and a fifty dollar bill appeared in its place. I went for a ride in a spaceship and when I looked out the window, I saw the planet Earth, a glowing blue ball of water. And once upon a time, before I entered the valley, I lived with Jeremy and his mother in heaven and the boy Mozart was there and Jeremy was teaching Mozart to play a concerto for our wedding."

The girls used to like her Jeremy stories the most. Until they started going to Sunday school that is, and discovered that Jeremy—their teachers explained—didn't exist. You couldn't be in heaven unless you'd died. Jeremy, they told her girls, was only a figment of their mother's strange and disordered imagination.

"Ma!" Ginny's voice leapt with alarm as Minnie began walking away from the house. "Will you come back?"

"Well, of course," Minnie said as she crossed the sidewalk in front of the house. Sleek foxtails brushed against her legs as she cut down through the gully and up onto the dirt road which was Ottawa Street, the street where she lived in the town of Agassiz. Ottawa Street went like this: it began in the river. And even though when the people in Agassiz used it and said, "We're going on down to the river," they were really going up to the river. And when they said they were going uptown, they were going downtown. Usually when they said they were going down to the river, it was with a load of junk concealed in the trunks of their cars.

So Ottawa Street had begun as grassland teeming with grazing buffalo and the stealthy movements of fur-clad nomads, the stone roasters who had crossed the frozen tundra and ancient ice and been stranded in the valley like stones left behind by the glacier's retreat. The valley became the place of tepees then and Ottawa Street a path beaten flat by horses' hoofs and eventually rutted with the passing of wagon wheels. The tepees vanished and the street became a narrow path leading up to the water, its hind end broadening at last with the arrival of settlers, among them the fathers of Standing and Campbell, young surveyors who became the founders of the town of Agassiz. They arranged the grasslands into neat, numbered squares of ownership, with allowances for roads and streets like Ottawa (which became, in the end, a dirt road with weed-choked gullies on either side). Workmen had begun to excavate the gullies near the river end of the street, and had dug trenches to lay down bigger pipes to accommodate the town's swelling effluence. They were waiting for the best possible time to haul the pipes in from the municipal yard on the far side of town. People were growing weary of waking after a heavy rainfall to discover their basements brimming with their neighbours' backed-up sewers.

At the far end of the street, closest to the river, was Olga Peter's house, where she lived with her elderly widowed mother. The spinster Olga white-washed their cottage once every three years, allowed herself time to weep yearly over her lack of marital status, and daily clipped the only pair of earrings she owned into place and set off to her job at the Bank of Montreal. "Olga" was an ugly name, it was admitted by her fellow Mennonites, who greeted her on the street and in the bank as "Ollie", but they had given her a nickname from early on and when they greeted her in church or at the prayer meeting, they called her "Teedle". She doesn't want anyone else to know this.

Beyond the Peters' house was a vacant field which went wild each spring with the growth of Queen Anne's lace, fleabane, and wild flax the colour of the northern waters. Across the road from that field was Joe and Alma Harder's house, a flat-roofed stucco house painted orange. The Harders were poor cousins to the prosperous Mennonites in the valley. They had immigrated from Mexico and decided to live in Agassiz where there were at least a few Mennonite families, those who had not prospered or who had married out of their faith or lost it. But when Joe—who was an easy-going man too used to his siesta, people said—had turned to the river for his occupation and not the land, so that Alma, his wife, had to in turn leave their two children to fend for themselves while she cooked at the hotel to supplement their meagre income, the Harders found themselves tolerated but not accepted by their own. Joe Harder didn't mind.

Beside the Harders' flat-roofed hacienda, and resembling more an outdoor toilet than a house, was Hendrick Schultz's place, where he lived with his mother, Elizabeth. The boy and his mother were recent immigrants, too, but even though they were not Mennonite, Elizabeth, because she spoke only German, had been welcomed with open arms by that community and she and Hendrick had become for a time the church's special "Samaritan Project". The church was small and their resources limited and so although the congregation had managed to purchase the lot of land for the Schultzes, the one-room house remained unfinished.

Across from the Schultz house and beside the vacant field was Annie Schmoon's shanty. Annie had built the house herself and it looked like a train boxcar with a lean-to added onto the back of it—Annie's mud room. Because stretching out behind Annie's place was a broad, damp piece of land which the river backed into every spring, giving Annie her own private pond and a good crop of frogs which she sold to the only Japanese in Agassiz, Taro Yamamoto. Taro took them on into the city and sold them to the finer restaurants there. This was Annie's only source of income.

A respectable distance separated Annie's place from the rest of the people on the street. Another road, Railway, cut across Ottawa at this point, even though the railroad bordered the opposite end of town. After that, houses popped up like mushrooms. Sandra Adam's bungalow was first, where she lived with her widowed father until she was forced to leave the town. Steven Adam had once been a hearty, athletic, outdoors man, an active Anglican who organized boys' camps and canoeing trips into the hinterland of the valley, but the loss of his wife had throttled his extroverted character. The final act of life's betrayal occurred several years later in a heart attack, and Steven, receiving a small pension, retired as Station Master and turned his grief and bitterness inward. At that moment, Thursday morning, he sat at the kitchen table scraping mould marks from a piece of ceramic greenware as Sandra, who had just recently graduated from high school, was beginning her three days at MacLeod's store.

She was crouched beside a display of kitchenware counting the number of pickle dishes when her boss, Mr. Newhoff, came up behind her, tapped her on the shoulder, and said with a puzzled expression in his voice, "The Head Office wants to talk to *you* on the telephone?" And Sandra, rising from her knees, cheeks flushed a bit more than usual because she was so new at this game of concealment, rushed off to meet her fate.

Then there was the Egg Hatchery Dorfmans' home, the first people in Agassiz to experiment with aluminum siding on their house. Across the road from the Dorfmans' was the well-kept house of Charles and Emma Standing. It was a solid two storey with a lightning rod and the Union Jack flag snapping to attention from its mast. Charlie Standing was a bitter, brown stick of a man who used his cane to shake at the Marchand children more than he did to walk. Charlie was the remaining son of the surveyor Nelson Standing, who had come from the east with Campbell's father as his second-in-command to parcel out the valley. Usually you could find Charlie sitting at his desk in the dining room, writing down the history of the North-West Mounted Police, or out in the collapsing barn where trunks held his memories, his helmet, his scarlet uniform with the gold braid at the shoulders. Or else he'd sit on one of the trunks and leaf through the yellowed pages of his father's ledgers, the records of speculation, land grants, townships, sections, ranges, and the names of those he had bought and sold. Charlie had been out on the front veranda reading when June's house exploded and the kids went flying, and so he'd gone round to the back and now sat on the porch in his wicker rocking chair, cane planted firmly between his knees as he leaned on it, fixing a rheumy blue stare on the barn, keeping watch.

Beside the Standing house was the Marchands' rambling assortment of rooms. June and August had only recently moved to Agassiz and had four lively children who were like their Métis mother, dark-skinned both summer and winter. "Métis" was a word June worked hard to remove from her vocabulary. When the enumerator came to the door and asked, June said, "French. But what's it to you, eh?"

Minnie and Albert's house came next. It was also two storeys, but not as tall as the Standing residence because at one time it had only been a storey and a half and Albert had added the second half after the girls had come along. Beside the Pullman house was the town's wonder of a clipped and cultured lawn, sprinkled with white swans with arched necks and their mismatched offspring, peeping yellow ducklings, rooted for ever in their strange procession by long metal spikes. Delta William's lawn was also where June and August's children, directed by Robin, the oldest, preferred to squat and relieve themselves during the day. Set back against this marvel of lush, thick, green carpet was the newest house in Agassiz. It belonged to Delta. Delta had cruised into town from the city thirty years ago in a pair of slacks, smoking a cigarette, and had snatched up the most eligible bachelor. She refused children and when Archie died of a heart attack up on his combine, she moved into town, built the house, and opened up a restaurant on Main Street. Delta's Hot Spot.

Across from Delta's, where Ottawa met Main Street, was the oldest house in town—the Campbell house. It had once been the house of the Surveyor General, the lackey of the Minister of the Interior, who, once the valley had been surveyed, turned towards commerce and speculation. It was now the house of J.P. Campbell, his son and the Justice of the Peace of Agassiz. A broad veranda sloped down to the street like a welcoming apron held in a curtsy, but not many crossed it unless, of course, they were summoned.

But Minnie Pullman was unaware of the order of the street as she hurried down the centre of it towards the river. What passed before her eyes were the tips of her galoshes and the road moving beneath them, a treadmill that carried her down and down to the water. So she didn't catch Emma Standing's friendly wave from the veranda or hear her comment that "Albert's woman looks a trifle more discombobulated today." Minnie didn't see Mrs. Dorfman out with the hose, washing down the side of her house.

"Albert's going to worry." Rosella's voice pressed against Minnie's back.

Minnie turned and saw the girl in June's garden. Rosella frowned, gathered her thick mousy blonde braids together, and tied them in a knot beneath her chin the way she did when she was afraid that something embarrassing was going to happen. She tied her head up into a neat bundle and kept everything around her out.

"Did you do what I asked?"

"Oh, I can't, I can't, I can't dooo it!" June's voice rose up the scale inside the house. Minnie smiled as she heard the sound of glass shattering against the wall. At least for June Marchand, this day was the same as the one before it.

Ta da da da da tum tum. Ginny's music followed Minnie down the street. "Oh yes, oh yes," she said, "I totally agree. He *was* such a middling composer." And then she turned sharply and looked over her shoulder, afraid that she might see the child in the white dress with the spatter of red strawberries across the yoke and hem. That she might be followed.

2

The valley unrolled into a wide view which spread vast and far; embraced by gentle green ridges and hills, it stretched north where the icy sea spilled into it and whales nudged its shore. And the valley's seasons could be charted by colours, like the way summer gave way to gold and a gradual pulling back of green into the colour of straw and then black spirals of earth inched across its floor until, once again, it became a clean white page, resting, waiting for another portrait to emerge.

Early in the morning, as the sun tilted down into the hollow of land, cars and trucks roared down its highways, going east, west, north, and south. And in the evening when the sun retreated, the process was repeated. The music that floated up from those cars and from the houses was a mishmash of sounds, but harmonious in the whole. From one town in the valley, a fiddle played a jig. In another, an accordion squeezed out a polka. From a Hutterite colony, the instruments were the voices of the bearded men and black-skirted women. Beside it, the twang of an acoustic guitar and the voice of a man who sang about dying for love. The eerie wail of bagpipes threatened to drown out all other sounds. But when the view narrowed down to the centre of the valley, to the town of Agassiz, the puddle that contained the overflow of all those other towns, the whole of the music was lost to a cacophony of sounds. And taken to its narrowest view, Ottawa Street—where the greatest pride its residents possessed was in their differentness from their next-door neighbours—here, discord ruled. And Olga Peter had brought some of it with her to the Thursday night prayer meeting at the Mennonite church.

"If you want my opinion," Olga-Ollie-Teedle said when the prayer meeting had finished, "the real problem with Hendrick Schultz is that he's spoiled. He's had far too much attention." She resented this, having another meeting over Hendrick Schultz, when she still had to sponge and press her navy skirt and wind up her hair before going to bed.

Jacob Friesen, their pastor, held up his hand for silence because the door had barely closed behind Elizabeth, Hendrick's mother. They could still hear the tap of her heels against the sidewalk as she crossed the church yard and walked towards the road. They listened as the soft crumbling of her step against loose stones grew fainter, and then they sifted from the corners of the vestibule and joined Alma Harder in the circle of chairs. It was Alma who had called the special meeting.

Earlier in the day, the weather had suddenly turned cool, dropping fifteen degrees in several hours, and even though it was late in the month of June, hopes for an early summer were dashed. The coils of the electric heater in the centre of their circle glowed, radiating heat, and the women pulled their chairs closer to it, making the circle tighter to trap the warmth. In the sanctuary, the twitter of the sparrow that nestled between the windowpanes echoed in the rafters and made Jacob think of the women's children. It made him uneasy to think that a child might go to bed unattended and wanting a touch before sleep.

"All right," Alma Harder said. "This is how it went. I heard a noise coming from the kitchen. A hard kind of whispering." She crossed her long bare legs, oblivious or uncaring—the women couldn't decide which—that the frayed edge of her underslip fell below the hem of her hotel uniform. She'd come to the prayer meeting directly from her job in the kitchen at the hotel, and her olive skin shone with perspiration. She also smelled faintly of onions and stale cigarette smoke and the women had danced around one another in their rush to sit in the chair farthest away from her.

She played for their full attention. She paused in her story to rearrange the wilted handkerchief in her breast pocket. A yellow bit of cloth, a careful folding of it, one corner pulled down to loll overtop her pocket like the tongue of an iris. The women waited and hid their annoyance—that she would waste time for the sake of appearances while the greying underslip told the truth of her life.

"Something told me to go and have a look. You know how it is, how you can get a feeling when something isn't quite right?" She felt the mole beside her nose, traced the outline of it with her onion-tinged finger, as though deep in thought. The mole had appeared, she'd told the women, the day her daughter, Maria, had been kidnapped by the monkeys.

The women sighed, shifted impatiently, plucked creases from their pastel laps. They knew her exotic story of the inexplicable. She'd told them the story of the monkeys several times. About the colony of monkeys that dropped down from the trees one hot afternoon while rust spotted the drinking can of water and lizards clung to light bulbs strung up inside the tent. They waited on mats in the shade in a drowsy state and waited for the heavy blanket of heat to lift. And one of the monkeys reached inside the hammock where Maria lay sleeping. The hammock swung once and Maria was gone, carried off into the far reaches of the trees, still asleep. The monkeys fled and the family gave chase. When they grew tired and stopped to rest, they thought all was lost, but the monkeys stopped as well and sat on their haunches and stared at them from the trees with beady eyes which looked unreal, like glass. When they moved, the monkeys moved. When they sat still, so did the monkeys. "They", she said, and "we", never saying exactly who, but leaving the impression that in Mexico, they were happier and life had been more of an ongoing party. And so Alma had got an idea and demonstrated it to the monkeys several times, laying a rag doll down on the ground until, finally, one of the monkeys mimicked her, bringing Maria down from the tree and setting her on the ground. "I wonder what effect something like that would have on a person later on?" Alma always asked at the end of her story, as though the question had only just come to her.

Well, the other women had their own stories too, which they recited from time to time. But it was not just for hearing themselves speak that they told the stories over and over, but to leave behind a message or to encourage.

Jacob's wife, Lena, told her story about her father being put in front of a firing squad in Russia. The way she told it was stark and vivid so that they could almost feel the night and taste metal as she ran barefoot, clad only in a nightgown, from house to house, urging people to call upon God for his deliverance. And how their prayers were answered miraculously even while she ran, imagining the sound of a bolt sliding a bullet into the chamber: the marauders grew tired of their game and rode off leaving her father with his wrists still bound, but unharmed.

But the story of the monkeys carrying off Maria disturbed them because they couldn't find its reason or meaning.

"Let us pray that our words tonight will be acceptable to Him who made us," Jacob said, interrupting Alma, wishing to set the correct tone for their discussion. The pitch of their voices grated at his ears.

"You know I'm not one to make a big stink out of anything," Alma said, "but when I went to see what was going on in the kitchen, I found Hendrick chasing my Maria around the table."

"You said, 'a hard kind of whispering'," Jacob said. "What do you mean by that?" Across from him, on the wall, Jesus the Good Shepherd clung to the side of an embankment, almost falling as he reached down to rescue a wayward sheep.

"Secretive like. I don't know," Alma said. "Almost angry, but not angry. A pushing kind of whisper. Like he didn't want to be heard."

"Well, of course," Lena said, impatience crinkling the skin above her nose. "Why does anyone whisper?"

More and more, the tension stretched between the women like an elastic band, Jacob thought. Quivering with petty indignation.

"What was Maria doing in the kitchen in the first place?"

"Well, excuse me," Alma said, "but she does live there. She had every right to be in the kitchen."

"Now, now," Lena said. "It's not necessary to be so sensitive. No one's blaming you for anything."

"Maria was washing the floor," Alma said. "Elizabeth and I were upstairs changing the sheets on the beds and the boy was waiting on a chair in the kitchen, as usual."

"When you caught him doing this, what did you do about it?"

"I gave him a good piece of my mind," Alma said.

Several of the women smiled and then Teedle-Ollie Peter could not resist and whispered in Hilda Penner's ear that she guessed that wouldn't leave Alma with much left to work with.

"However, talking didn't help," Alma said. "Because no sooner was my back turned when he was up to it again. Finally, Elizabeth could see that I was upset and so came and spoke to the boy, but that didn't help either. And then the fun started," she said. "Elizabeth broke a window. I'm going to have to dock her pay."

Questions leapt to the women's minds and they all leaned forward, startled.

Alma smiled. "I have to say, in all fairness, that the broken window part was an accident. She was just getting the spanking stick that was holding up the window. Anyway, she made Hendrick bend over a chair and she spanked him. Well, you could have knocked me over with a feather."

"I don't believe it," Ollie said. "At last."

"I didn't say for her to do it. I said I thought it was time she took the boy in hand, but I didn't say to spank him."

"Oh," Hilda Penner said. She pulled a tiny, lace-trimmed handkerchief from the wrist of her sweater and wiped her eyes. "Did he cry?"

"Not a whimper," Alma said. "At least not that I know of. But Elizabeth did. I had to send her home."

The women glanced at one another, at Jacob. Even though their eyes were trained to search out the first, faint lines of growth in the garden, and their fingers knew how to curl into the soil to find out if the beans were sprouting, they had all missed it: the pebbly skin, the suggestion of whiskers on Hendrick's adolescent chin. When he waited in their kitchens for his mother to finish cleaning, he couldn't sit still. And although they perceived these indications of future manhood in their own sons, they somehow thought that the boy, Hendrick, would remain a boy. They wondered among themselves now what Elizabeth could know about the feverish urging of a boy growing towards manhood. "I wonder what she knows about the nature of men, period," Hilda said, whispering discreetly so Ollie wouldn't hear. She reminded them that Elizabeth's marriage had been a short one. The women passed the thought through their eyes one to another: how could Hilda know anything about men either, having been married so late in life to that old tobacco-chewing fart of a man who spent more time in the barn with his animals than in the house with her?

"You've made your point," Jacob said. "And thank you. And I think we can manage to pay for the broken window."

Lena nodded her assent. The women began to gather up handbags from the floor and inch their chairs back into the cooler space behind them.

Alma remained seated. She uncrossed her legs and sat up straighter as though what she was about to say required this look of modesty.

"I'm not finished," she said. "There's more to it. The real point of the whole matter is that the boy was trying to hide something from me."

All movement ceased as the women waited, expecting to hear of some petty thievery. Something which would make them search their minds for instances of missing objects or loose change that could lead directly to Hendrick.

"He was trying to hide the fact that he had a stiff banana in his pants. If you know what I mean."

Ollie turned red up into the roots of her fair, curly hair.

"And it makes me wonder, that's all. You know. About what he was up to when he was chasing my Maria and whispering that hard kind of whisper. I don't think he had Bible verses on his mind, either." Alma thought it was plain nonsense—the big to-do that went on about the boy's memory of Scripture.

"It's pretty clear just what was up," Ollie said. The women gasped and stared at her. "No, what I meant was...," she said, and gave up the explanation in a fit of coughing.

"I'll deal with this," Jacob said. The women sighed in relief.

"Well, that's it then," Ollie said and jumped up from her chair. She gathered up her leather bag and sweater in one swoop and was out the door.

The women saw the wisdom in Jacob's smooth features as he blessed them. The stillness in his hazel eyes, the unlined youthful face, had always testified to them of the reality of his philosophy. That he found it possible in life to be content in any situation. Jacob raised his head and said, "Amen." His eyes met the sharp, furtive look of Alma Harder.

Jacob pulled the heater's plug from the wall and watched the coils dim. He stood in the dark vestibule and listened as the women's voices faded and then were replaced by the low grumble of a semi travelling out along the highway. Why would Elizabeth be moved now, at this late hour, to take the wooden spoon to the boy? This puzzled him and at the same time unsettled him because there was no part of those two which he didn't know or want to know. The door opened suddenly and a gust of damp air pressed in against his pantlegs. Alma Harder stepped into the wide strip of moonlight on the floor.

"Yes?" His voice betrayed the discomfort he felt when one of the women wished to speak to him privately.

Alma didn't speak at once. The only sound in the vestibule was that of the soft scuffle of her toe tracing out the perimeter of moonlight on the floor and the steady metallic click of the clock, seconds vibrating against his fingers. Let patience have its perfect work, he reminded himself. It was to be the topic of his sermon the coming Sunday. He often found that he'd be called upon to deal with the very thing he planned to teach. It was the Lord's way.

"It's the usual," Alma said at last and laughed. "I'm going to be a widow to summer again." The woman spoke in riddles, circled whatever it was she had in her mind. She was clever at gaining attention this way, he realized.

"I can tell," she said. "Joe's got that look. Ants in his pants. He won't be still."

The erring, straying husband. What did she expect him to do? "You could be wrong," Jacob said. "He could be harvesting the nets when he's away."

"All night?" Alma said and laughed once again, dry and bitter.

"No, no, of course not," Jacob said. "I'm sorry. Why don't you come to the house tomorrow? We can talk there." Behind him, the coils of the heater snapped as wires contracted in the cool air.

"I'm working tomorrow."

"Come on your day off then."

"I don't have a day off any more. I'm full time now," Alma said. "And I don't know where we'd all be without it." The strip of moonlight shrank to a thin line, retreating across the floor as she began to close the door. "I've been full time for a year now," she said, her voice muffled by the heavy wooden door. "Not that anyone's interested."

"Wait a moment," Jacob said, and once again the light cut across the splintered and water-stained boards.

He set the clock down in the strip of light between them and clasped his hands. "If you like, we could pray." He'd seen the silver trickle run down her cheek and over the top of the mole beside her mouth. "He said, 'Come unto me all ye who labour and are heavy laden and I will give you rest'," he quoted.

Alma plucked the careful arrangement of handkerchief free from her breast pocket and blew into it. "Thanks," she said, "but maybe more would be accomplished if you had a talk with Joe."

"God reaches hearts where men can't."

"I suppose so," Alma said.

"He may not stray this summer."

"Does the sun shine?" she said.

"One last thing," Jacob said.

"I know," Alma said. "Trust in the Lord with all your heart and lean not to your own understanding," she recited. It was her verse for the day. The one she'd pulled from a loaf of bread sitting on the windowsill above her sink as she'd watched Joe walking down the road towards the town.

Jacob smiled. "Well, yes, good. But there is something else. You could help me if you could give me any idea at all what made Elizabeth so angry that she would spank the boy. I'd like to know."

"Elizabeth?"

"Yes, I'd appreciate any ideas you might have." He waited. The sound of Alma's breathing filled the small room.

"Oh, I see." Her voice was a plane shaving free a curl of wood. "I see how it is," she said. "If I were Elizabeth Schultz with my precious Second Coming of a son, I'd say jump and you'd all ask how high. That's the way it is and that's the way it's always been."

The light was snuffed out as the door clicked shut.

Jacob's throat ached with the unfair comment. It was so unjustified. He freely gave his time to all of them, equally. He'd continually counselled them not to treat the boy differently or speak of his gift outside of their circle. The attention given to Elizabeth and her son was simple charity and nothing more. Slowly, the door opened once again but, this time, the woman didn't enter. She stood outside on the top step.

"I haven't the slightest notion what made Elizabeth angry," she said. "But there is something. Something else. I didn't want to bring it up in front of the others. But...don't you think that Hendrick is kind of old to be sleeping with his mother?"

The thought of their sleeping arrangements had never entered Jacob's mind before.

"Well, keeping in mind what I saw in the kitchen. Because they do sleep together. They always have and look at him—the boy's twelve years old, for pete's sake." She closed the door and once again Jacob stood in complete darkness.

He stepped outside, turned the skeleton key in its lock, and dropped it into his pocket. He hated having to lock the church. A church should be kept open for wanderers, strangers needing shelter from the wind. But, since the highway, there were too many strangers. Like the man who'd taken shelter one winter. Jacob had discovered him asleep on a bench behind the oilburner. "You have to let me stay," the man had said, "because you never know, I may be an angel." And Jacob—foolishly, he realized now—had allowed the man to take part in their service. Often, when he and Lena discussed why the husbands didn't come to church any more, they touched on this incident. The man, who they later discovered was an ex-convict only recently released, had disturbed their service by leaping up from the pew and chanting in a strange gibberish which he called the tongues of angels. Jacob had gone to the four corners of the building, praying away whatever residue of evilness had been left behind. But often he wondered whether his prayers had been sufficient.

The night air was unusually damp, more like early spring than summer, and cut through his jacket. He began to shiver. He walked to the end of the sidewalk and then stopped. It was cool. Lena would wonder where he was. And anyway, it was foolish to think that anything could be learned this way. But he could not help himself and he turned away from the huddled collection of buildings which made up the town of Agassiz. He walked quickly to get his blood flowing, but his body shook and hard spasms radiated outwards from his spine. A tethered dog rose from a back yard and yapped as he passed by. Its bark was answered immediately by other dogs in the town, and then a long plaintive howl arose in the south and the voices of the town dogs were silenced by it. It was a dismal sound.

By the time he reached the one-room house, its windows two rectangles of faint light pressing out against the black earth, his teeth chattered. The men of the church under his leadership had purchased the piece of land on Ottawa Street and had built the one-room house for Hendrick and his mother to live in. For several years they had taken turns keeping the place in order: painting, patching loose shingles, caulking windows to keep out winter drafts. But as their church attendance waned—except for Joe Harder, who hauled wood and water for her—their interest in the "Samaritan Project", as it was called, waned as well. Lena felt it was as it should be. That it was better to provide Elizabeth with work rather than things. He felt uneasy about being there, as though by walking past their house he'd pulled open a drawer that didn't belong to him. He saw the metallic sheen of the stove pipes and then the shelf above the table that held jars of flour, sugar, fruits, and vegetables, and below that, Hendrick, sitting at the table in his undershirt. He reached across the table for something. A long shadow crossed the wall behind the boy and Jacob saw that white head, white braids loose and swinging against her shoulders. Even from that distance and through the glass, Jacob sensed what seemed to be present whenever the boy and his mother were together. That it didn't matter what space he put between their chairs, when they were in the same room, he had the feeling that when one moved, so did the other.

Hendrick got up then and crossed the room where the bed rested against the wall. Then Elizabeth passed in front of the first and then second window. She reached up above the bed and the house fell into darkness. Jacob turned and walked quickly back towards the reflection of the town's lights glowing in the overhanging clouds. Perhaps she slept across the room on a bed put together at the last moment. Perhaps she made a place for herself on the floor. But then, why wouldn't the boy reach up from the bed and pull out the light and not leave his mother to stumble about in the dark? Why hadn't she come to him with her problem of the boy, instead of taking the spoon for the first time and spanking him? It was as though Jacob had just raised a kaleidoscope to his eye, twisted it, and watched the picture tumble into place. He had to do something. To help her. He had to figure out how to get the boy out of his mother's bed.

3

Sandra Adam hesitated before entering Ottawa Street. She heard the voices of the women who were returning from the prayer meeting at the Mennonite church. They sounded young, their voices high and clear, a bell tone in the air which was round and full with moisture. "Let that boy suck until he was four years old. Imagine." The sentence hung above their heads. "Shht!" one of the women cautioned silence and Sandra knew that they'd seen her. She saw them as they cut across Ottawa Street at Railway, walking in two tight clusters. She thought of the joke Sonny Ericson had once told in school. Why don't Mennonites make love standing up? Because they're afraid someone might think they're dancing. Prayer meeting did seem to be their only social activity. She never saw any of them at the movie theatre, for instance, or in Delta's Hot Spot, or at the skating rink. But still, unlike the Hutterite women who came into MacLeod's store all together with their designated spokesman and the remainder of the women hanging back and shy, these Mennonite women, both from the surrounding villages and in town, held themselves erect and a bit aloof, scrutinizing carefully each item, making Sandra feel like apologizing for its price or shoddy workmanship. She sometimes thought they felt they were above going to the movie theatre or Delta's Hot Spot.

She waited until the women passed into darkness before she stepped down into the street. It had rained during choir practice but the rain had passed as quickly as it had come, a sudden drumming against the church roof and then absolute silence. It had rained enough, though, that the muddy road had become sticky and pulled at her shoes. Despite this, she would not use the sidewalk tonight. She believed that she'd earned the right to make the decision to use the road, and not the sidewalk which would bring her closer to the women inside the houses. She no longer needed the reassurance of Delta out on the front steps in her chenille housecoat, cigarette glowing in the dark as she rode shotgun over her lawn; or Emma Standing either, who would glance up from her needlework and wave a friendly hello through the front window. Because of the telephone call from Head Office that morning, Sandra felt like a child sitting among a group of adults when a box of chocolates was being passed among them. Of course, no one expected her to refuse. The box passed and passed through hands into hers. Sandra looked down at the silver- and gold-wrapped candies with longing. And the great moment of realization of having passed from one state to another happened in the blink of an eye: she didn't have to do the expected. She could make decisions. No thanks, Sandra would say, feeling a bit sorry, but she would pass the box on, waiting for their recognition, their astonishment that she had grown up.

The first astonished person had been Mrs. Bond, the choir director. She'd rapped sharply on the top of the piano that evening and said, "For heaven's sakes, altos, pay attention. You're either in too early or too late." She'd fixed an icy glare directly on Sandra, but Sandra didn't feel like running from the musty-smelling loft to vomit over the toilet in the basement. She had answered back instead.

"I think you're playing too fast," she said.

"I beg your pardon?" Mrs. Bond said but the whole alto section noticed the flicker of doubt behind her glasses. Then she turned her back to them and slid the weight up the stem of the metronome slightly.

"Way to go, kid," June Marchand said and nudged Sandra in the side. "I may change my mind about you yet. The old babe sure can get her shit in a knot, eh?"

The waning day slanted across the horizon, cutting through the stained-glass window at the back of the United church, illuminating a glorious crimson and blue Christ. Someday, Sandra thought, she could even choose to believe or not believe in his existence, too. She turned to face June.

"Well, if she bothers you so much, why on earth do you bother coming?" There. She'd finally asked the question she'd always wanted to ask June. Why did the woman bother to come to choir practice if she never bothered to come to church? She was a thorn, Mrs. Bond had confided once to Sandra, but she believed some message in the words of the hymns might worm down inside June Marchand and, someday, she'd clean up her act. June sang a full octave lower than the sopranos and believed she sung alto.

"Well, what're we standing around waiting for?" June had said when practice was finally over. The choir members milled about on the front sidewalk, fumbling in shirt pockets and handbags for cigarettes. Moments later, a blue cloud of smoke billowed up as they exhaled with relief. "I appoint myself social convenor," June Marchand said. She stared at Sandra, her eyes fox eyes, glowing from the side of a road. "And I say that we all go down to the hotel for a beer. Those that don't drink can play shuffleboard."

"But what about Sandra?"

"Yes, it wouldn't be fair," someone else said and suggested that for the sake of Sandra who was not of legal age they stick to their routine of apple pie and coffee at Delta's Hot Spot.

June's caustic reply was lost as Mrs. Bond came alongside Sandra. "This girl and I need to talk," she said. "You'll do without her tonight."

"My dear, is something the matter?" Mrs. Bond asked. She'd led her back inside and they sat side by side on the front pew. The woman was too anxious and intimate—Sandra realized that now—and made her feel as though she were an insect on a slide about to be dissected. Like all the women in the town, Mrs. Bond searched diligently for blemishes on the girl's face, wanting, Sandra knew, to see a bit of acne there.

From time to time in MacLeod's store when she was busy dusting the kitchenware, a sunbitten farm woman would sidle up to Sandra and whisper, "Hey girlie, what kind of face cream do you use?"

"None," Sandra answered. It was the truth.

"Well, then what kind of cleanser?"

"Soap. Lifebuoy." She realized as she said this from the lines drooping down from their chapped lips that they thought she was being mean not to reveal the source of her healthy glow. She felt helpless and wished often that she knew how to tell lies and make them happy. And so she learned how to notice something special about them—how their earrings matched their purses, or she'd ask if they'd lost a bit of weight. She'd mention a special ornament she'd set aside—an unusual pair of salt-and-pepper shakers because she knew it suited their taste.

But the women of the town of Agassiz were different, especially the women who attended the United and counted on their good works to reserve a place in heaven for them. *If* there was such a place. They'd clutched Sandra to their hard bosoms ever since her father, Steven, had carried her home from the hospital. They had bathed her, rubbed oil into her creases (or so she imagined), hummed lullabies while Sandra's mother slept in the graveyard beside the highway. When it became apparent that Steven had turned his back on his faith, they took her along to the United Sunday school, arranged piano lessons when it appeared she was musically talented, persuaded Mrs. Bond to teach her a bit of voice and to hire her to lead the alto section when she turned fifteen. They still brought casseroles and muffins over to the house as though it were only last week when her mother had died giving birth. And when Sandra turned twelve like Hendrick, there was no need for a special meeting behind her back. One by one, the women visited.

"This is women's talk Steven, so take a hike," Delta said. She'd brought along a little booklet called "So You're a Girl!" Inside the book were drawings of tubes and frilly things and dots moving down those tubes, growing into little upside down babies. "You'll experience some mild discomfort," Delta said. "Pop an Aspirin and never wear white."

Mrs. Emma Standing clutched at the cameo brooch at her throat and the little circles of pink rouge on her cheeks turned scarlet. "Sex," she said and coughed, "is sacred. Always remember that."

Then Mrs. Dorfman—who was not United but Lutheran and who privately referred to the United people as being "wishy washy"—visited. "It's the curse, girlie," she said. She patted Sandra on the knee. "It's a woman's curse. We all get it. Just don't shampoo your hair when it happens."

Olga Peter, much to everyone's surprise, visited as well. It wasn't likely that Olga should notice that Sandra had turned twelve. She barely looked to the left or the right when she marched down the street every morning on the way to the bank. The Mennonites kept to themselves. Olga dropped a neatly wrapped package into Sandra's lap. "The instructions are inside," she said. "Read them and weep."

The day it finally happened, Sandra sat huddled against the fence down at the lumber yard, knees drawn up to her chin. Whenever she got up and tried to walk, a trickle of blood ran down her legs and into her white socks. She thought about those tubes and frilly things sucking up a dot and an upside down baby growing. It was all her fault for wearing the white dress. The worst of it was the idea that in every window someone watched, and whispers would rise up from the town and creep into every house. *Sandra Adam has started.*

"Oh my." Albert Pullman dropped down on the sidewalk beside her. "Oh dear, yes." He unzipped his jacket and slid free from it. He tied its sleeves about her waist so the jacket would drape down and cover the stains at the back of her white dress. He rolled down her knee-high socks and pulled them loose. He folded them down into two neat pads.

"Here," he said and handed her one. "I won't look. Put one of these inside your underpants." He turned away while she did so. He shoved the other sock into his pocket and winked at her. "Reinforcements. Tell me if you need it." She couldn't look at him. "Well, now," Albert said and chucked her under the chin, "isn't this a happy day."

"Happy?"

"Well, I believe so," Albert said. He took her by the hand and pulled her upright. "It calls for a celebration."

Albert led Sandra to the Dairy Milk Bar and bought her a double decker. She remembered it well. Strawberry and chocolate scoops melting together. He took time off from work to walk Sandra home and on the way he explained the dots and the frilly things and told her not to worry about the white dress. Soak it in cold water. And they made a deal. Every month, Sandra would come into the lumber yard and buy a package of 1/4-inch screws and Albert would know. He'd stop off at the Red and White on the way home and later that night, he'd hide the brown-paper–wrapped box in the lilac hedge at the edge of Sandra's yard.

Mrs. Bond slid up against Sandra in the pew until their thighs touched. "You don't have to tell me what's wrong unless you want to," she said. "But sometimes it helps to get it out."

For one second, Sandra almost fell for it. When she smelled the faint, safe odour of Mrs. Bond's baby powder, felt the warm swell of her bosom pressing against her side and the ample arm slip around her shoulders, Sandra almost grabbed Mrs. Bond, jumped into her softness, and told her. I sent a letter to Head Office. They received it. Today, they called me. And, as June would say, the shit's going to hit the fan.

She looked up and saw the network of spidery veins in the woman's cheeks. The arm grew heavy on her shoulder.

"I think I'm getting a cold," she said.

"Lemon tea with a spoonful of honey," Mrs. Bond said. Already she'd lost interest and reached for her sweater. She shrugged down into it. "And lots of sleep. You need to be up for your solo on Sunday."

Behind Sandra, the town glowed and hummed. The flickering neon sign above the hotel was reflected back in the wispy, trailing clouds. Sandra heard the squeal of tires—June Marchand, she thought, leading the whole choir astray. But that was not the case.

June swung into the curb, her boot heavy on the accelerator, pushing, always pushing to the limit. The car swayed for two seconds and she wanted to jab the accelerator and go straight clean through the hotel window. At the last moment her thigh jumped and she pumped the brake and the car rocked to a halt against the curb.

She watched in the rear view mirror as the other choir members entered the café across the street. Okay, so go on over to old Delta's, she thought. Pimple heads, the whole bunch. Do your little finger exercises. Deadheads. "Oh, you people are so sad, so very, very sad," she'd sung once, a little drunk. Leaving the hotel. Walking down a sidewalk flickering with neon light, a beer in hand, felt hat she'd borrowed from someone pushed back on her head. Banana earrings bounced against her jaw. August, stubborn, waiting out the last call inside. "Oh, this is very sad to see," she'd sung. Searching for her car. Sometimes they moved it. Sonny Ericson and his buddies would sneak out before closing, hook their cute little buns to the bumper, and push it around the block and then accuse her of being drunk when she couldn't find it. Or watch from the window and make bets on how long it took her.

"Why don't you people be happy?" she'd sung to the town. But the next morning when she rolled over in bed beside August and heard the kids downstairs already beating up on each other, she realized that she'd been singing to herself. That she was going to have to get out of bed again and keep doing those finger exercises. Which she could do with her eyes closed. And then she'd have to throw something. Would feel her hand squeeze against the side of a water glass, a plate, listen to it shatter against the wall. August had kept a box of polyfiller under the sink for years. Mixed it down into a smooth paste and buttered over the nicks and bruises on the wall. "Do that again," August said, "and I'll break your arm." But he never did. Because she'd hit him over the head with a dinner plate if he so much as tried. Or call her brothers out of the Pembina Hills and they'd wrestle him down. Threaten to cut off his balls again.

But after the satisfaction of glass breaking came the damned broom and dustpan—another finger exercise. When she thought of it—the sound of plastic bouncing off the wall—the thought made her swing her boot and kick the door open. Her narrow hips swung in tight jeans as she entered the beverage room. "Sassy ass", they called June.

Ernie stood behind the bar, washing glasses. "What, am I wrong?" he said. "Or is it Friday?"

June hiked up onto a stool. Emma Standing huddled in a dark corner, taking quick sips at a glass of sherry. The three old men who lived upstairs in the hotel sat together at a table in the centre of the empty room. Not speaking. Yellow fingers wrapped tightly around draft glasses measuring the level of the beer after each gulp. It was as though they counted. Twenty, thirty seconds, then their hands lifted the glasses again, Adam's apples bobbing beneath wrinkled brown skin as they swallowed another meagre portion.

"From now on, every day is Friday," June said. "Here's to prissy little Sandra Adam." Well, if it bothers you so much, why do you bother to come? Because she felt like it. Because when she'd first come to Agassiz and met Father Roy, the Catholic priest, on the street, he kept urging her to "look to her roots" and she knew he didn't mean her blonde hair either, which was turning out to be a regular pain in the butt to keep up. The black grew in so fast, most of the time she looked as though she'd been caught in a terrific dust storm. She came to choir practice because she studied them to try and figure out how they could keep doing the same things over and over. She and August had moved nine times in fifteen years and when August got hired on with the Roads crew in Agassiz, he said, "Enough." Except for Minnie the Spinny, who had gone batty trying, everyone in Agassiz seemed to be content to live in the same place and do the same things over and over.

Ernie wiped his hands and reached up for June's special beer mug. "Sassy Ass" the letters on it read. Ceramics was Steven Adam's hobby turned into a bit of cash.

"How's old Simon's hip?" June asked, nodding in the direction of the three men.

"Seems fit as a fiddle," Ernie said. "He managed to get down the stairs tonight, didn't he?"

"Some fiddle," June said. "Has the doctor been up to see him yet?"

Ernie's shoulders drooped beneath his sweatshirt. He had the look of a man so heavily influenced by the force of gravity that it drew the creases in his face down into his chin. His arms dangled at his sides. "Said he'd look in."

"I take it that means he hasn't?"

"Ah, come on. Get off my case," Ernie said. "Old Simon is well enough not to miss his treat night. Besides, I'm not their babysitter. They get a deal on the rooms as it is."

"Sure, and keep you in business at the same time. Minor detail." June picked up the mug, swallowed. If it weren't for those three geezers living up there in those drafty, filthy rooms, Ernie wouldn't be able to keep the beverage room open. Every time one of them kicked the bucket, Ernie scoured the bushes and flushed out a retired bachelor or widower. Or some battle-scarred leftover from a war. Always men. Women would want coloured towels and clean tubs. Complain about the noise of clanking radiators. As long as he had tenants, he fulfilled the basic requirement of the law for a hotel and could serve liquor.

On treat night, Friday, June and August's customary night to go flying, June would sneak upstairs and prowl through dark hallways and stand behind corners so she could look into their dimly lit rooms. She studied these men whose lives were arranged within four dingy walls containing a table, a chair, a bed. They pulled up the shade in the morning and pulled it back down at night. And she was puzzled. How did they keep on doing it. How? And why? And last Friday June had discovered Simon lying in a heap on the floor outside the bathroom. He held himself down there, trying to hide the stain in his trousers. June had carried him to his room and set him on the bed. And when she'd stooped to gather up his legs and swing them up, she saw the can of dog food underneath it.

"Hey, Ern," June said and watched those tobacco-stained hands lift the glasses and set them back down again, "you let those guys have pets?"

Ernie grunted as he stooped to count the cases of beer in the cooler. "No way," he said.

"I think old Simon must be putting one past you then," she said.

"Baseball team should be in about ten," Ernie said, still counting.

"Ernie."

He sighed and stood up. "Hell, no. Old Simon doesn't have a dog."

"He's got dog food."

"I know."

"Christ."

Emma Standing tipped back the last bit of her sherry, gathered up her straw handbag and raincoat. "Good evening," she said. Her face flushed beneath the circles of pink rouge as she slipped past them to the door.

"What's she doing here?" June asked.

"Thursday night is Emma's treat night," Ernie said. "Hey, wanna hear something priceless?" he said and dropped his voice as the door swung closed behind Emma Standing. "The old babe says to me, 'Ernest, I wonder if I might have a minute of your time?' So I says, 'Shoot.' And she says, 'Well, I might have another sherry first.' So's I bring it to her. And she says,

'Well, I thought you might be the person to talk to. You're a man, and, well, I guess you get to hear a lot.' And so she takes this magazine she's got in her bag and unfolds it. Points to some contraption in the ads. I can't figure it out. So she smashes back the sherry and says, 'It's Charles. I can't seem to get a thing out of him these days.' And I say, 'What, he's a bit into himself is he? A bit down?' 'Oh, how did you know?' she says. 'You hit the nose right on the head. It just doesn't seem to matter what I do. I can crawl all over Charles all night long and I can't get a thing out of him. Think this might help?' and it turns out," Ernie said, and gulped back his laughter, "that it's an ad for some kind of gadget that's supposed to keep his pecker stiff. A kind of erecto-matic." His laughter exploded and filled the almost empty room.

"So, do you think Simon eats it?" June asked.

"What?"

"The dog food?"

"Oh, that. Yeah. As Emma would say—you hit the nose on the head," Ernie said. "They all do. Hell, it's vacuum packed. Don't see any dogs keeling over in the street, do you?"

June's heart pressed against her ribs. Any one of the three elderly men could be Grandpops. The glasses rose. Fingers measured foam left at the bottom of the empty glasses.

"And now," Ernie said, "their treat night is over for the week and they'll all go on up to bed."

Her grandfather camping out in the shell of a rusting car in the sand dunes, dehydrated and gasping for breath.

"Like hell they will," June said and slid down from the stool. Her boots thumped against the worn carpet as she strode over to their table, fished for bills in her back pocket, and set them down on the table.

"Have another round," June said. "It's on me."

Their identical faces became strained, pinched, and then closed. One by one, they pushed the empty glasses into the centre of the table and struggled up from their chairs. "Don't take a hand-out from no squaw," a gravelly voice muttered in passing. And then one by one, they shuffled off through the darkened hallway that led to their rooms upstairs.

"What the fuck," June said. "I'm not black, am I?"

"You shoulda had me bring over a round," Ernie said. "Say it was on the house."

"Well, fuck it all to hell," June said. She reached and swept their glasses from the table. She listened to the sound of glass shattering. Ernie reached up to a pad of paper hanging beside the telephone and put down three marks. "I'll show them," June said. "I'll show everyone. I'm not black."

As Sandra Adam walked down the centre of Ottawa Street, her feet made soft sucking noises in the sticky, moist clay. The wind rose as she passed by the Pullman house. Up on the top floor, a faint light pressed out against the curtains. She saw a figure behind the curtain, looking out.

"What're you staring at?" Ginny asked Rosella, who stood leaning forward at their bedroom window, hands resting against the sill. Her bony rump shone ivory through her thin muslin nightgown. Clouds trailed about the room, dabbed at the flocked wallpaper, coaxing it loose at the seams until it gave up its hold and curled down the wall. Mist fingered their clothing hanging from a rod in the closet, imprinting it with a mustiness—fertile ground for mildew.

Rosella straightened and turned away from the window. The floorboards creaked beneath her long narrow feet as she crossed the room and squatted to adjust the water glass which served to catch little plops of water. Above it, a rust-coloured stain had spread across the ceiling and rain seeped through plaster which was as soft as toothpaste. Then Rosella sat down on the bed beside Ginny, who was slathering her arms and legs with Pond's Vanishing Cream. They heard their mother call out from the garden. Sing-song, high, her voice like their own. No firmness. Minnie had never raised her voice in anger. Rosella picked up *Anne of Green Gables*. A single lightbulb dangled from a wire above their bed and spread a circle of light across their chenille bedspread, chased shadows into corners of the room where soft grey balls, like clumps of woman's hair, nestled.

Ginny watched as Rosella's short brush-like eyelashes almost closed. But her eyeballs were still and did not follow any line in the book. Rosella sat beside Ginny on the bed. Ginny could feel the weight of her sister in the dip of the mattress and if she moved her foot two inches, their feet would touch. But it was as though Rosella was in another room. Sometimes Ginny felt as though she were standing on a rock and Rosella were in a boat, drifting away across the water, waving goodbye.

"Sandra," Rosella said. "I was watching Sandra Adam."

"Oh," Ginny said and watched her own hands rub and rub the cream into her shiny, impenetrable skin, a white slippery mess which rubbed off onto the sheets at night.

"What was she wearing?" Ginny asked.

"Clothes."

That Sandra. Always coming home from places, going places. Sandra had had her choice of any woman in town for a mother. She flew down the street, up the street, coat flapping, or hitching her arms through her sweater at the last moment as she ran, almost late, off to Guides, CGIT, calling out round breathless hellos because she was in a hurry, because she was going for her piano lessons or voice lessons or 4H.

They heard the back door slam shut.

"Oh," Ginny said. Her eyes flew open and she leaned forward, listening.

"Don't worry," Rosella said. "He's not going anywhere. He's got a cake in the oven."

Sandra helping the younger ones in school, bending down to button Rosella's coat in the hallway, saying, "What a pretty dress. Did your mommy make it?" And Rosella, snapping her head sideways, sank her teeth into Sandra's arm and hung on until her head ached.

"All right, all right, put up your hands then," Mrs. Clarence, the teacher, said. "Those of you who think you can bring something for the spring party, put up your hands."

Hands shot up all over the room. A chocolate cake. Rice Krispie squares. Peanut butter and honey sandwiches. Rosella bent over her notebook, making perfect Ms and Ns. She liked the roundness of the letters. Beads of perspiration popped above her lip as she made those letters roll across the page.

"Rosella?" Mrs. Clarence's voice. Rosella set the pencil aside. Her braids felt like corn silk against her chin. She leaned forward on her elbows and listened to the room that became the muffled roar in a seashell as she pressed her braids against her ears and hung on. The pencil rolled from the desk onto the floor. Sandra tiptoed from the blackboard where she'd been writing down who was going to bring what. The bandage on her arm had shrunk to a square of flesh-coloured plastic. She was going to explain why Rosella wouldn't be bringing anything. Rosella's arm twitched. She tried to hold it still, but slowly, against her will, she lost her grip on the braid and her arm raised itself.

"Yes? You'll bring something?"

Someone in the back of the room tittered.

Rosella saw the hand slide across the face of the clock above the blackboard and chalk dust sift down from a felt brush.

"It's all right. You don't have to," Mrs. Clarence said.

"A surprise," Rosella said. "I'm going to bring a surprise."

The air in the classroom rushed outwards suddenly as though the whole class had sighed with relief. "Oh," said Sandra Adam, who had volunteered to organize the party, "we can all use surprises."

The third day Rosella missed school, Albert called for the doctor. She lay in the centre of the bed curled in a tight ball, moaning and crying. The doctor shook the thermometer and pushed it under her tongue while Albert paced. The doctor said he suspected the nine o'clock flu and that the threat of cod liver oil would cure it. Albert left the house with him, running with relief down to the drugstore. Rosella clutched the sheets up around her neck and watched Minnie, who stood in the doorway smiling at the wall. The sun moved out from behind a cloud, pressed in against the drawn curtain, and a beam of light caught Minnie square in the face. She fiddled with the white buttons on her dress and smiled at Rosella as though she were anxious to make a friend. But anxious not to appear too desperate. Whenever anything unusual happened—chicken pox, or accidents— Minnie withdrew and hovered on the fringes of their ailments while Albert tended to them. "I just can't," she'd said once. "You're so much better at it, Albert. Crying hurts my ears."

"I think we should do something with the wallpaper in this room," Minnie said. "We'll strip it off and paint the walls. Something bright. What do you think of apple green?" And then her own idea caught her around the feet and made her waltz across the room, her galoshes tracing out her dance in black skid marks across the floor.

"And new curtains," she sang, the dance gaining in momentum, as though by waltzing and swinging her arms it was actually happening. Rosella ran, caught Minnie about the waist. "Stop that," she said and held her tightly until she couldn't move. She pushed her face into Minnie's stomach and felt her callused palm brush against her neck and she found the courage to tell Minnie what she'd done.

"A surprise?" Minnie led Rosella back to the bed and patted her lightly on the behind as she scrambled beneath the blankets. "A surprise for the spring party?" She sat down on the edge of the bed. "We used to have those."

Rosella leapt to her knees. "You did? When? Where?"

"Well, Jeremy and I, and…and…." Minnie hesitated. She knew what they'd been told: don't listen, don't encourage it. "And Mozart. In the grape arbour. Jeremy brought me a surprise. A starfish, I think."

Rosella flopped back into the pillow and turned her face to the wall. Minnie glanced down at her palm. "P". "I suppose I should get at the perogies," she said. "They take such a long time."

"It's Wednesday," Rosella said in a dull, flat voice. "It's 'B', not 'P'. Beef. A pot roast. Albert brought it home yesterday."

"SURPRISE," Rosella had written on large sheets of paper and taped them to lampshades, cupboard doors, in conspicuous places in every room in the house. SURPRISE.

Ginny sighed. She screwed the lid back on the jar of Ponds Vanishing Cream and set it on the floor. Rosella held the book. The words swam across the page, blobs of gelatin with flickering tails. Like the jars of tadpoles Minnie had brought to the spring party. Minnie, sweater fastened with a row of safety pins, shiny black galoshes trailing water down the aisles, walked between the desks, smiling, saying, "Surprise! Surprise!" as she set down on every child's desk a jar of flickering, ugly, swollen tadpoles. And now this. The horrible shame of it made Rosella cringe inside. Minnie, her mother, stark naked, swimming in the river.

Sandra saw the curtain up there shift as someone stepped away from it. As she passed by the Pullman house, she heard a whistling sound. Then she saw Minnie in the back yard, sitting in the garden. Minnie waved her arm and flicked it sharply. The whistling sound was the sound of a nylon fishing line whipping through the air, Sandra realized. Minnie flicked the line again and then leapt up from the stump. "I've got one," she called. "Albert, come and see."

The hinges on the door groaned as Albert stepped out and stood at the side of the house in a circle of light. Above him, moths fluttered. His round belly rose like a pregnant woman's beneath the white apron. Minnie held up the fishing line.

"How in heaven's name did you manage that one?" Albert said.

Sandra saw the phosphorescent glow of a firefly swinging from the end of Minnie's line. Poor Albert. She shouldn't really bother him with her monthlies any more. He had his hands full. The whole town was talking about Minnie's swim.

Albert heard the sound of clay pulling at Sandra's feet. He saw the light upstairs go out. He knew he should have gone up there and helped the girls with their prayers, but Minnie had called at the same time. Sometimes Albert felt pulled in too many directions. And so he sat on a stool just outside the door and played fetch with Katie so he could keep his eye on Minnie as well.

"How'd your day go?" he asked.

Minnie flashed him a smile which turned up the corners of her wide mouth and lit up her eyes. She dropped the firefly down inside a jar. She ducked her head over the jar and looked down at it, as though she'd been dealt a good poker hand and didn't want him to know it. She tucked her heavy black hair behind each ear and raised her head. Her face pulsed with green light. "Oh, the usual, Albert. Thursday, washday and pizza. Why do you ask?" The hair sprang loose then and that silver ribbon flashed down the side of her face, casting it into shadow.

He couldn't come right out and ask, "What were you doing down at the river today?" He had to walk softly in a large circle around the question. Unless she said, "Albert, I went down to the river today," he couldn't bring up the subject.

"Albert," Mr. Harrigan had said, "this is serious business." Mr. Dorfman had been dumping a crate of spoiled eggs over the side of the bridge and saw Minnie down there, floating on her back.

"And," Mr. Dorfman said, "she wasn't wearing a bathing suit. If you get what I mean."

Albert made an error and had to erase a full column of numbers. He blew bits of rubber across the page and started over.

"Albert, you're not paying attention," Harrigan said. "I believe this is serious."

"Not only could she drown," Mr. Dorfman said, clearing his throat and dropping his voice down a notch, "but someone might see her. One of the children of this town could just happen to wander down there and——"

"Look," Harrigan said, "some of us have kind of been wondering. Are you sure she's playing with a full deck?"

The bell above the door jangled and relief made Albert drop the pencil and rise to face it. Annie Schmoon stepped into the lumber yard store. She puffed and perspired heavily. She set her wicker basket down onto his desk. "I heard there was a meeting," she said and glared at them all.

"Now Annie," Harrigan said, "why don't you go home and nurse your frogs and we'll work this one out."

"You've worked out a few too many in your time, if you ask me," Annie said.

"This is none of your concern."

"Minnie Pullman happens to be my friend," she said and banged her fist against Albert's desk.

Albert was surprised, grateful, he didn't know Minnie had any friends. He stepped to one side, and then backwards until he stood directly behind the woman.

"It figures," Harrigan said. "That could be half your problem, Albert."

Albert moved away from Annie then and sat back down behind the desk. He picked up his pencil and began to scan a column of numbers.

"And you think what the woman did is just fine?"

"So, she took a swim on the river. It was a hot day."

"Naked," Mr. Dorfman said.

"Listen," Annie said. "What you don't know about Minnie is that she was a swimmer in her time."

"A what?"

"In her time, she was a swimmer."

"What's that supposed to mean?" Harrigan said.

Albert put his pencil aside once again, hope rising in a flush up the back of his thick neck.

"She was a channel swimmer," Annie said. "Swam the English channel twice. She misses it."

"Naked?"

"Of course. Greased her body, that's all. I don't think you realize the significance of it," Annie said.

"That's the biggest load I've ever heard," Harrigan said.

Albert's scalp tightened as his smile stretched up into his ears. He wished he'd thought of that one.

"Well, whatever's the truth," Harrigan said, "this is here and now." He jabbed Albert's desk with his finger. "And this river isn't any channel. Frankly," he said and studied Albert carefully, "maybe the problem is that she doesn't have enough to keep her occupied at home. If you get what I mean."

Albert's ears burned. He coughed into his fist. "The problem is solved," he said. "I want you to know that." He got up and walked over to the window, his fingers twisting and untwisting. He noticed the layer of dust on a row of bathroom fixtures and resisted the impulse to take a swipe at them with the sleeve of his shirt. "My Aunt Violet's coming for a visit. She'll take Minnie in hand," he said. "She'll know what to do because she's a nurse."

Albert threw the stick out to Katie. The rope uncoiled like a snake across the yard. He was careful never to throw the stick out of her reach. Minnie had gone back into the garden and sat down on the tree stump and began to sing softly. It was time, Albert thought, to go inside and write Aunt Violet a letter of invitation.

Minnie chewed on a fingernail as she hummed. Then she examined it as though she might find some clue to the mystery she was pondering beneath it. She stopped humming and took a deep breath. "Albert, love," she said, her voice clear and firm. Above their heads the windowpane shivered as Rosella forced its swollen frame downwards. Minnie waited.

"Yes, Bumkin?" Albert said.

"Albert, I hope you won't mind too much. But I'm not going to have sex with you any more."

Rosella's footsteps creaked in the floorboards as she approached the bed and then slid underneath the covers. She shivered and pulled the blankets up around her neck and waited to catch her breath. A dog barked.

"Ginny?" she said after a time.

"Yes, Rosella?"

"I want another mother." Rosella held her breath. Water plopped into the drinking glass on the floor. Wet plaster bubbled on the ceiling and inside their closet dust-coloured plants sprouted on a collar of a blouse.

"You didn't say your prayers," Ginny said and rolled over.

Everyone knew. Absolutely everyone in the whole town. Naked. She could just die of embarrassment.

"I think it's a sin to say that." Ginny's voice rose in the darkness, skinny and shivery.

"That's not in the Bible."

"Well, it does say to honour your father and mother," Ginny said. "Doesn't it?"

"Yes." At least that's what they were told in Sunday school. Rosella punched her pillow into shape and buried her head into it. " 'That *thy* days may be long upon the land'," she said. "Not *their* days, but *my* days. And really, I couldn't care less if tomorrow ever came and so I guess I've got a choice in the matter, eh?"

They finally slept. Their breath rose above the bed and mingled. A panel of wallpaper curled downward and slithered to the floor. Outside their window, trees stretched above Ottawa Street, branches straining upward to scratch an etching onto the sky where the lights began to flicker and flare into sudden brightness.

Sandra Adam passed by August and June Marchand's house, the Dorfmans' and Standings', fixing her eyes on the end of the road where a row of lanterns glittered from sawhorses, guiding her down to a safe landing. The Roads people, concerned about the safety of their partially excavated gullies, had placed the lanterns there and every night the men took turns carrying the can of kerosene, refilling, and turning up and igniting the wicks. Through eyes shot with wind, Sandra saw one of those lanterns move out into the centre of the road. It swung in an arc, steadied, and then moved towards her. Never show you're afraid, she told herself. Approach with boldness—her father's advice for dealing with stray dogs passing in the street.

"Put it back, Sonny," a voice said. "You'll just get into trouble."

Sandra's knees went rubbery with relief. It was only Sonny Ericson, and as they drew closer she realized with surprise that the other person was June's oldest daughter, Robin Marchand. Surprised because Robin was almost as tall as Sonny and it seemed to Sandra that the gaunt, tightly wired girl had sprung to full size overnight. Robin walked with quick, short steps, out of rhythm with Sonny, whose stringy long hair flipped up in the wind; in the light of the lantern the coppery flash of it was like licks of fire about his ears. Sandra smelled his strong, sharp odour as he came abreast of her and then hesitated. Sonny always smelled as though his head needed scrubbing, she thought. The lantern swung towards her as he turned slowly and faced her. As always, she fought the impulse to avoid his eyes. His face was dented, his blunt nose not quite properly aligned with the rest of his face, the thin scars across his cheeks and forehead a record of his travels across the valley as he roared through towns and villages in his battered truck with its forthright "Have Truck Will Fuck" message scrawled across its tailgate, name-calling people—frogs, polaks, knackzote eaters, chiefs, square heads—forcing his way into dance halls where he didn't belong. There were rumours about why Sonny and his parents were like seeds blown down from the lake shore, away from the Icelandic settlements, taking root among the cinders and hard soil on the other side of town beyond the railroad tracks.

"Hi yuh, Sandy," Sonny said. His voice was soft, a finger running lightly across her arm and making her shiver. The lantern dropped down to his side and her clay-encrusted feet were plunged into darkness.

"Yeah, hi," Robin said and Sandra thought that she detected a mocking tone in the girl's voice.

"You're out late," she said, feeling the bite of the girl's tone rise in her face.

"So, what's it to you?" Robin said as Sonny stepped to her side. They watched Sandra turn and walk down the road. "Going home to polish her halo," Robin said.

Sonny could still smell the faint odour of lily-of-the-valley. For as long as he'd known Sandra, she smelled like the ivory bell-shaped flowers that used to grow wild beside the train station. He'd attended school for as long as she had just to be able to slide up behind her in the cloakroom or hallway and smell the shape of the flower in her body and then, later, in order to be able to hold her closer to his nose, he'd salvaged the abandoned truck from a farmer's field and had pieced it together, the vision of her sitting beside him on its cracked, brown leather seat propelling him forward. "Sonny," she'd sung, "it's a perfectly wonderful truck, but I can't. Because. Because I need my exercise. Because my father would kill me. He wouldn't like it." Because Sonny wasn't good enough. Well, there were lots of girls who would ride with him and who had. He'd doused the patch of dark spear-shaped leaves and ivory bells with gasoline, crossed the tracks, and lobbed a flaming cattail torch into it and watched the ground burn.

"Okay, so show me the stuff," Sonny said. He stepped off the road into the gully in front of Charles Standing's house. If there was as much as Robin said there was, he'd make a pile. He'd been selling the Indians whatever bits of pottery or bones the backhoe had left intact. Cigarette money. But what he needed was a new truck. Robin had witnessed one of the exchanges made behind the hotel. "They pay you for that stuff?" she'd said. "Holy. We're rich."

"I can still see Sandra," Robin said "Wait. And cut the lantern, for pete's sake."

"She's clueless," Sonny said. There was nothing he could ever write about Sandra on the walls of the firehall. Nice tits, too. What a waste, he thought as he bent and snuffed out the light.

Robin and Sonny crossed the gully together and crept silently through the Standing yard, around the back of it, hesitating for a moment in the shadow of a crabapple tree to search the dark windows of the house for movement. "You're sure about this shit?" Sonny whispered.

"I told you. I've seen it hundreds of times."

"You better be right because I've already talked to the High Tree Band and the Porcupines and they're not interested in arrowheads and crap like that any more."

"So why clothes?"

"I guess they wanna wear them, eh?"

"Weird," Robin said.

"They've got the bucks, so who cares?"

"I get half." Robin crouched and darted across the back yard, down the side of the sagging barn, and then behind it. Sonny followed.

"Thirty per cent," he said, "because it's my truck. We couldn't get the stuff up to the chiefs without it."

Metal clanked as Robin pulled a wagon wheel away from the side of the barn and laid it to one side. "No way," she said. She lay down on her back and began to shimmy feet first through an opening in the barn. "Fifty, fifty," she said, "because you're too big to get inside."

"All right, all right," Sonny said. "But God, your ancestors must be having a shit fit. Rolling over in their graves. Selling their own stuff back to them." He gasped then as a warm ball of spit broke against his face.

"I'm no Indian," Robin said. "When're you going to get it straight?"

"Okay, so you're mischief," Sonny said. "I don't see the difference, though. It's all the same to me." Because June and August Marchand sometimes bought Sonny a round, his name for them was not unkind—it was "mischief", a play on words—rather than what the townspeople called them behind their hands—"breeds" or "mongrels" or "mulligan stew". "Your roots," Father Roy said. So Sonny resisted the impulse to grab a hank of the girl's long dark hair and yank it hard. The little brat. No bloody half-breed cunt spat at him and got away with it.

Sandra's step quickened as she neared her own neat cottage. Purple clematis climbed up a trestle beside the front door. Snow White and the Seven Dwarfs lined the front walk, welcoming her with their cheerful ceramic smiles. Inside, Steven would be sitting at the kitchen table sanding mould marks from greenware and the radio would be playing softly from the top of the refrigerator while he worked— something quiet, Schumann or Bach, to soothe his broken heart. Approach with boldness, Sandra told herself. And she would. Tomorrow, when she went into MacLeod's, she'd count the glass bowls as usual. She'd keep track of how many water glasses were sold, count the spoons, the cases of preserving jars. No one had asked her to do this. At first, it was simply good business to do an inventory often and never be caught short. Later, counting everything became her protection. Her neat inventories of how many Corningware casseroles were ordered and how many were sold tallied up at the end of the week and not a penny was unaccounted for. She'd been wise. She checked all her pockets before she left the store because of her boss, Mr. Newhoff. She imagined him, leaning back in his swivel chair inside that glass-enclosed office of his. He would dip forward, cup the telephone, and lower his baritone voice and Sandra knew that he was speaking to his brother. Making arrangements for his truck to pull up behind the store after hours. Then the two of them would throw tires up onto the truck or load up a washing machine.

"It's on his account," Mr. Newhoff said at first, turning away from her and in effect telling her to get back to kitchenware where she belonged. Sandra ran through the account file in the office when the man went for coffee and discovered that because Mr. Newhoff was a little short-winded, he'd skipped a note, and so she made out a card, labelled it, and recorded the number of tires that had gone onto the truck. She believed Mr. Newhoff would thank her. He stood before her later, the card in hand, and then ripped it up. You say anything to anybody, he said, and I'll plant a pair of stockings or something in your pocket and it'll be your word against mine. Mr. Newhoff, who sang in that beautiful Baptist choir, his voice blending with humility, allowing himself to become one with all the others, was a thief.

She could see her hand at the letter slot at the post office. The envelope slipping away. It was no mistake that Head Office telephoned today. She would approach with boldness, Sandra thought, as she bent to gather up the paper-wrapped box of sanitary napkins hidden beneath the lilac bush and slipped it under her coat.

Jacob Friesen saw the young girl stoop beside a bush in the corner of her yard and held back, not wanting to embarrass her. He waited until Sandra had entered her house before he continued on down Ottawa Street. The top half of the street rose to meet the broad, well-lit main street of town. But there were no street lights at the other end of Ottawa where it curved down and plunged into the darkness of bushes. If it were not for the lanterns placed at intervals by the Roads people, he would not be able to see his way. Whenever he walked down there during the day, it made him think of the strange beast mentioned in the Book of Job. The pathway to the river, that is. The reference to a large animal, the behemoth that could drink up a river. The opening down into the park-like area beside the river was ominous, a huge mouth. Often he knelt and peered inside before entering, seeing, there in the back, the river glimmering like a giant, wet tongue. It was always with relief that he passed safely through the opening, and entered the sounds of the secret and hidden. He entered Railway Street, his street. Beyond his house curved the roof of the skating rink, outlined clearly by the glow of street lights which lined the broad strip of Main Street. That street where square wooden buildings bordered each side. Where Jacob seldom ventured unless sent by Elizabeth to search out the boy who tarried too long. The blaring sound of a clarinet rose suddenly, wailing up above the skating rink roof, and then faded just as suddenly. The music was replaced with laughter and the sounds of people's voices. He was familiar with downtown by its sounds only. Sounds which changed with the seasons. Spring brought a sense of urgency and an almost hysterical relief in the voices of the young people who seemed to walk the streets both day and night. He was glad that Hendrick had never shown any interest in doing the same. A beam of light swept across the face of his house, swung in a half circle, and focused on a patch of earth in the yard across from his. It was Taro Yamamoto. The tiny man wore a bright straw hat as he knelt in the garden. Jacob crossed the road to greet him.

"There's been an animal in my garden," Taro said as Jacob entered his yard. He squatted and rocked back and forth on his haunches.

Jacob wanted to ask Taro: you've had many sons. Did you ever need to speak to them about careful, secret things?

"I heard the barking of a dog earlier," Jacob said. Taro flicked a clump of mud from a deep imprint. The animal had been a heavy one, large, Jacob guessed, but it did look like the paw print of a dog.

"What you see and what's there is not always the same." Taro drew the rake across the tracks, obliterating them. Jacob turned away, hiding in his smile the knowledge of the man's children, their haste to discover what had crept into their yard while they slept. What shape their father had pressed into the soil to try and fool them.

Taro took an envelope from his shirt pocket and unfolded it against his knee. "I heard from my eldest today. He continues to do very well."

"No, no," Jacob protested as Taro pressed the envelope into his hand. He felt the familiar crackle of bills. Since the falling attendance at the church, it had become more and more difficult to live on the women's offerings, nickels and dimes and the occasional dollar bill. "I can manage without it," he said. "In any case, the Lord will provide."

"That may be," Taro said. "But your Lord also provides for me today because it is me who has the need to give. And sometimes, you have the need to receive."

Elizabeth, Jacob thought—it was providence, an answer to whatever prayer he had unconsciously breathed out on the walk home. A way to prevent the boy, Hendrick, from sleeping with his mother.

The light above Albert and Minnie's door blinked out and the moths scattered in search of another light. Katie whined, curled into a ball, uncurled, whined once again, and then grew silent. June Marchand huddled down into an armchair on her front porch. August stretched out on a sagging couch, fast asleep. Across the street at the Dorfmans', a fringed shade slid down into place. At the hotel, three other window shades were drawn against the night in unison. At the corner of Railway and Ottawa came the sound of a screen door creaking open and then snapping shut. Steven Adam stepped out onto the sidewalk. A match flared as he cupped his hands and lit a cigarette. He stood for several moments looking up at the sky and then he turned in June's direction.

She sensed that he'd sniffed out her presence there on the porch. Well, fuck him and Sandra's prissy little mind. She got up and went into the house for another beer. Her hand met the light switch and the kitchen leapt forward to meet her. The yellowed enamelled walls, pock-marked with dull grey patches of polyfiller, seemed to mock her. Every kitchen cupboard was opened to cans—lids pried half off—and boxes—their flaps disgorging cereal or crackers. Plastic dishes. June switched off the light, but the light from the Standings' house overflowed into hers and cut across the table littered with leftover toast, jars of jam, peanut butter, and a strange-looking clay pot Robin had dragged home. She went over to the window and looked into the Standings' house. A varnished plate rail ran around the dining room, halfway up the wall, lined with flowered china plates. Above the plates, stern-faced people stared out from behind concave glass: Charles's ancestors and a younger Charles himself, wearing the Mounted Police uniform, glaring at her from a black oval frame. Emma sat at the table, her shoulders draped in an afghan, mending a sock. Across from her, Charles, his white back hunched over a sheaf of papers. So, the old geezer couldn't get it up any more, eh? "Here's to you," June said and lifted the beer in Emma's direction, "for still giving a damn. Here's to you," she said to Charlie. "May your pecker rest in peace."

Charles Standing was oblivious of June's toast as he bent over his journal. Heat pressed in all around him and the whine of flies was almost unbearable. Dust rose from the feet of the Indians, a tattered, bedraggled lot, as they marched before the mounted redcoats. The scout, Johnny on the Spot, dogged the heels of a few drunken stragglers. Charles reined his horse to a halt and stood high in the stirrups, watching as the first column of Indians began climbing the hills towards the reservation. Several of the riders flanked the squalid crowd, urging them to form lines and fall in. J.P. Campbell, always a spectator, reined to a halt alongside him. One gallon of raw alcohol cut three times, add a pound of tea and black chewing tobacco, throw in a quart of black molasses and a handful of red peppers and ginger. Trade whiskey. Fire water. "So far, so good," Standing said.

The two men's faces were so caked with dust that they appeared to be wearing masks. "Let's hope that they don't learn to read," Campbell said. "Or sober up."

The other men fell in then, and, but for J.P. Campbell, formed a scarlet line across the yellow prairie. A Union Jack fluttered from a lance. A child cried. "They say you can shoot a man through the heart and the brain when he's got a snoot full of that booze," Standing said, "and he won't die until he sobers up." He wheeled his horse around and gave the signal to advance. "Now all we've got to do," he said to Campbell, "is to wait for them to fall over." The land along the river had been secured for the white newcomers. And now the valley itself had been cleared.

June stepped back into the night. The earth absorbed what moonlight there was and except for those lanterns glowing at the side of the road, night was complete. She raked her fingers through the clump of platinum blonde curls at her neck, disliking the prickly dry feel of it. Once you start, you can't stop, a woman had warned her another time, in another place. And never perm on top of peroxide. Well, she had. You could hide dark roots better among curls. She heard the faint twitter of a solitary bird, late, out of its nest. She held the sound high in her breastbone, feeling at once like that late bird, solitary, out of her tar-paper nest and on a sandy road with Grandpops. His short, laboured gasps propelled her forward. He needed warmer clothing. She knew the story, how his family had returned from the hunt to find strangers' clothing hanging from a line strung up between two trees, and lanterns glowing in the windows of their house. She was young, but she was not stupid. She realized early that it was only fair that she and Grandpops clothed and fed themselves and her brothers with whatever they could find during these nightly raids along the edges of towns. It was fun. For a while. Until she grew older and realized that it would be fairer if she actually lived inside one of those houses. And then she met August.

"August?"

His thick snores rumbled across the porch. June went over to him and stood looking down at his slack features. As his stomach rose and fell, the moon glinted back at her in his bucking bronco buckle. Well, she was trying to stay put in one place, for the sake of August. His cowboy years were over. "August, you want to fly?" She nudged him with her toe. The snoring grew louder. Bad back from too many falls. August couldn't ride any more. June tucked the beer under her arm and crossed the street and headed off down the road to knock on Steven Adam's window.

At the end of Ottawa, where the road dipped down into blackness, granules of earth heaved and began to shift. A trickle of earth slid down an incline. Chunks of clay teetered, broke loose, and tumbled into the gullies on both sides of Ottawa Street. A sawhorse tilted and then toppled over and the lantern's flame was snuffed out, smothered by damp earth. Far below the road water gurgled, a puddle swelled, broke loose, and streamed on beneath the road. As June Marchand stepped down into the gully in front of Steven's house, she gasped with the shock of icy water pressing against her leather boots. Steven, you're not going to believe this one. He'd accuse her of being drunk.

"Minnie?" Albert whispered so as not to wake the girls upstairs. "Did you leave a tap running?"

"No," Minnie said. She lay rigid, listening intently. "But you can check if you want."

The mattress sagged beneath Albert's weight as he sat down. Minnie clutched at the side of it to keep from rolling into him. She had told Albert three times. I can't have sex with you any more. He never asked why. He hadn't heard. Albert's ears only worked when he wanted them to.

"No, if you say you haven't, you haven't," Albert said. Even though he didn't entirely trust her memory, he believed it was important that he never show it. It was his philosophy. Expect the best from a person and you got the best. He lay down beside her, pulled the blanket up over his chest, and then reached over and covered her shoulders.

They lay side by side, listening. Rosella's chart shone in the light of the moon. Friday tomorrow. Fish, probably. In the silence of the room, the sound of water running seemed to grow louder every second. "It's probably Delta," Minnie said. "Watering her lawn."

"Yes, it's probably that," Albert said. He sighed.

"What is it?"

"Rosella," Albert said. "She's changing. I can't put my finger on it exactly."

"Oh no," Minnie said. "Rosella seems fine to me. The same as ever."

Albert sighed once again. He wondered why he hadn't heard from Aunt Violet. This time, he would invite her to come and install her in the unfinished room. He recalled her sharp eyes diagnosing an illness in advance of any symptoms and the comforting smell of camphor and eucalyptus oil rising from her leather satchel. She wore a diamond ring given to her by the family of a soldier she'd nursed to life in the trenches. For her, Rosella would be as simple as a case of measles. Yes, the studding in that room was already in place. He only needed to order the drywall, plaster, and nails. He even anticipated the necessary measuring. But he couldn't see his hands grasping the hammer and driving those nails home.

"Minnie?" He reached, stroked the inside of her arm, and closed his eyes. Where was he? Oh, yes.

It's always summer and Ollie Peter wears the same dress, each time. She walks towards him carrying a blanket. Tonight, he fast forwards the picture and Ollie's lips are already brushing against his neck and her strong, thin arms reach up to clasp him. Hard. Too hard. His heart beats entirely too fast. She moans and nips his ear with her sharp teeth. He tries to hold Ollie still. Always, he tries to pat her into stillness and remind her that she is breaking her mother's heart. How impossible their love is. He, Albert Pullman, is English and she Mennonite and how could he ever be true to himself and become a Mennonite? He would never ask her to sacrifice what she is. He feels the fire of her pressing against him and prays for an asbestos suit. And then he reasons that it isn't his fault that he doesn't own one. He fast forwards the picture. He licks Ollie's small, hard nipples, then wedges his knee between her legs as she falls backwards on the blanket and he watches himself enter her.

Albert stretched into the picture. "Minnie?" It was time for her to roll over and climb on top of him and ride him to sleep. His hand met air and dropped down onto empty sheets.

In the kitchen, the light of the moon was blue and the empty chairs were skeletons. The clock ticked and the refrigerator gurgled, but Minnie wasn't there. He sat at the table in the dark. Maybe he should buy her a new nightgown.

Maybe he should have kept up the love play even when she insisted that she didn't need that. Maybe it was partly his fault because he was in love with two women. Because to Albert, it was still as though it had been a week ago, or even one year and not fifteen, when Ollie walked across the field towards him, swinging the honey pail filled with his lunch. She spread that blanket on the ground. Blue or grey? It was important that he keep the memory correct and not make up a single detail. Ollie unwrapped the wax paper packages. The sight of her small fingers moving so swiftly, efficiently, revealing thick sandwiches oozing mayonnaise, tart dill pickles, crumbling matrimonial cake, glistening slices of watermelon, made him perspire. How he laughed, surprised, amazed at how much energy he had as he thrust himself up inside Ollie. It made him want to sing, "Joyful, joyful, we adore thee."

Albert picked up a pencil one of the girls had left lying on the table and tapped out a beat against it. Joyful, joyful we adore thee, God of glory, Lord of love, hearts unfold like flowers before thee, opening to the sun above. But afterward—he made himself remember this as well—as Ollie curled into his neck and plucked a hair from his chest and spoke of love, of plans—he'd had to fight off an immense fatigue. Because he was so very fond of her, he had to protect her against herself. Albert gave himself to Ollie for a whole summer and then when the leaves on the trees began to wither and curl at the edges, he was walking past Harrigan's store and saw the pansy earrings and so he bought them. He lay beside Ollie on the blanket one last time while she unwrapped the package with her nimble, quick fingers and he explained to her that it was over. For her own good.

Albert waited for the first snowfall when he knew harvest would already be in and Minnie wouldn't be quite so run off her feet. He borrowed a car. He drove out to the Churchills' farm, where Minnie stood barefoot, ankle deep in fresh snow, beating a carpet on the clothesline. He'd seen her before, at the lumber yard, with the Churchills. She was quiet as a mouse, they said. But a very good worker. She says she's British, they said. Albert took the carpet down from the line. He dragged it through the fresh snow and demonstrated to Minnie how the snow made the colours leap up, bright and clean. And then he interviewed her.

"What are you?" he asked. "Nationality, I mean. Not that it makes any difference." Minnie poured him a cup of tea in the Churchills' bright farm kitchen.

"What are you?" Minnie asked and because he believed it was not only a sign of good manners but of intelligence when a person returned a question with another question, Albert knew she was the right person.

Albert told her. He set out sugar cubes on the table to demonstrate how his great-grandfather came from Ontario eighty years ago and started a sawmill. As the town grew and the trees receded until they were just a thin fringe following the curve of the river, the mill closed. Then his grandfather became a clerk in the lumber store. As did his father. And now, after several years of lending himself out to farmers, so would he. He believed that his great-grandfather was related to the Earl of Shaftesbury on his mother's side. At least, that's what his Aunt Violet had said the year she'd come over to live with him for a time, after…after…. His voice shook. "After my mother died."

Minnie listened carefully, never interrupting as he un-rolled his lineage, laid it down in a straight line of sugar cubes across the table. "So, I guess I'm about 100 per cent British," he said.

"That's exactly what I am, too," Minnie said and Albert did detect a slight British accent in her voice. The Churchills were right. Minnie was quiet and sensible and would not raise his heartbeat past the dangerous point.

"What's your last name?" Albert asked.

"Minnie."

"No, your last name." The whole town knew her first. The woman had been in the Agassiz district for one summer and whoever could had driven past the yard to catch a glimpse of this barefoot stranger with the silver ribbon of hair.

"Minnie who?"

"Fish," Minnie said. The word squirted across the table and landed in front of him.

"Fish? Fisher?"

"Herring," Minnie said.

"Herring?"

Minnie cleared her throat, leaned forward, and formed the words carefully. "My name is Minnie Heron."

"Will you marry me?" Albert said to save himself because even now, whenever he entered the Bank of Montreal, he felt a bit of that youthful energy returning. He felt the air rush inward. As though everyone in the bank had just inhaled at the same time with the memory of the near scandal between him and Ollie. Expecting a scene. He didn't notice the indifference of the girls as they sat at their desks flipping through stacks of papers, discussing what they were going to do on the weekend. Or else they fluttered about a bouquet of carnations on a certain desk and congratulated the lucky person on her engagement or birthday or twenty-fifth anniversary. Albert hesitated each time and then tiptoed across the shiny floor to the window where there was a desk with tidy stacks of deposit and withdrawal slips. He picked up a pen, selected one of the slips, turned it over, and pretended to write while he searched out Ollie's reflection in the window, to see if she still wore the earrings. "I'll wait for you," Ollie had said. "For as long as I live, I'll love you."

Albert waited almost five minutes sometimes until someone entered the bank and went over to Ollie's wicket. Only then did Albert set aside his doodling, take a deep breath, and go over to the second wicket and do whatever business he had to do for the lumber yard. He turned sideways so he couldn't see her or notice how curly grey hairs had sprung up among the blonde or see those tiny ears and the pansy earrings. No one had ever asked Ollie about the earrings. If anyone even noticed them any more it was to think that they were quaint, but too out-dated, and that someone should clue her in. Generally, the girls at the bank had stopped suggesting to Ollie that she try a new hairstyle, dab a bit of lipstick on her mouth. Occasionally, a new girl, flushed with the success of a recent engagement, would imply that if Ollie put a bit of effort into it, she wouldn't be a bad-looking woman. But Ollie's mother noticed the earrings and remained silent. When Teedle left for work with those earrings in place, Mrs. Peter bowed her head over a cup of tea and prayed.

Albert got up and switched on the lamp in the centre of the table. Then he got a dishtowel and draped it over the light. He took the writing tablet from the drawer beside the sink, the pen and ink bottle from the top shelf above the refrigerator. He sat down.

"My Dear Aunt Violet," he began. He dipped the nib into the ink and shook a blob loose onto his handkerchief before continuing. He rather enjoyed the rosy hue spreading across the linen paper.

> Rather a soft, cool day today with a little rain during the night. Wind about south-east.
>
> Went to church last Sunday.
>
> Mr. Black preached an excellent sermon from Matt. 26:53. Where he remonstrated with Peter for cutting off the man's ear (Christ that is). And informs him of the amount of angels he had at his command if he thought it proper to call them, but he suffered these things for

man's salvation. Took the girls down to the Dairy Bar for an ice cream afterwards.

Charles and Emma went for a drive on Sunday and Emma returned with a sick headache. In bed all the following day and so I visited with a shepherd's pie so Charles wouldn't go off his feed. He's getting thinner and thinner.

Minnie continues to give every appearance of being splendidly happy. And the girls as well.

A blob of ink broke loose and spattered down the page. Albert tried to sponge it up with his handkerchief but his hand shook and he spread ink instead of collecting it. And so he tore the page loose, crumpled it in his fist, and started over, his tongue moving with the effort, while outside the river twisted and almost turned on itself, currents rippling like flexed muscles beneath smooth skin. It lapped against the bank, leaving the clay dark with moisture; it licked at the tips of pussywillows bending too close to its side. The valley's night song drifted across its slippery surface, rose up into the hills, and clung to the branches of conifer, sarsaparilla, and juniper bushes where a herd of buffalo, calves in the centre, turned their flanks into a circle and faced the night. A bonfire leapt and crackled outside the buffalo compound and clam shells clattered at a woman's neck as she leaned over a steaming pot, stirring. The smell of fish soup hung in the air. Sonny Ericson squatted beneath a tree, smoking. Nestled between his feet was a six-pack of beer. Robin Marchand sat on the ground beside an elder, a man whose long, straight hair was streaked with silver. On the other side, a thin, dark man in a black suit squatted. He pushed his glasses up against the bridge of his nose and shuffled through several documents on the ground. Beside the documents lay a beaded rawhide suit. The old man stared into the fire and stroked the feathers on the bonnet cradled in his lap.

"You say you have many of these?" His voice was low and melodious.

"It's just the tip of the iceberg, Old Grey Hairs," Sonny said. He flicked his cigarette into the grass.

"We really don't need all that paraphernalia," the young man said. "We've got these." He motioned to the documents on the ground. "And they've got that," he said and pointed down into the valley where a road stretched straight and narrow for hundreds of miles.

Old Grey Hairs lifted the feather bonnet and set it on his head. "Huga-muga, oom-pa-pa," he said. "Me Moses-Drunk-All-the-Time-Bear-Claw. Me make treaty with the white man."

"You're perpetuating the stereotype," the thin, wiry man said. He stuffed the documents into his briefcase.

The elder took the bonnet off and set it aside. "I thought I was making a joke," he said.

"This isn't the time for it." The briefcase snapped shut.

"I know we don't *need* this paraphernalia," the elder said. "It's just the principle of the thing."

Bottles clanked as Sonny set the beer carton down on the ground. "Let's talk money," he said and cracked open a beer. He offered it to the old man.

"You'll ruin your liver with that stuff," Old Grey Hairs said. "And heart and kidneys. Not to mention your mental health."

"No kidding," Sonny said. He lifted the beer, tilted his head, and guzzled half the bottle.

"We're counting on it," the old man said.

Far below them in the valley, the light of a lamp flickered out through Mr. Campbell's vine-covered window, outlining leaves and curly tendrils perfectly against the glass. Down in one corner of the window, a spider's web quivered, bounced, and then jerked with the struggle of a fly trapped in its sticky net. Inside the room, Mr. Campbell bent over his desk and squinted at a letter lying open before him, trying to decipher the girlish script. The walls of this room were permeated with the bitter secrets of every dilemma which had come to him throughout the years. The valley's skeletons rattled in his closet. He'd kept his office in his home instead of at the courthouse and the house on Ottawa Street had become the centre of justice. Once his legs gave out, he was glad to have his bed moved down into this room. As long as the world outside continued to flow through his room twenty-four hours a day, he would be able to contain it.

A cricket chirruped beneath the bed and he called for Etta to bring the spray bomb so he could concentrate on this latest dilemma. Etta walked into the room backwards and excused herself as she got down on her hands and knees, pushed aside the ceramic thunder jug, and silenced the insect with a puff of spray. The two Mounties drummed their fingers against their knees and tried not to smile at the sight of Etta's broad, flowered buttocks jutting up from beneath the bed. Mr. Newhoff sat on a chair between them and saw nothing but the floor as he folded his hands across his lap and prayed. His fervent plea pushed out across his narrow forehead in beads of perspiration. The pendulum on the grandfather clock behind him swayed. Springs uncoiled and Mr. Newhoff's heart beat out the hour with it.

Etta smiled and bowed in the doorway and closed the door firmly behind her. The sound of its latch snapping into place assured the men of their privacy. She turned on the water tap in the sink and then went over to the door and put her ear against it.

"A fine kettle of fish," Mr. Campbell said.

Mr. Newhoff prayed. The prayer was a golf ball stuck in his throat. He thought of his people kneeling in the church, the largest and most stately in town with its Grecian columns lifting their thoughts heavenward when they entered. The bonging of the clock died and the gentle, hollow tick tock of the clock resumed.

"What's the matter?" Campbell said and looked out overtop his glasses at the praying man. "Didn't you pay the girl enough?"

He'd been weighed in the balance and found wanting. He prayed that they wouldn't fall asleep or fall into talk about crops.

"Twenty-four truck tires," Campbell read. "Seven cases of oil. Fourteen one-hundred pound bags of fertilizer."

"Yes, yes," Mr. Newhoff said. "It was a bad year for everyone. I was only doing what I could."

"You telling me that you gave the goods away?"

"Just a small handling charge." His voice clicked at the back of his dry throat. "For my time and gas."

"And the four washing machines?"

"For the women. To keep them happy. And there was no shipping charge."

Pain shot through Mr. Campbell's fingers as he picked up the inventory and handed it back to the Mountie. He reached for his pipe. His teeth clacked against its stem as he chewed and thought. He hated this piddling business. There were more important things to think about. "Well," he said, "your company says it recognizes that you've pulled the store out of the red in the past five years."

A bead of perspiration broke loose and trickled down Mr. Newhoff's long, lean face, down into the stubble of a day's growth of beard. Pray, pray, he urged the Baptist congregation.

"In fact, so much so, that they're agreeable to keeping you on. If you make restitution, that is. They'll be out tomorrow to see to that."

Mr. Newhoff coughed and then reached up to straighten the knot in his tie. "How much?"

"Four thousand."

Mr. Newhoff paled, stood up, and walked over to the door. The Mounties had already pulled their chairs closer to the desk and began to huddle down over a map spread in its centre. Mr. Campbell picked up his cane, hooked open a drawer in the oak filing cabinet, and set a bottle of Scotch onto the centre of his desk. Mr. Newhoff hesitated in the doorway, fiddling with the brim of his hat.

"You're free to go, man," Campbell said.

"Yes, thank you," he said. "But I was wondering.... The four thousand?"

"You've got a week." Campbell unscrewed the lid.

"I'll need a co-signer at the bank. I wonder if you might consider it?" Their laughter rang in his ears as he crossed the veranda and hurried down the road towards the church.

Mr. Campbell tipped whiskey into three shot glasses. Then he rubbed his aching fingers, still chuckling drily. He liked those people. Industrious, like the Mennonites who followed the first settlers, who had come with their green thumbs, cut back trees, hauled away stones, furrowed straight lines across the valley, prayed constantly, and the whole damned valley bloomed and flourished because of it.

"All right, gents," he said. "Let's get down to the real task. What do you make of those fires in the hills?"

"Bonfires," the Mountie said. "Huge fires. And the grass is always trampled down flat."

"A pow-wow." Campbell winced with the sudden pain shooting through his wrists.

"But we can never catch them at it. They're always gone."

The men huddled over the map at the desk and pointed out the source of the evening's blaze. How the site of the bonfire changed each night. Campbell leaned back into his chair and rolled the shot glass between burning palms, studying it. It had been almost a year since the town constable had reported hauling a drunken native off to the lock-up in the courthouse. Harrigan's sales of vanilla extract had dropped sharply.

"And this here's where we found the sweat lodge," the Mountie said and pointed.

Whiskey slopped over the side of the glass as Campbell leaned forward suddenly. Ukrainian territory. "What the hell they doing down in Easter-egg country?" he asked and felt a trickle of perspiration break loose and run down his spine.

"It's hard to say," the Mountie said.

The whiskey burned in the back of Campbell's throat as he swallowed. "I think we should bring in Charles Standing," he said. "See what Charlie thinks." In the same way that sharp pains in his knees and fingers predicted a storm brewing, he knew that what was happening out there could prove to be an embarrassment. He'd always realized the possibility of that. He just never thought that it would happen during his lifetime.

My Dear Aunt Violet,

During the night we were visited with severe thunderstorms and heavy rain. I'm afraid the muscuttos will be fearful. The day gives every appearance of being a warm one.

Lately I have been wondering whatever happened to that uncle of yours who went to Australia. The tennis player?

4

Katie yelped and bounded in wide circles around Minnie as she crossed Railway Street at Ottawa. Then they both stopped dead. Katie whined, cocked her head, and sniffed the air. Beyond, on both sides of the road, the yellow flames of the lanterns had become white, their light milky and diffused as though the glass chimneys had been swathed in cotton. Fog hovered above the black corridor of the road. Minnie hugged Albert's curling sweater against her body and stepped into the mist, following the sound of running water. She heard the hard swish of cotton pants as someone came up behind her, walking fast. She turned and recognized the man's face. But from where? What time?

"Good evening," she said softly. A ring of Allen wrenches jangled at his belt as he passed by. Of course. The MacLeod's man. She watched as he turned the corner and headed towards the south of town. She felt sorry for him. He always seemed rushed, answering a clock that ticked inside him, never straying from the road to wander across a field. Never even noticed the fog, she thought, which had begun to churn up from the gullies like white smoke. It floated across lawns and settled above flower beds—a soft, loosely knit blanket.

Katie dropped to her haunches and whined, looking for reassurance. Minnie slapped her thigh and the sound echoed sharply between the houses. "It's all right," she said and Katie got up and came to her side. Minnie looked up and watched as a V formation of lights passed overhead—silently, far among the stars, she thought. The lights always appeared to be drifting but, at the same time, they moved swiftly. She watched until they passed beneath the surface of the horizon. She heard the sound of water, as though it were being poured from a pail. She hurried towards it. To Annie's place.

Annie stood down in the gully. Water dripped from a tin pail hanging at her side. There was no need for a greeting between them. "This beats everything," Annie said. She held the pail up to Minnie. "Feel it. Go on." Minnie plunged her hand into the water and winced with the iciness of it. "Gonna keep my milk in it," Annie said. "Should keep it from going sour, don't you think?"

Minnie slipped the bar of soap from the pocket of Albert's sweater. She squatted, dipped it into the water, and rubbed the ink from the palm of her hand. She felt her face grow cool in the mist swirling up from the water. When she stood up, Annie gasped and stepped away from her. "Lordy, you look like a ghost," she said. "Your face—it's turned all silver."

"Boo!" Minnie said and laughed. She dried her hands on her thighs. The tin pail flashed as Annie swung it up onto the grass and climbed out of the gully. Minnie kissed for Katie to follow. The icy water pushed against her galoshes as she waded through it. She stepped out of the gully into Annie's yard.

"What in dickens do you make of it?" Annie said.

Minnie shrugged. She followed Annie to the front of the house and sat down beside her on the steps. "I came out here last thing thinking I'd see you coming," Annie said, "and there it was. Think it could be an underground stream come up to the top?"

"It's cold," Minnie said. "Like ice water in spring." The mist sifted across the grass, thinning out as it met warmer air, and began to rise, becoming a white vapour that made the air around them hazy so that Annie's face, the fronts of the houses across the street, the trees, lost their sharp edges and became blurred. A mosquito net, Minnie thought suddenly. That's how it must be, she thought. That's how it was, lying in a carriage and looking out through a white gauze net and seeing up there against the sun the flash of fire in maroon hair. A woman's hair. The woman's bare shoulders twisted suddenly and her slender arms opened wide to embrace the blue sky. A white clown face dropped down out of nowhere, shutting out the upside-down woman with maroon hair. A sad clown mouth opened and said, "Boo!"

Well, Minnie thought. Yes, it was like that. "I never say boo. Do I?"

"You just did," Annie said.

"I know," Minnie said. "Strange."

Annie took two cigarettes from her pocket and handed one to Minnie. "Good for what ails you," she said. "It's that kind of night."

"Nothing ails me," Minnie said.

"Nothing?"

"Well, except that I have come to some sort of decision today. That's all."

Annie fished in her pocket for matches. "Did you remember to write it down?" she said.

"I'm not going to have sex with Albert any more." Even to herself, her voice sounded stronger, more resolute.

"Goodness," Annie said. "So what's Albert going to do?"

"Without, I guess."

"Hah."

The match snapped against wood, flared, and Annie's cigarette glowed as she inhaled and passed a light to Minnie. "You and apple dumpling come to blows?"

"Oh no, no, no," Minnie protested. "Oh no. This decision has nothing to do with.... Oh no. It's not that I'm disenchanted with Albert or anything like that."

"I think you gotta be enchanted before you're disenchanted, girlie." She exhaled and closed her eyes. "He's bound to go elsewheres you know. Men being what they are. Apple dumpling or no apple dumpling."

"I can't help that," Minnie said. "I don't want it to happen, mind you. But I can't help it if he does. Albert's not everything," she said and couldn't say how she'd never expected or wanted him to be everything. "If he goes his own way, it's only fair, I guess."

Annie laughed. "You say that now, but wait."

They didn't speak for a time. They watched as the mist rose and blotted out the trees across the street, and listened to the frogs singing all around Annie's place in that dip of land behind her shack. They heard a woman cry out from Steven Adam's house, and then laughter. It was only June Marchand riding the night. They didn't speak of it. Throughout the years, during the long nights when neither woman felt the pull of sleep, they witnessed both the day and night dreams of the town, the real and the inexplicable, walking side by side in the street under the cover of darkness. Minnie welcomed these manifestations and regretted the amount of time she had wasted sleeping. Annie refused to acknowledge their existence.

Minnie inhaled and held the smoke in her lungs for as long as she could and felt the stars, Annie, the yard, take a giant step backwards.

"This decision about Albert," Annie said, "got anything to do with the ad I brought over?"

"Annie," Minnie said, "when are you going to go and see the doctor?"

"I asked you first."

"I saw you cough blood this morning. When?"

Annie grunted slightly as she stooped and picked up a wicker basket resting on the bottom step. "I found a little item in the newspaper," she said, "and it makes sense. So I've been trying it." She reached inside the basket. "Cup your hands."

Minnie felt the sticky wetness of a tiny frog skitter against the hollow of her palm. Katie whined and cocked her head. The frog, lulled by the coolness of Minnie's skin, grew quiet. She opened her hands a crack and the frog blinked up at her and its sides pulsed with air. It pushed against Minnie's hand as Annie plucked it from her palm.

"Watch," Annie said. She put her head back, opened her mouth, and dropped the frog down inside it. She held the frog in the hollow of her mouth for a moment and her cheek twitched with movement. Annie's throat contracted as she swallowed.

Minnie turned from the sight, her eyes tearing and her stomach going queer. "Annie," she said, "well, just how can that help? Swallowing frogs?"

"It's science," Annie said. "It's as scientific as penicillin." She set the basket down on the step and pulled a clipping from her jacket pocket. "It was in the letters to the editor." She read: "'Dear Sir: There is no superstition to the fact that swallowing live frogs is a cure for cancer. The frogs assimilate the disease and cleanse the system. It has been a cure in a definite case I know. It is as scientific as penicillin.'" She folded the clipping and put it away. "I've been at it a week now," she said, "and the lump hasn't grown a stitch."

"A week," Minnie said. "Why that doesn't prove anything."

Katie barked suddenly and rose up. The hair on her spine bristled. Moments later they heard what the dog had heard: the sound of a horse's hoofs drumming against the road in the distance, becoming louder. A white helmet flashed as the rider bent over the animal's mane. They heard the slap of a crop against the flesh of a satin thigh and the rider's urge for the animal to hurry, hurry. Chestnut flanks flashed as the horse galloped past.

The two women didn't speak of it.

Annie drew the last bit of smoke from her cigarette, pinched out its spark of fire, and chewed on the leftover tobacco. She hugged herself and rocked. "It sure is a big sky tonight." Her hoarse voice had become deep and full. "The stars," she said and hesitated. Her neck convulsed. "You might say I got a frog in my throat." Her laughter was forced.

"The stars?" Minnie asked and looked up. It didn't matter how far you got into the stars, they always seemed to move further and further away.

"The sky. It makes me feel about this big." Annie opened her fingers a crack. "I always feel I got a big hole inside me whenever I look up." Her chest heaved as she began coughing. She leaned over the side of the steps and spat.

"You all right?" Minnie asked.

"Ahh," Annie said and pulled the toque down over her ears. She leaned into the house. "It isn't fair."

"What, the sky?"

"Dying."

"I can understand why you feel like that," Minnie said. "You think so because...because...." She let the sentence trail off.

"Because I'm doing it," Annie said drily.

"And because you think that this valley is all there is to know."

"Because I don't believe in the hereafter, you mean," Annie said. "That kind of wishful thinking is for dishrags. People with no spines."

Minnie turned her face away from her friend's foolishness: the notion that saying something didn't exist made it so.

"Well, I guess we all gotta do it," Annie said. "Eventually we all die. I guess *that's* fair."

"Maybe not," Minnie said and patted Annie on the shoulder. "Maybe we don't all have to do it."

"Sure as night turns to day."

"Maybe not."

"You want the last word?" Annie said. She crossed her arms against her chest. "I'll give it to you. Now, tell me, who's this 'J' person who took out the ad in the paper?"

"Look," Minnie said and pointed to the horizon. A light flickered and then grew.

"Lightning bugs," Annie said. "Could rain later."

"Oh no," Minnie said. "Oh no, no, no. Not lightning bugs." She closed her eyes. The light came from Jeremy. "I had a pear tree in my bedroom once," she said through a smile. "It darn near covered the whole window. Jeremy planted it, I guess. He must have. Or else it was always just there. Maybe everything was always just there," she said. "If I had more time to think, I could remember."

"Yes, I know," Annie said. "You already told me that one. The room was on the second floor. Where you lived with that old lady and Jeremy."

Minnie fell silent. She loved Annie, but she didn't like the way Annie said Jeremy's name. Behind her eyelids she saw a starfish climb up glass. Green fronds swayed in the motion of bubbles reaching for the top of the tank. Through the water she saw an arm move up and down, up and down. Baby fingers curled over the strings of a violin. She saw the pout of pink flesh on their undersides. She looked closer and saw blue cords, sinew, flex beneath paper-thin skin on a wrist. The room turned slowly, bathed in flesh-coloured light, and with it, the boy's face, still and white like a statue carved from marble. On one side, the turn of the mouth looked like arrogance, on another, sadness. And yet.... And yet, mirth twitched at one corner as though the mouth held back a secret or a joke. An eyelid flickered. The boy winked. An old woman's hand reached out towards him; the spotted skin on the back of it was shiny and smooth, the colour of an old potato. The hand turned and opened and three sugar cubes tumbled across its worn palm. The music stopped. The boy laughed. A wet trickle of spit ran down his pronounced, pointed chin. Sugar.

"Jeremy," Minnie said. "The violinist. It *was* Mozart, wasn't it?"

Annie patted Minnie on the shoulder. She wondered if she should mention that the weed she grew behind the house—which they had just smoked—could sometimes cause the mind to make up things or make them seem bigger than they really were. "All right now," she said. "Think. Who's this 'J' person who wants you home?" Annie believed there was a scientific name for what Minnie suffered. Amnesia. Her strangeness resulted from not knowing who she was or where she'd come from. If you couldn't know where you were going, Annie thought, it was important to at least know where you'd been or else you wound up like Minnie, walking around in a permanent fog and a web of made-up stories which sooner or later would open the door to the loony bin.

"Jeremy," Minnie said. "Like it or not, it's Jeremy."

"Jeremy."

"My history." She could remember as far back as Frederick the Great now. And Mozart. Before he was born. Mozart had climbed down into the world and gone on to do exactly what he'd wanted to do. While she, Minnie, had only wanted to leave Jeremy so that she could see the valley. Well, she'd seen it.

"Before I was born," she said.

"Pshaw," Annie said.

Minnie circled Mozart as he stood on the chair in the kitchen, playing the violin. Taut strings vibrated with tension as his bow arm pushed and pulled music from its strings. The bow paused and the music stopped instantly. "Listen," he said, "I made this up while I was playing." He winked. "You can put words to it if you want."

"I hear silence," Jeremy said, entering the kitchen suddenly. "And *you* listen. It's 'hum, hum, tee hum'," he said, tapping the beat out against his leg, "*not* 'hum, tee, tee hum'."

"It's boring, that's what it is."

"If my music is beyond you, just say so."

"Listen," Mozart said and began playing.

"Gallant," Jeremy said, "but uninspired."

"I think it sounds a lot like Bach."

Jeremy's laughter echoed in the kitchen. "But without his harmony or imagination. Anyway, that's all I've been hearing for years and years. It's time for something new."

The boy's marble-like features closed and he resumed playing.

"When I want to hear your compositions, I'll let you know," Jeremy said.

"You don't want me to compose," Mozart said above the sound of the music, "because then you couldn't direct."

The muscle beside Jeremy's eye flickered the way it did when he was irritated or tense. "I wish Maria of Austria would get up off her knees for once and look behind her," he muttered as he began buttering thick pieces of toast. "I hardly slept all night. Frederick is up to no good." He poured milk into a tall glass, slopped over the top of it in his haste, and ran his long tongue up the sides before he handed it to Minnie. "Kinsky's a good man, but the rest of them are doddering fools. They'll be no help to Maria at all," he said. "And don't drink your milk standing up."

He handed her the plate of buttered toast. Cranberry jelly wobbled on the plate as she set it down on the counter. "What's that supposed to mean?" she said.

"The whole world's unravelling. I'll let you know what happens. Now sit. Drinking standing up isn't good for you."

"I think it would be," she said, "because it's easier for the milk to get into my stomach if I'm standing." The music skipped a beat and she saw the muscles in Mozart's stomach contract as he tried to keep from laughing and she was glad because sometimes she resented how Jeremy thought he knew everything. How he sat up there on the cliff on his chair for hours and wouldn't let her come up and have a look at what was happening down there beyond the trees.

"Sit," Jeremy said. "France and England are at each other's throats again, the Turks and Persians just won't quit, and Ivan's in trouble in Russia. The only good thing to happen lately is *Te Deum*. Bless Handel. He never lets me down," Jeremy said and kissed the top of Minnie's head.

She gathered her string into several loops and sat on the stool beside the counter. She'd become used to the string. Each year, the old woman had lengthened it and so now she scarcely felt its tug when she wandered too far away.

"Jeremy," Minnie said, "I'm bored."

Annie sighed. "I'd give anything to be bored." She reached for the wicker basket resting on the step below. "Knowing your days are numbered is not boring."

Annie took Minnie's hand into hers and opened it, turning the palm up. She dropped another frog down into it. "Hey," she said. "Wake up."

Minnie cupped the tiny frog into silence. Annie plucked the amphibian from her hand and swallowed it. Her throat contracted. And then, from her throat, came the sound of a child's cry. A sharp, quick cry.

Minnie stared at the woman and then her mouth opened into a horrified, round "O". She stood up and pressed her hands against her eyes. "No," she said. "No, no, no." Her voice rose to a wail.

"Slow down," Annie said. "There's nothing to be afraid of. It happens sometimes. I should've warned you. It's a natural sound."

Minnie dropped her hands but the look of dread remained in her eyes. Her mouth shivered. "No," she said. "I will not remember that. You can't make me." She plunged her fists into the pockets of Albert's curling sweater, turned and walked over to the edge of the gully and stared down into the mist rolling across its surface.

"Remember what, dear?" Annie touched her on the shoulder. "Tell me."

Minnie turned. She smiled, the pleasant round expression of peace once more in place. She bent and swished the icy surface of the water. "Look," she said and held up her hand. Mist trailed from the tips of her fingers. Katie whined and rose and came to stand at her side. Minnie looked up at the fire flickering in the hills. Its heat was melting the glacier into water. It was a signal for her to be ready.

"Where are you going?" Annie called as Minnie strode down the incline and through the water and up the other side. Katie followed. The mist covered them from view.

"I want to do something for my girls," Minnie said and Annie thought she heard her add, "for the last time."

It seemed to Rosella that all of night should have already passed when she heard the faint scratching at the bedroom door, but as she opened her eyes it was to darkness, to continuing night.

"Wake up." It was her mother's voice.

Before Rosella could caution Ginny to keep still, she rose up on her elbows and rubbed sleep from her eyes. "Is that you, Ma?"

"Yes, it's me. Come on, you two monkeyshines," Minnie said. "Wake up. I've got a great surprise for you."

Rosella's stomach turned. She pulled her braids together and knotted them firmly beneath her chin.

"They're sleeping, dear," Albert said.

The door cracked open.

Minnie felt the heat from their bodies rise above the bed. Rosella kicked Ginny beneath the blankets, buried her head into the pillow, one eye closed, one open. As Minnie stepped into the room the faint scent of a smudge fire entered with her. Rosella opened the other eye. A luminescent blue-green aura pulsed from her mother's body. The walls leapt forward and retreated. Ginny gasped.

"Ta da!" Minnie, a magician, pulled from her sleeve a bouquet of sparklers, stars, shooting and spitting.

Ginny squealed and pulled the blanket up over her head.

"Look, look," Minnie said and pulled their blanket free. She held above their bed a phosphorescent, pulsing mass. Heartbeats of cold light throbbed with individual rhythms and climbed up the sides of the jar.

Rosella swung with her fist. The jar shattered against the floor. Sparks billowed up beside the girls' bed and then became globes of light, blinking on and off as the fireflies circled the room and floated up to the ceiling.

Rosella cried and cried. And later, when she'd cried herself dry, she lay in the dark and thought of all the women on Ottawa Street. She planned on what she'd wear. The questions she'd ask and her answers to theirs. She'd start at the top of the street with Delta, or at the bottom with Olga Peter. But whatever she did, she was going to find another mother.

"Albert," Minnie said softly when she stepped into the kitchen. "I'm sorry."

"There's nothing to be sorry for," Albert said. "A little excitement's good for the heart." Albert had been hungry and so he'd made a pot of spaghetti after he'd written to Aunt Violet and was waiting for Minnie to return. He stood at the sink, scrubbing bits of dried spaghetti noodles from the bottom of the aluminum pot.

"No. What I meant was, I'm sorry, but I'm leaving you."

He'd left the pot standing and now had to scratch hard to pry the dried noodle loose. Bits of it wedged beneath his fingernails, sharp nudges of pain. He'd heard Minnie cross the room. She'd taken off her boots and her footstep was light and dry against the tiles. He picked up a spoon and scraped at the hardened bits of noodles and watched when they chipped loose—how beneath, the pot was brighter where they'd been. The network of spaghetti-noodle trails had somehow absorbed whatever metal was in the pot and left behind a wriggly track of something newer and brighter. He wondered if he left a whole pot of noodles standing to dry overnight, would the bottom of the pot become like new? If this just might be a way of cleaning aluminum?

Minnie's cool fingers trailed across his neck. His knees went wobbly, as though he'd carried several heavy bags of groceries home and had just set them down. A kind of relief. Because he'd known from her eyes that sooner or later something was going to happen. Minnie had always been a bit of a slippery thing right from the beginning. He'd tried to pin her down as best he could. In bed, for instance, he'd open his eyes and see that smile of hers radiating up to the ceiling, reaching up and up, and he sensed that the smile had nothing to do with his lovemaking. And so he gave in and let her ride on top because then, at least, she smiled down at him. Her refusal to marry him came from her desire not to be pinned down, he realized. She was like a ball of mercury rolling across the palm of a hand. You tried to pick it up and it slipped away, or became many parts which scattered across a lifeline and emerged once again into the single silver sphere. That was Minnie, Albert thought.

"But dear, where will you go?" he asked. He blushed to think what they were going to say down at the lumber yard.

"Albert," Minnie said, as though she was surprised by the question. She patted him lightly on the back. "I'm not going anywhere. I'm just leaving."

"Dear Aunt Violet," Albert wrote as the silence of the house fell heavily around his shoulders. He dipped the pen again. He heard Minnie's soft murmur outside as she gave Katie a last pat.

> Wind about east, quite a change, the rain falling very heavily at times during the night. This week I will commence to try and fix up that room for you as I am still expecting you to arrive before the summer blows in hot.
>
> I have been choring around, cleaning up the kitchen. On Sunday, I plan to help Rosella with her sewing.
>
> Lately, I have been experiencing some tightness in my chest. I have taken a dose of Epsom, but it hasn't brought relief.

"There, there, there," Minnie said and laid her cheek against Katie's head. She unhooked the rope from Katie's collar. "Hendrick Schultz needs a friend," she whispered. Katie bounded up and out of the yard. Then she stopped and looked back at Minnie, tongue lolling. "Go, go," Minnie urged. "Come back if you get hungry."

The ghost-like shapes of her family swayed on the clothesline. The laundry. She'd completely forgotten about the laundry. With fingers stiff from the icy water, Minnie pulled the clothes free and stacked her family in her arms. Oh, this day, it had started out as Thursday with the wash and.... Potatoes? Pizza? But it wasn't at all like the one before it. She began to sing.

FRIDAY

5

On Friday morning, Jacob Friesen was the first person awake in the town of Agassiz. As was the pattern, he awoke before Lena, his wife, and went into the kitchen to meditate. The absolute stillness of the morning, the hour that was his own before Lena arose and her bustling energy expanded to the far reaches of the house, was what he needed to set the tone for the day. Friday, the day he put together his sermon notes.

He raised the blind on the narrow window above the kitchen table expecting to see the garden and overblown spikes of pink and yellow hollyhocks straining to remain upright against the white picket fence, and beyond that maple trees, with bright new leaves concealing, for the summer, the corrugated, curved roof of the skating rink. But instead the outdoors had been erased completely by a heavy fog. He pulled the blind against it. The fog was as it should be, he told himself. That the Lord knew his need to feel enclosed, alone, and at peace. He reached for the writing tablet on the table, and his Bible. The Book of James. Counting it all joy when we fall into divers temptations; with temptation came the trying of patience and the way to perfection. He read for several minutes, making notes, and then felt by the pressing of light against the window blind that the sun had climbed and the day had changed.

And so it had. The light had become soft and diffused so that the trees had reappeared, although they were phantom-like, several landscapes transported from another place during the night, superimposed one on another. But the magic of the mist was quickly stolen by the blunt image of Hendrick Schultz teetering along the hand railing of the small wooden bridge that spanned the coulee between his and Taro Yamamoto's property. He drew the blind and sat down. He was simply not ready to face this yet. The boy and Elizabeth.

It was on such a morning as this, that the sudden knock had come at his door and his eyes had moved down from the immediate shock of Elizabeth's silver hair to her deep-set eyes, dark with worry, tanned skin drawn tautly across her cheekbones in a look of hunger. A blond child turned its face from him into the woman's neck where the pulse jumped as she began to speak to Jacob—low, halting, saying that someone had pointed out his place to her, that he spoke German. And he could not answer immediately because of his suddenly jumbled thoughts. It was impossible, but if it had not been for the fact that he himself had washed the stench of disease from her wasted body, carried her, and buried her in the ground beside their child, he was looking into the face of his first wife. She's exactly like the woman who died while I was out caring for others, he wanted to tell Lena. He'd almost told her several times. But Lena had taken Elizabeth to be the child they'd never had and so he'd remained silent.

The boy stood at his mother's knee in Jacob and Lena's kitchen, his face pressed into her lap. Lena rushed about, cooking porridge and toasting bread. Elizabeth slipped free from the jacket she'd draped across her shoulders and handed it to Jacob. A man's jacket, Jacob realized as he hung it on a hook beside his own. He fingered the sleeve for a moment, thinking. A man's jacket. She appeared to be watching him and smiling, but when he moved away her smile and gaze remained fixed on the jacket. She was caught by some inner thought or a memory whose picture she still looked into.

Jacob went out into the garage. He stood still, thinking. She was much taller than Louise had been. Thinner. But still, the hair was the same. It was unusual to see white hair on such a young woman. He climbed the ladder and reached for a shoe box in the rafters. He blew dust from its lid and went back into the house. The boy still stood at his mother's knee, face down, clutching fistfuls of her skirt. Jacob bent and held up a wooden block. The boy turned away. Jacob moved to the other side, holding up the varnished building block. The woman smelled of the outdoors, of dust that lingered on her shoes and in the folds of her skirt. The boy's angry screams erupted and spilled into the kitchen. He doesn't want anyone to look at him, Elizabeth explained and hitched the screaming child onto her knee. "Please don't look at him and he'll be fine," she said. Lena turned from the stove, astonished that Elizabeth would allow such behaviour. Jacob reached for his Bible and opened it quickly and read in German to the woman, "Chasten thy son while there is hope," he read, "and let not thy soul spare for his crying."

The boy lifted his head and turned his mottled face up to Jacob. His eyes were flecked with different colours of blue and had the look of a piece of cracked pottery. "Proverbs, chapter 19, verse 18," he said.

"Oh." Lena stood wide-eyed, the wooden spoon suspended over the bubbling porridge. Her face flushed with surprise. Jacob searched Elizabeth's face. She looked vaguely annoyed and shrugged her shoulders.

Jacob leafed through the Bible. "Train up a child in the way he should go; and when he is old, he will not depart from it."

"Proverbs, chapter 22, verse 6." The child could barely pronounce the word "Proverbs" and had put a "b" sound in the place of the "v", but he was correct. Jacob felt his mouth go strange and his lips began to tremble. He knelt beside the boy. "Psalm 23," he said. The boy's eyes widened. He slid down from his mother's knee, stood before Jacob, crossed his hands against his stomach, and recited the entire psalm.

"Acht, heavenly Father!" Lena exclaimed.

"Please," Elizabeth said and hiked the boy back up onto her knee. "This is why I left the other place and came here. He's only a child. People soon forget that."

Jacob's heart sang with joy. He tousled the boy's heavy blond locks. She hadn't taught him, Elizabeth vowed. It just happened one day when he was two years old. It was a gift from God, Jacob realized, and for some reason, God had entrusted this gifted child into his care.

"And what else?" Jacob asked the boy.

Hendrick turned his intense blue eyes up at Jacob. "*Mene, Mene, Tekel, Upharsin,*" he said.

Jacob sat now at the kitchen table, the Bible and notebook open on the table in front of him, and stared out the window. The mist had risen and was almost burned off by the sun— only wisps of it remained, trapped by the foliage of the trees. Lena had got out of bed and entered the kitchen, hairpins in her mouth and her arms raised as she walked and wound her hair up at the back of her head. "I'll put the cereal on," she said through the pins, as she did every morning.

"No," Jacob said. "Not today." Today he would spend the entire day out in the garage, praying and fasting and working on his sermon.

"How so?" she said, her plump arms still raised and her face still shiny with the sweat of sleep. "I wanted to wash my hair today," she said.

"Lena, Lena," he chided.

She blushed. "That's fine," she said. "I will manage somehow."

"You will do more than manage," Jacob said. "If you trust in the Lord, you'll be victorious."

The air was moist and fresh and he drew it deep into his chest before he went into the garage. He knew that Lena would brew strong coffee in their spotless, warm kitchen in the house he'd built before they were married, its rooms seemingly large enough for the years they had left. But the house had proven to be too small and so even though he'd never owned a car and didn't plan to, he'd built the garage. He'd also built the sitting bench for himself with its hinged lid, where inside he kept his books and the razor strap. It was where Hendrick had knelt at the age of six and, as only a child could, had opened his heart to receive Jesus. He had received Jesus again at eight and then at ten and because Jacob wasn't certain the boy really understood, once again at twelve. Jacob was concerned now that the pledges might be recitations like the verses of Scripture, because even though the child knew all of the words of the Lord by heart, he didn't seem to want to understand them. Perhaps reciting had become a trick, a way to show off, the same way a bully flexed his muscles. Jacob had kept a vigilant, careful watch over Hendrick and prayed each day that the Lord would reveal His purpose. But he was afraid now that his eye had missed something. That perhaps through his constant recitations, Hendrick had become immune to the conviction of the Holy Word and was capable of concealing deceit of the highest degree.

The garage was where he took Hendrick when he needed to counsel him or test the accuracy of his gift. It was where he had disciplined and admonished and instructed the child. Jacob would have him sit on the bench and turn his palms up to receive the strap while Lena stayed with his mother inside the house to prevent her from leaping up and interfering. And now she took the wooden spoon to the boy? Jacob turned to the concordance in his Bible. The word was a two-edged sword.

On that same Friday morning, the second person to get out of bed had been Mrs. Peter, Ollie's widowed mother and a faithful member of Jacob's congregation. Her day began as any other. She pushed up off her knees beside the bed, pulled the feather tick back into place, and then stepped into the pantry off the kitchen to the smell of flour and spices, where her dentures soaked in the chipped porcelain cup she'd brought with her from Russia. The cup was almost the only thing she had left and she clung to it. She refused to allow Olga to replace it with something new, like the pink plastic container she'd once brought home from the store, a container the shape of her dentures with a hinged lid which snapped into place so Ollie wouldn't be offended each night by the look of those teeth soaking in the pantry. Take it back to the store, Mrs. Peter told Ollie.

Her teeth in place, hair dampened and smoothed down, she unhooked her apron from the wall and hurried to the stove to set the water to boil for Olga's cereal. Upstairs, in her attic bedroom, Olga still knelt in prayer beside her bed. Mrs. Peter remembered and went back into her own bedroom to the bureau, where behind a photograph of her late husband she'd hidden three chocolate bars tied with a pink ribbon. She carried them into the kitchen and set them down on the table beside Olga's cereal bowl. It was the girl's fortieth birthday today. She'd made a special trip down to Main Street and that café place yesterday and had forgotten why she'd gone.

Mrs. Peter had stood looking in the window of Delta's Hot Spot for such a long time, hoping that she'd see something which would remind her why she'd gone uptown. She'd had to think: whereabouts were you standing in the house when you thought you'd have to go uptown? In the cellar. She'd been counting the jars of preserves left on the shelves—which amounted to forty—and that had reminded her of Olga's birthday and her need to buy a treat for the girl. And she had. Three chocolate bars. One dark one with almonds, one filled with fudge, and the other biscuit. She, too, reached for her well-worn Bible that rested on the table on the crocheted doily. She wondered what special message God might give her today for Olga. Something for her to take to work and think about while she counted money and listened to the foolish things people talked about. She unzipped the Bible and opened it quickly. Her eyes were drawn by a long verse. "So that they shall take no wood out of the field, neither cut down any out of the forests; for they shall burn the weapons with fire and they shall spoil those that spoiled them and rob those that robbed them, saith the Lord God."

She sat down in Olga's chair to think about it. What did it mean? They burned gas for heat and used electricity for cooking and there were no forests for cutting down wood. The floor above her head creaked as Olga shifted on her knees. Still praying, Mrs. Peter thought. Very long this morning. She got up and dumped the cup of cereal into the boiling water, flung in a pinch of salt, and stirred. She wondered what the girl might have in her head to keep her on her knees for such a terribly long time.

The last person to get out of bed on that Friday morning had been Sandra Adam. She did not reach for any Bible, but jumped up quickly and pulled a brush through her hair. She was late. She'd been awakened during the night by the sound of her father's voice once again crying out in his profound grief. Light was beginning to dawn before she'd fallen asleep and she'd slept through the alarm. She hadn't the necessary time to prepare for this important day. Just a lick and polish of cosmetics and she was off.

Whatever anxiety she'd had about facing the day vanished as she stepped out the door to the amazing sight of water flashing back the blue sky to her, and she heard the excited chatter of birds lining up on the Standings' roof and almost at the same time dust churned up from the wheels of a municipal truck as it sped towards her and skidded to a halt just beyond her house.

Men in yellow hardhats leapt down from the back of the truck and gathered at the edge of the gully, peering down into the water. Sonny Ericson, the only man not wearing the required green cotton shirt and pants of the Roads people, stood on the back of the truck. He'd ripped out the sleeves of his white tee-shirt and his tanned biceps bulged as he raised an iron rod from the floor of the truck and handed it over the side to August Marchand. August moved slowly, his beer belly supported by a wide leather belt. Sandra heard him grunt as he bent over and plunged the rod down into the water. Whatever it was that seemed to flow from their male bodies—their energy—intruded into Sandra's day. More and more, against her will, she felt herself being drawn into watching men. Studying the deftness of their fingers fitting things into place. She wanted to edge closer, look over their shoulders, smell them, stand in the way of that energy that churned outwards from their limbs.

Sonny vaulted over the side of the truck and joined the men who circled August, examining the water mark on the rod. August tasted his fingers. "It's water," he said.

The other men scratched their armpits, stroked whiskers, and waited for ideas.

"Ten bucks says it's artesian," Sonny said.

"Artesian watziz?" August spat into the water.

"Artesian well," Sonny said and held up his hands to demonstrate how water could get trapped between two pieces of rock. Like a sandwich.

"Yeah, well," August said, "how'd it get there? That's the sixty-four dollar one."

"It's probably always been there," Sonny said. "Something happened, like a fissure or something. In the rock. Opened up, I guess."

"For no reason?"

Sandra stood beside the water-filled ditch. There was only one way across it. She kicked loose her loafers and held them at her side and stepped down. Her muscles contracted with the shock of icy water. She stepped back into her yard. "It's freezing," she said and laughed, knowing that she showed too much of her legs as she held up her skirt.

"You want a boost?" Sonny said, and before Sandra could answer, he strode through the water and bent over in front of her. "Grab on," he said.

As she wound her arms about his neck, she could smell his heavy odour of unwashed hair. She felt the scratch of whiskers against her arms. He waded through the gully and up the other side. She blushed with the knowledge of her breasts pushing against his back.

"Thanks," she said. She released her grip and slid down his back to the ground. She wiped her reddened feet dry on the grass and squeezed back into the loafers. One by one the men had turned their backs on Sandra and kicked at the dirt or wandered off to examine the tread on a tire. Except for Sonny. Sandra's eyes searched for and then flickered briefly across that soft bulge in his jeans. She thought of the picture Delta had drawn for her. "Just so you know," Delta had said. "For your information, this is what men look like. Although my memory is fading," she said. When Sandra looked up, she saw that Sonny was staring at her and she turned away because he made her want to bring her arms up and cross them against her breasts.

The men all swung around at one time to the sound of Mr. Campbell's voice raised in anger as Etta pushed his wheelchair down the centre of the road. "God damn it woman, use the sidewalk," he said. But Etta just kept smiling and pushing. The wheelchair swayed and Mr. Campbell jolted forward as a wheel met a chunk of dirt. "Jelly for brains," he said and waved his cane. One of the men went over, kicked aside the clump of dirt, and wheeled Campbell over to the truck.

"We figure we've got an artesian well here," August Marchand said.

Mr. Campbell blinked. His eyes, unaccustomed to sunlight, began to tear and the tears ran down his face. He reminded Sandra of a salamander. If someone sprinkled salt on the man, his skin would shrivel and peel away.

"That's a pile of crap," he said. "Bedrock's about a mile under." His voice was a growl.

"Morning," Sandra sang. "How's your arthritis?"

"Don't stand near me," Campbell said. The end of his cane was sharp in her stomach as he nudged her away. "You're too hot. Can't stand hot people."

Sandra tried to catch Etta's attention, wanting to pass their common message of "Isn't he just the most loveable, cranky man?" Etta avoided the message and reached inside her dress to adjust a brassiere strap.

It must be the sudden appearance of the water, Sandra thought as she crossed the road. They were preoccupied. And she became preoccupied then with her own future. Her hair wasn't right for it. She'd get it cut. Or permed a bit. She'd suggest to Head Office that they promote her to appliances. It made sense after all: that a woman explain to another woman the advantages of sudsavers in the country. And the sales commission was higher.

Someone had been up early or out late, she thought, because several planks had been spread across the water in the gully in front of the Pullman house. Robin Marchand straddled the highest branches of the maple tree that bent over the sidewalk in front of Minnie and Albert's house. She could see the flash of Robin's brown legs scissoring up to the top. The girl stopped and hugged the tree with one arm, set a jar into a crook of a limb, reached down, and began reeling in inchworms dangling from strings. Just what did that girl and Sonny Ericson have in common? Sandra wondered. She felt something wet hit her arm. A circle of spittle bubbled against her skin. Sandra wiped it against her skirt, swallowing indignation because it was pointless, she realized, to say anything to someone whose mother sang a whole octave below the sopranos and thought she was singing alto.

Sandra passed by the Pullman house. Something new in the window, she noted. A lacy cut-out design of a fish climbed up the glass. The door at the side of the house creaked as it opened slightly and then closed, and then once again opened just wide enough for Rosella Pullman to slip through it sideways. As she walked across the yard, the flounces rimming the bottom of her dress bounced against her sharp, white shin bones. The straw hat she wore was pulled down about her pale face and tied into place with a pink ribbon.

"Morning Rosella," Sandra said, happy at last to see the girl outside. Dressed up as though she was off to Sunday school in another century—but outside.

Rosella flinched. The white gloved hands fluttered and she dropped the box-like purse she carried, white straw with a cluster of pink and blue flowers on the lid. Something Mrs. Standing would choose, Sandra thought.

"Where you off to so early?" she asked, thinking she'd offer to take the girl by the hand and walk with her part of the way. To instruct Rosella to be sure and approach with boldness.

Rosella was undecided. She glanced furtively down the street and then up the street. She crossed the yard carrying the straw purse tightly in both hands like a bridesmaid with a bouquet poised and ready to lead the way. "Which way are you going?" she asked.

"Uptown. To work, of course."

"Well then, I'm going the other way," Rosella said and headed off in the opposite direction to choose a mother.

"Oh wow," Robin's hoarse voice wafted down from the tree. "So look who's suddenly got a social life."

Sandra turned away from both of them. She passed by Delta William's property where sharp blades of clipped grass speared beads of dew and the whole lawn sparkled. I'll never in this life have a child, Sandra vowed as she thought of Rosella, of Robin, and how that sweet shyness had turned to outright snottiness overnight. Delta William had been clever, Sandra thought, and then realized that this was another decision she was free to make. Delta had shown her how babies happened. Had drawn that picture. She'd have to stop by one day and ask Delta how one went about stopping babies from happening.

She passed by Mr. Campbell's vine-covered windows, tendrils fingering up the roof and clinging to cracked mortar in the chimney. She felt her heart skip a beat as she entered Main Street. She slid her handbag up her arm and hooked it about her neck and slung it around behind her the way she'd seen a girl in a movie do it. The bag knocked against her back as she walked and her hair streamed in the wind and she swung her arms, happy, taking long strides, enjoying the confident, busy sound of her heels against the pavement. Sandra passed by the Bank of Montreal, the Red and White, the hotel, Urbanick's Baked Goods, and Delta's Hot Spot. Then she turned the corner at the cenotaph and thought briefly about Sonny Ericson. They'd never allowed her to have her own opinion about Sonny, either. He's a slow thinker, a teacher had once confided. And it seemed to her that he became slow then, gazing for hours on end out the window and sucking on his pencil. The boy's impulsive and wild; his mother's a Sigurdson; stay away from Sonny. And it was only after that that Sonny was chased down the highway by the police and roared home ahead of them and painted his truck yellow before they arrived and denied having ever been near the highway. Or, Sonny Ericson has a mean streak. And then he started blowing up frogs with a bicycle pump. He's becoming weird, they said his last year of school, because he doodled constantly. Pictures of daggers piercing hearts and blood dripping. Hooded skeletons peering out from his drawings, with lizards crawling out of their blackened eye sockets. And Sandra remembered Career Day, how Sonny had confessed to the whole room that he had aspirations of becoming a doctor. A surgeon, he said. An undertaker, you mean, someone said after everyone had stopped laughing. But Sandra recalled now the perfect anatomy of his skeletons— every bone in place—and the expression of suffering in his corpses' faces. But then, all these rushing thoughts of Sonny vanished instantly as beyond, near the end of the street where the grain elevator loomed up beside the railroad track, Sandra saw Mr. Newhoff as he stepped out of the store and bent over a display of truck tires. At his side stood a stranger wearing a suit. Head Office, she realized, and pushed forward to meet her fate.

"Well, I'm off," Olga Peter said on Friday morning as she entered the kitchen screwing her pansy earrings into place.

The smell of something sweet and soft entered the room with her. It was the smell of face powder, her mother realized, and noticed that the skin around Olga's eyes was red and that she'd tried to cover it over. At forty she'd carried Olga, her last child. She had picked up the Bible once again to find a better verse, something nearer to the back of it, when a flutter of movement in the window drew her away. There was a little girl sitting on a bench in the garden. She'd set a purse down on the ground beside her and had folded her white-gloved hands across her lap. Mrs. Peter blinked, expecting to see the child vanish. But no, there she still sat. White. Waiting for something. So she waited to see what would happen and got up, leaning across the windowsill. The girl shifted sideways on the bench, pulled her dress down over her knees, and scratched her nose.

Ollie sat down at the table. Mrs. Peter slid the pink-ribboned chocolate bars across the table towards her.

"Happy birthday," she said. "God bless you."

"Oh yes, thanks," Olga said. "It's that time of year, isn't it?" She crossed her legs and her nylon stockings swished as she swung her foot back and forth. The sharpness of her narrow white kneecap shone through the stockings.

"You've turned the hem up on your dress," Mrs. Peter said.

Olga coloured slightly and tugged the dress back down over her kneecap. "It's the way people are wearing them these days, Mother."

"Ollie, Ollie." The woman mourned in her heart the tone of voice her daughter had just used, like a bubble of water sizzling on the stove. The little girl in the garden uncrossed her legs and reached for the purse and set it into her lap.

"Listen, don't bother with my cereal," Olga said. "I'm trying to lose weight."

"At least read your verse," her mother said. "You need your spiritual food."

Olga picked up the Bible and selected a verse at random and read aloud. "Behold," she said. "It is come and is done, saith the Lord God; this is the day whereof I have spoken."

The little girl began to walk towards the house.

"There's a little girl in the garden," Mrs. Peter said and wiped her eyes which had begun to tear so suddenly.

Olga set the Bible aside and looked out the window. She gasped.

Rosella saw the door open and the swirl of blue paisley skirt flash as Olga clattered down the stairs.

Olga stopped short and stared at the girl, heart pounding. "Is something wrong?" she said.

Rosella's green eyes narrowed in the sun. She dropped the purse and flung her arms about Olga's narrow waist and hung on. Olga felt the heat of Rosella's breath against her breast.

"Please be my mother," Rosella said.

Olga patted the girl awkwardly for several moments. "You have a mother," she said. Rosella looked so much like Albert. The same freckled, milky skin. She pushed the child from her, crouched, and untied the pink ribbon, pulling the ridiculous hat free.

"What's this all about?" The girl wasn't a child, really. When Olga stood up, Rosella's head came to her shoulder. She plucked the white gloves from Rosella's hands. The girl chewed her fingernails horribly.

"She's not my mother," Rosella said.

Olga laughed. "Of course she is. But we could be friends."

"What would we do?" Rosella asked.

"Well, I could teach you things. Like, I could teach you how to sew." Some decent clothes, she almost said. "But we've got to make sure that it'll be all right with your parents," she said. She would send a note with the girl to Albert at the lumber yard and suggest that they meet and discuss how she could best assist with Rosella without interfering. Better yet, she'd go. With baking.

"Olga, what is this?" Mrs. Peter stood on the back step with her hands on her hips.

"My birthday verse," Olga said and took the child by the shoulders and showed her the path that led through the garden to Bison Street and not Ottawa. She would not take the chance of having Minnie see her.

"Your breakfast," Mrs. Peter said. "There's still time."

Yes, there was still time, Olga thought, as they walked hand in hand towards Main Street and Delta's Hot Spot. To celebrate her birthday. "You like donuts?" she asked Rosella.

Delta William saw Rosella and Ollie Peter's reflection in the mirror as they entered the café. Through the reflections of lemon meringue pies, a chocolate cake, and stacks of bran muffins, still warm, she saw the two of them sit down at the counter. She was too busy to relish the shock of it for long. She had other things on her mind. What was she going to tell Sandra Adam?

"One order of toast, brown," Delta called out.

Cindy Dorfman, the person responsible for the fresh baking every morning, looked up from the sink through the cut-out in the wall. The only condition Cindy had to getting up at 5:00 a.m. to bake was that she be able to watch them eat. "Gotcha," the girl said and popped the bread down into the toaster.

The mirror complements the baked goods and makes them look twice as delicious, Delta thought, as she reached up through the sound of cups clattering against saucers and the low murmur of male voices and plucked a bran muffin up into a serviette. Delta knew it was because of the fresh baking that her café was full every morning as soon as enough time had passed and it wasn't too indecent to leave behind jobs for the first coffee break of the day.

"I think I'll live dangerously," someone said. "Give me a slab of that apple pie."

"Hold your horses," Delta said as she sliced the muffin and covered it with whipped butter. Sandra, she'd say, there are just some things you don't do. Every single person in the café had made a deal with Mr. Newhoff at one time or another. All the sherbet glasses, water glasses, fruit juice glasses which gleamed on the shelves had come from Mr. Newhoff. A deal. She'd given the Baptist choir a hefty discount on their meals when they'd held their wind-up do at her place. As Delta rushed for the coffee pot, she was aware of white-shirted arms resting on the counter, stained fingers holding cigarettes, plaid shirts, a pocket with a pen and a pad of paper, and Rosella and Olga Peter, looking awkward and prim and out of place. But Delta never had time to see all of them. Just parts. This morning it was extra busy. Even the three booths along the wall were full of men who blew smoke up towards the fan on the ceiling and talked about the water filling the ditches alongside Ottawa Street. About artesian wells and how they worked. A hydrostatic principle. Equilibrium. And Sandra.

And then what Delta knew was going to happen, happened. The door opened and Sandra stepped inside, mascara running down her cheeks. The room fell silent and, except for the hum of the fan turning on the ceiling, it grew still.

"Oh Delta," Sandra cried, "I've been fired."

"She sang one solo too many," someone said, and then everyone rose, except for Rosella and Olga, leaving behind untouched muffins, a half-eaten chunk of pie, coffee mugs half full. Cindy stared out from the kitchen, stricken by the sight of a piece of chocolate cake abandoned, a fork plunged through its side. The men dropped change onto the glass counter-top, tipped their hats, and left.

"Well, what did you expect?" Delta said. "A bouquet of roses?"

"But what did I do?" Sandra twisted the brown pay envelope and then sat down on a stool and rested her head against the counter. Her shoulders heaved.

Delta lit a cigarette, leaned against the ice-cream cooler, and thought. If she hired Sandra, they'd all go on over to the hotel. Baking or no baking.

Cindy came out from the kitchen wiping suds on her apron. "What should I do with all the food?"

Sandra looked up at Delta. Her face was blotchy and swollen from crying. "He was stealing," she said. "And I get fired."

"The trouble with you," Delta said, "is that you're such a black-and-white person." She sighed. It seemed no matter how much you did for a person, it was never enough. Over and over, she'd seen children with a perfectly matched set of parents suddenly rise up and bite them in the ankles.

The trouble with you. Sandra was shocked because she never realized that there was anything about her which might be troubling.

"The trouble with you," Rosella said, "is that you think you're so much better than everyone else."

"Shht," Olga cautioned.

"Want some advice?" Delta asked.

"Oh yes, please tell me what to do."

"Leave," Delta said. "Leave the town and wait until this blows over."

"I can't leave my father," Sandra said. "He's got no one."

"Your father is capable of taking care of himself," Delta said. "And we'll keep our eye out. That's about all I can say. Now, I think you'd better go."

Sandra walked down the street, crying. She passed by Urbanick's where they had once tied a string around a wobbly tooth and pulled it out. They'd given her sheets of brown wrap to draw murals on. She passed by the Post Office and that fateful letter slot. Harrigan stood in the store window of the Red and White, adjusting a hat on a mannequin. But no one saw her. It was as though she'd never walked down the street at all. And when she crossed the new little bridge that her father had built over the water-filled gully, she saw him out in the garage, hammering a sign to the wall. "ADAMS CERAMIC WORKSHOP", the sign read. "I'm going to go into business and turn my hobby into money," he said. And then, "How could you make such an ass of yourself and embarrass me like that?"

When Sandra stood waiting for the Greyhound bus to take her away with nothing but the clothes on her back—she would bring little of her old life with her—and the pay packet in her handbag, she thought of it. That all the buildings on Main Street were just fronts. If she walked behind them, she'd see a wall propped up with two-by-fours. The whole town was only a set for a movie and the people players, and she was the only one who hadn't known it. Really, she didn't have any decision to make. They had expected her to stick to the script.

Sonny Ericson's battered yellow truck veered from the street and swung into the curb. The fenders rattled as he revved the engine. He rolled down the window. "Hi yuh, Sandy," he said.

She couldn't answer for the lump in her throat.

"You wanna go for a ride?"

"The bus," she said and searched for a tissue to wipe her eyes.

"Hey, no sweat," he said. "Hop in. I'll take you wherever you want to go."

And Sonny, Sandra realized, it was just like that for Sonny. They expected him to stick to the script too, she thought, and felt a rush of sympathy for the copper-haired young man. His crooked nose, the knife cuts, the imprint of knuckle-dusters on his chin—these scars were all part of the script.

She sat beside him on the brown, cracked leather seat, arranging her skirt across her lap, setting the handbag between them. And Sonny smelled it: the sweet, faint odour of lily-of-the-valley. That Sandra. She was so clueless.

The sky was high and faded with wispy clouds racing across the face of it and across the surface of the water that afternoon as Jacob Friesen turned at the corner and entered Ottawa Street. He needed to stretch his legs and rest his mind. Reflected in the water's surface was the flight of a hawk as it circled high above the street. Its wings stroked the air in a backward motion as it began its dive into the grass behind Annie Schmoon's shack and rose up just as swiftly, but not before Jacob had seen the shape of a small animal dangling from the bird's beak. He hadn't realized that a hawk would go for a frog, but as the bird wheeled above his head, he was certain that's what it carried. When he turned back to the road, it was as though something had shifted and the light had become the light of an overcast sky, the colours of the trees deeper, richer blacks and browns, and vivid bright orange fungi encrusted all the joints of the trees' branches. He heard the rumble of wooden wheels, of metal rims rattling against a worn path, and the low moan of a sluggish ox— but the sounds ceased as suddenly, when beyond, off to one side of the road, there was a flash of colour and Elizabeth stepped from her door and set a basket of clothes down on the clothesline stoop.

"Louise." His voice echoed in the empty street. He rushed towards the familiar, relief causing his breath to become ragged and uneven.

Elizabeth raised her arms and shook loose a green plaid blanket and began to pin it onto the clothesline. He'd made no sound, but she seemed to sense his presence behind her and she turned, arms still uplifted, and looked at him. Then Hendrick, too, who had been crouching beside a pile of freshly split wood, stood to face him, motionless. Their silence made him want to cry out, "It's I, me, Jacob." The blanket swayed gently. Jacob saw the curve of the woman's belly and the gentle swell of her breasts against it. She dropped her arms and walked several steps towards him, but seemed to change her mind.

"The Lord blesses us with the sun," Jacob said.

"Surely, he does," Elizabeth said.

"It's a fine day for doing the wash."

"Yes."

Hendrick walked towards the wood stack piled against the fence, his arms laden with split logs. Jacob saw the squareness of his shoulders, the back which had broadened during the winter.

"Would you like to go for a walk with me?" Jacob asked the boy. The boy pretended not to hear and began to lay the logs down, one on top of another, off-set, so the pile would not tumble—the way Jacob had taught him to do.

Elizabeth smiled and shrugged her shoulders in apology. "He refuses to talk," she said. "Two days now. Even Scripture."

Jacob turned from them and continued on, going straight down to the old park that led to the river. He knelt and peered inside the opening to the path. He strode through it, his heart thudding. As he passed through the entrance safely, he felt relieved. His eyes were drawn to the base of a tree, where among the dense growth something scurried away at the sound of his steps. He walked quickly towards the river bank because it was the time of year for wood ticks and he was afraid of the insects which hid in the grass that now brushed against his legs. He believed that only he ventured here—except, of course, for the strange Pullman woman. He stepped out onto the river bank and stood beside the water and prayed for contentment. When he lifted his eyes, he saw a flock of pelicans gliding silently along the tips of the trees, following the sweep of the river. He was looking into the setting sun and saw only their silhouettes at first, making them look ancient, like pterodactyls. They wheeled in a large half-circle and their backs became silver against the sun. They were far, far away from the northern sea where they belonged.

"Today I saw a flock of pelicans," Jacob told Lena as they undressed that evening. He reached for her in the darkness and his hand met her large, taut breast. As the last pink rays of the sun retreated to the rising bank of night clouds, Jacob fell asleep with the heaviness of Lena's head against his shoulder, her legs wound through his, and the sticky dampness of his own seed against his belly. He dreamt of Elizabeth. He stood before her, hands reaching for her face. As he reached, her face became a hard mask, as though made of china. He noticed the hinges on her nose and the brass clasp just behind her ear. His hands shook as he undid the clasp and slowly lifted one side of Elizabeth's face. Beneath lay another face, identical to the one on top.

SATURDAY

6

Dear Aunt Violet,

Wind south through the day but now east. With lightning. Dorfmans preparing their garden for potatoes. I suppose I ought to do as well, but I fear I must preserve what energy I have. Emma Standing very kindly set my dinner out yesterday, as Minnie has been a bit distracted.

On Sunday, we're having a visiting missionary. A Mr. Fife. "Come unto me all ye who labour." I have heard that he gives a very plain discourse. Rosella refuses to wear her gloves. She says she is going to try and stop chewing her nails.

Emma Standing says that sometimes fits can be caused by an overflow of blood in the head. Is this possible?

Minnie sat across from Albert in the darkened kitchen and listened as his pen scratched against the linen paper. On the table, tissue spilled from several boxes holding a frothy bouquet of nightgowns, slippery and shimmering—a light apricot one and a blue and a mauve. Minnie fingered a bit of lace and then pushed the boxes aside. "They're nice, Albert," she said. "But I can't eat them."

"Oh, my poor duck," Albert said, looking up from his letter. He leapt to his feet. "I got carried away. Today it's schnitzel, right?"

"Anything," Minnie said. "It doesn't matter." She watched a school of fish swim across the window. She didn't even know what day it was. She heard the whirr of the electric can-opener and watched Albert's freckled hands shake as he set a can of beans down into a pot of boiling water on the stove. She wondered why he didn't just dump the beans into the pot and heat them directly. But then the pot would need to be washed. And Albert was saving his energy now. She knew. All the cookie sheets and muffin tins in the bottom of the cupboard would end up being eaten by rust.

Above Minnie's head something heavy slid across the second floor. Rosella, likely rearranging her bedroom again as she had all day yesterday. Minnie reached for a square of paper on the table and folded it down and down until it was as small as the folds would allow. She reached for the scissors and began to nip sharp little cuts into the edges of it. Flakes of paper curled to the floor. Albert reached for a glass jar jammed full of wooden tongue-depressors on top of the counter. He pulled one loose and used it to butter thin slices of bread and then to spread a layer of cheese spread. He cut the sandwiches in two and dropped the tongue-depressor down into a paper bag on the floor. It was clear. Albert was saving his energy.

"Ginny? Rosella?" He called up at the ceiling. "It's ready." He set the food onto paper plates and glanced at Minnie and saw her head dip over the paper cutting. His thick fingers plucked at the knot in the string wound around the package Ollie had brought to the lumber yard. To be safe, he felt he should say something. "I wish Urbanick's wouldn't bother with string," he said, loud enough for Minnie to hear.

But it was Albert who had put the string around the package. He'd gone down to Urbanick's Baked Goods and had wangled a spool of white string from Stanislav and tied it around the square of brownies Ollie had brought. Albert had explained to Stanislav how there never seemed to be any string around just when you needed it. "Well, just the other day—" Albert had said, beginning to recite the story he'd memorized about the package he'd wanted to mail off to his Aunt Violet, but Stanislav excused himself and said he had a pan of bread he had to get out quick, quick. And so Albert had backed from the bakery, feeling a bit disappointed because he'd made the story up for nothing. He wondered, though, as he walked home, the spool of string clutched to his chest, whether Stanislav really had a batch waiting or if he'd guessed what Albert was up to and wanted to get rid of him as quickly as possible so that he could get on the telephone and tell his wife. The idea made the hair on Albert's chest tingle. "It's for your girls," Ollie had said as she slid the warm package across the counter to him. And he was very particular about not wanting to be misunderstood. "It's for the girls," he'd said. He wouldn't have taken it from her otherwise.

He didn't want to risk hurting Minnie either, and so he wanted her to believe that the brownies had come from Baked Goods. He set a brownie down on each plate. He carried the plates through the hallway to the stairs.

"Come and get it," he called.

Rosella climbed down, scooped up the plates, and pounded back up the stairs to the bedroom. "At last, some decent brownies," she said.

Albert set the heated can of beans down in front of Minnie. She watched his pudgy hands pour syrup into the centre of the can. A chair creaked. Albert had moved away.

She saw him sit down, his wide shoulders blotting out the fish swimming across her window. Cellophane crackled as he pulled free a new pair of Odor-Eaters. He ripped the old ones from his shoes, pushed the new ones down into their place. Albert bounced on the balls of his feet as he tested them out, crinkling the tips of the freshly shined shoe leather. He dropped stained foam soles into the paper bag. He sucked in his stomach and tucked his clean white shirt firmly in place under his belt. Then the comb. No more lick of salt-and-peppery hair falling across his shiny, unlined forehead. Albert wore his hair slicked right back. The way he'd worn it the day she'd met him at Churchills' out by the clothesline. And Minnie knew why Albert was conserving his energy.

"I'd like a spoon," she said. "You don't expect me to eat beans with a stick, do you?"

Albert's body flashed with tension. Everything inside him beat outwards against his skin. His face grew warm with the push of energy rushing from his pores. "I don't really have to go out tonight," Albert said. "I was just going to post a letter."

Minnie got up and patted his stomach. She brushed her lips against his chin. Aftershave lotion. Old Spice. "Of course you have to go out," she said. "Everyone has to go out now and then."

"Let me get you a spoon, dear," Albert said.

"I can get my own spoon—I'm perfectly capable," Minnie said and reached into the drawer behind her. She held up a fork. "See?"

"That's a fork," Albert said.

"It's what I wanted," Minnie said.

Albert reached and touched the ribbon of silver in her dark hair. "Of course, of course." He backed through the door, jingling the loose change in his pocket. "I won't be any later than ten," he said.

Katie lay out on the back step and Albert stopped to scratch the animal behind the ear. "Where you been, girl?" He didn't want to appear as though he was anxious to get away because, he reasoned, he really wasn't. Katie leaned into his fingers. Then she rolled over and begged him to scratch her chest. It came to Albert, as he tickled Katie and she slithered across the grass with pleasure, that maybe a stake driven into the ground would be the answer. If he gave Minnie so much rope and no more. Just for the summer. He nudged Katie with the tip of his shiny toe. He'd made a mistake by giving in to Minnie when she didn't want to get married. He should have been firmer and insisted that they meet with Campbell, the Justice of the Peace, and have him marry them instead of making up that tale of having travelled to another town in the valley and being married there. Being married would have given him more leeway to be firm, he thought. He reached for Katie's collar and the rope lying on the top step.

"No." Minnie's white face pressed out through the school of fish on the window. "She's okay now. You can let her run."

Albert stepped out onto the sidewalk. But on the other hand, he thought, not being married did give him the possibility of rethinking the choice he'd made fifteen years ago. Often a time came in a man's life when he began to think about the choices he'd made but couldn't do a thing about. The fresh Odor-Eaters put a bounce in his step and made him feel ten pounds lighter. Years dropped from his face. He was a lucky man. Because he could go back if he wanted to and do something about the choice he'd made.

He searched the street before entering it. There were several cars parked down in front of Steven Adam's place. Steven had been into the lumber yard yesterday buying supplies for his ceramics classes. Wiring for the lamps the women would make and lumber to construct shelves on which to set their fired objects. The women of the town had been round asking about the classes before the paint had hardly dried on his sign, he'd said. Albert wished Minnie would show an interest. An outside hobby could be the thing for Minnie.

The road stretched before him empty, clear down to the trees that screened the river. One of the Roads men walked alongside the gully and one by one the lanterns began to glow with light. An aura of cold air rose from the water rippling in the gully. It was much like standing in front of an open refrigerator, Albert thought. The water's presence would be a tempering influence on the heat of summer because so far it had not sunk—or risen—but looked as though it had reached its full swell and would remain that way. As the cool air met the warm earth, that early evening mist once again hovered above the ground. He walked towards Main Street, careful to keep his pace steady and unchanging in case Minnie had moved to the other window, and thought of Ollie. An image of a pearl button at her throat arose, and then her tiny hand curled against the counter-top at the lumber yard, and he saw that white crescent-shaped scar on her knuckle. Although the cool mist curled up about his knees as he walked, he was insulated against its dampness by images which propelled him forward.

A man, Albert Pullman, hurried in his heart towards a woman in the night. He walked slowly. Whistling. He resembled a boy who had put on inches, pounds, bigger feet, but was locked for ever into pre-pubescence. He planned what he'd say, not say. His slicked hair began to dry and strands of it sprang loose and stood straight up from his head as he walked towards a woman.

While the woman, Olga-Ollie-Teedle Peter, sat in her living room on a chair facing Jacob and Lena Friesen who had come to call, unannounced. Pink flowers the size of peonies crawled up Lena's lap. She twisted and untwisted several very old rings. They climbed up her finger to her knuckle and so Lena couldn't bend it without the flesh piling up around the metal.

"We believe that the Lord wants us to talk to you," Jacob said.

"We believe that we've been led by him," Lena said, and Ollie wondered if they meant her to think that it had been against their own will but that God had somehow dragged them by the scruff of the neck to lecture her.

"Something smells good," Lena said, and Ollie knew she was expected to offer them something to eat. Those were Albert's cinnamon buns cooling on a rack.

Ollie tried not to look at the clock above their heads. It was surrounded by a gallery of photographs. The grave faces of nephews, the cheeky, smart smiles of nieces laughed at her from beneath the tassels of graduation-day hats. The family portraits surrounded them—men standing with their hands on the women's shoulders and children arranged about their feet. And then there was the enlargement, a black-and-white photograph taken just after they'd come to Agassiz. A family gathering in the garden and Teedle, the youngest, sitting on the ground with her underpants showing and tousled yellow curls shining as she squinted into the camera and the wide space between her front teeth was a black dot on an otherwise hopeful smile.

Jacob cleared his throat and considered a crease in his black dress pants and then dropped his elbows to his knees and clasped his hands, as though in prayer. "Teedle," he said, "this is very difficult for us. But we believe that we should speak out. I think you should let Lena take on your Sunday school class tomorrow."

"What for?"

Lena smiled, gentle, meek, with not a hint of malice but of sorrow. "It's for the children's sake," she said. "We have to think of them, yes? It's better until all the talk is cleared up."

"What talk?" Ollie looked up at the clock and saw its hands inch closer to the hour.

"About you…and Albert Pullman," Jacob said.

"Oh that," Ollie said and laughed. Her earlobes grew hot beneath the clasps of the earrings. Above her head, her mother's slippers scuffled across the floor. Around and around. "My goodness," Ollie said. "You scared me. I thought it was something serious."

Jacob uncrossed his legs and leaned forward. "It is serious," he said.

Ollie pressed against the back of the chair, away from him. Her curly head rested against a lace doily and her fingers traced the wood carving in the chair arm. A fingernail twitched, scratched, and dug a mark into the soft, varnished surface.

"All I did was bring him some baking," she said. "It was brought to my attention that his girls could use a hand. They're practically on their own, you know." Her fingers drummed against the varnished surface. "And you know what that woman was up to on Thursday at the river."

Jacob looked uncertain. "Well," he said, "I have to admit that in this case, perhaps a little charity is not out of place."

But Lena stood up and put her hands on her broad hips, making herself look bigger, formidable. "Albert Pullman is a married man," she said.

"And so?" Ollie asked.

Jacob had an idea. He held up his hand. "It's simple," he said. "There's a way to avoid the appearance of wrong-doing."

"I'll deliver the baking," Lena said. "And if the girl agrees, send her to me and I'll give her some basic skills."

Ollie swung her foot back and forth, back and forth, barely missing the older woman's shin bone.

"I think that's a good solution," Jacob said. Lena had read his mind. "So, it's settled then."

Ollie's head throbbed as the clock's hand met the hour and the tips of her ears burned like fire. "If you say it's settled, then I guess it's settled," she said and leapt to her feet. "I have to go," she said. She stood at the kitchen door, breathless, the warm package held against her stomach. "And if you must have something to eat, I'm certain mother would be glad to fix you something. I'm sure she was expecting you."

Upstairs the slippers stopped scuffling and Mrs. Peter, realizing by the force with which the door had closed, knew that God had not yet answered her prayer. She dropped to her knees beside Ollie's bed. Ollie was going to keep on wearing those earrings and their house was going to be visited with a calamity. Wait and see.

Albert sat in the middle booth in Delta William's Hot Spot and waited. He watched his fingers unroll a straw, straighten it out flat against the grey arborite. He saw the wet smudge his fist had left behind. He picked up the straw, tucked under an end, and began to roll it up again.

"Refill?" Cindy Dorfman stood at his side. Albert was aware only of the yellow frill of her apron brushing against the side of the booth and the lemon odour of her hands as coffee bubbled up the sides of his mug. He watched his hand spoon sugar into the coffee, heard the tinkle of the spoon against the mug as he shook loose a drop and it sounded much too loud, like the sudden clanging of a church bell calling them inside. He set the spoon down carefully and then heard the sizzle of fat as Cindy dropped a basket of potato fries down into it. Except for Robin Marchand straddling a stool near the kitchen door, the café was empty.

Albert heard the door open and the tap of heels against the floor, followed by the swish of material sliding across vinyl.

"I'm sorry I'm late," Ollie said. She laid her hand on the table between them and he felt his fingers inch towards it. But the hand curled into a fist suddenly, turning the crescent-shaped scar on her knuckle white. "It's settled then," Ollie said. "I'm not to interfere. I'll lose my Sunday school class."

Cindy Dorfman peered out at them from the kitchen. Robin turned, still sipping on a milkshake, glanced briefly in their direction.

"But why?" Albert asked but didn't ask who had told Ollie that she was not to interfere.

The brown bow beneath her Peter Pan collar bobbed as Ollie swallowed hard. "Because you're a married man."

The door opened and Sonny Ericson, hands hitched into his back pockets, entered the café. He scowled as he walked towards Robin and Cindy.

"About time," Robin said. "Where in hell have you been? I looked all over for you yesterday."

"Would you believe choir practice?"

"No," Robin said.

"Well then don't ask."

Ollie leaned forward. She wished that for once Albert would lift his head and look her straight in the eye.

"I'm not married," he said.

He set the mug down carefully. Above their heads, the fan whirled silently, drawing strands of Albert's hair up from his head. Their eyes met. She was exactly as he'd remembered. That child-like space between her front teeth— the one you could slip a toothpick through—was still there. And her mouth was the colour of raspberry jelly. He saw himself in her flax blue eyes.

She clutched at the bow at her throat. "Not married?"

"No," Albert said. "She didn't want to."

Cindy plunked a plate of steaming fries down in front of Sonny. "What in hell happened to you?" she asked, and Sonny's hand came up to feel the scratches on his neck. They were long and deep and only just beginning to heal.

"Rough sex," Sonny said and laughed when Cindy blushed. "Well, you asked."

Robin snatched hot chips from Sonny's plate and stuffed her mouth. "We'll never get out of here," she said, her cheeks bulging with food. "Not if you're going to eat all that."

The door opened and they all turned. "I don't think you're going anywhere," one of the two Mounties said as they stepped into the café. Their yellow stripes flashed as they walked directly towards Sonny Ericson.

"Hey," he said. "What gives?"

"Left headlight out and both taillights."

"No way," Sonny said. "They were working five minutes ago."

"Well, they're not now." They lifted Sonny up off the stool and plunked him back down on his feet. Robin and Cindy watched the door close and then went over to the window. They watched as the Mounties threw Sonny into the back seat of their cruiser. Cindy sat down and stared at the plate of chips.

"Shit," Robin said and doused the plate with ketchup and began to eat.

"All that commotion over a broken headlight?" Cindy asked.

"Fat chance," Robin said. She would have to hitch a ride, go on up into the hills, and warn them to hide the stuff.

"We should talk," Ollie Peter said to Albert, breaking their silence. The Mounties had come and gone and neither one of them had noticed. Her fist uncurled and she spread her fingers across the table. Albert slid his hand towards hers. He nudged the crescent-shaped scar with his finger.

"Maybe it wouldn't hurt to talk," he said.

"On Sunday," Ollie said.

Albert detected some of that youthful energy in Ollie's voice and a slight bit of bossiness. He rested his arms against the counter, and felt the sudden release of perspiration trail down from his armpit and run across his belly—a cold trickle, making him itch. "Maybe," he said.

"Maybe?"

"Maybe we might talk."

"On Sunday."

"Maybe Sunday is a bit too soon," Albert said.

"Albert Pullman," Ollie said, throwing whatever caution she had to the wind, "I've waited fifteen years to talk. I'll see you on Sunday."

Albert reached for the box of straws resting beside the salt and pepper shakers. He chose a pink one and squashed it flat. It wouldn't hurt to talk. But that little edge in Ollie's voice, like a finger nudging him in the back, made Albert turn under the edge of the fresh straw and inch by inch roll it up into a tight little ball.

Minnie had waited until Albert's footsteps faded and then she spread the newspaper clipping down against the table.

MINNIE, IF YOU'RE READING THIS, IT'S TIME TO COME HOME.
Very Sincerely, J.

Boo! Jay. His smeary red lips turned up at the corners into a sad clown smile. The white gauze net covering the carriage billowed outwards. It quivered and grew taut. His face vanished. The woman's maroon head swung forward through the sky, bare shoulders flashing in the sun as they twisted in mid-air. The head lifted and a woman's face, flushed and bright, rushed forward towards the carriage in a smile and then she, too, vanished. Mary Ruth. Stop it, stop it, Minnie told herself and ground the tears which threatened to erupt back into her eyes. "Stop it," she said, but there was something about the sight of a can of beans plunked down in front of her, amber syrup slopped over the top of it, something about the hasty look of Albert's meal which spelled the word "uncaring".

"Get ahold of yourself," Annie Schmoon said from the doorway.

Minnie's shoulders shook and shook and shook.

Annie pulled a chair out from the table and sat across from her. She set a plastic container on the table and waited while the charcoal particles of night sifted down into the room and evening rose to their ankles beneath the table. The Big Ben clock on a shelf ticked off an hour. Annie picked up the clipping and put it into her own pocket. Minnie shuddered and a great sigh crept up in her chest and escaped into the room, leaving her with a numbness which allowed her to endure all things. The beans in the can had congealed and the syrup formed a thick crust.

"Okay, Min," Annie said. "Now tell me. This 'J' person. Who is he, really?"

"He used to say you're full of beans so you might as well eat them," Minnie said.

"Maybe you were full of beans," Annie said. She patted Minnie's hand.

Minnie pulled away from her touch. "He used to tie me to a chair in the basement." Mice whiskers twitched in shadows behind the furnace door. The rope around her chest was too tight and cut into her armpits. But the worst of it was the sound of Jay's feet on the floor overhead. Indifference passing through the hallway into his workroom where dusty speakers, twined wires, turntables lined the shelves in Jay's room. She heard the rasp of his turntable as he switched it on, and then static as the needle dropped down. The music of *Don Giovanni* . Hours passed by in the same music, over and over.

"I think he actually thought that if I didn't hear the fair going on in the grounds, and couldn't see it, that I wouldn't want to go," she said. "Or he put me down there to remind himself what a tragic figure he was. The man who'd suffered a triple whammy."

"This 'J'," Annie said, "suffered a triple whammy?"

"Everything always happened in threes," Minnie said.

That's what Mary Ruth had told her. That's what she'd said the day she packed her suitcase and threw it into the back seat of Billy's car. The saying was a parting gift from Mary Ruth, her mother—a farewell gesture. "I met Billy," she'd said. "I've fallen in love with him and now I'm leaving. This bird needs to fly," she'd said and then she'd kissed Minnie on the cheek and Minnie had carried the shape of her mother's mouth for a day until Jay made her scrub it off. It was all Jay's fault, Minnie thought as she watched the car drive away. Because Jay had bought the poor excuse for a house, parked their trailer behind it, and nailed Mary Ruth's feet to the floor. Green feathers gathered dust in the attic.

And the saying held true. Minnie watched for it. If she fell and scraped her knee, she was sure to bump her elbow and get a sliver in her bum from sitting out on the front stairs shortly thereafter. Mary Ruth took off, Jay brought his elderly mother to live with them, and Minnie grew up. He never forgave her for that. The saying held true for Minnie one day when the fair came to town. She was sitting in her room, reading, surrounded on all sides by books from the ceiling to the floor since Jay had built the shelves for them when it became apparent that it was necessary if she was going to continue to live and sleep in the room for the rest of her life. She was reading at that moment "that the situation of Cedric and of the Black Knight was now truly dangerous, and would have been still more so but for" the water glasses tinkling on shelves inside the cupboard in the kitchen.

She sat up, swung her legs over the side of the bed, and listened. She looked up at the hands sweeping across the words "Coca Cola" on the clock above the door. She'd been reading a full two hours and still Jay's mother had not requested her pot of tea. The water glasses became glass chimes rattling in a heavy gust of wind and then a sudden beast-like roar shook the floor under her feet. She threw the book aside and ran across the hallway into Jay's room to turn down the amplifier before the noise awakened the sleeping woman.

She stood in front of the tangled spaghetti mess of wires, speakers on the floor, turntable. She turned down the volume on the amplifier and choked back the sound. She held her breath and waited for the old woman to call. *The Magic Flute* had been playing and Jay hadn't bothered to take off the record before he'd slammed out of the house earlier. What would the woman ask for? Tea or pee? Callest thou me, oh withered one? "Minnie, I'm about drier than a desert dune in here." Every day Minnie prayed for a wind storm to blow her away. "Min, dear, I'm swimming in the Sargasso sea of pee." The player's needle had cut a nick into the paper label of *The Magic Flute* at its centre and the shape of that nick clicked like a dry throat in the speakers on the floor. "Minnie is the spinny one," Jay's mother said and laughed every morning when Minnie set the tray down at her bedside. Her laughter always had the sound of breakfast in it. Egg shells underfoot.

Minnie knelt on Jay's unmade bed and parted the curtains. A dragon writhed against a clear sky, its scales flashing gold in the sun. And then the face of the clown swept by, its exaggerated smile slightly mocking. The fair had arrived in town. It had arrived in boxes filled with bones, rigid metal skeletons stacked up on flatbeds or jutting out every which way from the backs of trucks.

She watched as the column of vehicles passed by on the road beside the house until they had all entered in at the gates and lumbered across weed-choked fields to the fairground's centre behind two rows of weathered bleachers. Then the dust settled back down and filled the tire marks imprinted on the road.

She turned from the window. Her stomach, suddenly gone tight, threatened to give up her breakfast. Mary Ruth's scarlet lips parted in a coy smile from the poster on Jay's wall, green plumage dipping forward as she nodded her head in a slight bow. She leaned backwards and pulled hard on ropes on either side of her. Silver legs shot forward and then Mary Ruth flew back and back up into one corner of the poster. "Go and find your sister." Mary Ruth's voice echoed in the room.

"Yes sir, two peas in a pod," Jay had said. "Just like you heard. And they're mine."

Mary Ruth cleared her throat noisily. "I was there when it happened, too," she said.

Jay's knees crinkled the legs of his grey flannel trousers as he walked back and forth, back and forth. Minnie and her sister sat side by side alongside the trailer on identical chairs. "Minnie" the gold letters spelled across the top of the chair and "Wanda" on the other. Jay had painted on their names so that he could tell who was who. Except that Wanda, playing their game, sometimes sat down in Minnie's chair instead of her own. Mary Ruth reclined in a canvas lounge under a tree, with a blanket thrown around her shoulders. She rested her maroon puffball head against the back of it. A large man dressed all in white sat at her feet on an overturned crate.

There were always men other than Jay around. The earliest memory Minnie had of Mary Ruth was of Mary Ruth, Jay, another man, and tension. Her mother's silver-stocking leg flashed up and down lazily, but Minnie sensed the energy exuding from her taut muscles. It seemed to Minnie that she was too bright. "She's too bright," Wanda, her sister, said then, speaking Minnie's thoughts. "It hurts my eyes to look at her." Their shoulders touched as they sat side by side on the chairs but Minnie didn't feel it. When she looked at Wanda, she didn't realize that she looked at herself. When she stood in front of a mirror, she thought that she was invisible somehow and that Wanda had come to stand in front of her. Wanda beat her foot against the rung of her chair. The silver button on the side of her black patent shoe flashed in a steady rhythmic motion.

"Identical's a definite drawing card," the man in the white suit said. His knuckle turned white as his finger curled and flicked away a fly crawling across his knee. "Wouldn't matter what they actually did. People would want to see them."

"Trapeze, eventually," Mary Ruth said.

"No sir," Jay said, still pacing. "No siree. Mary Ruth, we agreed. We stay put until we've got those two grown."

Mary Ruth yawned behind her hand.

"I don't want to be a drawing card," Wanda said.

The adults laughed. Jay stopped pacing. Mary Ruth reached up and plucked at the knee of Jay's trousers. "The parade," she said. "It wouldn't hurt to let them ride in a parade."

The man in the white suit stood up and whacked dust from his trousers. "Drive down next week," he said. "I'll meet you in Agassiz. The Wringle Brothers are a big outfit. Could be worth your time."

"It wouldn't hurt to look," Mary Ruth said.

"Even if we decided to get back into it," Jay said and scowled, "we don't need any manager."

Minnie was the spinny one because she daydreamed and walked into closed doors and off top steps and had more bruises than Wanda. Wanda won. The one year they went to kindergarten in a town where Jay parked the trailer while he searched for work and a place to live, Wanda won every single game she played. Even the lost child game. Wanda won. It was a game designed to test their memories and Wanda always knew who was missing from the circle when she came back into the room. "It's simple," Wanda told Minnie. "There's a hole where the person sat." And even if they closed in the circle to fill the gap or moved the kids around, the hole was still there.

Mary Ruth paused up in the corner of the poster, pointed her black slippers, and smiled. Minnie held her breath and waited, but she knew that Mary Ruth would not swing back down. She waited until the truck's engines in the fairgrounds had been silenced and then turned up the volume on Jay's amplifier. Its tubes glowed and the condenser hummed and the sound of waves beating against the side of the house rose from the amplifier's netted cloth front. An intermittent gust of wind washed through the microphones Jay had strung up around the yard outside. It was part of Jay's constant surveillance since the day of the parade, when Wanda had gone missing. He'd bought the house and parked the little silver trailer behind it and repaired electrical appliances for the people in Crocus, the obscure town he'd chosen to settle Mary Ruth and his remaining child in. The sound in the microphones suggested a wilderness, a wildness crouching down beyond the borders of Jay's domain inside its sagging chicken-wire fence. Minnie listened for the sound of her grandmother's voice. No tea or pee. Still the old woman slept.

She lifted the phonograph needle and silenced the hiccup in its speakers. Then she passed through the narrow hallway and, as she crossed the doorway to the woman's darkened room, the absence of sound yawned loudly. She bounced down onto the centre of her bed and reached for *Ivanhoe*, to press him against her new breasts. The sound of metal clanking against metal echoed in Jay's room, suggesting to her that the crew in the fairgrounds had already begun to assemble the skeletons.

Everything happened in threes and then the second thing happened.

Minnie heard Jay's truck, the throaty exhaust sound unmistakably his truck as it careened down the road towards the house, cut a wide swath through the opposite ditch before it swung into their narrow lane, up and over the culvert. The vehicle heaved and swayed—like Jay it was heavy in the belly—and then it thudded to an abrupt stop in Jay's room and glass exploded.

The back steps tilted under Minnie's feet as she ran down them. Steam billowed from the crushed radiator. Jay's truck was divided down the centre of its hood by the clothesline pole. The horn blared and then stopped as he raised his head. Blood poured from his nose down around his mouth, outlining it in red, and Minnie thought that her father's mouth had become like the mouth of the clown passing by on the road. He slid out from behind the wheel and limped across the yard towards her. He held a package up, splattered with blood. Another batch of books she'd ordered had arrived in the mail. "They were going to fall off the seat and I grabbed for them," Jay said. "I'm going to have to walk on down to the hospital."

At the sound of clanking metal, they both turned and saw the wedge of steel that would soon be the ferris wheel rise above the tanned backs of the working men. A red bandanna circled a throat. Jay's brow crinkled with worry. He no longer tied her up in the basement. Years had passed since she'd last asked to go to the fair. "Be sure you stay away from the grounds now, hear?" he said. His voice sounded squeezed and nasal. He pressed a handkerchief beneath his nose to stem the flow of blood. "You stay inside. You hear anything unusual, you tell Grammy right off." She watched as he walked down the road towards the town in his strange bow-legged, clownish manner, and she thought to call and tell him, Grammy's still in bed. But the thought was caught away by another sudden clang of metal.

By the time evening rolled in Jay had still not returned and already the sound of cars whispered loudly in the amplifier as they passed by the house and lined up against the barbed-wire fence in the fairgrounds. Minnie was on the couch finishing the last chapter of *Ivanhoe* and she heard the voices of the children and parents as they tumbled out of the cars. Wait for me. Hold hands, now. What I would like to do is. Snatches of their hurried conversations bleated out from Jay's room as they rushed through the gates, frightened that the midway might at that moment be rolled up like a carpet and loaded back onto the truck without their having had the chance to walk down its broad centre where the grass had been trampled and the mud oozed between toes in the women's sandals.

Once, in the middle of the night as Minnie lay in bed in her room, she heard someone say as they passed by the house, "Punch his way out of a paper bag." The woman's voice dripped with scorn. And, "You say you love me, but how can I believe it?" The voices came from across the road and the huddle of trees that screened the parked cars from view. She understood her father's need to be constantly on guard after Wanda went missing. But she wished he'd turn off the sound at night when she was safe in bed.

The sun had set. Minnie stood in the dark living room and listened to the sound of people's voices, the bright tinny sound of the merry-go-round. She looked out the window. The ferris wheel spun a ribbon of colour and the tents glowed like jack-o'-lanterns. She had waited long enough. She had kept her desire to go screwed down in place for so many years that she was careful now not to loosen the lid too quickly in case Jay came back at the last moment. She went into the old woman's room. The room smelled of unclean sheets, of sickness, of brown potato skin gone soft in a dark bin. She hardly ever noticed the odour, but it was strong tonight. She lifted the little brocaded change purse on the woman's bureau. It was chock full of bills—more than she could ever spend and so she didn't take them all. Just enough.

And so the third thing to happen that day happened. Minnie went to the fair.

She had studied people going to the fair for so long that she knew what not to do. She didn't, for instance, run. She didn't put on her white sandals, but rather her black tennis shoes. She didn't paint her mouth red or hang cherries from her ears because she wasn't looking for sly winks. She wore a clean blouse, a clean face. There were squeals of laughter as she stepped outside and heavy bass laughter replied. It floated down from the top of the ferris wheel where a chair rocked too sharply and the girl clung to the man and the pretence of fear in her cry made Minnie smile. She would not do that.

"Two dollars," someone said, and a hand reached out from the painted booth, bright yellow and red, the clown face, laughing at her. Minnie took the ticket that allowed her to enter with the others.

"Hang onto it if you want to get back in," a man's voice called after her, but already Minnie was gone, swallowed up by the stream of people, their warm bodies pressing in and around her, arms carrying soft, huge teddy bears, balloons bobbing, a crowd of pink, green, red, and white heads nodding in the warm air.

She leaned against the fence that enclosed the ferris wheel for a full hour, mesmerized by the flow of colour, the music, and the people. Couples stepped up onto the platform, the chair swung beneath their weight, and a tanned, muscular arm with a green snake crawling up the side of it pulled that bar down into place and locked people in. Over and over. And then his gloved hand eased a lever back and the couple moved up and the next chair swung down and so on and so on. Then the man glanced over at Minnie, briefly at first, but afterwards she noticed a new swagger in his hips as he went about his business, joking now, and using his hand to help tell the joke. When the wheel was loaded and turning, he smiled at a flash of pink in a girl's underslip and he laughed when they shrieked with fear.

He glanced over at Minnie again, winked, and pulled the lever with his leather hand. The ferris wheel spun faster, the lights a blur and the girls crying. He lit a cigarette, looked at his watch, and then at Minnie. The coloured lights spun their colours out across his lean, tanned face.

"Aren't you going to ride?"

Minnie shook her head.

"Scared?"

"I came to watch," Minnie said.

"What's to watch?" he said. "It goes round and round."

"You," Minnie said.

He grasped the lever and cries of disappointment rained down as the stream of lights became single coloured bulbs wheeling slowly to a halt. She watched as he freed them. He was jocular and jaunty. He took the money from the next couple to ride, scooped change from the canvas apron tied about his narrow waist. He unloaded the last chair but wouldn't let the two girls who had scrambled forward ride. Instead, he stuck his fingers between his teeth and whistled. A large man, belly swaying beneath a black tee-shirt, lumbered over.

"My break. You take over," the young man said and untied the greasy canvas money-apron. He vaulted the steel fence.

"What do you say?" He didn't wait for an answer but took Minnie by the hand and led her up the platform. Heat radiated from his body as she sat beside him. He slipped his arm about her shoulders. The chair swayed and lifted. She looked down and saw the shiny stub of skin on the end of his severed finger, a knot of flesh there, tying up loose ends. The chair rose up and up. They had climbed halfway up the bleachers, rising until she saw the show ring and mottled cattle on the other side and then the whole town, its streets hidden beneath rows of trees.

"Gene," he yelled above the noise. "I'm Gene Lacroix."

"Minnie," she said.

Behind her lay her own house. She turned. She could see black spots, tar, where shingles had been torn loose by the wind, and that crooked, splintered front step where she used to sit and watch in case Wanda should return home. In one corner of the yard was a sandbox with weeds growing up from it. She saw the silver trailer listing to one side on a flat tire in the back of the yard. She saw her house, so alone on its square of earth, enclosed by chicken wire, the glint of metal along the eavestroughs, Jay's microphones snuggling up against the fence posts, and the maze of wires criss-crossing in the air and funneling down into Jay's room, a siphon drawing off the sounds of the world. The sounds of Hallowe'en high jinks, lovers' quarrels, the intimate and banal details of strangers' lives entering their house. "What're we supposed to listen for?" Mary Ruth had asked. "Everything,"

Jay said. "We let it sneak by us once and it's never going to happen again." Minnie saw the old woman, a plum ripening in the heat of summer, about to split open in bed.

"Minnie what?" Gene shouted.

Minnie turned away from the sight of her house and saw the pinwheel of colour, the canvas-topped merry-go-round below, and she searched for the white dress with the spatter of red along the border of its hem. She was Mary Ruth up here and he was Jay, keeping their eye out for the two girls in identical dresses, riding identical Arabian horses on the merry-go-round.

She began to cry, short hard gasps which got away from her before she could stop them.

"Hey," Gene said. "Hey, you. What's up, eh? Want me to whistle us down?"

"No, no," Minnie said as she looked down at her house, flew above it, over it, beyond it. "Oh no, no, no."

But he whistled them down anyway and later they strolled behind trucks which hummed and sweated with energy. Coils of rubber hoses, thick electrical wire, throbbing veins, which they picked through and avoided.

"Hey, Gene, I see you got yourself another cutie-pie," a woman's voice, raw from too many cigarettes, called out from the doorway of a small tent. Kinky blue-black hair rippled from beneath a purple turban down across her bare shoulders. A silver star flashed on her dark forehead.

"Up yours," Gene said and was about to lead Minnie away but she'd seen the crystal ball resting on a piece of felt on a table.

And she remembered Mary Ruth urging the gypsy to keep trying. You see this girl, she'd asked hundreds of times in hundreds of small-town summer fairs in the valley. She'd push Minnie forward. The white dress, becoming too small, chafed at Minnie's armpits. I'm looking for her. She'd pull her chair in closer to the table and peer into their crystal balls, hoping to see what they could not. And sometimes the fortune-teller would stare at Mary Ruth as though she'd gone batty and say, well, you did just find her, point at Minnie and say, there she is.

"Don't waste your money," Gene said. "She's as phony as a three-dollar bill."

"Up yours, too," the woman said. Her smile was wide and her white teeth flashed. "This is private," she said and pulled the tent flap down into place.

The tent had trapped the warmth of the day's sun and smelled of damp grass and something spicy, like cinnamon. The woman motioned for Minnie to sit across from her. She slid the piece of felt towards herself and the crystal ball with it. Water, Minnie thought. That the ball was filled with clear water.

"Well," she said. "Gene's not in the picture at all. Because I see a man in a white suit."

Gene and Minnie crossed a baseball diamond, grass wet and glistening with heavy dew. They sat up on the bleachers enjoying the warmth of the wood. Gene lit a cigarette and talked quietly about the places he'd been in the valley, the string of little towns and the names she recognized from when Mary Ruth took her to the fairs. And Jay, trailing behind with a scowl, a giant fly swatter to keep away the men who would hover wherever Mary Ruth happened to light. But it was hard not to notice Mary Ruth with her maroon puffball head of hair, chewing gum too quickly, making those cherry lips of hers hard to follow. Minnie forgave her when she left, two years after Wanda. The town was just not large enough for her startling beauty which kept spilling over into other towns in the valley and attracting strange men like flies.

His people, the French, were big spenders, Gene said, they never bothered to count their change. He told her of crowds of Hutterites in their polka-dot dresses, black kerchiefs on the heads of the women, the bearded men, dressed all in black like priests, he said, standing around at the fair like Minnie had, content to watch it go round and round and seldom spending a nickel. Sometimes a couple of carnies would pick a fight and become rowdy to scare them off and leave more room for paying customers.

"And what about you?" he asked, wanting the story of her life.

She could say it in one sentence. "I stay in the house and read when I'm not in school. I have always lived in that house outside of Crocus."

"It doesn't seem like a bad place," he said and flicked his cigarette up and out into the night. She watched it smoulder in the wet grass and die. "I had a look around. I wouldn't mind staying."

"Here?" she said and heard Mary Ruth's voice in her own voice, saying to Jay, "What here? In this place? I had an idea that it would be more of a place," she had said, "and more of a house."

"It's out of the way," Jay had said. "About as safe as possible."

"I'd like to stay anywhere," Gene said. "For a change. You people always leave in the end and then we start pulling it down. And we're off, while everyone else is sound asleep."

"It's you who leave," Minnie said. The trucks had pulled out of Agassiz in the middle of the night. And even though the police had searched every single trailer and truck, Wanda had gone with them, Mary Ruth was certain. And Minnie wasn't saying. I don't know where Wanda is, Minnie said when they asked. And she didn't. But Wanda is the winner, Mary Ruth said to Jay. I don't understand it, she wailed. And Minnie knew that they weren't entirely happy that she'd been the one to return.

The following morning, after the fair, the field was once again a wasteland. And in the winter, a place of rabbit tracks and snow banks climbing up the side of bleachers. But no matter how many fairs Mary Ruth dragged Minnie to, they never caught sight of that matching dress, the white one with strawberries lining the yoke and a border of embroidered strawberries along the hem line.

"Think I could get a job here?" Gene asked.

Minnie picked up his hand and touched the shiny skin, the crimped little knot of flesh on the missing finger. He pulled his hand away. "Too many accidents," he said. "Another reason why I wouldn't mind pulling out of the game and settling down."

She lifted his hand again and singled out the wounded finger and pressed her mouth against it.

There was surprise in his eyes and then the look of a man remembering a dream or touch of something he'd once turned away from because he couldn't name it or hold it, do anything but feel and hope for its return.

She slid across the space between them, cupped his face between her hands, and kissed him. Then she pulled her blouse free and felt the cool air against her shoulders as she pushed it away from her. She looked down and saw her own new breasts, white and hard. Gene's tanned hand cupped her there. Then his dark, curly head bent slowly to kiss her breast and so Minnie arched her back. Her hands circled his chapped wrists as she drew him towards her. She lifted his hands and pressed them against her bared throat.

"Break my neck," she heard herself say.

7

Minnie chipped at the paper label on the can of beans. "So this 'J' person," Annie said, "he used to tie you to a chair in the basement. Why?"

"Fee, fie, foe, fum," Minnie said. She leaned forward and rubbed noses with Annie. "I smell the blood of an Englishman. The Churchills introduced me to Albert," she said. "They were nice people."

"For Limeys," Annie said.

"Gene Lacroix was French. And he took me home to meet his family. They didn't speak a word of English. I thought they'd be nicer. More generous, like he said. But his mother just glared at me the whole time and asked Gene if I was going to stay for ever. She nailed a crucifix up over our bed. It was one of those that glowed in the dark. We were living in sin, Gene and I. And so I left him and found John. John the Baptist. He had a restaurant beside the highway and handed out religious tracts with every meal. He baptised me in a rain barrel and taught me gospel songs which played on the radio in the restaurant all day long. 'Jesus, Saviour, pilot me,'" she began to sing and swing her fork in time to the music, "'over life's tempestuous sea; unknown waves before me roll, hiding rock and treacherous shoal.'" Surprise lit up her wide smile. "I remembered," she said. "John, he was nice, too," she said. "Quiet. But I couldn't stay. People came in from the crack of dawn to midnight. It hardly left me any time to think."

Annie fished into the pocket of her flannel shirt for a packet of papers and began to roll a cigarette. "Don't quit now, I'm listening."

"Then I went to work for the MacKenzie people. You ever eaten haggis?"

"Nope," Annie said.

"Well, don't."

Annie twisted the end of the cigarette. The match flared and her face leapt forward out of the darkness, her nose and bristly chin becoming more pronounced in the light of the flickering flame, her eyes cast into shadows, black holes. A skeleton, Minnie thought. Underneath that sack of skin Annie was nothing but bones. "And after the MacKenzies, the Epps, and then I went to work for the Churchills," she said softly. "That's about it. Now we both know." Jeremy, Minnie thought, Annie is dying.

Annie's cigarette glowed and the smell of the outdoors entered the room. Aha, at last, Annie thought. I'm learning something. But she felt a prick of disappointment. Nothing unusual, nothing that yet offered an explanation about Minnie. "What about before the Frenchy?" Annie said. "What about before Gene Lacroix?" She shook the match and the room went dark.

Minnie's hands found the manicure scissors and the square of folded paper. "I had a pear tree in my bedroom once," she said.

"Oh go on," Annie sighed. "Don't be into that one again. Just when we were finally getting somewhere."

"Well, I did," Minnie said. "And I don't think it's quite fair. Why can't I talk about Jeremy? Just because you and everyone else thinks Jeremy isn't real doesn't make it so, you know."

"Oh," Annie said, surprised by the quaver in Minnie's voice. "I'm sure he's real," she said and added to herself, to you.

"And I had an aquarium, too," Minnie said. "Some of the fish were so small they were like tiny blue sparks of fire." The scissors nipped at the paper and folded bits curled away and fell to the table.

"Let me get the light," Annie said.

"Oh no, no," Minnie said. "Oh no. I can see perfectly well." She shook the cuttings free, unfolded the paper, and held up a starfish. "I even had one of these."

"From the class of echinoderms," Jeremy had said as he lowered the starfish into the aquarium.

"It's from the class of echinoderms," Minnie said, waving the paper starfish in front of Annie.

"I found it last night when I was walking. I saw one with six legs once," Jeremy said, "but usually they have five. What do you want to call it?"

"Star Fish," Minnie said. "You should never call a starfish anything but Star Fish."

"Makes sense," Annie said.

Minnie closed her eyes. "Frederick the Great helped shape the face of present-day Europe," she said.

"Here," Annie said and reached for the lamp in the centre of the table. The table became washed in a soft pink light as the lamp shone through the towel Albert had draped over its shade earlier.

It was so unfair. Jeremy could go out walking and picking starfish while she was forced to stay with the old woman inside the house. Violin music floated down from the top of the house, the tower room, Jeremy's room.

"Time to talk," Jeremy said. "Behind the house, *schnell*." Minnie watched the starfish begin its crawl up the side of the aquarium through a swirl of bubbles and swaying sea growth. Jeremy paused on the staircase that wound past her room, cupped his hands, and called up, "I put you up there so you could see something and it doesn't seem to make a bit of difference. Look around you and think about what you see when you play."

"It isn't fair," Minnie said as they left the house and walked around its moss-covered roof to the back where Jeremy had built the tennis court. "I don't see why I can't go up to your room and have a look if he can."

Jeremy strode out onto the centre of the tennis court and took a piece of chalk from his pocket and began sectioning the court off into squares. Minnie sat on the edge and watched. Have a talk. He'll do all the talking, she thought. Jeremy looked up at her and smiled. The string attached to Minnie's ankle stretched far across the back yard, across the garden to the edge of it where Jeremy's mother sat on a chair with her back to them, a silver baton raised and swinging. At the far end of the garden, mice played in a dollhouse set down beneath a grove of trees. Leaves flipped in the wind, their colour changing from green to silver. Beyond the trees, the land appeared to drop away and disappear and appear once again in the far distance in a blue ridge. She saw a shower of sparks rise from the space behind the trees and then what appeared to be blue froth, like boiling milk cresting at the top of a pot. She got up. "Who is it this time?" she asked.

Jeremy looked up. "Oh. That. Nothing," he said. "That's Mount Cotopaxi. It's called a volcano. They happen."

"I want to see," she said.

"Stop whining," Jeremy said, "and pay attention here. This is what Europe looks like now; Maria is going to keep her crown, but Frederick will keep Silesia."

His voice was drowned out by a rumbling sound. An orange sun rose and broke apart; sparks flew upwards. She wanted to see what was happening down there. She looked up at the hill behind the house where trees marched up a steep incline. At the top of the hill was Jeremy's yellow canvas chair shining in the sun.

"Is that where you went last night?" she asked.

He followed her gaze. "No. Last night I went down. Not up. And the chair is off limits, too," he said. He sighed. "I'll be so happy when you're out of this stage."

"It lasts for ever." The old woman's voice rose up from the edge of the garden.

"Come over here," Jeremy said. "I can *show* you what's happening down there. England is the big winner this last round. Now they can begin empire building," he said.

"Hum, hum, hum," Minnie sang. She dropped back onto the grass and folded her arms across her chest.

"Pay attention and I'll teach you how to play tennis afterwards."

"Hum, hum," she sang and swatted at a cabbage butterfly that flittered in front of her face. "You'll have to find someone else to have a game with," she said. She looked up at the tower where Mozart's thin, white face pressed out from one of the dark windows that circled it. The tower cleared the trees and was about the same height as Jeremy's chair up on the hill, she realized. She pointed up at Mozart who bowed his head over his little instrument as he concentrated, his bow arm moving unceasingly. "How about him?" she said. "Teach him to play tennis. I'll bet he has a good arm."

Jeremy came over to her and sat down beside her on the grass. "Close your eyes," he said.

"They are closed," Minnie said.

"What?" Annie said.

"My eyes, they're already closed," Minnie said.

"Well, I can see that," Annie muttered.

Minnie stood in the centre of the garden. It was nighttime and the colour of the night was a soft mauve, like an African violet. Beads of light flashed in her long skirt when she turned quickly. Like fireflies, she thought. Mozart stood in the entrance of the grape arbour, his caramel-coloured instrument at his side. His blond hair had been combed straight back and he looked older. His face and white shirt reflected the violet colour as he stood looking up at Jeremy's hill.

Minnie saw a lantern swing and move quickly down the pathway from the hill. Jeremy stepped onto the edge of the garden and set the lantern down beside him. The mice in the dollhouse crouched, frozen, watching. There was a flash of colour as Mozart raised the violin. Minnie couldn't understand it—because there was no need for it—but she felt like crying. One moment she'd been fine and the next she had a sore which had begun to fester in the pit of her stomach. She pressed her hands against her stomach to keep any sound of crying inside. Spikes of blue and purple delphinium swayed in a breeze and Jeremy's face flickered with light and shadow. The need to cry pushed against cracks opening up inside and Minnie had to curl into the sound that had begun to climb up the back of her throat.

"Here," Jeremy said, at her side instantly. "Drink this." He tipped a cup to her mouth. She swallowed. The liquid was hot and thick. Music rose up through the violet air above the grape arbour and Minnie felt herself rise with it. She was being lifted in the circle of Jeremy's arms, up and up, carried to the sun by Jeremy and the music. The sun entered her chest and burned a spot in her heart. She was never, never going to come back down. She would stay up there for ever where there was no sky or land, just a blending of blue meeting blue and Jeremy's ribs pressing against her burning heart.

"Well, now you know," Jeremy said, "why I can't waste Mozart's time teaching him to play tennis. He's got to be perfect on the day of our wedding."

Minnie grabbed Jeremy through a shaft of sunlight and pulled him down onto her cone-shaped breasts. His head grew heavy on her chest. His thick hair was rough against the palms of her hands. "Jeremy," she said, "who are you, anyway?"

His laughter was muffled. He pushed himself upright. His lips were chapped and rough against her forehead. "Right now, I'm everything you need," he said. "I'm your father and your mother and your sister and your brother. And now, your brother wants to teach you how to play tennis."

"Show me again," Minnie said. "Show me the picture one more time, please. Then I'll let you teach me the game. Promise."

The old woman's voice rose up from the edge of the garden. "Jeremy, it looks like your prediction for England may be a little premature."

"What now?" Jeremy said and sprinted across the garden.

"A defeat," she said. "At Fontenoy."

Minnie watched as Jeremy stepped through the grove of trees at the edge of the garden and poised on the brink where the land dropped away. "That's bad news for Maria of Austria," Jeremy said.

"That's not news at all," the old woman said.

Minnie wondered what would happen once they got right back to the beginning of history. Start again? Was it all a circle?

Mozart tapped his bow against the glass. He smiled and beckoned for Minnie to come up and join him at the window. Minnie shrugged and pointed to the string at her ankle. He smiled. Take it off. He mouthed the words and pretended to slide something from his own wrist. The string sagged at her ankle. It had stretched with time and was grey and frayed from years of trailing across the ground. She bent and slipped her fingers beneath it, testing its slackness.

"Why do you keep on thinking about leaving?" Minnie imagined Jeremy saying, his voice touched with sadness.

"I just want to see, that's all," Minnie said.

"Try opening your eyes," Annie said drily.

Minnie dropped the paper starfish and it floated across the table and onto the floor at Annie's feet. "Because I didn't know any better," she said.

Annie bent and retrieved the paper fish and smoothed it out against the table. "Min," she said, "this 'J' person in the newspaper. It's not really Jeremy, is it?"

"Yes, I think so," Minnie said.

"But you're not absolutely sure."

"I think so."

"Couldn't be anyone else?"

"Well," Minnie said, "it's possible. It could also be Jay. J-A-Y," she spelled the name. "My father."

"Aha," Annie said and sat up straight on the edge of the chair, rigid with attention.

"He used to be a clown," Minnie said. "Mary Ruth was a trapeze artist."

"Your mother."

"But then she left. And so Jay brought his mother to live with us. And that's all," Minnie said. "I don't want to talk about it."

"Well," Annie said. "Yes." She picked up the can of beans, crossed the room, and let it drop into the paper bag. "That was a danged poor excuse for a meal, if you ask me," she said. "Saturday bean day this month, or what?"

"You shouldn't have done that," Minnie said. "Albert will notice. He worries if I don't eat."

"I'm sure Albert is worried silly," Annie said. "Albert's pretty busy looking out for himself, if you know what I mean."

"I know," Minnie said. Her voice dropped to a whisper. "You know, you'd think he'd have waited a bit longer, after fifteen years and sex every single night, period or no period, except for when the girls were born and even then, right up to the day before I went into labour and the minute I was up afterwards. Well, you'd think, at least I think, that it should have taken him longer than two days before he went courting someone else." She sighed. "I guess it doesn't really matter. But I just hope that man gets a stomach ache on that woman's baking, because it sure doesn't look like he's going to die of a broken heart."

"It doesn't really matter, eh?" Annie said. "Who do you think you're convincing?"

"It doesn't. I've got Jeremy," Minnie said.

"Smell." Annie pried loose the lid from the plastic container she'd brought with her. "Fresh this morning." She held it up. It was packed with plump, heart-shaped frog drumsticks. "Got some flour and milk? You go and call those girls of yours and the four of us will have a Saturday night feast." Her words were interrupted by a knock at the door. The two women stared at one another.

"I'll go," Annie said. She opened the door and the room became white with the light of the moon. Jacob and Lena Friesen stepped inside. Jacob coughed into his fist. "We weren't at all sure there was anyone home," Lena said. "It didn't look as though there were any lights on at all."

"Oh," Minnie said and pulled the towel from the lamp's shade. "Is that better?"

"Well," Jacob said and passed the rim of his hat through his fingers, "if you think I'm interfering, say so. But we have heard that there's a need here. We wondered if there was any way we might help?"

"Oh, I think Ollie Peter is already doing that," Minnie said.

"Oh," Lena said. "So then, there is a definite need?"

"I'm sure Albert would agree," Minnie said.

"Is there some way that I could assist in place of Ollie?" Lena said.

"Oh no," Minnie said. "Oh no, no, no."

"And this has your approval?" Lena asked.

"I asked for it," Minnie said.

As the door closed behind the elderly couple, Minnie leaned across the table and whispered, "J.... Jacob. Do you suppose it's Jacob Friesen who wants me to go home with him?"

"What do you think those women were up to, sitting in the dark?" Lena asked Jacob as they walked towards home.

"I don't care to speculate on the ways of the world," Jacob said.

"Still," Lena said, "Ollie or no Ollie, I'd like to do something for those girls. The women and I, we could buy a bit of cloth and patterns."

The envelope Taro Yamamoto had given to Jacob on Thursday night nudged against his breast as they entered Railroad Street. "It's good to care for others," he said. "But we have to take care of our own first."

"Who?" Lena asked. "What?"

Elizabeth, Jacob thought. He took her by the arm and they matched their strides. "There's always someone," he said.

Albert saw the elderly couple pass beneath the street light as they turned from Ottawa Street, and it was as though someone had taken a cloth and wiped them away because as soon as they stepped out of the circle of light, they were gone. It was five past ten o'clock. He walked quickly. He was late. Minnie would be waiting. The brown paper package Ollie had slid across the counter to him was warm in his hands. Inside it was a square of cinnamon buns. He'd lifted an edge of the paper and to his relief, saw that the icing on them was quite similar to those of Urbanick's Baked Goods. Now all he needed to remember was to tie the package with butcher string and the disguise would be complete. As he approached his house, he heard with some pleasure the sweet clear notes of the lullaby Ginny loved to play. He walked to the beat of it. Ta da da da da da da da, tum tum tum tum da da tum tum. Ginny's lullaby beat out, steady and sure. He stopped below the window, listening. And then the music stopped.

"Very nice, Ginny," Albert called up. "But why aren't you asleep yet?"

"Dad?" Ginny's face appeared at the window. "Ma's gone."

"For her walk."

"No. She's gone."

Rosella elbowed Ginny away from the window. "You're going to have to find someone to take her place," she said, "because I'm too young for so much responsibility."

"Rosella?" Ginny said, when the girl had turned away from the window. "I hate you."

Rosella sat down on the bed and pulled a pillow over her head. "I had to do something," she said. "Look at him. He can't take care of himself. And Ollie Peter is better than nothing."

"I'm going to find Ma," Ginny said. "I'm going to make her come back."

Rosella threw the pillow aside, turned and raised her hand as though she might like to scratch the scales loose from Ginny's white arms. "You do and I'll kill you," she said.

"That's one of the Ten Commandments," Ginny said.

"All right, all right," Rosella said. She walked over to the door, took its key down from a nail on the wall, and held it up. "All right. But it doesn't say anything about thou shalt not lock someone up." The door slammed shut.

Downstairs, Albert searched all the rooms. He pulled open closet doors and looked under their bed in the room at the front of the house. He went outside and searched the shed. He came back in and stood in the centre of the kitchen. The nightgowns had been folded, placed back into their boxes, and stacked on the table. Minnie's neat handwriting leapt forward from the piece of paper propped against the nightgowns. "I think Ollie would look good in the blue one," the note said. "It matches her eyes."

Albert sat down at the table. "Oh Min," he gasped and then the tears rolled down his face, making Minnie's words run all together. "Oh Min, Min," he cried. "It isn't fair. You never let me know you. You slippery little thing."

Dear Aunt Violet,

We have great need of your presence.

The weather changed suddenly tonight. Much wind, about the height of a tornado without becoming one. Then pummelled a full hour with hail stones as big as oranges. I may have a hole in the roof which could require mending.

I beseech you, Aunt Violet, to book your passage immediately. And don't forget to bring with you the little black bag.

The girls are alone. And I'm not married. I know you will find the latter information a bit upsetting, but, you see....

Albert laid down the truth for the first time, his tongue moving across his lips with the effort of it, while outside the moon washed the dish of the valley so that it shimmered in the night, silvery and snow-like, a bare stage onto which insects now crawled, singing their night songs, a steady rising and humming, their chorus interrupted occasionally by the burp of a frog.

J.P. Campbell worked through the singing in the night, interrupted only by Etta, who had entered his room, her wide hips swaying beneath the string of her apron as she picked her way among a heap of books lying open beside her husband's desk. Campbell opened a new book, scanned its text, and swept it to the floor. Then he wheeled his chair across the room to the bookshelf and pulled down the last two remaining volumes, glided back behind his desk, and leafed through the first one. His face shone with perspiration. Etta set a cup of coffee down onto his desk. He'd been up the whole night, reading and then snapping books closed and tossing them to the floor. She'd tried to sleep but the thump of books hitting the floor had prevented it. They lay in a heap about his desk, some of their pages crumpled and damaged. He closed the second book, lifted it in his twisted hands and threw it across the room. The book slammed into Etta's stomach, knocking the wind from her.

"Call Charles Standing," he said. "I don't see why he should miss out on all the fun." He knocked his pipe sharply against the ashtray and glared at her from beneath bushy white eyebrows which flared up at the ends like wings. "And put on a pot of coffee."

"I already have and I already did," Etta said and massaged her stomach. "You asked me to do that an hour ago. And Charles is already here, not at all happy about having to wait in the kitchen."

"Jelly for brains," Campbell muttered as he picked up the beaded tobacco pouch and examined the geometric design of the porcupine quills. Charles Standing stepped into the room. His cane rapped sharply against the ferns sprawling across the face of the grey linoleum. His pronounced Adam's apple bobbed as he swallowed his irritation.

"Sit, sit," Campbell said and hooked open the filing-cabinet drawer. "You'd better join me." He set the half-filled bottle of whiskey onto the desk.

"You know I don't," Charles said and chose a straight-backed wooden chair and sat on the edge of it, his sharp knees protruding. He pulled at his white moustache and twirled the ends of it between his fingers until they became a fine point.

"You may need it," Campbell said. He held up the tobacco pouch.

Charles Standing rose from his chair and thumped across to the desk. "By cracky," he said. "That's a good one. Where did you get it?"

"You checked out your barn lately?"

"It's secure," Charles said. "I check it daily. The locks haven't been touched."

"Check again. My boys have been running into all kinds of this stuff. They've tracked it back to Sonny Ericson. He's been selling this stuff— leggings, jackets, bonnets, the whole kit and caboodle. Still think the locks are secure?"

"Well, I'll just go and have a look," Standing said. His cane trembled beneath his weight.

"Sit," Campbell said. "I think, as they say, that the horse is already out of the barn. Sonny let it out. Know who's buying?"

"The natives," Charles said, his voice barely a whisper.

"You got it. Sonny's been unloading the stuff up at the reservation. But it gets worse," Campbell said. "I sent the boys up there to raid the place and get the stuff back." He tipped the whiskey up and swallowed and waited for a moment to allow for the warmth of it to seep into his arms and legs. "And the reservation was empty. Deserted. No hide nor hair. Not even the dogs."

The two men sat in silence. The springs of the grandfather clock unwound and the hollow bonging sound beat out from behind the glass. Charles Standing remembered clearly, as though it were only yesterday, his father telling him how once the leggings had given way to trousers, beaded jackets to proper flannel shirts, how when the women began to wear shoes and bear the Métis, the new race of half-white babies, the chance for proper settlement improved. Take people like June and August Marchand, for instance. They'd become French, or Black Irish, or Hudson Bay Scotch. They contributed something to the town. And the few lazy, shiftless, nonconforming Métis—well, his father had given their land to the more deserving. And so he'd known, when it came time to negotiate and resettle the Indians, to entice them out of their native costume, to trade it and then their land away. To him. For fire water.

"We've got to nip this one in the bud," Standing said. "You've got to do something. Find a law and slap it on them to prevent them from wearing the garb before they start thinking they're savages again."

"I've been looking for a law," Campbell said. "But I've gotta find them first before I can slap anything on them."

Etta entered the room carrying a tray with a pot of coffee and shortbread cookies. She spooned sugar into a cup, poured, and handed it to Charles.

"Maybe," Etta said, "you should slap a law onto Sonny."

"For God's sake, woman," Campbell said, "that doesn't make any sense."

"Well, for the future," Etta said as she backed from the room. "Make it illegal for anyone to sell the stuff and it would cut off their supply."

"Well, it is illegal," Standing said with indignation. "It's my property he sold."

Campbell cleared his throat and then grinned. "You don't want anyone to start asking how you came by it," he said.

Charles's moustache dipped into his cup. "I earned it," he said. "I cleared out this whole goddamned valley for you. I earned it."

"Preserve our heritage," Campbell said suddenly. "I believe that's the ticket."

"I beg your pardon?"

"That stuff, those artifacts," he said, pronouncing the word clearly, "are a part of the heritage of this valley." He picked up the tobacco pouch. "This should be preserved, kept in a building, a museum. I'll make it against the law to sell off these, these artifacts," he said. "Because no one group of people should have a monopoly on them. Some people would pay good money to see these—these artifacts."

"Like who?"

"Well, anthropologists, for instance. This is history, man."

"History began when our fathers entered this valley," Standing said. "And if you don't mind, I think I'll have a short snort." It would be a frosty Friday in hell before he'd pay to see his own property.

Etta ran into the room holding her stomach to keep it from jiggling. "The boys are here," she said. "They say they've found something."

With their yellow stripes flashing, the Mounties strode into the room behind Etta. One of them held up three feathers. "We found these beside the remains of a bonfire," he said. "In the same area as the sweat lodge. They're eagle feathers and they're notched."

"Warriors," Charles said.

"And they're on the move. Heading down towards Dauphin."

"I don't think their interest is the Ukrainian Festival, either," the other Mountie said as he unfolded a piece of paper and dropped it down in front of Campbell. "This was delivered to us. Sent it through the young Marchand girl."

"August's kid?" Standing asked. "That half-breed chit? What in tarnation is she up to?"

"Nothing," the Mountie said. "She was just handy, that's all."

Campbell pushed the official-looking document aside as though it were of little consequence. "You still got Sonny-boy down at the courthouse?"

"Technically, we shouldn't have," the Mountie said. "We can't keep him much longer for broken headlights." He took off his hat and scratched his scalp. "But what bothers me," he said, "is that there's blood in his truck. A smear of it on the side panel. And from the look of the scratches on his neck, I'd say he was in a cat fight."

"Love bites," the other Mountie said and laughed self-consciously.

"If we kept Sonny Ericson in jail for love bites or scrapping, he'd never see the light of day," Campbell said. "We can't keep him for a smear of blood in his truck, either. Impound it. We've got to cut off his legs, at least."

"On what grounds?"

"Unsafe, anything," Campbell said. His fingers itched to pick up the document. "My God, do I have to think of everything?"

"Well," Campbell said once the room had cleared and the two men had sat in silence for a moment, neither one wanting to say what they were thinking, "well, I guess they learned to read."

"I don't see what they can do," Charles said.

"Legally, they're entitled to the land. Ukrainians or no Ukrainians."

"Well, we can't very well send those people back to where they came from, can we? Besides, it's one of the better farming regions and the natives could never stay put long enough to harvest anything. Never could and never will." Standing thumped the cane against the floor for emphasis.

"I think we're going to have to meet with them," Campbell said. And dicker with them, give away another piece of the valley instead. Something further up in the hills.

Minnie held the flashlight steady for Annie. Its beam revealed a slippery, spotted back and a yellow throat ballooning with air. Annie reached for the bull frog. She pinched it just in front of the forelegs on each side so it wouldn't grab hold with its powerful hind legs and squirt through her fingers at the last moment. Once she'd had a big one do that and it hit her square on the shoulder and knocked her flat onto her back. She dropped the squirming amphibian down inside the basket.

"Over here, over here," she urged Minnie to swing the light. Annie stooped, grabbed, and plopped another huge frog down with the others. She stopped to shake the pain of the cold water from her hands.

"Dang it," she said. "Can't keep at it. That underground stream must've found another route, because look," she said and pointed to her boots. "It's up to my ankles now and awful cold. Never up to my ankles unless in spring."

Minnie wondered at how the frogs all fell silent at once. They'd stood at the edge of the marshy dip of land behind Annie's shack and listened to frogs calling to each other like a bunch of children in a schoolyard at recess time. But the second Annie had stepped down into that moist coulee, it had been like turning off a light switch, the silence that sudden. And now, as they waded back up the side of it and stepped into Annie's back yard, the chorus of frogs erupted again, ear-splitting indignation. Those inside Annie's basket thudded their limbs against it in answer.

"It was just the opposite," Minnie said.

"What was?"

"When I was born. It was just the opposite. At first, it was quiet, but the minute I started to slide down, I could hear sounds and then they fairly rushed up at me and it got so noisy that it hurt my ears until I got used to it."

"Really," Annie said. She pulled the navy toque from her head and wiped perspiration from her face with it. "Tired," she said. "Could hardly get out of bed this morning. Think I'll go in and make a pot of special coffee." She groaned slightly as she lifted the basket from the ground. "One consolation," she said. "I won't have to be doing this much longer. Yamamoto will have to find someone else."

Minnie went around the house and sat down on the top step and plucked at the button of Albert's sweater. She didn't know what she'd do without Annie. Above, the silent V formation of lights appeared over top the trees, gliding in perfect unison. She watched until they passed centre sky. When she'd been up there and looked out the window at the stars, she'd felt as though the pulsing lights moved around and, at the same time, away from her. That she was still, while they receded, wheeling away and away. She hadn't been afraid to watch the glowing ball of planet Earth become smaller and smaller.

"Jeremy," Minnie said, "what'll become of Annie and Rosella, Ginny and Albert?" She closed her eyes to see. A boulder tumbled down a cliff of blue ice, bouncing, turning end over end, falling through the roar of water and the silver curve of flat-bodied fish and the bones of a mammoth, falling through clouds of mist, down and down, crashing to the floor of the valley. Don't worry, she imagined Jeremy saying. She opened her eyes and saw fire leap in the hills. She stood up, turned, and saw another bonfire on the opposite shore. No wonder the water had risen in Annie's pond. The ice was melting faster. She sat down, hugged her knees to her chest, and began to hum softly. Once again, she heard the hollow drum of horses' hoofs, a rhythmic fast gallop along the road. She saw the flash of a yellow braid on shoulders and a white helmet with a curious-looking spike in its centre which, as the rider bent over his mount, made her think of a unicorn. Puffs of dust exploded at the animal's hoofs as the shiny chestnut flank passed by on the road and then the flick of a tail and the animal was covered by the mist rising above the gully. Gone.

The door opened and Annie stepped out onto the stairs carrying two mugs. She set one down beside Minnie and then sat beside her.

"It's not helping, is it?" Minnie said. "The frog cure?"

"There was blood in my stool this morning," Annie said.

"Is the pain bad?"

"I can manage the pain," Annie said. "It's just the idea of the whole thing. No one gave me any say in the matter. The minute you're born, you start to die. So I think a person should have the right to choose whether or not to be born. Before people take their pants off, they should ask," she said. "Think about being responsible for another person's death. Instead of the itch they intend to scratch." The coffee and rum warmed the back of her throat as she swallowed. She sighed. "Don't listen to me. Seen a cat corner a mouse once, and the only danged thing the mouse could think to do was to start gnawing on its own tail."

"I chose to be born," Minnie said. She slid her hand down her leg, feeling for a ridge of string at her ankle.

Annie peered down into Minnie's coffee mug. "Stuff and nonsense," she said. "And you've only had one mouthful. Me, I'm about ready for a refill," she said.

Mozart stood at attention beside Jeremy's chair on the hill, the violin at his side. "I have my own landscape," he said. "I really don't need to look around when I play."

"Jeremy tried to keep me from seeing the valley," Minnie said, "because I guess he knew what would happen."

"Begin playing," Jeremy said. He stretched and put his arms behind his head and leaned back into the canvas chair and gazed up at the sky.

Annie stood at the door of her house about to go back inside. She thumped the empty coffee mug against the palm of her hand. "Min," she said, "this Jeremy person. Is he really Jay? Your father?"

"Oh no," Minnie said and began to laugh. "Good heavens, no."

"Who's he supposed to be, then?"

Minnie slid the string up and down, up and down. Caramel wood shone as Mozart raised his instrument. His arm moved slowly. Jeremy slid further down into his chair, his posture indicating that he was relaxed, pleased for once with the boy's efforts.

"Jeremy," Minnie said to Annie, "is my father and mother and my sister and brother. And I think…," she said, her voice becoming tight as her throat constricted. Her fingers played with the clasp on her galoshes. "I *know* that one day, I was supposed to be Jeremy's bride." Her chest ached and ached.

The string slipped up the bare arch of Minnie's foot. She wiggled her toes and felt it drop free. She bent slowly, picked up a rock, and pulled the string taut. She placed the rock over top the string so the old woman would not feel the difference and would think that she was still at the end of it. She crept around the front of the house and mounted the stairs. She tiptoed past the old woman's room hardly daring to breathe. The woman's breath was even as she slept, little short, squeezed hisses of air being released, a quick gasp for more air, and then the gentle hiss once again. Minnie counted twenty before she passed by the old woman's door and up the stairs to her own room. She stood in its doorway for a moment, looking up the curve of the stairs. Then she pried free her tennis shoes and began to climb up. A strange blue light flickered against the wall behind her as she climbed the spiral stairs. An aquarium, she thought—that Jeremy had one, too. But his would be the size of an ocean, no doubt. Her foot met the top step and Jeremy's room opened to her in a flash of light. Windows circled the room and below stretched land, a valley, where inside a galaxy of lights wheeled, a fire at its centre, feathering up the sides of the land in lights which twinkled, jumped, and sometimes darted suddenly across the face of it. The glass was cool against her palms as she pushed against it, drawn by the sight. Tears formed behind her eyes. Stop it, stop it, she told herself. There was no need to cry. There was simply no need for it. But she wanted to reach down there and nudge every light with her finger. To open doors and look inside. Being able only to look was too awful. The violin climbed up the scale, a high thin note prevailed— her desire, which would not be satisfied unless she finally did it. Until she slid across the garden on her back, scrambled through the grove of trees, and climbed down.

She crouched among the shadows of the dark trees and watched how the lights blinked on and off, how some of them seemed to shimmer different colours while others flared brightly and then sank into sudden darkness. Several swept across the dish of land with regular swinging motions.

The music stopped. "It's not bad," Mozart's voice said. "It's not baroque. What is it?"

Jeremy started forward in his chair. "Minnie."

Minnie turned and waved. "I have to see." Her voice echoed back to her from his hill.

"Don't," Jeremy said, his voice echoing in the far ridge beyond. Don't, don't.

She dropped to her knees and rolled onto her belly and began to slide downwards. As her feet found crevasses and her hands clutched at weeds to ease the speed of her descent, his voice became fainter, like the sound of water gurgling in a stream trickling over stones. The stream stopped moving and when she reached out to touch it, it was unpenetrable, solid and cold. Like ice.

As she slid further and further down, the sounds of the valley rose. A gentle humming at first, then the hum became the thunder of many different sounds. Before she hit the bottom, she hung on for a moment, looked up, and saw up there that sheet of blue ice rearing above her, solid and thick.

"Jeremy *represents* all those things to you," Annie said, as she stepped back out onto the stairs with a fresh mug of coffee. She sat down. "For some reason, you need to make up a Jeremy."

"No, he *is* all those things," Minnie said.

"Well, that would make him, a—a god."

"It's never come to me to call him that," Minnie said. "You'd never think that God would play tennis. He always said that he was Jeremy."

Annie jammed the navy toque back onto her head and pulled it down over her ears. "I never figured to have much use for the idea of God," she said. "I never wanted a scapegoat to pin all my troubles on. Or to avoid facing them."

"Oh no," Minnie said. "Oh no, no, no. You don't think that I blame Jeremy? Oh no."

Laughter beat out from Steven Adam's garage. His ceramics class threatened to go on for all hours. June Marchand, trying her hand out at not breaking things.

"I had a girl once," Annie said after a time.

"Who, you?"

"I did." Her watery eyes blinked in their sockets and the bushy eyebrows gathered and met across the bridge of her nose.

"Well, so what happened to her?" Minnie asked.

"Gone."

"Run off?"

"They took her from me."

"Who did?"

And Annie indicated with the sweep of her hand: the valley, the town, the people on the street. "I was only fifteen. Five days after she was born, Harrigan and the lot marched into the house and dang near ripped her off my breast. Poor wee thing. Said I wasn't fit."

"And did you...," Minnie said, "did you ask her if she wanted to be born?"

"Hah!" Annie said. She sat up and flung the remainder of her coffee over the side of the steps. "Think you got me, eh? I wasn't in a position to ask," she said. "I was flat on my back with a hand crost my mouth so's I wouldn't squeak."

They heard Katie whine and saw the animal skirt the edge of the gully, looking for a dry path across it. Minnie kissed for the dog. She complained, but then splashed down through the water and up the other side. Silver beads flew from her black coat as she shook the water free.

"Anyway, it's all under the bridge," Annie said. "You could be that girl, you know. That would make you one-half Irish. The other, a dog's breakfast like that mutt over there."

Minnie slid up against Annie, took off Albert's sweater, and draped it around her emaciated frame. Annie's eyes squeezed shut as she sucked at the sudden thrust of pain. Her shoulders fell forward as the pain passed. She squinted up at Minnie. "No one could be all those things to you, unless they were God," she said.

"Well, you are," Minnie said. "You're all those things. To me." She put her arm around the woman and smelled the smell of an apple gone soft. She pulled Annie's head onto her shoulder.

"Jesus, God, yes," Annie said. "We may as well love each other because no one else does."

Minnie held the woman and watched the white mist drift up off the water, rise, and gather in clouds beneath the limbs of trees.

"I'm curious," Annie said, her tongue slow from the effects of the rum. "What might a person do in heaven all day?"

And Minnie told her. Lessons. Tennis. A swimming pool. A garden. Jeremy. You'll have exactly what you need.

"I hate pears," Annie said. Her head dropped and then she slept.

SUNDAY

8

On Sunday morning, Jacob Friesen awoke from a restless sleep to the sound of a dog barking. From four o'clock on, he'd been pulled to the surface by the harsh, insistent bark. In the living room, delicate springs began to uncoil as the hinged door of the cuckoo clock sprung open and the bird called the sixth hour. The clock belonged to Jacob. It was the one thing that he'd brought with him from his previous life with Louise. The furniture, the basement full of trunks filled with linens, a porcelain set of dishes, feather ticks, Lena had brought with her. He lay in the semi-darkness, listening to the bird swing in and out of its door, and tried to recall what it was he'd been wrestling with in his sleep. But it was as though the fight had been a physical one because his legs ached and a dull pain had spread out across his lower back. At the window, a grey kind of daylight outlined the blind and cut through the fringes of it along the bottom of the sill. Finally, the bird's door clicked shut for the last time, the sound replaced by the steady, rhythmic drum of rain against his roof. The weather had turned. He reached for Lena beneath the blankets and shook her gently. "I'm going ahead," he whispered.

Lena sat up suddenly and pushed the blankets down around her knees as though she were about to get up. Their night odour, the smell of sour milk, billowed up from the warm sheets. "What time is it?" she said.

"No, no," Jacob said. "I'm going to go early. The church may be damp. I'll plug in the heater for a bit."

"You know I won't sleep," she said.

He sighed. "Try."

As he dressed, the sound of rain against his roof and windows made him grateful for the warmth of their narrow room—the source of it their own bodies. It made him think suddenly of the woman Elizabeth and her son. Lena had huddled back down under the blankets and Jacob studied her curled shape and wondered how they slept. Back to back, curling away into themselves, or, during the night, did the boy turn and curl about his mother's body? The temptation of imagination was too strong and Jacob was there, standing beside their bed looking down at them. The boy waited, he knew, and listened for the sound of his mother's breathing to subside until it was barely a sound and only a slight movement in the springs of the mattress. With a slow stealthy movement, the boy began to slide his hand across the soft flannel of his mother's nightdress. The hand was a white wedge, its fingers squeezed together as it moved down towards the mother's hip. The hand began to slide across her flat belly, up towards the curved mound of her breast, the clenched fingers still a solid mass, still an innocent movement should she awaken. With that image, Jacob's eyes flew open to the curled form of Lena beneath the blankets. He knelt before the bed and prayed.

The gate creaked on its hinges and snapped shut behind Jacob as he stepped from the yard. The cool wet air met his flushed cheeks and he felt released by it. Perhaps, he thought, it was like the growth of a calf—how if you carried the animal around each day, you became used to its growing weight until, it was said, you could actually carry a full-grown animal in your arms. It was like that for Elizabeth. She didn't think twice about having the boy in her bed. But what about the full-grown animal? he wondered.

He slid the umbrella up its stem and it snapped open above him. Except for the rain pelting against the umbrella and the crunch of his footsteps on the road, there was no other sound but his thoughts. He saw Taro Yamamoto out in the yard and waved his greeting. I wonder what walked across your garden last night, he thought. Once Taro said there had been strange hoof marks; a deer or a goat had crossed through during the night. Taro waved and smiled. Jacob knew the man understood that it was the Lord's day and that his mind had to be still and listening. He crossed Ottawa Street and saw the Pullman man outside in his housecoat. Albert stood at the doorway of the shed in his back yard looking inside. He was looking to see if Minnie had come home. June Marchand saw Albert as well, through her kitchen window where she stood pinning her hair up into sections, thinking, God, bloody drag, but she had to do it to get the peroxide right down to the roots. And after the peroxide had bleached away the black of her natural colour, she'd have to apply a toner to get rid of the orange and her scalp was bound to get all bubbly.

"Mom?" Robin entered the kitchen.

"Where in hell you been all night?"

The girl's face was smeared with what looked to be charcoal and she smelled of wood smoke.

"Around."

"You hungry?"

Robin set a black leather-bound book on the table and opened it at a dog-eared page. "I want to show you something."

June poured a glass of milk and set it down in front of the girl. The streaked face and smudge-fire odour of her daughter's clothing threatened to bring back memories June was trying to bleach out. Grandpops and her brothers, fringe dwellers camping out alongside dozens of small towns and villages until August had come along and made her legal. "Clean yourself up," she said.

"Look," Robin pointed to a column of spidery handwriting. "I think we own land."

"What now?" June returned to the mirror without looking at the book and wound up a large remaining section of hair and pinned it flat against her head.

"I found this in old Charlie's barn," Robin said. "In a trunk. It's a record of some kind."

"Jesus," June said. "I have told you and told you to stay away from Charlie's place. You're going to get into trouble bringing that crap home."

"Françoise Vandal, Napoléon Vandal, Roger Vandal, Hélène Vandal." Robin read from the ledger. "Thérèse Vandal, Josephette Vandal."

June grabbed the book from Robin's hand. Napoléon. Grandpops. The second oldest in his family. He had been only fourteen the autumn his family had returned from the hunt and found their cabin occupied. Eventually the homeless family scattered in order to survive. Several of them wound up in the city and sold their lives and the lives of their children to a meat-packing plant for a measly hourly wage. Others had changed their names and disappeared. When June's father vanished into a hospital with tuberculosis—and her mother, into the bottle—Grandpops' face had dropped down out of nowhere through the flap of their tent and he had moved in. He brought with him a strong-box of tools and a wad of papers tied with a strip of rawhide. "See this," he'd said once and the bundle of papers sprang loose. The paper felt like money. "It's worthless," Grandpops had said, "but I keep it because it looks good. I like the look of my name." June flipped through the ledger and stopped at a page with a sketch of the river. Parish 16. Range East. Including the town of Agassiz. Each brother and sister had been granted a section, side by side. Numbers sixteen through to twenty-one. Beside each name was the word "unclaimed". And then, below the Vandal names were the Richards names. Marie Anne, Margaret, Alexander, John, Andrew, and Thomas Richards. Granted the same land.

"We never got any land, did we?" Robin asked.

"Nope," June said. "But what's this 'we' business? Those names don't have much to do with us. That's Grandfather and his family."

"It has lots to do with us," Robin said. "Napoléon Vandal—was *your* grandfather. My great-grandfather. I'm a Vandal, too."

June shivered and gathered her housecoat around her body. "Don't get in a snit over that one," she said. "It happened, as they say, many moons ago."

"But it's not fair," Robin said. "We're related. If the land went unclaimed, then we should claim it."

"It's not that simple," June said. "Grandpa probably sold the land grant to the first person who came along," she said. "The old man liked his booze."

"I don't believe it."

"That's because you're young."

Robin took her jacket down from the wall and slipped into it. She rummaged through cupboards, found a box of Oreo cookies, and stuffed her pockets.

"Where are you going?"

"Do you really care?" Robin said as the door slammed closed behind her.

So it was Sunday morning when Robin stepped out onto Ottawa Street. She carried the ledger beneath her arm. Clouds had spilled down into the valley and settled in during the night. The light wash of rain earlier made the roof tops of all the houses in Agassiz seem brighter, as though freshly painted. Beneath those roofs, women combed children's hair, plaited braids, unrolled curlers, preparing for church. In the basement of the Baptist church, the choir had already assembled and loosened up their vocal cords with scales. Inside the Lutheran church, the minister carried a stack of red hymnals, blowing dust from their covers before he slipped them into place in the pews. The organ sounded wheezy and off, but he smiled in passing and said good, good, to the young farm girl who peered intently at the notes as she practised the hymns for the service. As he passed by, the minister smelled the odour of chicken feathers and hay. In the choir loft at the United church, Mrs. Bond urged the altos to move in closer and fill the space Sandra Adam had left behind; they'd manage without her.

But Jacob Friesen's congregation was only a small group of women and several of their younger children, and it was growing smaller every year. It did not warrant an organ or a choir, only Lena at the keyboard of the warped and out-of-tune piano, their voices, and the voice of the sparrow. Oh Heavenly Father, Jacob prayed as he crossed Ottawa Street and headed out towards the little wooden church on the edge of town. Forgive me this day my wicked imagining and open their ears to receive something from you. He treaded the water of his responsibility to rightly divide the word of truth.

Robin Marchand stood on the sidewalk with her hands in her pockets, ledger tucked up beneath her arm. The air drifting in off the water in the gully made her shiver. She would have to get back inside Charlie's barn. She could use the musty old tent he had up there in the rafters. Parish 16, Range East, included the town. She couldn't determine exactly where from the sketch, so she'd have to choose. She chose. Delta William's place. That of all the pieces of land along Ottawa Street the one she'd most like to claim for her great-grandfather was Delta's place.

An hour later, Albert stepped from the house, fully dressed, with a freshly starched shirt, his hair still wet. "Beauty of a day," he called to June Marchand, even though the sky threatened rain again. June sat out in the garden with a plastic bag on her head in hopes that whatever light there was would hasten the process of bleaching the colour from her hair.

"Hey Dad, where you going?" Ginny's voice sang down from the top of the house.

"I'm not going anywhere," Albert said. He watched June. A fine figure of a woman. He was surprised by this thought— that suddenly he would notice the compact, trim little body of June Marchand and just why the men at the lumber yard called her Sassy Ass.

"You are so going, I know it," Ginny said. Her voice quavered.

The bedroom door opened and Rosella, her hair freed from the braids and looking like unravelled wool, said, "Shut your face." She bumped Ginny away from the window.

"If you want to go for a walk, I'll manage things," she said to Albert.

"Well, thanks," he said. "I just might do. But I won't be long."

Grass whipped against his polished cotton trousers as he crossed the field towards the empty fairgrounds. It had begun to rain again, just enough that he and Ollie wouldn't be soaked but enough that they would only have a short time to talk before they'd have to head home for shelter. He didn't know if this thought made him feel better or not. Bluebells nodded against his knees as he pushed through a shallow growth of bush and stepped into a clearing. Ollie had found shelter beneath the wooden gazebo where the town's band had once played during the fair. The building was tumbling down and here and there boards were missing. It had been years since the band had played anywhere. Ollie waved. Albert hurried across the sea of grass towards her. He felt the gazebo give a bit as he stepped up onto it. She'd already spread a blanket over the floor planks. Albert leaned into the side of the gazebo to catch his breath and felt a sliver press against his flesh. He jangled the contents of his pockets, fingers examining the loose change, a couple of finishing nails, a nut and bolt.

"All right," Ollie said and sat down on the blanket. "Let's talk."

"Okay," Albert said.

"Sit." She patted the blanket. The pansy earrings flashed at her ears. His knee bones cracked as he bent and sat beside her. They were hidden from view by the gazebo's siding.

"Have some," Ollie said, and Albert watched as her tiny, efficient hands unscrewed the cap from a Thermos and splashed coffee into a plastic cup. "Sugar and cream already added," she said and passed the steaming brew up to him. "Just the way you like it."

It was exactly how he liked it. Thick as syrup.

"Okay," she said. "Now tell me why."

"Why what?" Albert asked and noticed how she'd only allowed him two sips of the coffee before she'd ploughed in.

"How come you and Minnie never married?"

"She didn't want to," Albert said. "She said no one ever needed to know."

"And does anyone else know?"

"Only you," he said. "And my Aunt Violet in England. I'd appreciate it if you didn't say anything."

"Well, I'm not about to take an ad out in the paper," Ollie said. Although it was a good idea.

"There's another thing," Albert said.

"And the girls really aren't yours?"
"She's left me."

As Jacob Friesen mounted the three steps to the pulpit, he searched the window-ledge for the sparrow. The women's voices were high and child-like as they sang the last verse of the children's hymn and he longed for the sparrow to appear at that moment to remind them of so great a love that it cared even for the falling of a single sparrow. He prayed silently.

He turned to face them. Ollie Peter was not there. Had she been unnecessarily offended by his visit? The widow Peter bent over her hymnal, not singing, and the muscles in her face worked to keep herself from crying. But the face of Hendrick Schultz leapt forward to meet him and all the others receded. The boy stood at his mother's side. His head reached her shoulder but Jacob knew he was taller than that. Hendrick's habit of walking stoop-shouldered as though always deep in thought made him appear shorter, younger. The boy raised his eyes at that moment and his piercing blue pottery gaze met Jacob's over top of the hymnal. A feigned innocence, Jacob realized. He wondered how long he'd been blind to it.

"Today we will begin in the Book of James," he said. "James, chapter 1, verses 2 and 3."

Hendrick's lip curled and his face grew red.

"James, chapter 1, verses 2 and 3," Jacob said. The women glanced at the boy and then at one another.

So the boy still refuses to speak. Jacob opened the Bible in front of him and read the verses. Elizabeth turned her face up to him and when he'd finished and looked down at her it seemed to him that her features had dissolved and become a still white mask. Alma Harder and her two children, Maria and Rick, sat directly behind her. The Harder woman chewed at a strand of hair and through eyes narrowed almost to slits, she studied the back of Elizabeth's head.

Rain pelted against the window suddenly. Jacob arranged his sermon notes, rearranged them. He couldn't seem to find the opening paragraph. His ink letters ran together on the page and became unreadable. The women shifted uneasily because of the delay. Lena smiled encouragement from the front pew. They all heard the swish of wings fanning the air and the thump of the sparrow's body as it landed on the sill and hopped down between the windowpanes. Several of the women smiled as the bird began to chirp. The sudden appearance of the bird was like sunlight blasting a hole through the roof of the church: Jacob realized that he was not meant to deliver the sermon. Instead he would tell them the story that presented itself to him in its entirety. It was a story he'd heard a Haitian missionary tell at a conference, years ago.

He stuck the sermon notes into the Bible and closed it. "I want to tell you a story this morning," he said. "It's a story about a man who wanted to sell his house." He leaned forward and rested his arms against the pulpit in order to speak more directly to them.

"But there was a problem," he said. "And the problem was that the person who was interested in buying the man's house didn't want to pay as much for it as the man wanted." He raised his voice to be heard above the voice of the sparrow and it echoed back to him. It seemed to him that his voice was stronger and deeper than it had been for a time. Hendrick stopped fidgeting. Jacob stopped to drink from the glass of water Lena had set at the side of the pulpit before continuing. He studied the slightly swollen features of the boy, the hint of blond whiskers on his chin, the pout of his mouth. It was the face of a man, he realized.

"Well, the owner decided that he would sell the house at the lesser price, but on one condition," Jacob said. "That he could retain ownership of a single nail above the door of the house."

Elizabeth's face became clear, each feature defined and in focus as she leaned forward to listen.

"Time passed," Jacob continued. "And by and by, the man wanted to purchase his house back from the new owner, but the new owner refused to sell it. And so the man went out and killed a dog and hung the carcass on the nail above the door. And by and by," Jacob said, "the stink of the animal spread throughout the whole house, filling it and forcing the new owner to give in and sell."

Alma Harder clapped her hands against her mouth and a slight gurgle of suppressed laughter rose in her throat. "I would love to try that," she said. The women turned and stared at her. Jacob felt a flash of anger. Hendrick had swivelled about and stared at the woman as well. Their attention was scattered, the mood broken.

"The story," Jacob said, straining to be heard above the commotion, "illustrates how important it is for us to make sure that we've given our whole hearts to the Lord. That we don't hold back one single thing." But even as he spoke, the real truth of the story became clear. That someone in his church had left a nail above the door of his heart and the stink of the dog had spread throughout the house. It was witnessed in his falling attendance, the absence of the women's husbands and older sons, the women's continual plucking at discordant strings, and Hendrick Schultz.

Who was it? The boy leaned over at that moment and whispered something in his mother's ear. She appeared not to listen and remained attentive although the woman, Alma Harder, still tried to suppress her laughter.

"A fool returns to his own vomit," Jacob said, his finger wagging directly at Hendrick. Don't forget your promise. The one you made to God. "And a dog to his folly."

195

Hendrick smiled. "A dog returns to his vomit," he said. "The fool to folly."

"Yes, yes," Jacob said. The boy had flexed his muscles, Jacob thought, choosing to speak to draw attention to error. Elizabeth continued to look up at him, as though expecting he would say more. She alone remained the same, Jacob thought, untouched by what went on in the town around her, untouched by whatever had caused the falling away. She'd remained faithful and unswerving. He wanted to reach down and trace the contour of the deep cleft at the base of her neck, the slender fragile stem which held the silver head so erect and alert in a girlish way. He would like to feel her face between his hands. And lie with her. To search out the moist centre of her and enter it and watch that peace in her face, that uncanny stillness, change and move with something else. To hear her cry out from beneath him.

Albert sat beside Ollie on the blanket in the gazebo. He felt her lean towards him. It was as though the world had tilted suddenly, Ollie thought, shifted to one side and caught her unprepared, causing her to lean towards Albert. She'd lain in bed last night drawing up the agenda for their meeting. How she would measure out her affection in words only. Not like the last time when she gave Albert everything he wanted too quickly with no strings attached. But she hadn't counted on this happening, that the world would suddenly tilt.

Albert's ears began to burn with fire as he sat very quiet and still, allowing Ollie to cross the space between them. He would not move first. And then she reached up and wound her arms about his neck. He felt her arms tremble and her breath at his neck become quick and ragged. So suddenly, just like that. He patted Ollie on the back and felt the soft curve of her breasts press harder against his chest. He patted and patted and thought how fond he was of Ollie, while Ollie began to shake. She reached up and kissed him behind the ear, burning him there.

"Oh, I can't wait," Ollie said and suddenly she was grabbing at Albert's shirt, pulling it loose. Buttons sprang free and rolled across the blanket as she pulled it open. Both of them tugged their garments free, kicked them loose, not thinking where they landed. Albert was amazed at how white his belly was and at how well it fit against hers, cupped by the wing of her pelvic bones. "Oh, I can't wait," Ollie cried as she flopped back onto the blanket and her knees fell outwards. Albert watched in amazement, watched himself enter that pink wound of Ollie.

A woman's cry rose up from the roof of the wooden gazebo. They heard it inside the church, faintly, but definitely the voice of a woman crying out. Jacob stepped back in shock and his arm flew up as though to ward off a blow. His hand swept the Bible over the side of the pulpit and the sermon notes scattered across the floor.

Albert lay beside Ollie on the blanket. From beneath the gazebo came the sound of a small animal scurrying away in the grass. Ollie's belly heaved. Albert wanted to cover her and hold her close for a moment. She moaned then and slid her leg over top his and nestled her head into his shoulder. Light knifed through the cracks in the roof and the sound of soft rainfall made Albert feel tired. His jaw ached with the effort not to yawn.

"Oh Lord," Ollie said. "God." She buried her face in his armpit so he wouldn't know she was crying.

Albert thought about how on Monday he'd do an inventory at the lumber yard. He'd spend the day out back, counting two-by-fours. He hoped it wasn't raining on Monday.

"I could still have a child if you wanted one," Ollie said. "There's still a bit of time."

Albert patted Ollie's shoulder. A combination of fond-ness and sadness made his chest feel full and heavy. He was sad that there were so few men available for someone like Ollie. She deserved someone really nice.

Ollie felt that spongy pat against her shoulder and wanted to turn swiftly, bare her teeth, and bite his hand to make it stop patting. "In any case," she said, "I'd be good for your girls. I know I couldn't take the place of Minnie, but Rosella and I could be friends. She needs a friend." She rose up on one elbow and plucked at a hair on his chest. Albert winced as she pulled. "There wouldn't even be the mess of a divorce," Ollie said.

Energy trickled from the tips of Albert's fingers and toes. It seeped from his body and ran through the cracks in the floor, dripping down into the grass below.

"Promise me that we'll talk again, soon," Ollie said.

"I'm going to be pretty busy at work this week," Albert said. "There might be some overtime."

"In the evening."

"I'm always so tired after overtime."

"The weekend."

"I promised the Standings that I'd have a look see at their drainpipes on the weekend."

"Sunday. Promise me that we'll talk next Sunday."

"We'll see," Albert said. "I don't know. Maybe Minnie'll come back and it might be hard to get away."

"Do you want her to come back?"

Ollie's curly hair tickled the palms of Albert's hands. "Oh Ollie, let me tell you," he said. "You're such a good person."

9

Hendrick Schultz stood in front of the open door of the church vestibule and waited for his mother. And although, as usual, she seemed to hang back from the circle of women, it was as though she had her own private circle. That today she carried everything she needed inside her. As the boy looked at his mother standing there, separate, a full head taller than most of the women, her face saying that she knew something that they didn't know, his resolution not to talk to her began to dissolve. Unable to gain her attention and signal his impatience to be gone, he turned back to the open door. Beyond stretched a field of grass and, beyond that, the sky hanging too low with clouds. He yearned to move out across that field and keep going until the muscles in his legs became cramped and his thighs ached, until finally that constant, nagging urge to stretch and yawn disappeared.

"Well, my boy," Jacob Friesen said, "I've invited your mother to come for a visit this afternoon. You will come as well?"

The man's false joviality rose above the women's voices and Hendrick became aware immediately that all movement froze for several moments. And then the women turned back to one another—but their voices had become stiff and unnatural and their movements jittery. *Isaiah, 39, 4,* Hendrick recited in his mind to keep from thinking, Maria? *Then said he—then said Isaiah—behold—carried—Hezekiah—* he recited. The fierce hunger that clutched at his stomach whenever he was in church was replaced by nausea and a gush of salt water at the back of his throat. *Amos, 4— hear this word—and I also have given you—*Maria Harder. Maria Harder had told the women what had happened in the kitchen on Thursday morning. He was certain of this.

"Around three o'clock," Jacob said and turned from Hendrick.

A sharp cry drew the boy's attention. The girl, Maria, and her younger brother, Rick, were wrestling over an umbrella. Muscles knotted in Maria's wiry, dark arms as she twisted it free from her brother's grasp. Even when she stood still— which was rare—Maria had the appearance of motion in the energy humming in her body and the sparks crackling in her blue-black hair. Her dark eyes met his, and Hendrick, feeling Jacob's careful studying of his reaction, turned away. *Luke, 24—Now upon the first day of the week, very early in the morning—*Elizabeth touched the boy on the shoulder and he sagged with relief.

Jacob stepped past them and stood to one side of the door—his formal position for leave-taking, the official signal that they could leave. Elizabeth yawned suddenly and attempted to hide it, but Alma Harder saw that movement and pushed over through the circle of women to Elizabeth's side.

"Something kept you from sleeping?" she asked. Her green eyes glittered out from their slits.

"I slept well, thank you," Elizabeth said and smiled at the woman—a safe, polite, self-contained smile.

"Just don't forget that you owe me for half a day's work because of the behaviour of that boy of yours."

The women shushed Alma, shocked by her tone. "Don't be so bossy," Hilda Penner whispered.

"I'll boss who I like," Alma said.

"Hallelujah," Maria Harder said as she dashed towards the door, but at the last moment, Rick, her brother, darted in front of her and escaped first. Maria turned and looked at Hendrick. Her tongue flickered and then darted out, once, twice. Maria Harder is a cockteaser, the older boys said. Jail bait. But just you wait, Maria Harder will be the town bicycle inside a year. It was wishful thinking on their part.

"We'll have a nice long visit for a change," Lena said and patted Hendrick on the shoulder as he left the church. "I baked your favourite square," she said, and hope flared in the boy that maybe he was mistaken and they didn't know anything. But the hope was quenched beneath the probing of Jacob's eyes that were the colour of ice on the river in winter reflecting back the sky at the end of the day, the white ice becoming a colder tinge of blue, shadows only differing shades of blue, growing darker as the sun waned. The boy stepped past the couple without answering, out into the rain-heightened colours and moist air.

He turned his collar up against the rain which had become a steady drizzle. Ahead on the road, Maria and Rick began to run. Their legs churned awkwardly as they both sought shelter beneath the umbrella. Its taut black skin, wet and shining, looked like a giant spider, Hendrick thought. Maria's laughter rose from beneath the umbrella as they ran and leapt in a great stride across a water-filled pothole. She was like her Mexican-born father, Joe, thick-lipped and eyes heavy-lidded and jumping with the taunts she carried. Rick was pasty-faced, long-faced like his horsey mother. A touch of the peasant, the women said of Alma Harder's shape, and that even though she'd come from Mexico, if you put a babushka on that one you would see the Ukrainian there, pretending to be Mennonite.

"I don't think I'll ever get used to the idea of snow," Alma Harder had said to Hendrick's mother the summer they arrived from Mexico. It was the first week and the family had traipsed about the town introducing themselves.

"It's not an idea," Elizabeth said. "It's real. They bring it in in truckloads, month after month."

Joe Harder laughed. Hendrick was startled by his mother's sudden humour and then drawn by the sound of merriment in the man's deep voice. Joe's gold tooth shone in the sun when he laughed. And then Elizabeth laughed too—a short outburst, quickly stifled. "Don't worry," she said. "Winter isn't as bad as you might think. Everything is so clean when it snows."

The three adults had stood on the road. Maria sat cross-legged in the centre of it. The soft, powdery soil tinged her legs and coated her bare feet, making them even browner than they were. She looked like an Indian child, she was so brown. She wore a long skirt of brightly coloured material and several necklaces of dried corn and black wooden beads which rattled as she scooped up the soil and sifted it from hand to hand. Later the women said that the Harders were worse than a pack of Indians and they had to teach them not to walk into their homes unannounced, or enter when they were absent and cart off whatever it was they needed at the time. They had to know their place, the women said of the Harder family, and how things worked around here.

Hendrick had tried to ignore the girl. He played catch, throwing the ball as high as he could towards the sun and watching it fall like a stone towards him. And then he heard the unmistakable sound of the girl farting. But when he turned to look, she laughed at him and he saw that the sound came from her armpit. She clasped her bare armpit tightly with her cupped hand and pumped her arm up and down furiously, and the result was long, drawn-out wet farts interspersed with short dry ones. Alma Harder laughed. "That one," she said, "did you know that she was kidnapped by a crowd of monkeys, once?" she asked Elizabeth. Joe Harder cautioned her with a dark look to stop speaking, but she seemed oblivious of his silent message and told the whole story.

Hendrick was mesmerized by the sounds Maria could make. He dropped the ball, put his hand inside his shirt, and clasped his armpit. He pumped his arm. Nothing happened. She laughed. His arm began to ache and his armpit chafe. Like this, Maria said, and showed him how. He felt his face burn with defeat. He squared his shoulders and crossed his hands against his stomach. *In the beginning God created the heavens and the earth—and the darkness was upon the face of the deep. And the spirit of God moved upon the face of the waters. And God said—*

"Enough," Elizabeth said. "You'll wear your tongue out."

Hendrick watched as Maria picked at a scab on her knee. He was fascinated and then repulsed when a stream of blood ran down her leg. He reached for his handkerchief just as Maria picked the crust free and put it in her mouth. "Show off," she said and stuck out her tongue, wiggling the black scab. He desperately wanted Maria to be his friend.

"And so what does your husband do?" Alma Harder asked his mother that day on the road.

"I.... He...." Elizabeth had stammered. Everyone in the town knew; she wasn't used to explaining.

"He's somewhere in Russia," she'd said at last. "I'm not sure where. The Red Cross is searching for him."

"He's dead," Hendrick had said.

Hendrick heard his mother's step on the church sidewalk. "I don't want to go to the Friesens'," he said. He lengthened his stride when he reached the gravel road. He brought his foot down, enjoying the sound of water splashing up and over his polished boot. A crow flapped up from a tree beside the road, cawing harshly.

"Well, so you've found your tongue at last," Elizabeth said. "It's a good thing, because I was beginning to get used to the peace and quiet."

"I'm not going."

"I already said that we would."

"Well, you go then."

Elizabeth stumbled as her foot slipped on the loose gravel. "Wait for me," she pleaded, and he turned to wait while she stooped to dab spatters of mud from her stockings. He looked down at the sharp pink line of her scalp, a cross dissecting her head where her hair was parted tightly into braids. When she straightened, she reached for him and dabbed a spatter of rain from his face. Over her shoulder, Hendrick saw the whitewashed church and the people filing from its front door and one by one, except for Alma Harder and old Mrs. Peter, they all turned and walked in the opposite direction. He saw movement at the church window. It was Jacob Friesen, he realized. He recognized that haystack of grey hair.

The floor in the church creaked as Lena skirted the aisles between the pews and each time she dropped a hymnal back into its place, the dull thud of it echoed in Jacob's head. He was cold and yet the whole of his chest and the spot between his shoulderblades had grown slick and clammy with sweat. Beyond, on the road, the boy Hendrick and Elizabeth were wavering images behind the glass. And beyond them, where the road curved slightly, the two Harder children, colourless stick figures, rounded the bend and were screened from view as they turned the corner and headed towards Ottawa Street. Jacob had seen Elizabeth stoop suddenly and dab at something on her legs. The movement was lithe and quick. He cursed the devil silently, commanding him to leave.

Lena pulled the drawstring of the bag that held the day's offering, closed it, and handed it to him. His fingers touched hers as he took it from her and their eyes met. He wanted to tell her that today he'd heard the voice of the devil. That the evil one had come to stand beside him in the pulpit.

"Here," Lena said and thrust a book into his hands. "One of the women said it might be helpful. It might give you some idea of how to tackle Hendrick this afternoon."

A Guide to a Christian's Growth towards Manhood. Jacob felt that his smile was forced as he thanked her and followed her from the church. As he pulled the door closed behind him and fit the key into its lock, the sound of the sparrow echoed in the building. Someone had thrown a rock through the window early in the fall. When the building was heated for service, the sparrow took shelter and nestled between the broken window and inner glass. They'd grown accustomed to the dry, fluttering sound announcing its arrival, and to the bird's song which accompanied their own. But today, as Jacob listened to the bird, he questioned whether it was always the same bird that visited them, because sparrows all tended to sound the same. Only the pitch and volume changed. Bright and happy. And he wondered then whether the birds were cursed or blessed because they had no choice but to sound always happy.

Hendrick and Elizabeth, turning, saw the elderly couple leave the church yard, and continued on their way.

"It's our duty to visit with them," Elizabeth said. "I think they're lonely people."

Hendrick felt a sudden push of the old anger return. "You hit me," he said. "In front of everyone, you hit me," he said, speaking for the first time of that thing which had entered their house and hung in the air all week.

"I spanked you," she said and sighed deeply. "I regret that. But there are some who would think it was long overdue."

"Why?"

"Let's say I lost my temper."

She urged him to take her by the arm and they continued to walk side by side, her coat brushing against the heavy wool fabric of his trousers, and the touch of it sealed the bond between them once again. He felt light-headed with relief. *He maketh my feet like hinds' feet, he setteth me upon my high places.*

"It's just that I can't stand changing that woman's bed," Elizabeth said. "It's the one thing I hate." She was lost in her thoughts and the boy knew that she'd spoken them aloud without thinking.

"So you spanked me?"

"There was more to it than that," she said.

"What then?"

"Never mind," she said. "There must be a few things left in this world for you to wonder about."

They turned the corner and entered Ottawa Street, going away from Main Street towards the river. The houses were reflected back to Hendrick in the water shimmering in the gully. Behind his house was an empty field and on the other side of it, the number 44 highway that crossed the bridge over the river and then climbed on up to St. Mary's Road, which, since Hendrick had come to the town of Agassiz with his mother, was the farthest he'd been outside of it. The Harder umbrella collapsed suddenly as Maria and Rick veered from the road and waded down into the gully.

"I waited for you last night," Hendrick said. "Hours."

She pulled him into her stride, but didn't answer.

Sometimes when his mother disappeared, he would pull a blanket from the bed, swaddle in it, and wait on the floor under the window. It was what he'd done last night. And he'd seen the Japanese, Taro Yamamoto, pass by wheeling a wheelbarrow. And, of course, he'd seen Minnie Pullman. Often, he and his mother would listen to the steady plodding of her galoshes on the road and he'd say, "There she goes." And Elizabeth would reply, "They say the Lord loves a fool."

And Hendrick had seen the woman, Alma Harder. He heard her at first, talking to herself. She was having an argument, raising questions and answering them and contradicting the answers. "Why aren't you in bed?" she'd asked, stopping suddenly in front of his house when she saw movement at the window. But he didn't answer because he wasn't speaking. Alma's eyes widened and her mouth opened in a sudden, surprised "O", as though she'd suddenly been punched in the stomach. Her arms fell to her sides and she turned and walked back to her house.

Hendrick awoke later to find himself back in bed. He had opened his eyes to the faint first light of Sunday breaking and the sound of water tinkling in a wash basin. His mother stood naked in the centre of the room, foot up on a chair, and water ran in a stream into the basin as she dipped a cloth into it and twisted it dry. He saw the cloth move amid that puff of hair between her legs. He pretended to sleep. Then she slid in beside him beneath the blankets, shivered, turned to face the room, and slept immediately.

Maria and Rick swept through the water with their feet, going back and forth. Then Maria rolled up her sleeve, plunged her arm into the water, and came up with a beer bottle.

"Those little Indians," Elizabeth said. "Just look at them. They're going to spoil their Sunday clothes." She started forward, arms swinging, oblivious now of the mud splashing up about her ankles. She stopped and came back, measuring each step with care.

"I think you're the one to tell them," she said. "You're older than they are. They should have to listen to you for once."

His throat went dry. *First John, 3, 12. Not as Cain, who was of that wicked one and slew his brother.* He felt his mother's hand at his back, pressing him forward.

"Their mother will thank you for it," Elizabeth said. Hendrick saw the hint of a smile in her eyes. He knew she wouldn't be smiling later. That after their visit with Jacob her eyes would become two embers sinking back into her head. He'd have to hang blankets over the windows to keep back the light. Put a slop bucket beside the bed to catch the vomit. Wring out rags and place them against her raging headache.

The Harder children stood knee deep, the ice-cold water inches from overflowing into their boots. Maria looked up in surprise and then, seeing Elizabeth, hid the beer bottle behind her back.

"My mother says to warn you that you're going to spoil your Sunday clothes," he said. His voice came out too high and unnatural. All about him, rain fell, dimpling puddles in the gullies where the children stood. The sound of it was like the sound of worms chewing leaves from trees. His eyes moved down from Maria's shoulders and flickered across those mounds, searching for the thrust of the acorn he'd felt in the centres. She dropped the beer bottle and brought her arms up to cover her chest.

She was different. Like he was. And Hendrick had followed the girl around that first summer. He lay in the grass in the field behind their house and watched her moving about the yard, jumping rope, pulling weeds from the garden. He whistled like a grasshopper. He cupped his hands and blew into a piece of grass and made a kazoo-like noise. He hooted like an owl and then he was a fox yapping. But she never seemed to notice.

He was an Indian scout, creeping among the trees beside the river, following Rick and Maria through the forest and ducking out of sight at the last moment, silent, never bending a twig or snapping any branches. He chattered at them, a squirrel, then the magpie's haughty sound, and waited, desperate for the first signal of friendship. He crouched behind a tall growth of nettle and cupped his hands and sang her name. But he never knew if she'd heard or answered because he'd slipped and fallen forward and grabbed at the nettles and he'd had to run home from the sting of them.

But unlike Hendrick, Maria was not compelled to be different and she shed it quickly. By the time school began, her brightly coloured skirts gave way to the more common dress of the other girls, the beads had vanished, and despite their different ways, Maria and Rick were accepted quickly at school. This acceptance had to do in part with the day when something sinister and black dropped down from a fresh shipment of bananas hanging from the ceiling in the Red and White. Maria chased the creature down and cornered, behind the potato sacks, what proved to be a large tarantula.

When Maria had stepped out on the road the first day of school, Hendrick was standing at the edge of his yard and waiting for her to pass. Further down Ottawa Street, Hendrick saw the diminutive figures of Rosella and Ginny Pullman, pale china figurines walking hand in hand, and behind them, the flash of Sandra Adam's red coat as she turned and waited for the heavy, plodding figure of Cindy Dorfman to catch up. He rehearsed what he'd say. Maria, he'd say, what has four legs and can't walk? Why are elephants grey? Maria, he'd say in a light-hearted tone as though he'd said it every morning for years, wait up Maria. I'll walk with you.

"Maria." His tongue felt heavy and swollen. Not a tongue, but a woollen sock.

She turned. "Genesis, Exodus, Leviticus, and Deuteronomy," she'd said. His mind went blank. He heard the words of scripture inside his head, a flood of strange language, words leap-frogging one overtop another, or sometimes a single word, a domino tumbling over and causing a chain reaction of myriads of dominoes, words, tumbling out and out and down and down, leaving his knees shaking, his back bathed in sweat. He stuck his fingers into his ears so he wouldn't have to listen.

"Weird," Maria had said. "You're weird." And went to school to brag about being neighbours to the boy Hendrick who had the amazing memory. She learned that first day not to refer to Hendrick's talent again. That largely, because it was not understood and was feared, it must be ignored.

"What business is it of hers, what I do or don't do?" Maria asked Hendrick, and swished her boots through the water so that he could see that she didn't care if it flooded them or not. "What makes you and your mother think you're so much better than us?"

Hendrick felt his mother's eyes on the back of his neck and then the dry heat of her breath against his neck as she came and stood behind him. "Did you tell them what I said?"

Hendrick turned on his mother suddenly, anger pushing against his skull. "Mama, leave me be," he said. He raised his hand as though he intended to strike her. Elizabeth winced, stepped back, a look of shock on her face. Between the fingers of his raised hand, he saw cracks of grey daylight and he squeezed the light out and let his hand fall to his side. He turned from his mother as she walked away from him, surprised by the force of his words and their effect.

Maria jostled the bottle from hand to hand. "Enrico Schlitz," she said. "Why do you think your shit doesn't stink? Just because you can recite the Bible doesn't make you any different. You're just like all the other boys."

The boys had begun to write about Maria Harder on the washroom walls. Some said that Maria had gone inside the boy's washroom and written on the walls herself. That once she'd lifted her skirt and shown her twat to them. One of the older boys had strolled through the hallway saying, "Smell my new girlfriend," and shoving his finger beneath the noses of the other boys. "Maria," he said with a swaggering confidence which vanished to a sense of injury and bewilderment when he found both his bicycle tires slashed to ribbons with a carpet knife. But oh, they were just a bunch of pups, grabbing onto and humping any passing leg, dry runs as it were and harmless.

"You're a bloody stool pigeon," Hendrick said.

"I don't know what you're talking about," she said. She flung the bottle and it arched up over a clump of bushes. Knobby branches pinged against the side of it as it fell through and bounced against the hard ground.

"Go home, Hendrick sauerkraut," Rick's thin voice bleated up from the gully. "Go home and sleep with your mommy."

For a moment, it appeared as though Maria might jump on Rick and beat him. But then she smiled at Hendrick and said, "Yes, baby, go home and suck your mommy's titty."

It was as though a fist had slammed into Hendrick's chest.

"Well, you do sleep with her," Maria said. "Everyone knows."

"Hendrick fucks his mother," Rick chanted. "Hendrick fucks his mother. Hend—" he began once again, but was jolted into silence when Maria punched him between the shoulder blades.

The words leapt forward and froze all motion for several moments. Hendrick saw the boy's mouth move. He heard the words. But the meaning only became clear in their echo inside his head. He ran to catch up with his mother. He reached and grabbed a fistful of her coat to make her slow down.

"You raised your hand against me," Elizabeth spat out the words. And then she saw his face. "What is it?" she asked. "What did that girl say?"

Hendrick reached for her hands. The knuckles were chapped from cleaning their houses. He felt the heat of his mouth against the roughness of her skin.

"Mama," he said. "I hate this place."

"What did she say? Tell me. Did she say something about me that upset you?"

"I hate this place." His voice echoed among the trees that lined the river.

"Quiet," she said. "They'll hear you. Now tell me, what did that girl say?"

"There must be some things left in this world for you to wonder about," Hendrick said in English.

Elizabeth stood for a moment and stared after the boy as he walked on ahead of her. "Hendrick," she called, as he passed by the turn-off to their house, his shoulders squared and determined. "Hendrick."

"I hate this place," he said. "I'm leaving."

"Child!"

His shoulders slumped forward as he stopped and turned. He plunged his hands deep into his pockets and bent forward at the waist as he walked towards her. "As soon as I can, I'm leaving," he said.

Elizabeth patted him on the shoulder as he stepped across the boards which Jacob Friesen had brought to lay across the water. "We'll write another letter today," she said. "Maybe there's some new information."

It was useless, the boy thought. Sometimes he believed that his mother had made up the story about his father, a German soldier missing in action in Russia, and had grown to believe it. There were never any replies to her letters. The boards wobbled beneath his weight. He turned and waited for her.

"I'm sorry," he said, and hated the sound of that word immediately. I'm sorry, he'd say when Jacob Friesen confronted him. I'm sorry, sorry, sorry, he'd say to his mother while he sat at her side and laid rags across her forehead. I'm sorry, he felt he should say to the whole church. I don't think there's a reason for my gift at all. So stop looking at me. I'm sorry, he would like to say to Jacob Friesen this afternoon. I don't think God even likes me.

"There's nothing to be sorry about," Elizabeth said and patted his cheek. "There's enough being sorry and unhappiness in this place to last the whole world a lifetime."

"Then why do we stay?"

"Go and bring in some wood and I'll fire up the stove and we'll have something hot to eat."

"Why?"

"Well," she said as she entered the house, "so far it's not a strong enough reason to make me want to leave."

Hendrick went out behind the house where the woodpile leaned against the fence. Letters were useless, he thought. He stacked wood against his chest until the rough bark of it scraped against his chin and the muscles in his arms ached, working against the temptation to go out into the field where he knew he'd see the ground festering, pustules of spittle bubbling from tiny pink mouths. He heard the groan of a pump handle and looked across the yard and saw Rick Harder. He wanted to swing hard with his fist and feel glass shattering, feel the pain of his knuckles splitting open and running warm with blood. *These also are the chief of the mighty men whom David had, who strengthened themselves with him in his kingdom, and with all Israel, to make him king and—this is the number of mighty men—and after him—and they set themselves—* Rain beaded his hair and dropped onto his shoulders. *Now three of the thirty captains went down to the rock to David into the cave of Adullam—* The muscles in his arms hurt with the weight of the wood while he gasped to hold back the flood rising inside his chest. He heard a noise behind him. A soft whistling sound. He turned. The wood tumbled from his arms at the sight of Katie. The dog had crept up on him and wasn't more than three feet away. Hendrick dropped to his knees and held out his hand. Slowly Katie's tail fluttered and she dipped her head down into the weeds and raised it again, jostling something between her jaws. Hendrick saw the rat's tail first, faintly pink and raw-looking beneath grey fur, and then the limp carcass held firmly between Katie's teeth. She wheeled and loped steadily across the field. He stacked the firewood in his arms and watched as she disappeared behind a sagging barn. He waited for the dog to emerge from the other side. He waited several minutes. He realized that the dog was still there. That Katie had slunk back down onto her belly and waited for him.

"Hendrick sucks his mother's titty," Rick chanted softly from his yard.

Also the valiant men of the armies were Asahel the brother of Joab, Elhanan, the son of Dodo of Bethlehem—

"Hendrick sucks his mother's titty."

And Abishai the brother of Joab— No, he thought, and stopped reciting. He watched as Rick teetered along the boards across the gully. The boy walked down the road, beating the ground with a stick. Quietly, Hendrick eased the wood from his arms and followed.

10

When Minnie stepped into the yard, it was to the sound of Ginny's smooth touch at the piano and Johann Kirnberger's simple lullaby beating out, steady and sure. Albert's petunias, their starry throats washed clean by the rain, shone as the sun pressed through the thin clouds and two hummingbirds, their iridescent bodies suspended on invisible wings, dipped their beaks and drank. Ginny's music was a welcoming sound, warm, after a night of wandering. She felt lightheaded and off balance from lack of sleep, but there was no way around it if Albert wouldn't take her seriously. If she was not going to have sex with Albert any more she'd have to keep moving at night and sleep during the day.

She leaned into the side of the house for a moment, crossed her arms, and closed her eyes. Ta da da da da da tum, ta da da da da da tum tum. A tawny calico cat entered the back of the yard and the hummingbirds skittered up and across the side of the house. The cat stopped, blinked at Minnie, and then padded through the patch of phlox, across old bones and shards of a clay pot and the crumbling leather of a porcupine roach buried in the mound.

Minnie tugged at the door and heard the hook rattle inside its loop.

"Albert?"

The music stopped.

"Ma?" It was Rosella's voice at the playroom window.

Minnie backed into the garden and looked up. "Hurry," she said. "My teeth are chattering."

Rosella crossed her arms against her flat chest.

"Be a good girl and unlatch the door," Minnie said.

"No," Rosella said.

"Oh. Is there a password?" Minnie asked and then heard the muffled, sniffling sounds Ginny made. "Is something the matter with your sister?"

"She's fine," Rosella said. "I'm fine. Albert's fine."

"Well, good. But why is Ginny crying?"

"Because you're an embarrassment to the universe, that's why."

"That's not the truth," Ginny said. "Don't lie."

"Where's your father?"

"He's not here."

"Rosella, come down and open that door," Minnie said. "I'll tell you a story if you do."

"Another tall story," Rosella said. "What can I say?" And then she slowly drew the blind, shutting Minnie out.

Minnie went through the garden into the shed and pulled down the axe and a burlap sack waiting in place for Katie's next litter of indiscrimination.

The muscles in Minnie's calves tightened as she descended the hill that led to the river. The axe inside the sack nudged against her spine as she stooped, parted the willow branches, and stepped down onto the narrow path that cut through the trees and down to the river. She would miss those girls, their little warm bodies which were like round balls, a presence that seemed to roll away from her just as she reached to touch them. She'd miss the sight of a mousy blonde pigtail shifting suddenly across a narrow back. Those girls of hers, they had somehow found a crack and slipped on through.

Beside the path, flies buzzed above a heap of rotting garbage. And beyond the path, among the trees, the litter of spent car batteries, tires, and discarded household appliances spread out among the toadstools, wild rhubarb, and bushes of nettles. Branches pulled at Minnie's hair as she bent and stepped out onto the river's bank. Large birds wheeled above the trees on the opposite shore. They glided silently towards her, following the green curve of the river's path. Their wings teetered slightly as they passed overhead, as though they were signalling the knowledge of her presence below them. A branch snapped, and Annie stepped down beside Minnie. "I saw you pass by," she said.

"What do you make of that?" Minnie said, as the pelicans wheeled in a half circle and began their approach once more. They could hear the wind in their wings as they passed overhead and this time disappeared.

"Could be lost," Annie said.

"Could be that they're waiting for the water," Minnie said.

"You're out and about early," Annie said.

"I've been locked out, it seems."

"It's come to that, has it?"

"Rosella."

"Well," Annie said, "a fine pickle. I'll be right back," she said. She began to head up the path. "If you're going to camp out you'll need...." Her voice was shut out by the sudden whine of the town's siren from the firehall. She came back and grabbed Minnie by the arm. "A fire," she said.

The siren climbed to its full wail, reached its highest point, and held it for several moments. The sound circled, came back on itself and echoed, a sound turning within a sound. It dropped, died, and once again rose.

"Not a fire," Minnie said.

"What then?"

"A missing child."

When a child went missing in the town of Agassiz, news of it would spread like a fire and sweep through the streets. The women would run from their houses still wearing their aprons and call for the missing child. But seldom was anyone lost for longer than an hour and usually it amounted to nothing more than a child having taken a wrong turn on the road—a matter of heading east instead of west. Or a child, feeling the heat of summer and without its mother's knowledge, had dragged a blanket out into a corner of a yard and, lulled by the buzz of flies and humidity and feeling safe in a nest of uncut grass, had fallen asleep. The discovery of such a child, sometimes forlorn and crying but usually blissfully ignorant of its state, brought intense joy to the women for several moments afterward because the hole which had opened up in the air when a child went missing had been filled in once again.

There had been several other incidents of missing children before now. A few in the town could remember vaguely an incident of a missing girl. Belonging to gypsies, it was rumoured, or to low-life carnival people who used to come and go each summer with the fair, parking their trailers and cabanas in the field beside the fairgrounds and pulling out again a week later. But the memory of this incident had almost faded and had become a story which the women used to warn their children against straying. A kind of bogeyman story. The other incidents of missing children were of children who had gone as far as the town's outer borders. They recalled, as they searched the streets for Hendrick, that he'd been one of those. That he'd been the first and the youngest to get that far. He'd only been seven years old at the time. He'd wandered away and a farmer on his way into town for supplies had been passing by Horseshoe Lake and had seen the boy crouching beside the road, almost hidden by cattails. He'd had to chase Hendrick down to bring him back, he'd said, and his pant legs were stuck with burrs to prove it.

The boy said he'd been going downtown to mail a letter when he got lost. He still carried it in his pocket. But what was he doing way over on the other side of town, the opposite side from the post office? Taking the long way, Hendrick had said and it became the joke of the town for a year or so. Whenever anyone was late home or delayed for a meeting, it was said that they'd taken the long way.

The women had hugged the boy and then led him down the street to Jacob and left it up to him to impress upon the seat of Hendrick's pants the dangers of wandering. They warned him as well. That the next time, the Indians might cart him off and put him to work on the reservation in their moccasin factory and he'd never see his mother again. Like the missing child story, they told this story in jest— a bogeyman story. They didn't see any harm in instilling a wariness of these dark rovers. They themselves looked over their shoulders twice and locked their doors whenever a dusty, gaudily dressed band of Indians straggled into town.

No one had ever gone missing in winter and no one had ever run away before Hendrick Schultz. He'd been seen on the bridge, someone said. Someone else said an entirely different direction, heading away from the town. But it was Joe Harder who had alerted them to the seriousness of the situation.

"Some fool kid was rafting on the river," he'd said to Alma. The door swung closed behind him, almost catching him in the back of the knees. When he was surrounded by the chrome and steel of the hotel kitchen—Alma's domain— he felt that he should take off his boots. Alma stood at the counter and a knife flashed as she trimmed pastry from the lip of a pie.

"Seems the Golden Prince is missing," she said. "The women came asking about him earlier." The knife zinged around the edge of the metal pie plate. "Got a guilty conscience about the monkey business with Maria and took off."

The cigarette wobbled between Joe's lips. His face went stiff the way it happened sometimes when he'd be sitting at the table, coffee cup raised, about to drink, and he'd see Elizabeth pass by. He thought about Maria and monkey business and that the girl was growing wild and then a line of Scripture about the sins of the father skipped across his mind like a flat stone and he let it drop beneath the surface. He wished he hadn't stopped off with the news. That instead he'd gone straight home as he'd intended, to stretch out in bed and recall Saturday night. How he'd been coming back from Taro Yamamoto's place where they'd sealed their usual bargain for the coming season of goldeye with a glass of saki. On Saturday night he'd been whistling, thinking of all the hot evenings in store for him once summer became more entrenched and predictable, when it would slide over him, the hot evening of summer, too quickly, but nevertheless, the silver waters of those hot nights, when he would lie with Elizabeth, would part for him, thick and slippery like mercury, and then he would swim through them slowly, lazily, stretching them out until she'd laugh and beg him to stop saying she'd be sore in the morning. And Saturday, while walking home from Taro's place, Joe had seen the first of his summer signals. Elizabeth's blanket swaying from the clothesline.

"Well, if Hendrick was out on a raft, he's more than missing," Joe said and instantly felt shamed by the surge of relief he felt. But as the boy grew older and needed less sleep it became more and more difficult to meet. And Hendrick was Elizabeth's sun and moon.

"And wouldn't that be convenient?" Alma said.

Joe turned away from the bitterness which drew her mouth down at the corners. "Coward," she said, her voice a hard slap against his back.

Joe pushed out into the day at the word "coward", before she said what she knew.

"You're not going to help look for that boy," Alma said, as the door closed behind him. "Not after what he did to Maria. Go home and look after your own," she said, her voice cut off by the heavy door.

Alma stood for several moments behind the closed door, a pie held in mid-air. Her instinct was to heave it. But she'd be short of pies tomorrow if she did and would have to mix up a single batch to make up for it. So she set the pie down carefully beside all the others on the butcher block. Then she ran water and soap into the sink and dropped bowls and the blades of the pastry-cutter down into it. She swept a cloud of flour from the floor. Then the wooden stool cracked beneath the weight of her dimpled, ample buttocks. She pulled the handkerchief loose from her breast pocket, the one she carried for the times she peeled onions, and cried into it. Her cries grew and grew until they became the sound of outrage. She threw the handkerchief to the floor, grabbed the paring knife from the butcher block, and brought it down hard into an apple, twisting it until white pulp and apple juice spattered the front of her uniform.

Joe had hurried on over to the firehall and it had been his finger on the alarm sending the siren climbing for the second time. Its wail echoed in the cinder-block building. The walls of the building had been painted flat green but moisture and lethargy had done their work and where the paint hadn't peeled, it had faded. The run-down condition of the place was an invitation to the children of the town to scrawl their messages on the walls.

The door opened and Jacob Friesen stepped inside.

"I saw a piece of raft on the river," Joe Harder explained. "Upside down. I hear Elizabeth's boy is missing."

"Yes," Jacob said. "Soon after church. We have been scouting the streets, looking. It's time for an honest effort to find him."

They waited in silence for whoever was inclined to aid in the search to arrive. The door opened and several husbands of women in Jacob's congregation entered. Filing in behind them were several men whom Jacob knew by name only. He nodded a stiff greeting and turned to read the writing on the wall. "Here I sit in murky vapour, god-damned toilet has no paper...." He turned from the words quickly, without finishing, and saw the hint of amusement on several of the men's faces. Overhead, water pipes gurgled and moisture dripped from them, spattering against the concrete floor.

"M.H. fucks like a monkey." Joe read one of the messages scrawled on a pipe overhead, and frowned.

Jacob was glad now that he'd forbidden Hendrick to loiter about this place. When he and Lena went over and over the same ground, the reasons why so many of the women's husbands had begun to sleep in on Sunday mornings or work their fields instead of coming to church, they could never come up with a clear answer. Even the sons balked at attending as well, and few, except for Hendrick, came after the age of twelve. Lena had suggested that maybe Jacob should begin to preach in English. But Jacob rejected the idea as being unfair to Elizabeth. No, Jacob kept reaching back to the year the highway came to town, connecting them with the city. Changes came with the highway, like the truckloads of Texas watermelons, huge striped fruit, sweet and juicy, spilling from the backs of those trucks. But the seeds of the fruit had somehow been treated on the vine so that no matter how hard they tried they couldn't coax a single Texas watermelon to grow.

The sound of the siren dropped down to a low growl and climbed for the third time. Its sound vibrated in the floor and Jacob felt the buzz of it through the soles of his shoes. Today was the day, he realized, when God would take this occurrence and use it for his divine purpose. What had happened in his church had been insidious and gradual. It was clear—the effect of the highway—in this building alone. The children whose parents took them into the city came back disgruntled, filled with garbage ideas which were satisfying for the moment and then discarded. It left them frustrated, kicking holes into walls and writing out their vicious sayings. The wail of the siren grew suddenly louder as the firehall door opened and several more men stepped inside.

"I know in my heart that Hendrick is safe," Jacob had told Elizabeth when she'd come flying in through the gate with the news that the boy hadn't come in for lunch. She said she was certain Maria Harder was behind it. That Hendrick had stopped to talk to the girl and she'd noticed how upset he was afterwards. "Please," Elizabeth said, her eyes darting with worry, "send someone to speak to Maria. I must know." And so, Jacob, seeing the tension creeping into her eyes, sent Lena home with her and then asked several of the other women to go over to the Harder household. From there, they were to go to the church and pray for the missing child.

Wouldn't life be a bowl of cherries, Lena thought as she hung blankets over Elizabeth's windows to stem the light, if they could all just crawl into bed the moment anything unpleasant happened. Wouldn't that just be wonderful.

Maria Harder opened the door and let the women in. Alma seemed surprised to see them. "Well," she said when Maria showed them into the living room. "Go and have a look, will you—there must be a blue moon." She was clad in an underslip only and had one foot up on a stool. Her uniform hung from a hanger in the doorway and they had to stoop beneath it as they stepped into the room. The speeches, questions the women had rehearsed on the way over, scattered. Trees grew in wooden tubs set on the floor all about the room. The height of them reached halfway up the wall. Their glossy leaves were tongue-shaped and cast a lacy shadow against the pink walls behind them. As the women stepped into the confusion of colour, they were enveloped by a heavy sweet odour. Like the waxy smell of a funeral, someone said later. A hint of decay among the flowers. But it was only the smell of the sticky syrup coating thick clusters of pink and purple hyacinth set among the trees on overturned crates. Beside them, nodding from long slender tubes, were deep-throated amaryllis, reaching up through the trees like scarlet-feathered birds.

"You caught me getting ready for work," Alma said. She quickly began to roll a stocking up over swollen toes which were blueish-looking and separated one from another by bits of cotton wool jammed between them. "Citrus," she said, as she stepped into her white hotel uniform and slid it up over her hips. "I grew them myself." The women turned from the sight of her heavy pear-shaped hips and melon-shaped belly. For the most part, they themselves were small women, dainty hands and feet, given later in life to spreading across the buttocks and adding inches to bosoms. And so the woman's large bony hands and feet and the width of her shoulders were unusual. The frame of a work horse, they said, and that it was just as well, because poverty would probably walk by her side the rest of her life. And so the room startled them because it jarred with what they'd assumed about her. A woman who spent more time out of her home than inside it—who let her children run free with a house key dangling from their necks on a string, who smelled strongly of perspiration and onions, and who had come from Mexico—would be slovenly. They didn't need to verify this assumption.

"Rub the leaves," Alma told them. "You can tell what kind of citrus by the smell that comes off." They seemed reluctant, almost shy to do this and so she showed them how and made them smell their fingers to see whether the tree was lemon or orange. Goodness, the women said. They hadn't realized that it was so long since the last time they'd visited. "About five years," Alma said and turned from them quickly while she fussed with a handkerchief in her breast pocket. "The week we came here from Mexico." Well, they said, thinking how like the woman to try and pin them against the wall. But they mutually and silently agreed that they shouldn't rush into anything about Hendrick missing and the girl. They sat down instead on the edge of the turquoise couch and fingered the brightly flowered slipcover. The room felt steamy and lush and tropical and they expected to see monkeys swing down from the trees. Inwardly, they fought and railed against the short growing season and looked for ways to hang onto green things throughout the winter and add some colour to that bleak white landscape which stretched time to the outer limits. But this growing of actual trees inside the house seemed excessive to them, almost unnatural. If she wants a jungle in her house, why doesn't she go back to the one she came from, they said later.

Maria sat down on the floor and gathered her skirts up beneath her. She rested her pointed little chin against her knees and leaned against the wall, almost hidden by the foliage of trees. She studied the women with her sharp quick eyes when they weren't looking. When they were, she seemed unconcerned and chipped away at the nail polish on her toenails. Alma tugged at the hem of her uniform but it failed to conceal the hem of her underslip. "They don't make these things long enough," she said and laughed, almost shyly, and offered to make them a cup of Russian tea.

"They didn't come here for tea," Maria said. "King shit from turd island is missing and they somehow would like to pin the blame onto me."

Elizabeth heard the siren and reared up in bed, eyes wide and haunted looking. Had the women returned from the Harder household yet? Did Lena have any idea at all what Maria had said to Hendrick to make him so upset? She wrung her hands and cried and Lena had to take her by the shoulders and push her back into the pillows and remind her that the tension of tears would only serve to make the pain in her head worse. That they had learned very little from Maria in any case, nothing which would give them any clues about where the boy might be.

"But it can't be six o'clock already," Elizabeth said. "He'll be hungry. Look, his lunch. It still sits, accusing me."

"Now, now," Lena said and was almost going to tell her not to be so sensitive. She couldn't tell Elizabeth that it was already past six and in between the supper-hour siren and the nine o'clock curfew warning and that seven and a half hours had passed since they'd spread out through the streets calling for Hendrick. The sound of the siren died and then climbed for the third time. Elizabeth pushed Lena's hands from her shoulders and swept back the blankets as though she were going to get up and run from the house, but nausea claimed her and she leaned over the side of the bed and retched into the pail beside it. Lena wrung out a cloth and wiped the woman's mouth and then rinsed the cloth and set it against her forehead. Elizabeth closed her eyes and once again drifted into the pain. "Oh Lord," she whispered. "It's hell having to live with a nail in the heart."

Lena's own heart lurched with those words. Nail in the heart. Dogs hanging from doorways. Jacob's unusual story told in place of his sermon that morning. A picture of Christ hung above Elizabeth's bed, tilted down so that it seemed to hover in the air. The sepia-coloured Christ didn't look into the room but off to one side instead, as though he didn't want to look at her. The clock ticked on the windowsill, its sound making Lena suddenly feel isolated, cut off, and totally alone the way it happened when Jacob was out in the garage working on his sermons. She would stand outside the door, hand raised, thinking what she would ask of him before she knocked. Or the way it was when she needed to wash her hair but could not stoop over the basin with her back turned to the room because of the fear which would sneak up behind her and poke its index finger into her spine, or stand poised about to brush the back of her neck and so she would have to call out for Jacob, that she needed another pail of water, that she needed wood for the fire, or some such excuse so she wouldn't be alone. She peeled the cloth from Elizabeth's forehead, amazed that it had already grown hot. Elizabeth muttered and groaned but didn't open her eyes and Lena saw that she slept. The ticking of the clock grew louder, overwhelming all other sounds, and so she got up, slid a folded blanket from the foot of the bed, and wrapped the clock in a bundle and set it on the floor. She turned to face the room. When she sat back down, she was aware that her palms were sweating, her throat parched, but she didn't reach for the glass of water on the apple box beside the bed. The windowpane behind her cracked sharply and then it seemed that she could hear footsteps, a faint, soft noise of someone standing just outside the door. She could hear the creak of bones. "The Lord is my shepherd," she recited silently, "I shall not want." The chair was hard and her tailbone ached. She felt the pressure of the fried potato and blood sausage lunch push against the belt of her dress. "He maketh me to lie down in green pastures." Some of the fear began to subside. Gas pinged deep inside her guts. She rubbed her belly. The overhead light reflected in the glass of the picture of Christ and she saw herself. Her face was even wider in the distorted reflection, bloated looking and a sickly false smile turned up the corners of her mouth. Was this what the others saw when they looked at her? She reached up, pulled the light chain and the room became dark. She went over to the window and, one by one, pulled the blankets free, not wanting the light and not wanting total darkness either. Then she went over to the table at the farthest end of the room and picked up the breadknife and set it on the floor beside her chair.

The women at the church had arranged their chairs into the accustomed circle. The grey walls reflected with a soft sheen, the light coming from a bulb suspended from the ceiling. The light reflected in the eyes of the Good Shepherd and on his hand, which reached down into a bramble bush to rescue the single lost lamb. The sound of the siren was a sobering one; it drew their thoughts inwards as they waited.

"Where's Ollie Peter and her mother?" someone asked, but Hilda Penner held up her hand for attention.

"I have something to say," Hilda said. "And it's going to sound like a complete and total lack of faith, but I have to say it. When Hendrick disappeared like that after church, well, for a moment, I thought he'd been taken."

"Kidnapped?" someone asked, thinking about Indians or strangers passing through on the highway.

"No," Hilda said and laughed self-consciously. She worked busily at pushing the cuticles back on her fingernails and they winced with the way she showed no mercy, scraping and pushing with her thumbnail at the tight band of white tissue.

"People from another planet?" The women laughed nervously. From time to time there had been sightings of strange things in the sky. A case of two moons once. A case of reflection. Over the years, several among them had been out walking at night and had looked up and seen a silent string of lights pass across the sky in the shape of a V. They didn't speak about it and kept their heads down when they walked at night because they didn't want to see any apparition the devil might conjure as supposed evidence of life in another galaxy. They knew from Scripture that it was entirely possible for him to do so because he ruled the air above their heads. And wouldn't the devil just love to have them look up and begin to question and doubt the mystery of being the apple of God's eye in the universe?

The door opened. "Carried off by a horde of monkeys?" Alma Harder said as she stepped into the vestibule. She'd been coming home from the hotel and had seen the light on in the church. Could she join them or was the prayer circle closed? Did she, in their opinion, smell okay?

"Now, now, don't be so sensitive," Hilda said, mimicking Lena Friesen, and the other women laughed and moved their chairs to allow one more. One of the women patted Alma on the knee and said that she would like a slip from one of those trees she grew in the house. Alma was going to explain that they wouldn't start from a slip, and that she soaked the seeds in a bit of toilet tissue in a shallow dish of water, but that she did know of a method of cutting into the plant and packing the wound with peat moss so the branch would begin to send out roots, when Hilda cleared her throat and said they should remember, please, that this was a serious time and would the person in charge of the prayer record please take it out, and then she continued on with what she'd been saying.

"No, I was thinking," Hilda said, "about the story the pastor told in church this morning."

"Ahh," the women sighed in unison, that strange story. Jacob's sermons were not what they used to be. This was something they could pray about and so the woman took out the prayer record from her handbag. It was a green notebook filled with their weekly requests. Praying was much like doing housework: it was too easy to think that nothing had been accomplished unless you kept a record. And like housework, where you repeated the same chores over and over, you had to keep praying for the same things over and over. "The pastor's health," the woman wrote, "for strength to preach a good sermon."

"And I was thinking, as I was remembering his story," Hilda said, "about unconfessed sin."

The women glanced at one another warily.

"It's easy for you to think about unconfessed sin," Alma said and laughed, "but I can't, because I don't have any."

Whatever newly formed charitable feelings they'd convinced themselves to feel for the woman fled. The kindest reaction would be to ignore her, as usual. If any man says he's without sin, they reminded themselves, the truth isn't in him and he's a liar. Their wariness was replaced then with an urgent desire to search their hearts for unconfessed sin.

"When Hendrick disappeared, well, I was at the house," Hilda said. "I saw that pile of wood beside the door. And there wasn't even a boot mark in the dirt, nothing to show that he'd walked away from the house. It was raining, you know— you'd think there would be a mark. And for a moment, I thought that maybe the Lord had come. That he'd caught Hendrick to be with him and I'd been left behind."

She had voiced their secret, innermost fear. They had all from time to time been standing at the sink or crawling beneath a bed looking for a missing shoe and heard the whistle of a train or a child walking by on the road practising his trumpet and thought that it was the sound of the Lord returning and had stood there, waiting and waiting to be snatched up to him. Or they had witnessed a strange cloud formation on the horizon at night and tiptoed through the rooms of their houses peeling back blankets in cribs and beds, seeking reassurance in the presence of their sleeping children that they had not been overlooked.

"But when I saw all the people out looking for Hendrick, I knew it wasn't so," Hilda said, "because there were little kids there, younger than Hendrick. Just as innocent," she said.

"Hendrick is past the age of innocence," someone said. "Lena said it happens around the age of twelve."

"Well," Hilda said and fiddled with her fingernails. Although she'd never say it out loud, she sometimes thought they were far too certain about how things worked. That when she said her prayers at night, she sometimes prayed that there would be surprises in heaven. She'd asked the pastor once if he thought a Roman Catholic might get into heaven, and he'd said that it was impossible to know the heart of a man. Who could know what a man thought the moment he died? And so, it was possible.

They heard a rustle in the sanctuary and leaned forward, fear bristling outwards in a halo from the circle of chairs. The sound was dry, like autumn leaves stirring against a sidewalk. And then they heard the faint chirrup of the sparrow and they smiled at one another and drew their chairs in closer.

"I have a confession to make," Hilda said. She began to rub her eyes with her knuckles. She stood up then and folded her hands across her abdomen. They knew about Hilda Penner's confessions. They usually amounted to a hill of beans. She'd confess impatience with her slovenly husband who insisted on honking his horn on the sleeve of his shirt, or brought manure into the kitchen on his boots. It was going to be a long night.

"I think we should really pray for Hendrick now," someone said, reminding them why they had assembled. The woman with the prayer record wrote down the boy's name. "Missing," she wrote. "Safety." But they noticed how Hilda's dress shook and that her knuckles had turned white and so the woman closed the notebook and slid it back into her purse.

"I was once responsible for the death of a child," Hilda said. "That's why I've never had any." The women's faces paled and they held their breath high up in their chests, grabbing shallow gulps of air so as not to overshadow anything Hilda said with the sound of their own breathing. The sparrow twittered and then fell silent as well. She'd only been twelve years old when her parents sent her to work for a young couple who had just bought a piece of land from her father and had begun to farm it. She hadn't wanted to stop going to school and she'd been peeved about this. Several other times her parents had farmed her out to someone for housework, and you know how it is, she said, how children concoct fake illness or spend the day playing in the trees beside the river, rather than going to school? Well, she had played hooky from work and gone to school instead and her father would come with the team and drag her off. But this farm was close enough for her father to keep watch and her brother dropped her off every morning and didn't leave until he saw that she'd gone inside the house. But the work turned out to be pleasant, she said, because the couple had a baby girl.

Her voice shook at this point but then she grew determined and lifted her sharp chin and her voice became stronger. She stared straight ahead, trance-like, and began to recite the story to them in an almost musical way. She described the great beauty of the child and of its nature. The language she used was exquisite and lyrical, like the poetry of the psalms, which drew them in and made them see the blush of the child's cheeks and feel its chubby arms wound about their necks.

"The parents said I spoiled her," Hilda said, "and it's true. I found it hard to deny her anything. But they were glad to have her out of their hair and to be free for once to do the chores without needing to wheel her about the yard with them in the wheelbarrow any more. I dressed her and undressed her and combed her hair. At night, I cut apart my own dresses and hand-stitched garments for her to wear. The parents said I could do what I wanted but there were only two things I was not to allow the child to have and those were peanuts and watermelon."

"And you did," someone said.

"I was slicing watermelon for their noon meal and she was sitting on the floor and kept reaching for it."

"And so you gave her a piece." They wondered where this was leading.

"Several pieces," Hilda said. She had to tell the whole truth. Now that she'd started, there was no sense in going half way with the confession. She told them how the child cried for more after she'd eaten the first piece of watermelon and so she'd given her another and another.

"Many, many pieces," she said. "I don't know to this day what got into me. But she kept crying and begging for more and before I realized what I was doing, I was on my knees on the floor beside her, pushing pieces of watermelon into her mouth until she gagged." She shook so badly that her knees gave way and she had to reach for the chair behind her and sit down. She turned her back to the women and rested her forehead against the chair. The women looked down at the floor, up at the ceiling, wiped bits of tears forming in their eyes. Even Alma Harder remained silent and stared at a spot on the wall, never thinking that Elizabeth was slipping in her cleaning of the church. Forgetting for a moment that she hated the woman.

"And so the baby girl choked?" someone asked in a whisper.

Hilda swivelled about in the chair to face the circle. She looked smaller, as though telling the story had deflated her. She took off her glasses and laid them in her lap. "During the night," she said. Apparently, during the night, the child cried and cried with stomach pains until the parents, facing the prospect of milking the cows and the sun rising before they'd had a single hour of sleep, closed their ears to the child's cries.

"The girl vomited and choked on it," Hilda said, her voice flat and dead.

The parents waited for Hilda the following morning. She'd passed by the barn and was surprised not to see them on stools, leaning into the side of a cow, or to see the little girl on a blanket in the straw, holding her arms up to be carried. Instead, the woman sat at the kitchen table and the man stood behind her with his hands on her shoulders. Upstairs, he said and jerked with his head towards the stairwell that led to the attic room where the child slept. And be sure to look in the cradle, he said, which, she told the women, she thought was strange because where else could the child be?

She stepped into the room and immediately knew something was wrong. The cradle was empty. And then she smelled something sickly and sweet and saw the pool of vomit among the sheets, speckled with black watermelon seeds and undigested rind. She turned and saw the box. He must have been working like a demon, she said, because already he'd made a wooden box and when she turned, she saw it set up between two chairs and the little girl inside it, her hair combed just so, so that the curls stood straight up and the sun shining through the tiny window near the ceiling spun her hair into gold.

"I knew the little girl was dead," Hilda said. "But even so, I couldn't believe it. And so I stepped up close to the box to see if her chest moved. And something ran across the child's dress," she said. "Something grey. It must have been a mouse, because I noticed then that the little girl's eyelashes had been chewed right off."

They gasped and nausea clutched at their stomachs.

"Huh," Alma Harder said, as though she resented this part of the story. "Don't tell me you've been blaming yourself all this time. It was the little girl's time to go, that's all."

"Oh, I know, I know," Hilda said. "But where does that leave me?"

Lena Friesen sat facing Elizabeth's room and listening to the muffled tick of the clock in the bundle at her feet. Elizabeth's twitching and moaning decreased and then ceased altogether as she fell deeper into sleep. "The Lord is my shepherd," Lena recited. Even though I walk in the valley of the shadow of death. Jammed behind the picture of Christ was a palm branch tied with a bit of red wool. It was the only attempt at adornment in the room. Beside the bed, covering the rough boards, was a braided rag mat, washed so many times that the rags had become frayed and the colours bled together. She looked up, surprised to see a spider web in one corner near the ceiling. The whole room had a feeling of impermanence. Of a summer holiday cottage and not a house. Beneath the window rested the treadle sewing machine she'd given Elizabeth, its peeling veneer covered partially with a star-shaped doily. It was as though she saw the one-room house they'd built and furnished for Elizabeth and Hendrick for the first time: the bed with its sagging mattress, metal posts once painted white but now chipped with marks like teeth marks along the top railing. Hilda Penner's husband had rescued it from the nuisance grounds. Her intestines sang and crawled with gas and she feared that if she didn't get some relief her bones would fly apart. She picked up the knife at her feet and the slop bucket and tiptoed across the room. She placed her ear against the door and listened, hearing only the soft backwash of the night lapping up its hardwood grain.

She stepped outside onto the platform and felt the boards sag beneath her weight. The fear had stayed behind in the house and she felt better now as she stood for a moment looking across the flat field behind the house. Above it, a V formation of lights slid silently towards the horizon. She looked away. It brought to her mind the foolish notion, appealing only to those without sound beliefs, that when a child died its soul became a star in the heavens. It was a strange idea, a cold thought, she told herself as she swung the bucket, emptying its contents into the field. She would prefer to think that the child was in the earth for always, rather than in the sky.

A dog began to howl, a long, drawn-out cry. The sound of it made her flinch and think of Jacob's story and the idea of a dog hanging from a spike above the door. It would have to be a spike, after all, because an ordinary nail wouldn't be strong enough. Whose dog was it? And how had the man killed the animal, she wondered, and that if he hadn't bled the dog, there would have been much blood dripping down the door for a time, dirtying the owner's property. And what about that, she wondered, the owner's rights? And anyway, why hadn't the man just kept his door closed to prevent the smell from spreading? She had meant to point these things out to Jacob, but it had slipped her mind with the excitement of Elizabeth running into the house with the news that Hendrick had gone missing. As the V formation reached the rim of the earth it suddenly broke apart and flared up and out, and then one by one the pinpoints of light arched down into the horizon and disappeared. She shivered and looked back at the dark house. She buttoned her sweater up and set the knife down on the platform beside her. She rocked into the sound of the dog barking and waited for news of Hendrick.

The women gathered around Hilda, who wept. The hard knot of tears, carried for so many years, was picked loose now in short bitter cries, giving way then to wails of sorrow. They clasped her about the shoulders, knelt beside her, and patted her knees. They told her, "Hush, stop crying, you were only twelve years old when the little girl died, and probably still innocent." That girls stayed innocent longer than boys. It was too much responsibility. And anyway, the Lord loves a contrite heart and he's taken what you have done and thrown it away further than the eye can ever see and forgotten it completely. Even now, they said, it's as though it never happened.

They were overwhelmed by their own spirit of for-giveness and felt uncommon generosity and kindness one towards another so that when another woman stood up and said that she had a confession to make as well they bent their ears to listen, ears which were now tuned to the spirit of com-passion. One hour would bleed into another hour and, except for the occasional chirrup of the sparrow, the world outside the room would retreat into the night and they would confess jealousy and envy and bitterness of spirit.

Only Alma Harder would refuse to kneel and refuse to confess, still maintaining steadfastly that she had nothing to say that God didn't already know. They turned on her. What about the story of Maria and the monkeys? Would she have the audacity in the face of the Holy Spirit to deny that she'd fabricated the whole thing? Huh, Alma said, she'd only told them the half of it. And they felt sorry for her—that God had for some reason refused to bless her and prayed that he would bring some sin to her mind that she might be relieved of the burden of it.

The men at the firehall had waited for a signal from Joe Harder. So, the mommy's boy, the little boy wonder, Hendrick, actually had enough spine to squeeze a titty, the men thought. Not a very big reason to run away. He'd copped a feel. Bully for him. The smell of urine rose from a wooden cubicle in the corner where wads of wet paper clung to the ceiling above and the messages inside were more vicious, carved into wood with everlasting anger. "M.H. does it with a broom handle." "H.S. sucks cocks."

"It'll soon be too dark for anything," Joe Harder said, "lanterns or no lanterns." He glanced at Jacob. "Do you want to say a few words before we go, or what?"

"Yes," Jacob said and their hearts fell. He wanted to tell them to remember that we wrestle not against flesh and blood, but against principalities, against powers, against the rulers of the darkness of this world. He wanted to leave them with this verse in their hearts as they prepared to scour the river bank, but there were unbelievers present, and besides, the others were backsliders, and it would be beyond their spiritual awareness to realize that this was in fact a wrestling match with the evil one.

"Trust in the Lord," Jacob was saying when the door opened. One of the older town boys stood in the doorway, red-faced and panting from running. He'd been out on the bridge looking over the side of it and something black and shiny had bobbed near the shore. It looked like the head of an animal, he thought. But it was too black for a muskrat or beaver and anyway, it didn't plough the water with its snout the way a beaver does. And so he'd scrambled down the embankment and fucking near—oops, he said, seeing Jacob among the men—almost fell—he corrected—reaching for what it was. And this is what it was, he said, and held up a dripping rubber boot.

Lena Friesen was squatting in the field behind Elizabeth's house when she heard the music. The knife was set down on the ground beside her where she balanced delicately on her heels, groaning and straining to empty herself of seaweed and water. The music had begun as a single, high, wavering voice and then grew into two, then swelled into three- and four-part harmony. A chorus of women's voices, singing "Jesus bids us shine with a clear, pure light, like a little candle burning in the night. In this world of darkness," they sang.

Still carrying the knife, Lena followed the music out onto the road. For they wrestled against rulers of the darkness, Jacob had reminded her before she left. But he'd failed to finish the verse off. The final part of it, about people in high places. The stars were reflected in the water-filled gully as she walked along Ottawa Street. She turned off Ottawa and began to walk towards the church, slowly at first, not at all certain she'd actually go that far. As she rounded the bend in the road, the church came into sight; the two windows on each side of the front door blazed with light. She thought that her eyes played tricks at first, she told them later. That it had been a case of over-tiredness, or being worried which made her eyesight fuzzy so that it appeared that the air above the church moved. I had been sitting with Elizabeth, she said, and thinking about the story Jacob had told us and I looked up and there, above the roof of the church, the sky shimmered, oh, so delicately at first, like the opening bars of the aurora borealis. The closer she got, the more certain she was that she could actually see something up there, fluttering like hundreds of silver wings moving in time to their music. Like moths, they would want to know? Yes, like a blizzard of moths, she said later, only it wasn't moths.

She dropped the knife and began to run.

The door swung open, startling the women into silence. Lena stood in the doorway, purple-faced and gasping for air. Her hair had pulled loose from the severe bun at the back of her head and strands of it were plastered by perspiration against her neck. And for the first time, the women saw the girl in Lena's face. What she must have looked like. And they all thought that she'd been a happier person once, the kind of person who would brighten up a room when she entered just by smiling.

"What's happening?" Lena asked.

And they told her of their confessions and renewals and how they loved her and how they couldn't stop singing.

"Well," Lena said and sat down on one of the chairs. "I've been thinking as I was sitting with Elizabeth. About Jacob's story. And I have to tell you that it wasn't really my efforts that saved my father from the firing squad in Russia. It was the silverware."

His heart filled with dread by the sight of the dripping boot, Jacob had hurried on home, leaving the men to go down to the river without him. He knelt beside the bed, his head bowed into the feather quilt and in a moonbeam that bathed all the room in a cold white light. He heard a dog barking and the peace he'd carried with him to the firehall fled and in its place a tumult of questions and conflicting emotions collided inside his heart. There was no denying the evidence of the boot. What you see is not always what's there—Taro Yamamoto's voice crept into his mind, and Jacob saw the man bent over the garden, raking paw prints from the black soil. Yes, he must continue to have faith, he realized, but every time he closed his eyes to pray, he fought an overwhelming desire to sleep until at last he gave in to it and let his head grow heavy and his eyes close.

Jacob slept, kneeling beside the bed. A trickle of saliva ran down his cheek into the spread. His eyeballs flickered and darted behind closed lids. He dreamt that his house was full of boxes. We must clean our house, he told Lena. If we do, our Father will give us this purse of jewels. He held the blue velvet pouch in his hands and undid the clasp. Inside it, tiny rubies and pearls and blue sapphires rolled across the satin lining, like bits of coloured glass. He closed the purse quickly without showing her, feeling the prick of disappointment. It seemed so little. He cleaned and cleaned. He could feel himself perspire and grow hot with frustration. His eyeballs darted back and forth. His house was so full of boxes. Every time he lifted one and carried it outside, another appeared in its place. They had too much clothing, too many dishes, too much silver. Closets began to appear with more and more clothing. Jacob lifted an armful of clothes from a rod in a closet. Behind it, a cross hung on the wall. The image of the cross jumped forward and the clothing disappeared as he reached for it. And then he flinched. Someone had filed the corners of the cross down so that they were sharp as daggers. His hand reached for the cross once again to take it down and then he saw the goatee, the hooked eyebrows, and flaring nostrils. The face of the devil laughed at him from the cross. Vanity, the devil said. It's all vanity.

Except for the swirling halo of insects around the men's lanterns which were held up over the water and the flicker of light dancing in the hills, there were no colours to the night. Minnie and Annie crouched in the entrance of Minnie's shelter, listening and watching the men search for the boy. Annie had helped Minnie construct a lean-to with a canvas tarp and branches which would keep Minnie dry in the event of rain. Annie had brought along an old Sterno cooker, a frying pan, and a length of fishing line. The water, reflecting the bright light of the moon, was white and the men standing at its shore were black silhouettes against its surface. They looked out over that stretch of silk and thought of a mouth opening, hoping for air and gulping water instead, of limbs churning and jerking in surprise beneath the surface. They'd seen the remains of a rope tied to a stake, its end severed, and the fresh imprint of boots leading down to the river's edge.

"We'll have to wait until morning," Joe Harder said. "Bring the grappling hooks at sunrise."

"Maybe he's taken the long way home," someone said. But no one felt like laughing.

"They couldn't find their own noses," Annie said as the men turned and pushed back up the path. "Let the women look," she said, "they'd find that boy."

"Mary Ruth never had any luck," Minnie said.

Jacob's eyes flew open as the voices of the men grew louder. Pain shot through his knees as he leapt to his feet. He could still see that leering face. He clasped his arms to keep the tremor from spreading throughout his body. Darkness moved across the face of the floor, retreating as the men's voices, low and tense, passed by the house. He heard the clicking sound of an animal's claws against the sidewalk and a soft thud. Jacob rushed to the door to ask the men, "What news?" He opened it, stepped out, and then stopped dead. On the top step, starkly vivid in the light of the moon, was the carcass of a rat. He saw its ivory-coloured teeth, the tips of them bared and bloody, as though snarling at him in death. Jacob shrank back into the deep shadow of the door, the knowledge coming swiftly. The men fell silent and all he heard as they passed by was the swish of their pantlegs. He remained hidden. He was certain this day would end in tragedy. And that he had somehow set it in motion. Beyond the town, the piercing sound of a dog rose up, clear, singular, and the hair on the back of Jacob's neck prickled with the sound of it. Then the discordant voices of the town dogs rose up as well, and from another street Jacob heard a string of oaths and a window coming down hard. Then the wailing sound of the clarinet spiralled above the curved roof of the skating rink, its hollow sound echoing. The men had stopped at Taro Yamamoto's yard and Jacob heard the man's low voice, a question. Jacob would like to ask now, "What was it? What was the shape of the prints you saw in your garden the other night?" His chest grew heavy so that it became difficult to breathe as though the room held too much moisture. He realized now that the story God had given to him that morning in the pulpit had been sent for himself.

The women fanned heat from Lena's face with a hymnal, fearing her heart. She shooed them away and her voice grew soft and gentle and she thanked them, but said that she was fine now. That for the first time in years, there was nothing wrong with her heart. And she told them the real reason that her father had been tied up and set before the firing squad in Russia was because God had singled him out. Because of his greed. While others in the village had shared their possessions or sold them to buy medicine and food for all, they'd buried silverware and hid trunks of blankets and dishes in the orchard. And it was because she'd dug up the silver and brought it to the marauders that they'd spared her father.

"Well," Alma said, "I would say then that it was a good thing that he did keep it."

"It was greed which caused him to do so," Lena said. "And it's the same spirit which made me encourage you to be stingy with Elizabeth." Beginning next Sunday, she told them, they would begin to have a second offering, a love offering to begin to repair and spruce up Elizabeth's house. They were going to resurrect the Samaritan Project.

"You can count me out on that score," Alma Harder said. She got up from her chair and walked over to the door. "I've already given that woman enough," she said. The windowpanes shivered in their frames as she slammed the door behind her.

"Let's continue to pray," Lena said. "And let our first prayer be that our offering doesn't have to go to pay for a funeral for that boy."

As they dropped to their knees one by one, the women felt that inside they were clean pages and hesitated before forming their thoughts, being careful, wanting the first marks on the page to be beautiful ones and pleasing. If they all agreed that Hendrick would be safe, he would be. The Lord had said, had promised, that where two or three were gathered in his name, so was he. There were such things as miracles. They'd just witnessed this in their renewed love for each other and in what Lena had seen on the road. They closed their eyes and each one waited for the spirit to tell her whether or not she should be the first to speak. Then they heard the sound of someone whistling outside and then the sound of feet hurrying up the sidewalk. Alma Harder opened the door and beckoned to them.

"You can stop praying," she said. "It looks as though the Anointed One has returned."

They ran to the windows and pushed against one another to look out. There was Hendrick Schultz, hands jammed deep into his pockets, collar turned up and around his ears, bent forward at the waist, whistling softly. He walked past the church without acknowledging them. They watched as he rounded the curve and emerged after a time as he cut across the road heading towards Ottawa Street.

11

"All that commotion over nothing," Annie said. She struck a match and bent over the pile of sticks. The women had seen the boy, Hendrick Schultz, as he had crossed over the bridge from the opposite shore and had heard his carefree whistling. "Siren and all. Enough to wake the dead." Fire leapt in crumpled newspapers which cradled a nest of twigs.

"We may have started the tradition," Minnie said. "Wanda and I." The dried wood pinged and snapped as it caught fire and a puff of blue smoke curled upwards. "I think I can remember hearing it. Three toots of the siren."

"Whoa," Annie said. "Who's Wanda?"

"The other pea in the pod," Minnie said. "My sister."

"I see, I see," Annie said quietly and moved around the fire slowly, as though Minnie were a bird she didn't want to startle. The heat of the fire had caused an updraft and the wind gathered in the leaves above their heads, the sound, gentle waves rushing up to meet the land and falling back. She set a log across the leaping fire and sat down beside Minnie in the entrance of the shelter. "Your sister."

"Wanda. When she went missing they alerted the whole town with the siren. I guess they had to. It was the only way they could get anyone's attention. The sound of the fair was

loud, you see, that god-awful, tinny, fake steam-organ music."
She took the cigarette Annie offered and lit it.

"Well," Annie said.

Minnie stared out over the river into the tangled darkness
on the opposite shore.

The thin tinny music had pressed against the sides of
the fortune-teller's tent. She could hear Gene whistling a tune
while he waited for her outside. "No," Minnie said to the
fortune-teller. She reached for the piece of felt and slid it
across the table until the crystal ball was directly beneath her.
She wanted to look into it herself. She saw that the ball was, in
fact, fake, one of those things you could buy at the drugstore,
filled with bulging red roses, their petals coated in something
which looked like gelatine. Which made you want to throw
up because they reminded you of something dead. But she
looked down inside the ball anyway and she saw Wanda.

"Up and over," the man's face glistened with perspiration
as he swung Wanda over the side of the car and into the back
seat. And then Minnie felt his hands at her armpits and she
was being lifted through the air down into the car with its
shiny red leather seats.

"Two peas in a pod," the man said as he stooped,
reached for his white fedora, and jammed it onto his head.
The acrid smell of cigar smoke clung to his stubby fingers.

"Be sure and smile now," Mary Ruth said, reaching over
from the front to straighten the pinafore on Wanda's dress.
Three peas in a pod. Mary Ruth flicked at her maroon hair.
She wore an identical dress. White, with strawberries around
the yoke and a border embroidered around the hem line.

They moved through the street slowly, and pulled up
behind a horse-drawn trailer covered in fake grass with a
funny little house in its centre. Hands fluttered and clapped,
and Mary Ruth blew kisses off the end of her white gloves.
The sound of a trumpet pierced the air and then the clash of

cymbals gave the signal and brass instruments flashed in the sun as a band stepped into place behind the car.

"Smile, smile, you two cutey-pies," Mary Ruth's shiny lips said. Minnie saw Jay, his red clown's mouth turned down into a scowl as he ran along the street. He stopped suddenly, swung a silver bucket of what looked to be water. The crowd shrieked and moved back in one big swell as paper confetti swirled through the air. The sky opened and peanuts rained down inside the car. The noise pressed against Minnie's ears. It's too noisy, she thought. "It's too noisy," Wanda shouted and kicked at the back of the seat for Mary Ruth's attention. A balloon popped. A white bird fluttered up from Jay's chest.

"We're almost there," Mary Ruth said.

And then the gates, draped with festoons of yellow and red bunting, opened and the parade passed through into the sound of the fairgrounds, the brass music blending all at once with the cries of the people, the cajoling voices of men in straw hats, crying out as they passed by the brightly painted booths and the thin tinny sound of the merry-go-round.

"What you'll need is a different name," the man said. "Like the 'Flying Zarzyckis'. Create the illusion that you're exotic foreigners."

Mary Ruth's laughter cut through the clanging cymbals. "You'd need a mouth full of marbles just to pronounce that one," she yelled. "Anyway, poor Jay looks like a thunderstorm about to happen. A new name is the last thing I'll need to slip past him." She leaned across the seat towards the man in the white suit. She left her mouth behind on his cheek.

Minnie saw lightning flash from Jay's ears and thunder roar out of his mouth.

"I'll take them for a ride on the merry-go-round," the man said through his cigar, a funny, crushed, brown wiener jutting from his mouth.

And then Wanda was there in the crystal ball but Minnie saw only fragments of her, the red strawberries spattered across her dress, Wanda's patent shoes, the silver button on the side of it, flashing as she walked on the other side of the man. Minnie saw the man's white shoes, the tips of them turning black with mud from the midway.

The man's hand cupped loose change. "Your choice," he said. "Which horse?"

"You choose," Wanda said. The animals pranced and it was hard to choose because they were never still.

"You choose," Minnie said. And then they both said, "The black one with the red and gold saddle."

Mirrors flashed and so there were six of them, two Minnies and two Wandas and two of the man in the white suit standing between them, his hand rising and falling on the horses' backs.

A cow mooed suddenly from across the river, long and plaintive. The sound echoed in the steel girders of the bridge.

"Mary Ruth had those dresses made," Minnie said. "She must of had them made especially for the parade."

"Shht," Annie cautioned. "Listen."

"What is it?" Minnie listened and heard at first only the wind fanning the fire, the groan of the solitary cow. But then she heard a sound from deep among the trees across the river, faintly, a sound like someone coughing. She got up and moved away from the roar of the fire. It was the sound of a child, crying.

"No, no." Her mouth began to quiver. She stepped into the shadows of the trees. "Oh no, no." It was the sobbing cry of a lost child. Her jaw ached and spasms of shivers ran up and down the length of her body.

"It's Wanda," she said.

"Go away," Annie said. "It's your imagination. If you had a sister Wanda and if she went missing, that was years ago. And she wouldn't be here."

"Well," Minnie said, "well, it depends. You see, after we went on the merry-go-round, he, that man, took us for a ride. We drove and drove. I was crying, but Wanda was yelling and kicking the back of the seat and asking to go back to Mary Ruth and Jay. She held my hand. The top was still down on the car and the wind was like ice on my face. And then," Minnie said through clenched teeth—the words, squeezed down to a thin line, were barely audible—"and then, we were here. Right here. Beside this river. In this exact spot. The man in the white shoes and white pants and white jacket, Wanda, him, and me. Only his shoes weren't white any more. And he said he had a bit of magic. He wanted to show it to us, but one at a time. Minnie first, he said, because M came before W in the alphabet." Minnie closed her eyes and her fists clenched the air. "And Wanda stepped forward instead, playing our game. And it wasn't long before there was no magic at all, because she started to cry. And I saw those god-damned strawberries on the border of her dress as it landed on the ground. And then Wanda cried out, quick and fast, the sound choked back so suddenly, and so I went to look where he'd taken her behind a clump of bushes, and I couldn't see anything of her at first, just him, his back. He was kneeling on the ground. And then," Minnie's voice dropped and became soft and quiet, "and then I did see Wanda. Just the bottoms of her muddy little shoes. They were up in the air, kind of funny looking, on each side of the man, bobbing, up and down, up and down," she said.

"Noo," Annie wailed. "Noo." Her cry echoed across the water. "Stop, no, stop."

"I was only five," Minnie said, "but I knew enough that it wasn't magic and so I ran away. I think I must have followed the sound of the siren back to town."

"Stop," Annie cried. "My heart is breaking."

Minnie sat down beside the weeping woman. The heat of the fire pressed out, warming her face. "I guess he must have broken her neck," she said. "And thrown her in the river when he was done."

"Oh, be quiet, do be quiet," Annie cried.

Minnie felt at peace, quiet. The glacier, after all, was melting. "Shh," she said and patted Annie on the back.

Annie reared up, her fists clenched tightly against her chest. "This goddamned and stinking world," she said. She began to shake violently. "It makes you want to kill somebody."

"No," Minnie said.

"At least be angry," Annie said. "You have the right to be angry."

"I didn't have to go through that," Minnie said. "It was my choice."

"Oh," Annie said and her head dropped to her knees. Her shoulders began to shake as she wept. "Oh, oh, oh, you poor wee thing."

"Shht," Minnie whispered and held up her hand. "Listen. The crying. It's stopped."

Dear Aunt Violet,

Wind south-east with an unusual chill. I covered the petunias for fear of frost. Dorfman claims this happens every seven years.

I have a question of a female nature. I was wondering, at what age does a woman go into the change?

Minnie and I—

Minnie and I. A great tiredness settled between Albert's shoulder blades as he bent over the table. Steam billowed up from the ironing board as Rosella ironed a dress. When Albert had opened his eyes that morning, he'd expected to see Minnie beside him, wrapped like an Egyptian mummy in the sheet, her hands folded across her chest, so silent and still.

"Ollie says that she's going to start me on a skirt first," Rosella said. "They're the easiest to sew."

"That's nice, dear," Albert said. He pushed the letter aside and reached for the book and opened it at its marker.

SYMPTOMS OF MENOPAUSE
hot flashes
dry vagina
insomnia
weird dreams
sensory disturbances
funny sensations in the head
sore heels
vertigo
disturbing memory lapses
chills

Poor Minnie, Albert thought. It was Minnie to a tee. "I believe," he said and pushed up from the table, "that maybe I might go down and see if the men have found that boy yet. Maybe I might just go and have a look."

Rosella's green eyes narrowed as he left the house.

"Dad?" Ginny called down from the window as he stepped out into the yard. "You going some place, Dad?"

"Just for a minute," Albert said. "Only for a minute. And then I'll come up and hear your prayers."

"Will you go and talk to her and try and get her to come home?" Ginny whispered. "Get Ma?"

"Well," Albert whispered back, "it's a thought. I just might do." And he walked from the yard, whistling.

He saw the fire beating out from among the trees and then the white tarp spread over branches and sitting in front of it, her silver ribbon of hair shining in the light of the fire, was Minnie.

She saw him coming and smiled. Albert squatted beside the fire and poked at it with a stick.

"What is it, dear?" Minnie asked "Are the girls all right?"

"They're doing just fine," he said.

"I thought they would."

"Min?"

"Yes, Albert?"

"I was wondering. Do you ever have sore heels?"

"Well," she said. "Yes, sometimes, yes, I guess my heels are sore fairly often."

"Oh," he said and poked the fire. A piece of log broke loose and tumbled to one side, its embers flaring with sudden heat. "I'm so sorry," he said.

"Don't be sorry," Minnie said. "It happens."

"Bumkin," Albert said, "would you like to come home with me?"

"Yes," Minnie said, "I really wouldn't mind. But I don't think Rosella would go for it."

"Rosella could be won round," Albert said. "Do you think you might try, for the sake of the girls, to—," he searched for the word.

"To be normal? Less of a joke of the universe?" Minnie said.

"I understand everything now," Albert said. "About hot flashes and chills and all that. And there are things you can take for it, you know. Like bee pollen for instance."

"Bee pollen?"

"And evening in primrose oil."

"Albert, what day is it tomorrow?"

"Monday."

"Do we have cabbage for the borscht?"

"Ah," Albert said. "That's another thing. It gives me gas."

"Oh," Minnie said. "I'm sorry. You should have said something."

"If you don't mind," Albert said, "I'd really prefer meat and potatoes and vegetables."

"Every day?"

"Every day."

"Well, fine, Albert," Minnie said. "That shouldn't be too difficult to remember. But Albert, love?"

"Yes?"

"I still can't have sex with you any more."

Albert jumped to his feet. "Oh no, no," he said. "I understand perfectly." Dry vagina. In time, that could be cured, too.

MONDAY

12

The fiery band of the sun's first rays lifted the grey rim of night clouds that were strung all along the horizon. A hawk wheeled above the valley, waiting for the first sign of movement in the patchwork quilt of fields below. Vegetation, thick as moss, bordered the limits of the villages and towns and crept towards the centre of the fields which darkened now with the shadow of the hawk's wings as it passed over. The air was cool and thin, waiting for the breath of those below to fill it and make it round. In the north, a flock of pelicans swept across a pod of beluga whales breaking the surface of icy waters.

Near the centre of the valley, the town of Agassiz was still. Overnight all its streets had become lined with mirrors which flashed back the fiery first band of light. The quick-silver look of the gullies was water, still canals outlining the town and mirroring the flash of sky.

The hawk glided above Ottawa Street, above the stillness inside Annie Schmoon's shanty; the only words ever again to enter its dank and hollow centre were in the newspapers lining its windows. She had slipped away into death during the night and her absence—as was often the case with the elderly or unwanted—would not be noticed until corruption raised its smelly finger at those passing by. Water glimmered in the cattails in the coulee behind her house and submerged grass bowed into a current which rushed on towards a culvert beneath Bison, on into the coulee that lay behind Taro Yamamoto and Jacob Friesen's houses, passing beneath a foot bridge and making its way towards the river.

Delta William had arisen for an early morning trip to the bathroom and had flushed the toilet and cursed silently as she watched the water brim to the top of it and overflow. She went out into the kitchen for the rag mop and stood at the window in shocked surprise at the sight of a tent pitched in her back yard, its white canvas walls washed pink by the early dawn.

A chickadee called from the maple tree in front of the Pullman house and suddenly the air exploded with bird song and mixed with it the excited chatter of people as they rounded the corner of Ottawa Street. All at once—with the exception of Elizabeth and Hendrick Schultz—the entire congregation of Jacob Friesen's tiny Mennonite church—the men along with the women and children—hurried in a cluster with Joe and Alma Harder and Maria leading the way. Jacob Friesen, who brought up the rear, lagged behind them, and even though Lena called for him to "Hurry, hurry", the gap between himself and the others grew wider.

"My Rick is a strong swimmer," Alma said, her voice unnaturally high-pitched and her cheeks red with the fever of sitting and waiting for the sun to rise. "I thought the boy was at home with Maria," Joe had said when he'd returned from the search on Sunday night. "Oh," Alma had said and fingered the mole at the side of her mouth. "So did I." Maria said that she was sure Rick was at the hotel with Alma. And all three fell silent.

"When Rick was only a baby," Alma said, her voice coming in short spurts as they hurried down the path single file, "I dropped him in a river in Mexico," she said, "and he swam. Just like that. As a matter of fact," she said, turning to speak to the person behind her on the path, "he rolled over onto his back and looked up at me through the water and laughed."

The women glanced at one another as they stepped out beside the river bank, embarrassed for Alma—that even now, at this dark hour, she would make up stories.

Hilda Penner's husband unwound the rope from his shoulder and the grappling hook thudded to the ground at his feet. The men righted the over-turned boat and slid it down towards the water, working silently, respectful of the tension drawing the skin tight across Joe's cheekbones.

"You don't have to go out there," Hilda's elderly husband said. "That's why we're here."

Joe kicked at the boat. "Vultures," he said. "That's why you're all here."

Jacob Friesen stepped onto the river bank. He came up behind Joe and touched him on the shoulder.

Joe wheeled around on him and raised his fist. "You tell me this is the will of God," he said through clenched teeth. "Go on. And I'll give you five. I dare you." He punched the air in front of Jacob's nose.

Tears streamed down Jacob's face. "No, no," he said. "Forgive me. It's all my fault."

"And not only that," Alma said, pacing up and down in front of her audience, "the monkeys had my Maria for three days," she said. "That's how long we chased them. Once I heard her crying and I thought my heart was going to break. You can't imagine what it sounds like to hear your baby crying in the middle of the night from the top of a tree. It would be the same as," she hesitated, "well, the same as standing outside a burning house and not being able to get inside it to rescue your children," she said. "Like that." Ollie Peter stepped forward and tried to stop Alma from pacing, but the woman shrugged her off. "Those monkeys had Maria for three days and when I finally tricked them into setting her down on the ground, she was naked," Alma said.

"Mom," Maria said, her voice an anguished cry, "shut up."

"And she was bleeding between her legs."

Lena Friesen gasped. Hilda Penner caught hold of Alma and held her close. "What a liar," someone whispered, and that it was no wonder that this calamity had visited their house.

The men eased the boat down the bank and climbed into it. "Oh no," Alma said and pulled away from Hilda's embrace as they began to push off from the shore. "Not without me," she said. She clambered down the sticky bank towards the boat. "Ricky is my son and I'm coming along." Several of the men on shore tried to restrain her, but she untangled herself and began to wade through the water towards the boat.

"It's all right," Joe said. "Let her come."

The men reached for Alma, pulled, and the boat tipped sharply as she slid into it on her stomach. Those on shore saw the flash of pink underpants as the soaked uniform rode up about her hips. The men winced as she crawled over them to the bow of the boat. She leaned out over it and cupped her hands to her mouth.

"Ricky, Ricky," she called. "Yoo hoo. It's Momma."

"Here now," one of the men said gruffly and tugged at her arm.

"Ricky," she called. "Baby, don't worry, I'm coming."

"Mom?" A sleepy voice rose up from among the trees on the opposite shore. Those on the bank stood rooted, thinking at first that the boy had somehow called forth from the deep.

"Mom?" The voice was stronger and sounded surprised. "Mom? I'm here. Over here."

"Oh, darling," Alma said. The boat rocked as she stood up. "I'm coming, I'm coming."

Those on shore saw the woman stand up. They saw the boat rock sharply. They saw Alma's legs scissor in the air as she leapt into the water.

"I'm coming, I'm coming." She began to sputter and pant and flail her arms wildly in her attempt to swim.

"Mom," Rick called out, loud and clear. "I'm here. Come and get me. Hendrick tied me to a tree."

The men in the boat sat frozen for an instant. Alma turned and looked back at them, through strands of wet hair pasted to her face. They saw the look of sudden awareness dawn in her eyes and then fear. "Joe. Help," she said. "I forgot. I can't swim." The words bubbled at the surface as her dark head sank beneath the water. Several of the women on the shore began to wail.

One of the men swore, grabbed the oars, and pulled hard. The boat veered further away. They sat transfixed, staring at the spot where the water had closed over. Suddenly, Alma's white arms thrashed up through the surface and she arose, coughing and sputtering. The boat teetered as Hilda Penner's husband stood up and swung the grappling hook. The hook sliced through the air—fear had made him strong, he said later—high, high, it flew and splashed down far beyond the struggling woman. The rope smacked against the water in a straight line, inches from her head.

"Grab hold," Joe's voice rang out.

"Dad? Dad? Come and get me. I'm freezing," Rick cried. The people on shore held their breath. Alma reached for the rope. Once again her head disappeared beneath the water.

"Keep the rope taut," Hilda's husband cautioned. The oars pulled. The hook sank and skidded along the muddy river bottom and finally held fast. Alma broke the surface again, gasping for breath but clinging tightly to the rope.

Then, hand over hand, she began to pull herself towards the boat. Joe kicked off his rubber boots and slid over the side and swam out to meet her. The people on the shore sighed with relief.

"Forgot she couldn't swim," one of the men in the boat muttered, anger taking up where fear had left off. The elderly Penner grunted. "Weighs as much as a baby elephant," he said.

Alma shot forward through the water. Her hands grasped at the side of the boat. She was safe. "Did you think you were the apostle Peter then, wanting to walk on water?" one of the men attempted a joke. Joe pushed from behind and they pulled, and finally she lay squirming and soaked, a landed fish. The elderly Penner tugged at the grappling iron as Joe Harder treaded water, waiting for a hand up. The rope sawed against wood as Penner pulled hard. Joe felt something soft slide up his leg. "Jesus," they heard him exclaim. They looked over the side. Sightless eyes peered up at them through the water. Then a nose, mud trickling from its nostrils. A bloated, bruised face with muddy weeds for hair rose to the surface. It was only when they saw the brassiere that they realized it was the corpse of a woman.

"Well," Lena Friesen said, "if you won't go down there and deal with that boy, then I will. He owes an apology." She was down on her hands and knees in the garden, weeding the radishes. Even though the sun beat down hard and she felt the heat of it in the soil as she worked, Jacob stood on the walk beside the garage wearing his overcoat, its collar turned up. Beyond their picket fence water lapped against the sidewalk and the damp air cut through the coat into Jacob's bones. He stared at the potted plants set out against the side of the garage.

"What that boy did was the same as pushing that woman out of the boat," Lena said. And then, "So, was it an older woman or a young one?" she asked, hoping to catch Jacob off guard. The men had tied a float marker to the body and rowed to shore. They'd chased the women away and called for the Mounties to take care of this terrible business. "They say she was wearing only underwear. Is this so?"

"Spindly," Jacob said suddenly and knelt beside his potted plants. "Far too. And growing too fast."

Lena looked up, expecting to see someone at his side, but he'd spoken out of a daydream. "It was a mean prank with a terrible ending. The boy owes the entire family an apology. It's a wonder Rick didn't come down with pneumonia," she said. And then, "Jacob, do they have any idea yet who it was who drowned?"

"What have you done with my plants?" Jacob asked. He'd examined them and discovered each to be in the same state. The growth of them was wild and out of control; the translucent stems twisted and curled from the main stalk and flopped over the sides of the pots.

"I fertilized them," Lena said. "That's all. If there's something wrong, it wasn't my doing."

"Now, now," Jacob said. "Don't be so sensitive."

Lena glanced up quickly. His voice sounded as though it came from the bottom of a barrel. She'd noticed the tone of sarcasm as well, but saw nothing of it in his placid features. Jacob sat down on the bench beside the garage and leaned into its side and stared at the garden.

Through heat waves shimmering from black soil, Jacob saw the paisley backside of Lena turn towards him and then waver and dance as her voice faded from his hearing. Viewed through half-closed eyes, the world took on a rose-coloured tint. His night had been filled with dreams. He had dreamed that he'd knelt beside Taro in the man's front yard and seen Elizabeth's footprints pressed into the soil.

He'd dreamt that she'd stood beside him at the table in her nightdress and that as she leaned forward her white silky braid had brushed against his bare shoulder and he'd smelled her scent—the light, powdery, dry smell of a baby—as she bent to kiss him. And then her face had changed, had become Louise's face—soft, swollen, as she looked up at him, pink and shining with her love—and her voice became Louise's voice, saying "Ahh." Jacob heard himself say "Oh, oh, oh." "A girl," Louise said. "I'm swimming with you and it will be a girl."

He'd dreamed of Lena's death. In the morning, when they'd awakened to the pounding at the door, he'd been shamed by the remembrance of the dream of Lena coming up the stairs from the cellar. He heard her puffing. He was there, at the top of the stairs, looking down at her. Her arms were full of linens and dishes. "It's time to put these to good use," she'd said, just before she fell backwards. Her eyes had flown open and stared at him as she'd receded down and down into the final crack of her head against the cement wall.

Jacob stared at Lena's dancing paisley buttocks. She had over-fertilized the plants. The plants would simply grow and grow until they burned themselves out. It came to him that that was much the same as what he'd done. He'd given his people too much. He sighed and rested his hands against his knees, the pose that of a meditating man, at peace. But the sinews beneath the skin on the backs of his hands writhed beneath blue veins thick as earthworms. He closed his eyes and tried to rest in the explanation of having given too much. Red and yellow pinwheels turned beneath his eyelids. He heard that deep laughter and felt the bench sag beneath the weight of the devil. "Jacob Peter Friesen," the deep voice whispered in his ear. He felt the breath of the words against his neck, hot, fetid, like the breath of a sickly animal. "Vanity," the devil said, "surely God will not hear vanity."

"We should have a meeting," Lena said, "and make that boy stand up and speak. He should be made to make things right, first of all with the Lord, and then the Harder family," she said.

Jacob stood up.

"Where are you going?" she said.

"I have things to attend to," Jacob said and his voice was softer, gentler than it had been all week. He went into the garage and stood looking at his toolbox, deep in thought.

Jacob startled Elizabeth, who was out spading the garden plot, and Hendrick, who huddled down beneath the blankets in bed.

"Don't pay any attention to me," Jacob said as he set his toolbox down on the ground. "I've just come to take a few measurements so I'll know what lumber to order."

Hendrick heard the thump of the ladder against the side of the house and sat up.

Jacob began his climb towards the sun. His arms ached as he pulled himself upwards. He felt his knees shake as he neared the roof's edge. He crawled up onto it cautiously and on all fours moved up its incline towards the peak. Beyond, the trees followed the river, a blue-green belt of growth. On one side he saw the little town, the houses, their roofs bright and safe beneath the boughs of maple trees. On the other side, his church, brilliant white in the glare of the afternoon sun. They were his imperfect sheep, he the flock's imperfect shepherd. Freed from the constraint of the heavy black earth and all that struggled to grow from it, he felt freer, lighter than he had for years. He realized that all he'd ever tried to do for Elizabeth and her boy was to be a roof, a covering against inclement weather. He saw himself, arms spread out like a roof, protecting this time those whom he had once neglected and lost because he'd carried to them the disease from the houses of those he'd ministered to and helped bury. Tell me that is vanity, he thought, and I will say that God is too hard to ask a man to deny his own for others. He stood up slowly, and felt his knees grow steady and his face shine with the heat of the sun radiating from the shingles. Tell me it is vanity to be a roof, he thought. He waited for the devil's voice. Silence. He smiled then and raised his arms and breathed deeply, taking into himself the clean air. He would finish off the Samaritan Project, build the boy a room, and get on with the task of discovering the Lord's will for the boy's gift. "Praise God from whom all blessings flow," Jacob sang, his baritone voice deep and full. "Praise God all creatures here below." While below, the mirrors winked and sparkled with the life of the sky.

Hendrick looked up from the bed to the sight of a shadow crossing the window. He thought it might be a giant bird swooping past the window, but at the last moment the shape became as limp as a rag doll and fell like a stone. He heard his mother cry out and, at the same time, a hard thump against the wall of the house rattled the dishes on the shelf.

Elizabeth stood in the doorway. "Get up, hurry," she said. "Go to the doctor's and then to Lena. Tell her Jacob has fallen."

These are the generations of Esau who is Edom. Esau took his wives of the daughters of Canaan; Adah, the daughter of Elon the Hittite, and Aholibamah, the daughter of Anah the daughter of Zibeon the Hivite. Hendrick's mind churned as his arms pumped and his chest burned with the knowledge that Jacob Friesen had fallen.

"This is a cleaning tool," Steven Adam explained to Minnie Pullman, as he had to every woman who attended his ceramics class for the first time. He'd be patient, he assured Albert who had visited and requested that Minnie take part.

"She needs an outside interest," Albert had said. "It's all part of the change. She needs more than house and children." Steven agreed to give Spinny Minnie a try, but privately he didn't expect too much.

"The cleaning tool is an essential tool," Steven said and held it up. "Put your name on it. It'll become your friend for life. Each tool has its own feel, so never lend it out or use anyone else's."

Minnie nodded. "Cleaning tool," she said. Her fingers itched for the pen in her breast pocket. "C.T." she would scribble on the newspaper that was spread across the work-table. But it was important, she realized, if she was going to be less of an embarrassment to the universe, that she try and remember without it.

No one had looked up when Minnie had stepped into the garage or noticed that she'd bathed, wore a new dress, and had tied her hair back with a ribbon. The women had been warned she'd be attending and had promised themselves, for the sake of the sweetheart, Albert, not to make a big thing of it. They worked on their projects and exchanged recipes and bits of gossip around the table in the centre of the garage. Fragments of their talk jumped forward as Minnie listened to Steven Adam. "Thought she could walk on water— Harrigan thinks about a week— Bloated. I think—" Emma Standing's voice leapt forward, "about the water in the ditches. Unhealthy for old bones."

"Here," Steven Adam said and set a sparrow down in front of Minnie, its clay mouth opened to receive toothpicks. "Start on this."

"Hey," June Marchand said. "What gives, eh? I've been working for days on this little fart of an ashtray and she gets the bird right off."

"You promised to watch your language," Mrs. Dorfman said.

"I said I wouldn't use my 'f' word," June said. "That's what I said." She combed her fingers through her platinum blonde hair. She wore a pleated white skirt of silky material, pearls around her neck, and the cowboy boots had been replaced with a pair of Sandra Adam's spike-heeled pumps. She'd passed Father Roy in the street yesterday and he didn't even recognize her. No one noticed that June was wearing Sandra's clothes. Everyone just thought how at last some of their influence had rubbed off and June had cleaned up her act. The saying "Out of sight, out of mind" held true for the people in Agassiz and the girl, Sandra Adam, seldom entered their thoughts. Even Steven Adam seemed to forget that he'd had a daughter. He'd been too busy. Judging from the attendance at his classes on Friday and Saturday, his business was going to exceed his expectations. He would extend his classroom hours. Perhaps make Tuesday night a "French Ladies" night. They would bring exotic dessert creations for the break, and occasionally, for a birthday or for fun, a bottle of wine. Thursday night, he'd host a "Mennonite Ladies" class. These women would go for huge projects, such as whole sets of mushroom canisters to line their shiny kitchen counters. He'd keep Monday afternoons open for the ladies of Ottawa Street. He'd buy some Easter egg decals which would draw the Ukrainians' eyes. He envisioned in all the houses in Agassiz, on mantels or beside a bed, a pair of Pinky and Blue Boy statues keeping watch over a table, or a couple in bed making love, the expressions on their sober, delicate faces never changing. He'd teach the women how to paint faces. But only he would do the lips. He wouldn't trust anyone to have a steady enough hand to paint the lips on the Smily Dolls, Pinky and Blue Boy, the Elves, Snow White. He'd make their cheeks blush with lipstick, left-overs from Sandra, tubes of lipstick that rested in the centre of the table in a glass bowl.

And in almost every house a ceramic frog would squat beside a sink, a scrub pad in its mouth. His students would prepare for the festive season and paint and stain Mary and Joseph and the Christ child, attempting to achieve the look of polished wood, making them appear ancient, rare antiques. They would brush thick glaze onto Christmas trees, dab the tips of them with the lava that frothed and bubbled in Steven's kiln and would come out looking exactly like real snow. Oh, everyone, he thought, as he watched the women work, would be busy glazing and arranging crystals on the backs of turtles so they'd melt and run down evenly, making the turtle more realistic, giving it depth. And when they became tired of frogs and turtles and peeping, immature birds, he'd keep ahead of them. He'd order chess sets, the Virgin, Venus de Milo, the Thinker, St. Francis of Assisi.

"Oh fart!" June Marchand said as the clay ashtray exploded in her hands.

Steven frowned and turned to a shelf lined with greenware. He set another ashtray down in front of June. "That's why you can't start with a bird," he said.

The door flew open and Delta William stepped inside, still wearing the chenille bathrobe she'd put on when she got up to go to the bathroom. "June Marchand," she said, "I've been looking all over creation for you. You go and tell that half-breed brat of yours to take that tent down, this minute. It's killing my grass."

"I beg your pardon?" June said, rising up from the table slowly. "What kind of brat?"

"You heard what I said," Delta said and stepped back when she saw the look on June's face. The clay ashtray shattered against the wall behind her head.

"You fucking white bitch," June said and her hand flashed in front of Minnie's face and then Minnie's sparrow smashed to powder on the other side of Delta's head.

"Now, now," Mrs. Dorfman said. "Such filthy language."

"You smarmy, obsequious whore," Delta said and snatched up the vase Emma Standing had been sanding smooth and heaved it across the room. Shards of clay flew across the floor to Steven Adam's feet.

"Hold it, hold it," Steven said as June rounded the table and headed towards the shelf of greenware. She gathered several raw clay mugs to her chest.

"Oh dear," Emma said and slid from her chair to crouch beneath the table.

Delta's breasts heaved beneath the housecoat as she took a deep breath and crossed her arms over her chest. She spread her legs and held her ground. "You don't scare me," she said, "and you're not fooling anyone with your bottle-blonde hair, either. So why don't you do yourself a favour and go back where you came from?"

June raised her hand, about to hit the woman with a mug, and then she stopped, turned, and one by one, set the mugs carefully back onto the shelf. "All right," she said with uncommon sweetness. "All right. I'll do just that." The door slammed shut behind her.

"Well, Steven," Delta said, "let that be a lesson to you. A leopard doesn't change its spots," she said as the door opened once again.

Mr. Harrigan stepped into the garage. He pulled off his hat. "Steve," he said, "I'm afraid I may have some news for you. About Sandra."

"Yes?" Steven said, thinking instantly about the girl's room, the moulds stacked up on the bed, on top of the bureau, the bags of clay piled in the centre of the floor, the washing machine in the kitchen filled with another batch of clay. There was simply no room in the house any more for Sandra.

Harrigan fumbled with his pocket and took out a bit of mauve silk. He held it gingerly between two fingers and shook it open. He set it down on the table. Panties. Mauve panties with the word "MONDAY" embroidered in white satin stitching. "We're hoping it's not so," Harrigan said, "but the body pulled from the river today? Could these belong to Sandra?"

"Oh!" Delta William exclaimed. "I gave her those. For Christmas. A pair for every day of the week."

Clay shards crumbled beneath Steven's feet as he stepped over to the table. "No," he said. "They're not Sandra's."

"Steven," Delta said, "I should know because—"

"MONDAY," Steven said and pointed to the underwear. "It was Friday when she left. Not Monday."

"Steven," Delta said, "what difference does that make? Wait," she said, "I'll go inside and look."

Harrigan removed his glasses and wiped his eyes. Steven went over to the shelf and took down another sparrow. He set it down in front of Minnie. "Monday," Minnie said. "Today is Monday." She'd remembered, without any cheating at all.

They heard the scuffle of Delta's slippers and then she stood in the doorway with a look of anguish twisting in her face. "Oh Steven," she said, "they're all there in her drawer, except for Monday."

"Oh no," the women cried. "Oh no. Poor Sandra."

Their cries rose up over the town, across the hazy face of the valley, up into the smoke-filled hills. Then they descended once again, scraps of paper fluttering down into the streets, becoming the size of newspaper which hands reached for and read. And the news was received with sorrow. Harrigan remembered now how sweetly she'd sung "The Old Rugged Cross" at Easter time, her voice pure and clean without any false tremor. Others remembered that she would babysit past midnight and had volunteered a hand with the youngsters at the school. The people unfolded the newspaper in Delta's Hot Spot and read the message while they stirred their coffee and turned away from half-eaten cinnamon buns.

"Drowned?" Steven said numbly as they sat him down on a chair. "What could have happened?" The women hovered over him and exchanged uneasy glances.

"Well, she did take this whole MacLeod's thing kind of hard, Steve," Harrigan said. "When she walked past the store, she looked upset. Crying. So, you never know."

"I loved that girl to death. Didn't she know that?" Delta said and wept into the hem of her bathrobe.

"Ever since she was a wee one," Emma said.

"Our Heavenly Father." The United Church minister sat at his desk in his study and began to prepare what he would say at the funeral service. He remembered, as though it were only yesterday, Sandra singing "Oh Holy Night", her voice soaring up in the rafters of the ceiling. "Our Father who art in heaven," he prayed, "you know that we loved Sandra dearly."

"Dear God," Mr. Newhoff prayed as though he were beginning a letter. He knelt in his office in MacLeod's store. He remembered the girl singing at the cenotaph, her voice high and clear in the chilly air. Perfect diction. "Faith of our fathers," she'd sung, as though she'd really meant it. "I have failed, I have failed," Mr. Newhoff said. "By my behaviour I have failed to show her the way to salvation. And now, I can't be sure where she is." The office door opened and an astonished clerk stared at the kneeling man. Mr. Newhoff leapt to his feet. "I dropped a quarter," he said and coughed.

Mrs. Dorfman covered her face in her hands and wept silently. It was just so like the girl, she thought, and saw Sandra folding her clothes neatly and setting them aside before she leapt into the water.

"It's all our fault," Delta cried. "We didn't prepare her for real life and she cracked under the first pressure."

"Well," Minnie Pullman said softly. "A triple whammy." Jacob Friesen, Sandra Adam and— Her stomach felt sick. And Annie. She could feel it in her bones. "Everything happens in threes." She pushed away from the table, walked across the room, picked up an ice-cream pail filled with moist clay, and left the garage.

Dear Aunt Violet,

Beauty of a day with slight winds from the north. The petunias fared the night well. A bit of storm brewing west of here, but I believe it should pass us by.

Minnie gives every appearance of being splendidly happy and the girls as well.

Minnie sat across from Albert at the table, rolling out ropes of clay.

"What're you making?" Rosella asked as she entered the kitchen with a bounce in her step and the smell of apricot bubblebath emanating from her bony limbs. Albert had taken her shopping and she wore her purchases proudly. Her first pair of blue jeans and the apricot bubblebath. The faint strains of Kirnberger's lullaby beat against the ceiling.

"I'm making a snake," Minnie said. She saw the apprehension in the girl's eyes. She laughed. "Watch," she said and began to build a coil vase.

"Neat," Rosella said. "Is that what you learned today?"

"No," Minnie said. "You used to do that. And Ginny, when you played with Plasticine. I remember. And today is Monday," she said. "And tomorrow, Tuesday, and so on and so on."

"Neat," Rosella said, using her new expression for the umpteenth time that day.

"How was your first lesson?" Albert asked.

"Neat," Minnie said and dipped her head. The silver flash of hair slithered down the side of her face, casting half of it into shadows. Her eyelids fluttered. "It was just fine, Albert," she said. "But, if you don't mind, I'd like to try my hand at something here at home."

"You must go out," Albert said. "Everyone needs to go out now and then."

"Yes dear," Minnie said. Her throat clicked as she swallowed. "Terrible thing about Sandra, Albert. And the Reverend Friesen." And Annie.

"Yes, terrible," Albert said. "Don't think about it." He reached over and covered her hand with his own.

"Well," Minnie said and tucked a strand of hair behind each ear, "I have to, don't I? If I'm going to be less of an embarrassment. I don't want to think about it, but I have to."

"Well, you mustn't forget these," Albert said and reached for a shoebox on the table filled with vitamins, minerals, and herbs. He unscrewed caps and hard yellow tablets, white capsules with tiny milky beads inside, amber oval pieces of jelly that looked like cat's eyes, dry-tasting tubes of roots, pink papaya footballs, rolled across the table top. He scooped them up and pressed them into her palm. "Something for your sore heels," Albert said.

Minnie crushed the coil vase down into a lump of clay, rolled it into a round ball, and began to smooth it with a tongue-depressor. "If you don't mind, Albert," she said, "I just might stay up all night and work on this. If you don't mind."

"My dear," Albert said and stroked the inside of her arm. "My dearest Bumkin, I don't mind in the least."

13

The sky opened up that night and blocks of rain thundered down, hammering the plants in the garden flat against the earth. Hendrick Schultz stood in the damp, crowded room and stared at Jacob's hands which seemed to have grown in death so that they covered almost all of his chest. Against the black gaberdine of his jacket and in the dim light of a lamp burning in a corner of the crowded room, the hands seemed to glow white with their own inner light. *Their webs shall not become garments, neither shall they cover themselves with their works, their works are words of—* He felt giddy. He knew it was not appropriate, but laughter threatened to erupt from his stomach. Their works are *words*. He'd made a mistake. *Their works are works of iniquity.*

The whole congregation had gathered in Lena's cramped parlour to say goodbye and to witness in Jacob's smile the evidence of his homegoing to the Lord. The men, self-conscious in their outdated Sunday suits, wiped their brimming eyes against the sleeves of their jackets. Taro Yamamoto took up little space, standing separate from them in one corner of the room. "He was a great man," Taro whispered and tears slid down his face. They were touched by this—that Jacob had reached people outside of their own community—and, suddenly, the dead man became larger than they'd realized.

"Truth has fallen in the street," Hendrick recited from Isaiah. While laughter bubbled in the pot below, his throat constricted with fear. He was free.

Lena sat with a stiff spine on the edge of a chair, feet planted firmly on the floor as she posed, waiting for Hilda Penner to take the last photograph of her and Jacob. The flash bulb popped, its blue light illuminating the deep worry lines in her face.

"This would be a good time for us to say a few words," Hilda said, but already one of the men had stepped forward to speak.

"I never heard the pastor say an unkind word about another man," he said.

"You have caused grief in the heart of your saviour," Jacob had said when Hendrick lied about the number of peppermints he'd taken from the cup in the cupboard. Jacob had set one of his little traps. He'd counted before and after.

"Jacob was always there when you needed a hand," another man said. "Often before I'd ask, he'd appear by my side with an offer to help."

He was full of eyes, before and behind, Hendrick thought.

"He was generous."

They were supposed to speak as they were moved to do so, but as one stepped forward the other beside him felt obliged to take a turn or risk appearing to be carrying a grudge or wrestling with a spiritual or habitual sin. Who hadn't spoken was often noticed more than what was said.

"He was spirit filled and his sermons always made me think," Mrs. Peter said.

The heat emanating from their bodies into the room made the moisture in the air swell and the enamelled walls began to perspire. Hendrick's giddiness subsided as the heavy, warm air pressed in on all sides. His forehead beaded with clammy perspiration. He would escape into the Word. *These are the generations of Esau the father of the Edomites in Mount Seir—the names—and the sons—and Timna was concubine to these dukes that came of Eliphaz.* His mind raced as he stared at Jacob's hands which appeared unreal now, carved of marble, ornaments which they'd placed against his chest for show. *And these are the sons of Reuel—* His knees ached and he kept rising to his toes to stretch the tension from the muscles in the back of them.

"Jacob always kept his word, you could count on that," Ollie's voice trembled.

"When I was in the hospital so terribly ill, Jacob came every day and visited, often stopping by the beds of those who were not of his flock to bring a cheerful message."

"He taught me to trust in God."

"He never tied anyone up." The circle shifted and all glanced at Hendrick who stood transfixed, staring at Jacob's hands. They saw him teeter slightly. Someone snickered. The sound came from the direction of several of the boys who leaned against the wall beside Maria and Rick Harder. *Arise, shine; for the light is come, and the glory of the Lord is risen upon thee.* Jacob was gone and he was free.

"When I was hungry, he gave me food," Taro Yamamoto said, his voice climbing up the wall where he stood huddled in a corner. "When I was unhappy, he comforted me. When others refused to speak to me in the streets and threw stones at my children, he rebuked them. When there was a need, he met it. He alone came when my sons' mother died. He was a great man," Taro said as he squeezed through the crowd, stepped to the door, and left them behind.

The room fell silent.

Yes, Hendrick thought, even when he spanked me it was with sadness, never anger. His eyes met those of his mother across the coffin. She appeared to be pleading with him for something.

"Jacob taught me how to pray," the woman next to Hendrick said softly.

It was Hendrick's turn to speak. He took his mother's plea to mean that he must say something nice about Jacob Friesen.

Once, Hendrick thought, he gave me a coin after I'd dug the dried corn stalks from the garden, burned them, and spaded the entire plot. Here, he said, every man is worth his labour, which made me think that every chore I had done for him up to that point had been worthless. He flipped the coin to me and I hesitated, not wanting to grab for it and wanting to as well. Wanting, not wanting. I am like a teeter-totter inside, he thought. I wasn't quick enough and the coin fell to the ground and slipped between the cracks of the dried mud pats on the road. I waited until he'd gone back into the house before I began to look for the coin. I must have ripped up half the road before I gave up. When I did, I got up from my knees, trying not to cry; if there's one thing I will change about myself now, I will stop crying. I saw Uncle Jacob. He stood at the window. He'd been watching the whole time.

"None calleth for justice, nor any pleadeth for truth," he recited, *"they trust in vanity and speak lies, they conceive mischief, and bring forth iniquity."*

"Hush, boy," someone said. That Hendrick would show off here and now was a disgrace.

Hilda Penner rushed in to fill the awkward silence that had followed. "Once upon a time," she said, "Jacob chased a mouse from my flour bin. It ran up his pantleg and he grabbed it and held it and walked all the way home like that. It looked so funny."

"It bit him," Lena said. The shadow of a smile crossed her face. "He had to have a tetanus shot, and his arm swelled up the size of an apple."

The smell of strong coffee brewing in the kitchen made Hendrick's stomach queasy. He felt the gush of salt water at the back of his throat. Lena reached for him and wound her arm about his waist and drew him to her side. He smelled the tension in her heavy body and in the acrid perspiration caught in the crepe fabric of her mourning dress.

"He loved you with the fierce love of God, as his son," Lena whispered. "Just as I do. Now is the time to do it," she said. "In front of all, in Jacob's presence. You owe Rick and his family an apology."

Hendrick could see the pores on her nose as she leaned towards him. "I don't owe them anything," Hendrick said.

"Mrs. Harder could have drowned."

"I don't care." About Elephant Harder. He looked up and his eyes met the fierce glare of Maria.

"First John, chapter 1, verse 9," Lena whispered. Hendrick saw the sandy cowlick on Rick's forehead rise and then the boy's mouth. Rick puckered his lips and began to move them in a rhythmic sucking motion. Then the boy yelped suddenly and stopped sucking as Maria pinched him.

"First John, chapter 1, verse 9."

"If we confess our sins...." Hendrick recited the entire verse. The words, coming from far off, sounded hollow inside his head.

"Mama."

Elizabeth heard her son's sharp cry and felt him move around the foot of the coffin. She shrank as he rounded it and pushed towards her. He raised his hand and hit her across the stomach. And then, both arms flailing, he beat against her hips and then her arms, crying all the while, "I hate, I hate, I hate this place." After the initial shock, one of the men intervened and pinned the boy's arms to his sides. He lifted him off his feet and carried him out into the kitchen. "Stop crying," the man urged. "What do you want to go and make such a fool of yourself for?"

Elizabeth turned from the people and pressed her face against the cool, damp wall. She was aware of Alma Harder standing beside Joe, their fingers entwined.

The women stayed behind in the house to sit with the widow Friesen. The men and children filed through the door into the night. The sky, a magician's cape flung open wide, swept about their shoulders, its black satin lining brilliant with the movement of millions of sequins sewn into place, yet wheeling in silent precision around them.

Leaves dripped rain onto their shoulders as they passed beneath the trees. Elizabeth and Hendrick stepped from the house and walked past the men on the sidewalk. Hendrick pushed on ahead of his mother, head bent, walking away from them rapidly. The men watched the darkness cover him from their sight. Without Jacob's influence, the boy would soon go to the dogs, they thought. An apple turned quickly.

The gate groaned on its hinges. "Good evening," Elizabeth's voice was barely a whisper as she stepped from the yard. She nodded to them briefly and then followed Hendrick into the darkness.

"Still waters run deep," one of the men said.

"I wouldn't mind discovering just how deep," another said and laughed. He took a flask from his suit pocket and, as Joe Harder approached, offered it to him. They wanted to talk a bit, about the woman they had pulled from the river. Sandra Adam. And speculate.

"No," Joe said as his eyes followed Elizabeth into the night. "The children will be alone," he said and hurried off.

Elizabeth walked swiftly and as she heard the sound of footsteps behind her she walked faster, her heart beating against her breastbone and pumping blood so strongly that it echoed in her ears. Always, the glint of the moon shining in her son's blond hair remained before her. But Joe began to walk faster and then to sprint and he caught her from behind. His arms were tight around her waist, warm, strong. Once again, the boy was swallowed by darkness and the path before Elizabeth's feet vanished. She shrank from the darkness and leaned against Joe. "I can't stand it," she said. "You were touching her."

"Shh," he said. His breath was warm in her hair. His touch was eager and sure from years of knowing her. The only sound for a moment was in the swaying and creaking of heavy branches above their heads, the sounds of Joe's hands moving against her clothing, and their breath. She caught his hands and held them tightly, still.

"No," she said.

"I need you," he said.

"Oh," she sighed. She turned into him then, reached down, and placed her hand against his hardness, rubbing it gently. Then she touched his face. His gold tooth shone as he smiled. He kissed each hand and squeezed them between his own.

"You *know* what that was all about," Elizabeth said. "My boy tying your boy to a tree. He knows," she said. "I'm sure Maria knows and told him. They all do. I don't see how things can be the same any more."

"But I can't be without you," he said.

"The boy hates me for it."

The trees swayed and light dappled Joe's narrow, strong features, tension drawing sharp lines. "If…," he said, "if only old Penner hadn't had such good aim with the grappling iron."

"Don't say it," Elizabeth said. "I've thought of it, too; but I don't think we should say it."

"I could have been a father to the boy."

"He has a father," Elizabeth said.

The night passed as Jacob slept with his hands folded across his chest. The smile on his frozen features began to curl up at the edges of his mouth until his teeth were bared and the smile began to resemble not so much a smile but a grimace of pain. The women had put Lena to bed and gathered around the table in the kitchen and waited for night to pass into the next day. The cuckoo clock sprang out of its house in the living room, shocking the women from their drowsy state as it had every hour.

"Jacob looks so natural," one of the women said. That phrase had at first expressed what had amazed them—his smile, the peacefulness there—but had now become but a refrain for each passing hour of waiting.

When their thoughts turned to Lena alone in bed and how she would be for the remainder of her life, they tried not to allow a feeling of smugness to creep in. Instead, they imagined themselves asleep, alone. And their husbands dead. But despite their imaginings, the feeling that they were safe would return. That the angel of death would pass them by because one day they'd be out getting supplies at the store, or working in the yard, and hear the sound of the last trumpet, and they and their husbands' flesh would never need know decay. That somehow they'd managed to be born at the right time, or had done something right.

"He lived a long and full life," someone said.

Unlike the poor Adam girl, they thought, and dreaded to envision where it was her soul lingered tonight.

Thick strong coffee gurgled in the glass knob of the percolator as one of the women rounded the table, refilling cups ringed with many coffee lines. They were shocked into stillness then by a cry behind the bedroom door and the sound of bare feet against the floor. The door opened and

Lena stood in the hallway, a fist full of flannel nightgown balled up against her mouth, her eyes staring at them, but unseeing. "He's here," she said. "He came through the window while I was sleeping and threw chloroform onto my bed."

Who, they wondered silently with crashing hearts and furtive glances behind them and into all corners of the room, even though the air was clean and they didn't detect the sickly sweet odour of chloroform. They reached for the swaying, terrified woman and led her to a chair. One of the women tiptoed past the living room door to reassure herself that Jacob still slept in the coffin. Hilda Penner entered the dark bedroom cautiously and switched on the light. But it was as she suspected: the window was shut tight and, except for a warm, tangled mass of blankets which testified to a restless sleep, the room was perfectly normal and in order. She opened the closet door and poked about in the clothing. She knelt beside the bed and looked under it.

When Hilda stepped back into the kitchen, Lena sat on a chair, eyes still wide and staring, arms frozen in a crooked position, as though to ward off a blow.

"When Lena was eight years old," Hilda said, "her father was awakened by the sound of hoofs pounding on the road. When he went to the window, he saw a flash of sabres in the moonlight as a band of hoodlums rode towards their village at full speed, drunk with alcohol and bad intentions and slashing telegraph wires along the way. He woke the family and took Lena and her older sister, Erica, out into a field and hid them in a haystack. He said to make sure that they didn't utter a sound. He was frightened because it was common knowledge what the marauders did to young girls. And so the girls hid in the straw, holding hands, rigid with fear as the sound of the men's footsteps approached. And then it happened," Hilda said. "Lena sneezed and a man, lusting after blood, thrust his sabre into the haystack, missing Lena by inches, but killing her sister."

Lena's arms fell into her lap and her chin dropped to her chest. "I can't sleep alone," she whispered. "I can't ever be alone at night."

Hilda offered to stay and led Lena back into the bedroom, undressed, and climbed into bed beside her, holding her close until her shivering limbs grew still.

"I never told you this," Lena whispered so the women in the kitchen wouldn't hear. They'd think she was boasting. "I never told you about a dream I had once. I dreamed about this. That Jacob had died. My grief was so terrible that I wanted to die as well and so I asked God to let me die. And do you know what? He took me into a wonderful place," she said. "It was very green. There were sycamore trees, and cedar; I can still smell it. I think it was a place just outside of the gates of heaven. And God said that he would give me my wish, but he wanted me to look at two tombstones that stood in the centre of that place. And I did. The first one had my name on it and that was all. But the second one had my name, and underneath, many, many names. And God said, 'Do you see that? If you decide to live, you could become a great Prayer Warrior and all those names there are the names of the people who will owe their presence in heaven to you.' And do you know what?" Lena whispered.

"What?"

"Hendrick's name was at the top of that list." She pulled away from the heat of Hilda's body and rolled over to face the wall. "The boy will come and stay with me tomorrow night."

TUESDAY

14

Minnie cradled the bread board in her arms and waited for
Jacob Friesen's funeral procession to pass by. She stood on
the road where Railway intersected Ottawa Street as they
approached two by two, the maroon wood of the coffin
gleaming as it swayed with the even pace of its bearers. A
black coat flapped at a knee suddenly, dark skirts swung
against the women's calves, and the soft pad of their feet
against the powdery soil was all the sound they made. The
widow Friesen walked behind the casket wearing a heartsick
smile, her eyes fixed carefully on the sprig of roses on the
coffin's lid in case it should slide free and fall. As she crossed
Ottawa Street, she sensed Minnie's presence and turned,
nodded slightly, and said, "I will pray for you."

"Thank you," Minnie said. As those around the widow
had not heard her speak, they were irritated for a moment—
that the strange Pullman woman would intrude in the
solemnity of the occasion.

Minnie watched as they walked away, going down
towards their church on the edge of town. On both sides of
the road, their reflections walked with them. Elizabeth broke
her stride, stepped forward, and fell into place beside Joe
Harder. And it seemed to Minnie, as she watched the funeral

procession walk up and up into the watery horizon, that the dark line became a single dot in the figure of Hendrick Schultz who walked at the end of it, alone.

The bread board bounced against her stomach as she headed towards Steven Adam's Ceramic Shop. In the board's centre, swathed in plastic wrap, was the clay figure she'd stayed up all night to finish. She passed by Annie's shanty and felt her chest tighten. The windows were only half covered with newspapers. But it didn't matter, she knew. Daylight would not prevent Annie from sleeping any longer. She was stopped by the cry of a seagull which suddenly became the raucous cries of many seagulls. The sky rushed away from her as she watched them dip and soar, their white wings almost colliding in mid-air. Food, Minnie thought. The birds believed she carried food on the bread board. She hunched over to protect it and hurried across the bridge and entered Steven's yard.

"Minnie Pullman," Delta said as Minnie stepped inside the garage. "What are you doing here?" Her eyes were red from crying half the night and her voice sounded as though she had a cold coming on. She and Emma Standing and Mrs. Dorfman had spent the entire night in the garage, each of them working on a piece of ceramic to pass the time, while Steven prepared the piece he'd put on Sandra's grave. All night he'd worked feverishly, scraping away mould marks from Cinderella's gown, scouring the seams on her arms flat, wiping down her ruffled petticoats with a damp sponge to assure himself that the mould marks were invisible and Cinderella looked as though she had emerged perfect and whole from beneath his hands and not in two pieces.

Steven, they'd told him, you've come through this once before and you'll come through it again. No amount of guilt or grief would bring the girl back. They were sad, but they had to concentrate on the living. They worried about Steven's heart.

Even though Minnie had sat up all night in the kitchen working, her cheeks blushed on their own and the blueish circles under her eyes had been wiped clean. She set the board down on the table, turned, and flashed a wobbly smile at Steven Adam. "I made a surprise," she said. "For you." Her fingers shook as she peeled the plastic wrap away.

Delta gasped. Mrs. Dorfman looked up from the praying hands she'd been cleaning. Emma Standing adjusted her glasses and peered down the table. "Oh my," she said.

"What is it?" Steve asked as he sanded the toe of the glass slipper.

"Steven," Delta said. "You've been holding out on us. You never showed us that mould."

"Oh no," Minnie said and laughed with embarrassment. "I made this."

"Go away," Delta said. "Tell us another."

The slim figure of Sandra Adam, bent at the waist, her skirts extended on each side of her in a curtsy as though she were accepting an invitation to dance, sat on the centre of the bread board.

"Smooth cheeks," Mrs. Dorfman said. "How did you manage that?"

"A spoon," Minnie said.

"And the hair?"

"A fork."

"What about the dress?" Delta said. "How in heaven's name did you manage the pattern?"

"A bobby-pin."

"Well," Delta said, recognizing the hook marks in the skirt as being just that.

"But what's she doing? What's that young girl doing?" Mrs. Dorfman asked. There was no place you could put an air fern or stick a pencil, nor a hole to fill with cotton balls for the bathroom. Her cleaning tool was suspended in the air above the praying hands.

Young girl. None of them had recognized that it was Sandra Adam.

The lettering on the masking tape that circled Mrs. Dorfman's cleaning tool jumped forward. Something was wrong, the woman realized. The name on it was wrong. It wasn't her own cleaning tool. "Delta", the letters said. She'd been using Delta's cleaning tool all night and the hands hadn't shattered. It hadn't made a bit of difference in the look of the piece. It looked exactly like the other three sets of praying hands she was making for Christmas presents.

Delta sat back down at the table, but like the other women, she didn't feel like working. They scraped at mould marks for several moments but kept glancing at the young girl bent in a curtsy. One by one, they set aside their tools. Discontent circled the air in Steven Adam's ceramics shop.

"I thought you might like to have it," Minnie said and slid the bread board across the table towards Steven.

He lifted his head slowly. Then he picked up the girl and balanced her on the palm of his hand. "It's quite nice," he said, "but unfortunately, useless."

"Why?" Minnie asked.

"I can't fire it," Steven said. "It's not hollow."

Mrs. Dorfman pushed aside her work, suddenly tired. She leaned towards Emma and whispered, "I've been using Delta's cleaning tool." Emma's eyebrows flew up above the frames of her glasses. She reached for her cleaning tool where it lay to one side. "And I've got yours," she whispered.

"Did you know?"

"Not until this very minute."

"Neither did I," Mrs. Dorfman said. "And it hasn't made a bit of difference, as far as I can tell."

Steven balanced the girl on the palm of his hand. Mrs. Urbanick, he realized, would want to make her own Easter eggs. Paint them with weird geometric designs instead of using his decals. She'd find a way to spoon out the inside of the egg and patch over the hole. Delta would begin to shape blocks and spheres from clay, pierce them with a pencil, and design a necklace. Emma Standing might roll out a piece of clay with a rolling pin, bring along a heart-shaped cookie cutter, and show them how to make the wind chimes, and his moulds would never be used again.

"If I fired this," Steven said, "it would just crack and shrink."

Minnie watched as Steven's long fingers contracted and tightened slowly around the little girl. She watched the girl become a thick lump of clay oozing out between his knuckles. He let it drop to the table.

Minnie picked up the squashed mass of clay. The walls crackled and waves washed up against the sides of the garage and then the sounds of the town pressed in—a flag snapping from the top of a house, a cricket singing. Once I had a sister. Her name was...Annie...Sandra.... Wanda. The click, click of a dry throat in speakers. I had a girl once; you could be her. One tiny hand emerged from the ruined figure, imprinted now with the whorls and lines of a man's fingertips. She turned the lump of clay over and there was her own face, cheeks pinched together and lips puckered, as though she'd just blown out the candles on a birthday cake. Once, I was a girl.

"I have every right to be angry," she said, her voice not more than a whisper. Her fingers shook as she rolled the lump of clay into the plastic wrap and picked up the board. "I have every right to be angry." Her voice grew stronger. They stared as she walked across the room to the door. At the last moment, she swung around to face them and the swiftness of her movement caused her heavy hair to spring loose from behind her ears and fall forward, the silver ribbon flashing down the side of her face. Minnie lifted her chin and smiled at the wall in front of her. "I'm very angry," she said. She turned and left.

"You're probably all wondering why I'm doing this here at the church, instead of later at the house," Lena Friesen said. She stood at the front of the church, directly beneath the pulpit where the coffin rested, and placed her hands against its polished sides as though to warm them. The sight of the men—the husbands and all their older sons—standing so meekly in among the two rows of pews, and the coffin itself, the rich grain of its mahogany, its heavy brass handles which they had insisted upon and had dug deep to purchase from Harrigan, comforted her. What Jacob hadn't been able to accomplish in life, he'd accomplished in death. It was the will of the Lord.

They were amazed by the new softness in Lena's voice, how overnight the harsh, grating sound of it had vanished.

"It was a way to make certain you'd come," she said, referring to the table set to one side on which Hilda had placed Jacob's mementos. "Many of you haven't been inside the church for years," she said. "It was a great source of pain and prayer for Jacob."

The men tugged self-consciously at the lapels of their suits but didn't protest, allowing at this time for grief to press its advantage. They wondered silently what kind of pie-in-the-sky pronouncement the woman would burden them with. They had in the past complained among themselves about the real world and how they had to live in it. How the money they sweated for in the real world had bought Jacob and Lena the luxury of living in the old one. But for the most part they had only been half-hearted in their complaints because, while they could never be like the deceased or live his life, they had at times, when they felt good about themselves and satisfied, welcomed the sight of him walking down the road on Sunday morning in his outdated black suit, carrying the ridiculously large Bible beneath his arm, to prick them with guilt. It had made them feel like better people if they could, from time to time, feel guilt. But it was over now. With Jacob's passing, the church would probably close down. They were more or less attending the funeral of that, too.

"Jacob wanted me to give each of you a little something and I didn't see any reason why it couldn't be done here."

The casket's hinged lid had been opened and removed. Jacob lay nestled in the diamond-tufted satin; the original smile which had turned to a look of pain during the night had changed to a slight expression of annoyance now, as though he resented this delay in his leave-taking. The blinds had been pulled against any of the town's curious and so the light was grainy and they had to strain for a sharp picture of his features. Lena began to weep softly as she looked at Jacob, and Hilda came forward and led her over to the front pew and the table with Jacob's mementos. Lena wanted one of the men to receive Jacob's penknife with the mother-of-pearl handle, another the fountain pen he'd used to write down his sermons. As she called a name, each stepped forward, feeling awkward and burdened by the gifts and fearing that she was being hasty and would miss the man's presence in the items. She gave away Jacob's hammer and saw, bags of nails, his reading glasses. She gave away his carpenter's hat and apron, his brush and comb. At last, she lifted the great leather Bible.

"Joe Harder," she said, "this is for you." She stood up and stepped towards him. "I've marked a piece of Scripture for you to read," she said. "It was his favourite." It had come to her during the night that Joe might be the man to replace

Jacob. That God would make him a fisher of men instead of a fisher of fish.

Joe flinched as though he'd just touched a hot stove. "No," he said, "I couldn't."

"I'll take it," Alma said. She took the heavy book from Lena's hands. "She'll probably use it for a doorstop," Ollie whispered into Hilda Penner's ear.

"Hendrick?" Lena had only one gift for the boy. And that would be to take up where Jacob had left off.

Elizabeth nudged the boy forward. "Psalm 24," Lena said. "It was his favourite."

The sisal runner in the aisle squeaked beneath Hilda Penner's feet as she backed away as quietly as she could. She wanted to go down into the basement and plug in the coffee urn so the coffee would be ready when they returned from the cemetery.

Hendrick lifted his head and squared his shoulders and clasped his hands in front of him. "Psalm 24," he began. His eyes met the dancing dark eyes of Maria Harder. He saw the muscle beside her mouth twitch. Her lips parted suddenly and her teeth flashed white as she smiled, wide and bright. At him. Hendrick felt the room retreat and his face was bathed in a cold sweat.

"What has four legs and can't walk?" he said. "Why are elephants grey?" And then his knees gave way. Had not one of the men noticed and caught him, he would have hit the floor.

"Good Lord," Hilda exclaimed from the doorway. They all turned and stared at the woman. "I don't know what we're going to do," she said, "because there's at least a foot of water on the basement floor."

Hendrick Schultz lay in bed that night beneath the feather quilt, eyes closed, feigning sleep as from the foot of the bed came the sound of Lena drawing her funeral dress up over her head and shaking creases from it, and then the sudden clatter of metal hangers in the closet as she searched for one and pulled it free. She had not turned on the light; she would not disturb him when she came to bed, she'd said, but Hendrick saw her anyway, in the sounds she made. He saw white flesh popping free as she pulled a rubber garment down to her knees and sighed with relief as it snapped loose and she stepped out of it. The room contained the smell of Jacob. It smelled of something moist and round, an unpleasant clean odour which said nothing of its owner, except that he was clean.

The bureau drawer squealed suddenly. "Sorry," Lena whispered. She pulled a nightgown from it, shook it loose, and dropped it on over her head. Hendrick held his breath, kept his eyes and face still. Lena's knee joints cracked as she bent, slid a pot out from beneath the bed, and lifted its lid, releasing in a billow a sharp antiseptic odour. She squatted over it, clutching at the bed to steady herself, and he felt her hand move in the mattress.

Elizabeth had stood at the door of their house watching as Hendrick walked away from it. At the last moment, she'd called to him and he'd turned, hopeful, but she ran towards him with a tiny white bundle, a stack of peppermint disks wound into a handkerchief. "For your pillow," she urged. "Take it." Her square toes stuck out the end of her brown sandals, the large toe curled up and crooked. Hendrick wanted to push his face into his mother and smell her because his own odour was not complete without hers. His remained steady, predictable, stronger if he hadn't washed his hair for a week. Hers changed regularly. And he'd grown familiar with its cycle. Sometimes it was thick and sharp, the smell of rust in the water pump, becoming drier later, like the pages of his notebooks. But on the nights that she left him, she brought back another smell: the mustiness of toadstools or a bed of moss growing in the dampness beneath the bridge. As he reached for the handkerchief and the peppermints inside, he realized that he could no longer run and leap and straddle her waist. Because he was too old. Because she was a woman. He hated her for that. He shook open the handkerchief and the white disks rolled free, scattering across the ground between them.

Lena groaned and passed wind, a stingy, pinched sound. He heard the clink of her teeth dropping down into a glass of water beside the bed. He opened one eye and saw the clock—a pinwheel of green light—as she wound it. She sighed. Hendrick clutched at the side of the bed as she pulled back the feather quilt, sat down, and the whole mattress tilted. She rolled into bed, her back turned to him and her knees drawn up to her stomach. He heard the growl of her intestines. She belched into her fist.

"Oh God, oh God," Lena whispered. "Why did you have to take Jacob away from me so soon? Why did you have to go and do that?" she asked.

Hendrick felt the tension in her bunched shoulders as she stiffened and pressed her fists into her stomach to still the motion of her belly so that her cries would not shake in the mattress. After a time, the movement stopped and Lena rolled over onto her back.

"Blessed are they whose iniquities are forgiven," she whispered, the words loose and open because her teeth rested inside the glass jar. "Thank you for forgiving me all my sins," she whispered.

Hendrick held his breath and kept his face clear of any conceivable emotion.

"That was sacrilege," she said. "A terrible thing to do. And to poor Jacob. Are you sorry, child?"

"No," Hendrick said.

"If we confess our sin, he is faithful and just to forgive us," she recited.

Hendrick felt himself sink down and down into the plump mattress, sleep almost claiming him when, in the distant background, he heard the sound of Katie, barking.

"Confess...if we confess," Lena said, the words slurred with sleep. She rolled away from him and her breathing grew still and even. Hendrick crawled from bed, almost tripping on the nightshirt she'd given to him to wear, and stood at the kitchen window. Beyond, Taro Yamamoto's cottage was a dark block set against the sky. The road passed between the two houses, its dry, powdery soil luminescent, like dust from a miller's wings. The road bordered that shallow dip of land where a silver wave lapped against the bottom of the foot bridge.

"Can't you sleep, child?"

He climbed back into bed.

"It's your conscience," she said.

He pretended that he'd fallen asleep instantly and began to snore, but the wool socks she'd given him to wear to bed prickled against the soles of his feet, making it almost impossible to lie absolutely still and his muscles ached with the attempt. He felt like kicking out against the blankets, rising up suddenly in a scream, grabbing the ticking clock from the dresser, and throwing it against the wall.

"The wages of sin is death," she whispered.

Revelation, chapter 1, he thought, and began reciting, the words unrolling all by themselves and filling his head with their sounds. *Of the testimony of Jesus Christ, and of all things that he saw—John—to the seven churches which are in Asia. And from—And hath—behold—come—I was in the Spirit*—he recited silently behind squeezed-shut eyes. The words leapt and jumped and knocked about in the back of his head.

He recited into the sixth chapter until Lena's breathing once again became even. He slipped from beneath the blankets and went into the living room to look out the front window. The shadow of leaves moved on the sidewalk. The half-moon curve of the skating rink arched behind their branches. The water in the ditches rippled in the wind. He heard people's voices—young, like his own, children still out and about, playing games. Maria? He heard the thump of boots growing louder and saw Minnie Pullman pass by Taro Yamamoto's gate, the silver ribbon of hair swinging rhythmically against her face.

He slid back in bed beside Lena. The clock's numbers glowed eerily from the bureau.

Hendrick fell asleep and dreamed. He dreamed of people—flat, like paper cutouts, and one-dimensional. They slipped through the walls of his house and passed silently in waves over his bed and out again. He dreamed of Maria Harder, who was not a girl, but a woman with full breasts and a round ripe belly. "I have something for you," Maria said. "Please don't tell my husband." She set down on the floor a dappled grey horse which pranced across the splintered boards towards him and up and across his fingers into the palm of his hand. It reared and pawed the air with its black hoofs. Maria's hand opened once again and two children rolled from her fingers and tumbled across the floor. They were pink-skinned children, chubby and bald-headed. They laughed and chased one another and did somersaults in the doorway of the room. "Look," Maria said and held them up for him to see. The boy had a stiff penis and the girl an opening. Maria fit the children together and their lips met in a kiss. "Come," she said, urging him to play with them, but Hendrick preferred the horse and took it to his bed and set it down on the face of his patchwork quilt and marvelled at the tiny hoofs as it trotted across multi-coloured fields of cloth and rough edges of wool stitching that held the plains together.

The mattress sagged, and Hendrick awoke with a start and clutched at the side of it. Lena sat down on the bed. "I had to get a drink of water," she said. "I hope I didn't wake you."

Perspiration ran in a trickle from under Hendrick's arm, down his side. Don't scratch, he told himself.

A light swept across the window momentarily and with it deep shadows vaulted up and over the walls and once again the room became as dark as the cloud-covered sky beyond the window. His feet were swollen with the heat of wool and prickles ran up his leg to his shin bone. He stiffened as Lena reached across the space between them and patted him lightly, a soft marshmallow touch against his shoulder.

"Hell is a terrible place," she said. "There will be much weeping and wailing and gnashing of teeth."

Revelation, chapter 7: And after these things I saw four angels and I saw another—saying—hurt not—sealed forty and four thousand— He recited the seventh and eighth chapters while the night passed beyond the window.

Hendrick walked with Maria in the coulee. She held the two children. He watched how they fit together, the boy's stretched-out penis slipping neatly between the little girl's legs, out of sight, their mouths coming together in a kiss. She passed the children to him. He felt their tense, rigid bodies in his hands, their life beating out from their ribcages against his fingers. He fit the penis into the little girl, withdrew it. Put it back inside. The dolls kissed and kissed. "Here," Maria said, "that's enough." She grabbed the children from his hands and knelt in the grass. He watched in horror at how she tore the grass free, scooped out a hollow, and dropped the children down into it. She buried them with the sweep of her hand. She rubbed her hands together to rid them of dirt. "I had to do that," she said and turned her mouth up to him, for him to kiss.

The boy's moans woke Lena with a start. She listened to him groan as he rolled over onto his stomach and then she felt the movement of his hips pitching against the mattress. She listened intently for several moments but as the movement became quick and hard, she called out.

"Hendrick, wake up."

His eyes flew open. He was aware instantly of the warm fluid on his stomach, how the nightshirt stuck to him there. That he couldn't, must not, move, or she would smell it.

"You were dreaming," she said. "And you woke me up."

Hendrick chewed, feigning a dry mouth, and once again pretended to snore. *Revelation, 13: And I stood upon the sand of the sea and saw a beast rise up out of the sea, and the beast—and the dragon—his deadly wound—forty and two months.*

He rose to the surface gradually, aware immediately that the darkness of the night had reached its fullest point and surrounded the bed. At the same time, he became aware of a suffocating heaviness and, fully awake, realized that Lena had rolled over in bed and in sleep had flung her arm over his hip. Her limp fingers dangled inches from his member. He barely dared to breathe as he recited. *Revelation 20 and 22: And if any man shall take away from the words of—God shall add—God shall take away—Amen, even so come—surely I come quickly—the grace—Amen.* His fists were clenched and his eyes squeezed shut with the coming of the end when there was a loud pounding on the door.

"What is it, oh Lord?" Lena said, awake instantly. She sat up in bed and clutched the blankets up around her chin.

"It's me. Elizabeth." The door flew open with a bang and she strode through the kitchen, the narrow hallway, and into the bedroom. In the light shining through the curtains,

Hendrick saw his mother's hair, freed from its severe braids, rippling in silver streams across her breasts.

"Get out of bed," Elizabeth said.

Hendrick's feet met the damp floor.

She peeled back the quilt and climbed into bed beside Lena. "I'll take his place," she said. "For tonight only. And then you're on your own."

She flipped over onto her side and rested her head into the crook of her elbow. "Go home," she said. "I think I have enough reason now to leave this place."

Hendrick tore the woollen socks free, felt the shock of the cold linoleum against the soles of his feet, and entered the world.

The river's current swept around the base of the bridge, its force, a tremor in the skeletal frame, reached up to the very top of it where Hendrick straddled the span. He felt the shiver of the current pass through his body. Beneath him along the bank, willows bent into the river's flow as the water inched up the shore. Branches of overhanging trees snapped free and were pulled swiftly downstream. Katie scouted among the trees and barked as she caught scent of a family of ground squirrels fleeing the rush of water inside their burrows. Hendrick looked out over the town and waited. Here and there lights had been left burning above doorways, beacons guiding late returners home for the night. And beyond the town, at its outer edge in the south, light danced in the sky as fire licked up from the roof of the church. He watched as the fire's reflection in the sky grew suddenly, becoming like the volley of sheet lightning in a summer storm and illuminating the outline of puffy cumulus clouds. He waited for someone to notice.

Minnie Pullman squatted at the entrance of the crude canvas shelter. The boy's silhouette, all hunched and crouching up on the bridge, made him look like a huge barn owl, she thought. Katie barked up at the sky.

"I'm leaving this place." Hendrick's voice rang in the steel girders.

"So am I," Minnie called. But her soft voice was over-powered by the sound of rushing water.

Sparks jumped and snapped and the pages of hymnals curled and turned brown. The sisal runner between the pews exploded into flame and turned to powder. In the vestibule, *The Good Shepherd*, its glass black with smoke, crashed to the floor. The whole sky pulsed with the rage of the inferno. And finally the whine of the siren on the watertower behind the firehall rose up above the town. Up the scale it climbed and the sound, trapped by the low-hanging clouds and the smoke, did not press out over the rest of the valley, but hung above the town of Agassiz, the sound turning on itself and becoming a sound turning within a sound.

WEDNESDAY

15

The last day of the valley began as a thin note, a sustained high C, a thread sawing back and forth between two teeth, the rawness of the day's first light, white, spare, transparent as water, and gradually the sky became defined by the rush of colour into it, the rising sun and the clouds pressing against its surface.

The note was a taut wire running through Mr. Campbell's room as he bent over the map spread out beside his desk. The two Mounties stood at ease across from him. The dark vines climbing the window flipped in the breeze and the ferns on the floor moved with light.

"Cree, you say, and Ojibwa?" Through flashes of daylight at the window he could see across the broad Main Street into the schoolyard where newspapers, Popsicle wrappers, and potato-chip bags were pressed up against the fence.

"And some Assiniboine and Sioux."

"Sioux? What in hell they doing over this way?"

"Support, I guess. They're all wearing buckskin, head-dresses, some in breechclothes," the Mountie said. "And get this—face paint."

"They've got both ends of the highway?" The hollow tick of the grandfather clock echoed in Campbell's breastbone.

Etta rapped on the door sharply. "There's someone here to see you," she said.

"Not now," Campbell said.

"Jelly for brains," one of the Mounties murmured and laughed.

"No one can get in or out of the valley," the other Mountie said. "They've barricaded both ends. I think we're going to have to have a talk with them soon."

"You'll have to wait." Etta's muffled voice beat against the closed door. There was a dull thud and the door flew open. Delta William elbowed her way around Etta into the room.

"Campbell," she said, "we pay you good money. Now earn it. You just better do something about that Marchand woman this minute. She's camping out on my lawn, for God's sake, cooking out there, first thing this morning, blankets strung up all over creation, and a slough of garbage," she said but then stopped, seeing the men's look of astonishment as, behind her, Charles Standing tottered into the room leaning heavily on his cane. His head had been shaved clean.

"Took a ride up there to put them straight," he said.

"Looks like they got the message," Campbell said and chuckled wryly. "At least they left your scalp."

Light dappled across Standing's bald pate as he bent forward to draw up a chair. "Savages," he said.

"You should leave things to the boys here," Campbell said.

"I was only going after what's rightfully mine," Charles said and thumped his cane against the floor.

Etta's voice rose up behind the door. "No, no," she protested. "You can't go in there!" But Mr. Newhoff, the MacLeod's store manager, ignored her protest and stepped inside. He hesitated, but then pushed his shirt sleeves up to his elbows and strode into the centre of the room.

"Look here—" Campbell said and was about to ask the Mounties to clear the room.

"I'm a thief," Mr. Newhoff said. "I confess."

"Yes, well, we all know that," Campbell said.

"Listen here," Delta said and crossed her arms against her breasts. "I'm not budging an inch until you send the boys down there."

"But you don't know how big of a thief I am," Mr. Newhoff said. Perspiration formed a row of shiny beads across his forehead. "It's in the bookkeeping," he said.

Outside, the short, round Harrigan had to step around Albert Pullman, who stood on the sidewalk in front of the Campbell house, reading a letter.

"How's the wife and kiddies?" Harrigan asked but didn't wait for Albert's reply as he bounced up the stairs, crossed the veranda, and knocked on the door.

Albert read:

Dear Albert Pullman,

In reply to your frequent letters of this past year.

I must remind you once again of the fact that your dear Aunt Violet passed away ten years ago. As executor of the deceased's estate, I am the party who sends the apparel for your daughters each year, as instructed by your late aunt in her Last Will and Testament.

Sincerely,

James A. Taylor
Barrister

P.S. What in the devil are muscatos?

"What is it now?" Campbell asked as Etta showed Harrigan into the room.

"I figured one more wouldn't hurt," Etta said.

"At first," Mr. Newhoff said, "it was because I couldn't live on my salary. But later, well, we, Betty and I, we liked having a new car every three years or so."

"You're not paying attention," Delta said. "The oldest brat seems to think she's entitled to a piece of land and so she's claimed mine."

The cane thumped against the floor. "Heathen savages," Charles said.

Harrigan crossed the room quickly and leaned over Campbell. "Listen," he said in a hushed voice. "I think you should know. Two things. One, the Adam girl, Sandra, well, the doc thinks she has a few too many bruises for a fall into water; and second, the fire last night? Pretty sure it's arson."

"Eek," Etta said as she ran into the room. She threw her apron over her head. "Go and have a look."

All of Ottawa Street was reflected in water. From the bottom of the street where it joined Main and up to the top and the river, reflections of the faces of the houses, the passing of clouds, and the sweep of birds and the quivering lines of telephone and electrical wires, weathered grey poles, and twinkling glass conductors, shimmered in the water— an upside-down world and a rightside-up world and, as the astonished group filed out onto the veranda, for a single instant none of them could determine which was which. Water lapped at the veranda's latticed sides and stained dark the wood of the bottom step.

They gaped at Albert Pullman who stood on the side-walk, still reading the letter, oblivious of the water rising up around his ankles, and at the sight of Minnie, strange, vague smile in place, her knees rising and falling in a steady march to the music of an invisible band rounding the corner at Main Street with a sign held aloft.

THE VALLEY ENDS TOMORROW

Minnie smiled and waved the sign and saw dinosaur bones, bleached by the sun, jutting up from the box of a truck. They slid to one side in a dry hollow clatter as the midway truck turned the corner in front of her, at Ottawa Street. As the truck turned, a golden dragon unfurled across its side. The dragon's mouth opened, its red split tongue darted forward, and fire scorched the sky. She saw the rippling reflection of its gold scales in the water and heard the rush of waves against tires as the truck ploughed down the centre of Ottawa. She stepped into its wake. Blue satin shimmered amid the glint of brass as the band stepped into place behind her. The trumpet blared and then the French horns; the trombones and the tuba joined in—a bright, happy march, its melody an expectant one that made her feet fall into place. She saw Etta standing behind J.P.'s wheelchair and then Campbell himself, brown and wizened, with his green blanket spread across his lap to hide his puny, shrunken legs. She saw Delta William's face screw up into its usual haughty expression. Harrigan. Albert. Pudgy, doughy, soft Albert. His freckled white hands pressed up against his mouth.

"Hello Albert."

"Oh dear," Albert said.

"Smile," Mary Ruth said as she fell into step at Minnie's side. She raked scarlet nails through her maroon puffball curls and flashed them all one of her brilliant smiles. Peanuts rained down on them and dimples of water spurted up around their legs as peanuts hit the surface.

"I am smiling," Minnie said.

"Yes, I see that," Albert moaned. "Why?"

"Well," Mary Ruth said, "I must say, you look a bit like me. I'm surprised. You were such a homely kid."

Jay's soaked pantlegs clung to his shin bones as he fell into step on the other side. His white clown face shone silver in the sun, the button nose a bright cherry. He smiled his sad clown smile. "I saw you wink at the trombone player back there," he said to Mary Ruth. "The minute I turn my head, you're at it."

Water splashed as Minnie stamped her foot. "All right, all right," she said. "You can be in the parade, but there's to be no fighting."

Iridescent green feathers brushed against Minnie's face as Mary Ruth spread her arms wide and bowed low to the people on the veranda. "That'll be a change," she said.

"What I don't think is fair," Annie Schmoon said, coming up from behind, "is that you had the choice." Her grey hair, a woolly frazzle, bristled out from beneath the navy toque.

"Here, give me some of that," Mary Ruth said and plucked the cigarette from between Annie's fingers, sucked on it, and handed it back. Annie passed the cigarette to Jay. Mary Ruth stopped to pull the wrinkles from her silver stockings. "What's not fair?" she asked.

Minnie looked over her shoulder and saw the bearded John the Baptist fall into place behind the band. Oh, she thought, that was nice. He nodded a solemn greeting. And then beside John, the lean Gene Lacroix, and then, all the people she had ever met since she'd come to the valley, young girls with streamers fluttering in their hair, the swish of the black skirts of the Hutterite women, the silky sheen of a kimono, men with red sashes wound round their slim waists circling in a dance, and there was the flash of white and green, an Irish jig, a yarmulke reflected back the sun, red kilts bobbed at knees, oh, they were all there, like a swarm of mosquitoes hovering at the end of her parade.

Ta da da da da da da tum, ta tum ta da da tum tum. Minnie heard that simple, contrived, uninspired melody above the clash and clatter of the band. She saw Ginny's face at the window, peering down at her. Minnie waved; Mary Ruth waved; Jay waved. Their feet swished through the water, sending ripples out towards all those houses, wrinkling the faces of reflections. They walked through the sky, the clouds, the silent sweep of pelicans, cranes, seagulls, the quiver of lines across the water.

"Ma? Is that you Ma?" Ginny called down as they passed by the house.

Annie grew short-winded in the effort to keep up with them. Jay passed the cigarette back to her. "So, was it you who put the notice in the paper, then?" she asked.

"I don't know what you're talking about," Jay said.

Minnie's laughter shivered, a brass chime swaying from a tree, its exotic wind sound the patina of another world creeping into the empty street. She heard ice groaning and splitting, water rushing into the valley.

The dragon writhed around the corner onto Railway, heading south towards the fairground. Beyond, at its sagging gates, a white dress fluttered and an arm raised in a wave.

"Wanda!" Mary Ruth said. "Oh, I knew it. I just knew she'd find her way back to the fair."

"This is where we leave you," Jay said to Minnie. He turned and swung a shiny tin pail and confetti, a cloud of tiny moths, dotted the blue sky. Wings unfolded and spread as a white bird fluttered up from Jay's chest. "So long," he said.

"Ta ta," Mary Ruth said and blew Minnie a kiss. "Be good."

"I had a dollhouse in my bedroom once," Minnie said. "Jeremy would never allow Mozart to take much of a break and so I played with the mice. Dressed them in funny little skirts and hats I made from hollyhocks growing in the garden."

Annie rounded the corner, turned, and walked backwards behind Mary Ruth and Jay. "If there really is a Jeremy," she said, "then it's not fair. Everyone should get the same treatment. Everyone should be able to choose to be born."

"Come on, old girl," Mary Ruth yelled and beckoned to Annie. "We'll spot you a ride."

"Maybe you did have a choice," Minnie said. "And you just can't remember." But Annie didn't really want an answer, Minnie realized. She saw the old woman link arms with Mary Ruth and Jay while beyond at the crooked gates the little girl in the white dress with strawberries embroidered around the yoke and hemline, watched and waited.

"Well," Delta William said. "Did you get that!"

"Albert," Campbell said, "it's a shame, but I think it's time to do something about that. She's gone loony."

"Oh dear," Albert said. "Oh, Bumkin."

They watched as Minnie walked away from them down the centre of the street, heading towards the river. Her flower-spattered dress, its hem hanging askew on one side, rode the top of her black galoshes. Her sign flashed its message back to them.

THE VALLEY ENDS TOMORROW

Albert looked down at the crumpled letter in his hands. "Oh dear," he said and let it drop. His feet splashed water up around his knees as he ploughed through it towards Main Street and stepped up onto dry land. Water squelched inside his shoes as he hurried on towards the bank. He rehearsed what he'd say. He could not, of course, get down on one knee. He tried to calm the tripping of his heart against his ribcage as he entered the Bank of Montreal. The air rushed inward as he stepped inside and he felt the girls' quizzical glances as he trailed water across the shiny floor. He went over to the little table beside the window and selected a deposit slip and then searched in the reflection in the window for Ollie. The girls need a mother, he'd say. For the sake of the girls, will you marry me? But Ollie was not there behind the counter.

"Albert?" Ollie's voice was steady and sure at his elbow. He turned and noticed the pattern on her brown dress, how the little pink flowers were all upside down.

His hands fluttered and knocked a stack of deposit slips to the floor. As he knelt to gather them, they slid away from him and no matter how quickly his hands could grasp and gather, it only made it worse and they spread out across the floor.

"Oh dear," Albert said, as Ollie squatted beside him. "Look at what I've gone and done."

The pansy earring was inches from his mouth. Ollie, he'd whisper, would you, could you, will you, are you willing, please, to be my wife?

"Albert," Ollie whispered. "The lumber yard was in looking for you. There's a call. From Rosella. It appears that Minnie's about to take another swim on the river."

Albert saw his own hands, his white fingers twisting and untwisting. He supposed he ought to have bought a ring first.

"Albert," Ollie said, as her quick nimble fingers snatched up the deposit slips and stacked them into a neat pile, "you'd be a fool not to marry me."

Albert felt the sharp nudge of bossiness between his shoulderblades.

"Next Sunday," Ollie said. "There's no reason to put it off."

"Well, I don't know," Albert said. "We're having a visiting missionary on Sunday."

"Well, miss it," Ollie said.

"Well, maybe," Albert said. "Maybe. I might do that."

He got to his feet and went back to the little table. Ollie pushed the stack of deposit slips into their slot. "No maybe," she whispered. "Yes or no."

Albert turned away from the sight of Ollie's bare arms, the fine blonde hair, like cornsilk, sweeping across them.

"No," Albert said.

"Oh!" Ollie cried. "I hate you."

The typewriters stopped clacking. A girl lifted her head from a bouquet of carnations. The bank manager rose from his chair as Ollie Peter walked across the floor to the door. She turned, faced them all, tears splashing across her face and down her tiny jaw into the creamy lace collar of her brown dress. She lifted the hem of her dress and held it against her face. Her knees shone out through black lacy cut-outs of her silk underslip.

"Albert Pullman," she cried, "you're a coward, that's what you are. And I wouldn't have you for a husband if you were the last man alive." She pulled the earrings free. The yellow and purple flowers bounced across the floor to his feet.

The girls in the bank stared, mesmerized, astonished at the sight of the black underslip, lace, the flash of trim legs.

Dear Aunt Violet,

It has been raining almost continuously for a fortnight and so the gardens are well flooded. But tomorrow promises to be better with the wind blowing in hot from the south.

He'd turned on the oven and hung his pants on the door to dry and the smell of them was like a wet dog. He heard the clink of glass in the basement as quart sealers and empty jam jars bobbed about in the water, coming to rest against the second step. The air was damp and it was hard to control his shivering fingers.

Dorfman informs me that he is going to build a boat and has asked for advice. I would appreciate any information you might gather on boat building at your earliest possible convenience.

THURSDAY

16

the grey cornea of water curves up and up, bending the blue
back of the sky until its stretched skin splits and the blue and
grey melt into one and Minnie floats free

a lantern hails from the shore

ABOUT THE AUTHOR

Sandra Birdsell was born in Morris, Manitoba and moved
to Winnipeg in 1967. She is a successful scriptwriter,
playwright, and filmmaker, and has won many awards for
her writing, including the Gerald Lampert Award for new
fiction, the National Magazine Award for short fiction,
and the Canadian Book Information Centre's 45 Below Award.